PRAISE FOR J … AN

"This twisty, intriguing … phere, heartbreak, magic, and ultimately a bright spark of hope!"

—RACHEL LINDEN, BESTSELLING AUTHOR OF *THE MAGIC OF LEMON DROP PIE*, FOR *THE VANISHING OF JOSEPHINE REYNOLDS*

"In *The Vanishing of Josephine Reynolds*, Moorman deftly weaves her trademark everyday magic into a tale of time travel, mystery, and romance. At the heart of the story is Josephine, a young woman so stricken by grief that she wishes to no longer exist. Transported to the 1920s when she passes through a magical door, Josephine has one last chance at life—if she can find the courage to live and love again."

—KERRY ANNE KING, BESTSELLING AUTHOR OF *IMPROBABLY YOURS*

"An ancestral home holds stories, secrets, and maybe even the ability to rewrite history in Jennifer Moorman's latest enthralling must-read. *The Vanishing of Josephine Reynolds* seamlessly blends the present day with 1927—and a splash of Moorman's signature magic—in a moving, unputdownable race against time. A testament to family ties, the power of love, and the indomitable human spirit, Moorman's latest proves that, sometimes, the impossible can become possible. I was hooked from the very first enchanting page."

—KRISTY WOODSON HARVEY, *NEW YORK TIMES* BESTSELLING AUTHOR OF *A HAPPIER LIFE*

"*The Vanishing of Josephine Reynolds* drips with lush Jazz Age detail, a vivid cast of characters, and a protagonist whose future literally depends on her ability to navigate the past. In one novel, Jennifer Moorman gives us a time-bending tale of both suspense and self-discovery and a heroine we can't help but cheer as she learns what she's truly made of—and perhaps, how to love again."

—BARBARA DAVIS, BESTSELLING AUTHOR
OF *THE ECHO OF OLD BOOKS*

"*The Vanishing of Josephine Reynolds* is absolutely mesmerizing! Jennifer Moorman expertly weaves a story of time travel, suspense, love, and the 1920s into a book with twists and turns and an ending I never saw coming. I stayed up WAY too late for too many nights simply because I couldn't put it down. It's magnificent!"

—MADDIE DAWSON, BESTSELLING AUTHOR
OF *LET'S PRETEND THIS WILL WORK*

"Jennifer Moorman charms readers again with this time-traveling delight. Join Josephine Reynolds as she visits the 1920s, trying to right a wrong that set into motion a series of life-threatening events. Fanciful and fast-paced, *The Vanishing of Josephine Reynolds* is another winner for Moorman."

—ELIZABETH BASS PARMAN, AUTHOR
OF *THE EMPRESS OF COOKE COUNTY*

"*The Vanishing of Josephine Reynolds* charms all the way from the enchanted door and its whispered passwords to the raucous speakeasy. It is impossible not to root for Josephine as she fights against the sands of time—and her own vanishing—to save her family and unearth her truest self in the process. Jennifer Moorman shines."

—GRACE HELENA WALZ, AUTHOR
OF *SOUTHERN BY DESIGN*

"*The Magic All Around* is brimming with lyrical Southern beauty, page-turning mystery, and delightful magic. With a house built of enchanted wood, a mother-daughter bond that changes a life, a family saga that brings you home, and a captivating love story, *The Magic All Around* is a work of storytelling-art. For readers of Sara Addison Allen and Lauren K. Denton, this is your next captivating read. If we have eyes to see and ears to hear, Jennifer Moorman is here to remind us that there really is magic all around."

—PATTI CALLAHAN HENRY, *NEW YORK TIMES* BESTSELLING AUTHOR OF *THE SECRET BOOK OF FLORA LEA*

"Brimming with love, and crackling with magic, this story will feel like home on a page—whether it's the home you miss or the home you're hoping to find."

—NATALIE LLOYD, BESTSELLING AUTHOR OF *A SNICKER OF MAGIC*, FOR *THE MAGIC ALL AROUND*

"Charming, enchanted and delightfully Southern, Jennifer Moorman's *The Magic All Around* is a cozy story of family, love and finding yourself. Perfect for fans of Heather Webber and Sarah Addison Allen!"

—LIZ PARKER, AUTHOR OF *IN THE SHADOW GARDEN*

"Full of Southern charm, second chances, and an opinionated old house that's as (lovingly) meddlesome as a well-meaning aunt, *The Magic All Around* is sure to delight. Jennifer Moorman's latest is equal parts magical and hopeful, revealing the healing power of love."

—SUSAN BISHOP CRISPELL, AUTHOR OF *THE SECRET INGREDIENT OF WISHES*

"Combine four parts love, two parts excitement, a dash of humor, and a pinch of magic, and you have Jennifer Moorman's delightful *The Baker's Man*. Moorman's sweet, heartfelt confection will please anyone looking for a charming, witty, utterly delectable read!"

—LAUREN K. DENTON, *USA TODAY* BESTSELLING AUTHOR OF *THE HIDEAWAY* AND *A PLACE TO LAND*

"Jennifer Moorman's *The Baker's Man* is a teaspoon of love, a dash of magic, and a whole heaping cup of Southern charm. Anna's legacy of unconventional romance and luscious baked goods is a treat from start to finish. Perfect for fans of Amy E. Reichert and Jenny Colgan."

—AIMIE K. RUNYAN, BESTSELLING AUTHOR OF *THE SCHOOL FOR GERMAN BRIDES* AND *THE MEMORY OF LAVENDER AND SAGE*

"*The Baker's Man* is a charming recipe of magic, romance, friendship, and the importance of staying true to yourself."

—HEATHER WEBBER, *USA TODAY* BESTSELLING AUTHOR OF *MIDNIGHT AT THE BLACKBIRD CAFÉ*

"*The Baker's Man* hits my sweet spot with mouthwatering baked goods and an enchanting romance. Jennifer Moorman's scrumptious tale has all the magical ingredients: best friend banter, small town drama, and the mysterious arrival of the perfect man!"

—AMY E. REICHERT, AUTHOR OF *ONCE UPON A DECEMBER*

The Vanishing of Josephine Reynolds

ALSO BY JENNIFER MOORMAN

The Magic All Around

THE MYSTIC WATER NOVELS

A Slice of Courage Quiche

The Necessity of Lavender Tea

The Baker's Man

RETELLINGS OF FOLKLORE, MYTH, AND MAGIC

Nina, the Bear's Child

The Vanishing of Josephine Reynolds

A NOVEL

Jennifer Moorman

HARPER MUSE

The Vanishing of Josephine Reynolds

Published by Harper Muse, an imprint of HarperCollins Focus LLC.

Library of Congress Cataloging-in-Publication Data

Names: Moorman, Jennifer, 1978- author.
Title: The vanishing of Josephine Reynolds: a novel / Jennifer Moorman.
Description: Nashville : Harper Muse, 2025. | Summary: "Can an entire life be erased by one thoughtless wish that changes a single moment?" —Provided by publisher.
Identifiers: LCCN 2024030101 (print) | LCCN 2024030102 (ebook) | ISBN 9781400343638 (paperback) | ISBN 9781400343645 (epub) | ISBN 9781400343652
Subjects: LCGFT: Magic realist fiction. | Novels.
Classification: LCC PS3613.O575 V36 2025 (print) | LCC PS3613.O575 (ebook) | DDC 813/.6—dc23/eng/20240712
LC record available at https://lccn.loc.gov/2024030101
LC ebook record available at https://lccn.loc.gov/2024030102

Printed in the United States of America

24 25 26 27 28 LBC 5 4 3 2 1

To Josephine—I've never forgotten that day on the riverbank, you and me watching the sunset in Florida, you wondering if anybody ever really saw you, asking if you were a ghost. This book is for you because I saw you then and I see you now, and you are absolutely unforgettable.

If the house of the world is dark, love will find a way to create windows.

—RUMI

PROLOGUE

Couples moved around them, swaying to a sensual rhythm of brushes on drums, the steady thump of a bass guitar. Feathery high notes on the piano accentuated the lightness moving through her. The singer crooned about love and flying and blue skies. With her cheek pressed against the warmth of his chest and his arms wrapped tightly around her, she wouldn't have believed that in a couple of hours this would all be gone. All the people, the music, the joy.

The sway of their bodies mesmerized her, temporarily tricked her mind into believing that everything would be okay. Days and days would stretch out before them. Hours to laugh and love and make a future together. Endless kisses and parties and more dancing just like this. A thousand more moments with his body pressed against hers.

She looked up at him and smiled. "I could do this forever."

His grin fluttered her heart, and he leaned down to press his lips to hers, pausing only long enough to ask, "Promise?"

She didn't answer with words. She didn't have to. Their kiss made a promise she'd never be able to keep, though she wanted to. Because keeping that promise to him tonight would unravel the entire future.

CHAPTER 1

Josephine Reynolds was a ghost.

She moved through life like an untethered being, a shadow on the periphery. If you turned your head to catch a glimpse, it was gone. *Gone.* That word played on a loop in her mind, had been playing for months. Her previous life. Gone. Her purpose. Gone. Nathan. *Gone* in a heart-stopping moment.

Josephine stood in the sticky warmth of the sunroom among the ZZ plants, the ferns, the Meyer lemon tree that ached to be repotted this year. A lone orchid drooped, heavy with crisp white blooms. The Christmas cactus showed off at least a dozen exotic bright pink blossoms. Even with all the suffering, she'd managed to keep the plants alive. Most of them. The peace lily in the corner sagged as though it was in the throes of giving up, too weary to go on. No peace around here. That feeling she knew intimately.

Josephine stared out the windows at velvety smears of pink and violet reflecting on the surface of the swimming pool during sunset. If she stared hard enough and closed her eyelids just enough, she could imagine Nathan doing laps in the pool just before sunrise. After precisely half an hour of gliding through the water, back and forth, back and forth, his toned body would rise out of the pool, water droplets beading on his skin, and reach for the folded towel on the end of the chaise nearest him. Then he'd towel off before coming inside to shower. She could almost smell the chlorine on his tan skin, almost see his wet footprints marking his path from pool to house.

Her cell phone buzzed in the living room, startling her out of the vision and forcing her back into now. Now, where every moment stretched toward nothing, heavy and meaningless. She turned her back on the sunset, on the memory of Nathan's routine, and walked into the living room. Her bare feet sank into the plush rug, which softened her steps. Grabbing her phone off the coffee table, she swiped it open to see a text from her sister, Katherine.

Hey! Let's grab dinner. I'll be there soon.

Josephine's sigh slumped her shoulders. She texted, Not tonight. I have . . .

What did she have? What excuse could she make up this time? When declining her sister's weekly invitations, she'd said she had paperwork to review, accounts to close, arrangements to make, a house to clean, laundry—a never-ending to-do list of inconsequential tasks. Anything to keep her from reengaging in anyone's life.

Before Josephine could draft a reason, Katherine sent another text. Open the door.

Josephine glanced through the living room toward the front door. The chiming doorbell caused her to flinch. The peal reverberated through the grand two-story foyer. Josephine stood still. Maybe the person would go away. Unless it was her sister.

A banging sounded against the door. "Open up, Jo!"

For a terrible second, Josephine considered ignoring her sister. Then she crossed the living room and padded across the cold marble-tiled foyer. She unlocked the front door and opened it slowly, hesitantly, as if her sister might spring through in a defiant manner. But Katherine stood on the front landing, long dark hair flowing around her shoulders, with an expression of kindness that quickly shifted to concern. A canvas grocery bag hung on one shoulder.

"Hey," Katherine said. "Assuming you would turn down my invitation to go out, I already picked up dinner. Can I come in?"

Josephine paused with the door halfway open and nodded. "Of course." Her voice sounded hoarse, unused. When was the last time she'd actually had a real conversation with someone in person? Had it been weeks? She couldn't recall. She cleared her throat. She fully opened the door and stepped back to allow Katherine to come inside.

Katherine walked past her toward the kitchen, and Josephine closed the door, flipping the deadbolt to lock it, and followed her. Katherine pulled clear containers of prepared food from Whole Foods out of her bag and displayed them on the island. Josephine stood awkwardly in her own kitchen.

The pendant lighting created pools of soft white light on the granite island. Nathan had chosen the lacquered bronze pendants from Restoration Hardware when they'd built the house five years ago. He preferred the classic-modern combination with its geometric angles and industrial vibe with a hint of timelessness. Josephine slid her fingers across the beveled edge of the counter.

With the last container removed, Katherine stilled and locked her gaze with Josephine's. "I want to ask how you are, but it's obvious. Selfishly I wanted to come over and see you were doing better, finding your way back, but you look—"

"I'm doing fine." Josephine's defensive tone revealed otherwise. A bit too punchy. Her stomach cramped. Heat rose up the back of her neck and flushed her face. She wasn't fine, unless *fine* meant something sunken. But to try not to appear like the heap of sorrow she knew she was, Josephine added, "I like to wear comfy clothes on Saturdays."

Katherine didn't speak for a few moments; then she exhaled. Placing both hands on the island, she stared at her splayed fingers. "Jo," she said in a quiet, gentle voice, "you're wearing Nathan's shirt, and it looks like you've been wearing it for days. I don't want to sound like Mama, but did you brush your hair today? You look like you've lost weight, and you didn't need to, and it's Thursday. If this is you doing fine, then I don't think I have the heart to see you doing badly."

Josephine swayed on her feet. She reached for the edge of the island to steady herself. Glancing down at her—no, *Nathan's*—rumpled button-up shirt, she saw she'd misaligned the buttons, so the right side of the shirt hung lower than the left. Was that a coffee stain near her hip? She finger-combed her long, messy hair, which resulted in her fingers snagging tangles. When she gazed up at Katherine, tears stung her eyes.

"I'm okay, sort of," Josephine lied. "Today has just been a bad day." Actually the last few months had been a string of bad days that each bled into the next like a bloodstain.

"It's been six months," Katherine said, coming around the island to stand close to her sister. "I know there's not a time limit on grieving, and I'm not suggesting you 'look at the bright side' or any of that other garbage people blubber when you've lost someone, but, Jo, you *have* to move forward. Nathan wouldn't want this for you. If the roles were reversed, would you want him in this state?"

Josephine laughed a dreadful, bitter sound that ripped up her dry throat. "Nathan would *never* be in this state. He'd be doing what he always did, work. He'd fill up his days with patients and parties and working lunches at restaurants where people hero-worshiped him." Josephine clenched her jaw. The acid of her words felt like blisters on her tongue. Adored, handsome, wildly successful Nathan had *left her* to deal with this gaping hole alone. She'd poured everything into his life, molded herself into the perfect polished wife, and now . . . Now she was no one but a grieving widow. Someone people pitied for a while and then forgot like last year's fashion.

Katherine touched Josephine's arm. "Hey, it's going to be okay. We can get through this. You and me, we can get through anything."

A stabbing sensation choked her breath halfway up her throat. Josephine nodded, not trusting herself to speak.

"Maybe today isn't the best day to catch up over dinner," Katherine said. "How about I put this in the fridge, and you eat when you're hungry. Let's make a plan for this weekend, though, okay? You need to get out of this house."

Katherine looked around the kitchen. She bit her bottom lip the way she always did right before she told Josephine something that had a high probability of hurting her feelings.

"You might consider selling this place," Katherine finally said. "It's not really your style."

Nathan had spent as much time choosing all of the fixtures and furnishings as he did working his practice. This house was a labor of love—or a labor of something. A status symbol. A way to showcase his ambition and impressive lifestyle. Josephine hadn't offered many opinions on the house's style or décor because Nathan's fondness for top-of-the-line, extravagant possessions was hardly something she wanted to argue with him about. He reminded her that his taste was impeccable, which included his choice in marrying her. Now she was just part of the collection he was no longer around to admire. This house was a museum dedicated to Nathan's prized belongings, including her.

"Nathan loved this house," Josephine replied.

"I get that, but what do *you* love?"

Josephine *heard* the words, but she didn't understand them. "I love this house too. It has everything I need." Everything except Nathan. Without him directing life and filling the house with his presence, Nathan's absence eliminated Josephine's purpose and direction.

Katherine's sigh betrayed her frustration. "Do you love this house because Nathan did or because you actually think this is your dream home?"

Josephine's expression slid downward. This time, heat akin to anger flared up the back of her neck. "What are you trying to say?"

Katherine pushed her long hair over one shoulder and leaned her hip against the counter. "Remember Seth?"

Josephine's mind squealed to a stop, then riffled through years of memories as if they were files in a drawer. "The guy I dated freshman year in college?"

Katherine nodded. "That's the one. He was obsessed with Pink Floyd and gas station burritos. I think the only clothes he owned were band T-shirts and ripped jeans. He played air guitar *in public* all the time. It was embarrassing."

Josephine's memories of the young man rose up in her mind like fog, barely formed and wispy. "How can you remember any of that? All I remember is that he was tall and cute."

"He was cute," Katherine agreed, "if you could ignore all the other things not as attractive, which I couldn't. And the only reason I remember him is because *you* started loving Pink Floyd and dressing in grungy T-shirts and faded jeans. You thought his air guitar was endearing, but the day I saw you eating a lukewarm burrito from Circle K, I nearly flipped my lid."

"Why?" Josephine asked, not able to recall the moment.

Katherine sighed and pushed herself away from the countertop. "There's a pattern here, Jo. Whenever you dated a guy, you always became whatever *he* was or what *he* needed. You stopped being Josephine. You were Seth's girlfriend or . . . Nathan's wife. You lose yourself in them. You give up your friends, your preferences, your identity." She motioned to the house. "Like this house. It's a beautiful home, sure, but it's all Nathan, and I can't help but wonder if you even know who you are without him. After all these years, who's Josephine? What does *she* want? What does *she* love?"

Josephine's fingers crept up to her collarbone and rested there on clammy skin. A twinge of nausea, the faint yet staggering awareness that Katherine was right, alarmed her. Who was she without Nathan?

No one.

Katherine moved toward Josephine. "I can help you get this place on the market, find the right buyer. Not that you need the money, but you'd bank a lot for this house based on the Green Hills neighborhood alone. It would probably sell in less than a week, and I wouldn't be surprised if there was a bidding war.

Think about it." Katherine pulled Josephine into a hug. "I love you, Jo-Jo."

"I love you, Katy-bug," Josephine said, surprised to hear the childhood nickname for her sister rise from the abyss.

•••

AN HOUR LATER, Josephine had showered, brushed her hair, and changed into a pajama set. Nathan's shirt lay on top of a growing pile of laundry in the basket. She wandered the second-floor hallway, recalling the worry marking her sister's face. Katherine wasn't the only person in her life who'd voiced concerns about Josephine's downward spiral. Her mama called every other day, and Josephine only answered once a week. Her neighbor had just yesterday dropped off a gift basket with not one but *five* business cards for therapists, ranging from grief counselors to energy healers.

Josephine had no desire to talk to anyone about anything; she didn't need their advice or their easy-step plan to getting on with her life. When had she become a burden to everyone, a nagging worry they carried around, a thorn in their side? She brought discomfort and worry to her family and friends. This was not the woman she'd dreamed of becoming.

Her feet dragged her toward her bedroom. As she passed Nathan's home office, she paused in the doorway, breathing in the scent of him that still lingered in the room. Her laptop had replaced his on the oversize mahogany desk, and it was open and facing the windows that overlooked the backyard.

A surge of sorrow caused a realization to hit her like a slap across her face. "I can't do this anymore," she whispered. She sagged beneath the weight of her grief, beneath how meaningless her life had become. "I wish I'd never been born."

The lights in the room flickered like a pulse. Off, on. Off, on. Off, on. The electricity continued this heartbeat rhythm for a few seconds before darkness prevailed. Her entire body tensed. Her lungs squeezed out the last of her breath. The steady hum of electronics and the air-conditioner—ordinary sounds that no one ever noticed—ceased, leaving the house in a stillness so complete that Josephine heard her next intake of breath. She stood in the silence, almost as invisible in the darkness as she felt in life.

A ding sounded from her laptop. Within seconds the power kicked back on, and the house whirred to life again. Josephine's body unclenched, and she opened and closed her hands, flexing her fingers. She walked into the office, slid behind Nathan's desk, and sank into the cushy leather chair. She gripped the edge of the desk and pulled herself closer. Reaching for the nearest lamp, a Tiffany replica that Nathan loved, she pulled the cord and illuminated the desktop. Josephine slid her finger over the laptop's touchpad, waking up the screen. After keying in her password, she saw her email inbox was open, and one unread message waited for her. Katherine had forwarded an email. The subject line read Fw: Foreclosed Homes in Nashville, TN. In the body of the email, Katherine had written: Look what's on this list! Josephine clicked open the email.

Distractedly she scrolled through the houses and wondered about the people who had lived in these homes. Were they as lost as she was? Had they loved their homes? Had they spent more than they should have? Had someone died and left no one responsible?

A historic Victorian home in Belle Meade caught her eye. "It can't be," she said, leaning closer to the screen. Josephine's heartbeat quickened as she speed-read the information, clicking through the blurry photographs, which confirmed she recognized the home. The Carter Mansion was in foreclosure?

The Carter Mansion had been a wedding gift to her great-grandmother Alma when she married in 1916. Josephine hadn't set foot inside the house since she was a little girl, but seeing these online photographs resurrected delicate memories. After her grandmother's death six years ago, Josephine's mother, Emily, and her mother's brother, Donovan, had inherited the house. A disastrous family squabble ensued, and Emily had relented to Donovan, giving him complete ownership. When Josephine questioned her mama about it, Emily refused to discuss it, not wanting to further break her own heart over her brother's selfishness. Seeing the confusion and distress on her mama's face, Josephine hadn't brought it up again.

Josephine and Katherine were probably seven and five the last time they'd been inside the Carter Mansion. That was right before their dad's job moved the family to Atlanta. With its large rooms, narrow closets, and unusual storage spaces, the house had been ideal for endless games of hide-and-seek. Katherine would often give up because she tired of searching for Josephine, who Katherine swore became invisible. They ran wild through the back garden and helped Grandma Dorothy clip roses to place in Mason jars around the house. If she closed her eyes, Josephine could still smell the sweet mix of blooming flowers, lemon furniture polish, and dusty books that permeated the house.

Now, five years after Uncle Donnie's underhanded act, here was the Carter Mansion in foreclosure. A barrage of questions rushed through her. What happened to her uncle? Had Uncle Donnie sold the house to someone who couldn't afford the upkeep? Had he not been able to maintain it himself? How could a historic home in the gorgeous Belle Meade area go into foreclosure? If Uncle Donnie hadn't been able to keep it, why hadn't he sold it? Why hadn't he reached out to the family?

Josephine inhaled slowly, remembering Katherine's suggestion about selling her house. She reached for her cell phone and stared at the lock screen that lit up when she lifted it off the desk. An image of her and Katherine taken last year smiled up at her. They'd been caught laughing, and Josephine remembered the moment. She knew her sister fretted about her, which twisted her stomach. She opened her texts and typed a message to Katherine. Hey, just read your email. That's Grandma's house!

Katherine's reply vibrated Josephine's phone. Yep, the one Uncle Donnie stole.

Josephine surprised herself by laughing. She wouldn't have phrased it as such, but Katherine wasn't wrong.

I loved that house, Katherine texted. Remember that time you hid in the armoire, and I gave up searching for you?

Josephine texted, Which time? You always gave up. She could almost hear her sister laughing.

The time you found me an hour later eating cookies in the kitchen. You were furious. Until I shared my cookies.

Another question ballooned within Josephine, a question so startling her back went rigid and her breath held. She put down the phone. Should *she* buy back her family's home? Tingles moved over her skin, pushing goose bumps to the surface. Was that a yes? A confirmation from the soul fighting for survival within her? Josephine pushed back from the desk and spun herself around in the chair to gaze out into the moonlit backyard.

Fireflies winked off and on in the darkness. Situated on just less than two acres, this home was on one of Nashville's most coveted streets. Although Nathan hadn't been into gardening or yardwork, he wanted a gorgeous backyard with landscaping, a pool, and a shaded patio.

He insisted on a house with excess room for entertaining friends and family, and they'd hosted incredible parties, lavish holiday gatherings year-round, and more intimate pool soirees in the summers. Josephine couldn't even—and didn't *want* to—imagine hosting anyone in this house ever again. Maybe Katherine was right; this home no longer fit her. Maybe it never had. Maybe this had always been Nathan's desire.

Would Katherine think Josephine had completely lost her mind if she did something outrageous and bought their ancestral home? She picked up her phone and typed, I think you're right about me needing a new start. I'll need your help selling this place.

Three little dots hovered on the screen while Katherine typed a message. Just reading this makes me want to cry. Is Jo-Jo back?

What if I buy the Carter Mansion? Josephine's finger hovered over the phone before she sent her final question. Am I crazy?

Three bouncing dots had Josephine holding her breath. Then the dots disappeared, and Josephine frowned. She startled when her phone rang in her hand. Katherine was calling.

"What do you think?" Josephine said in a rush of breath.

"Let's do this, Jo-Jo."

CHAPTER 2

TWO MONTHS LATER

Metal scraped against metal and the rolling mechanism groaned when Josephine shoved up the garage door on the storage unit. "I can't even remember what's in here."

Katherine stood beside her, swiping the neck of her Vanderbilt T-shirt against her sweaty brow. "Says pretty much everyone who owns a storage unit." As the door lifted completely, she gasped and stepped forward into the half-filled space. She went immediately for the oversize armoire and ran her hands over the intricate inlays and the polished wood. Her fingers left streaks in the layer of dust coating the furniture. "Why have you been hiding this beauty?"

Josephine's eyes moved from one piece of furniture to the next. Along with the armoire were upholstered chairs, a sideboard, a few end tables, lamps, a framed full-length mirror, and a few stacks of boxes and clear plastic containers.

Josephine rested her hand on the back of an antique wingback chair upholstered in a soft tan fabric. "Nathan wasn't into antiques. He preferred shiny and new. But I couldn't bear to give away these family heirlooms. I guess I thought maybe one day I could find a home for them."

Katherine gave Josephine *a look*, and the meaning was clear. The abandoned antiques were yet another indicator that she had molded her life to suit his. Instead of commenting, Katherine said, "I'd forgotten how gorgeous these pieces were, Jo. They'll be perfect in the Carter Mansion." Katherine smiled at her.

"You know they were all originally there, don't you?" Josephine said.

Katherine's smile widened. "Of course, and we'll return them to where they belong." She stepped back out into the sunlight and glanced toward the parked U-Haul truck they'd rented. "Let's load up what we can reasonably carry. We'll pay the movers extra to swing by and grab the rest of these items. What time did they say they'd be finished at the Green Hills house?"

Katherine had taken to calling Josephine's previous home, which now belonged to a local attorney and his family, "the Green Hills house." It was as though she was trying to separate Josephine as much as possible from her former life. To help ease her sister out of the old and into the new. Katherine made it seem like slipping out of her old life was as easy as slipping off a pair of heels. To Josephine it felt more like wrangling off a sports bra.

"By three," Josephine said. "I'll call and give the movers directions here, and I'll ask the attendant to open the door for them since we'll be gone."

"I'm sorry Mama and Daddy can't be here to help," Katherine said. "And if Neil wasn't showing the Eastwoods a dozen different houses today, he'd be here too."

Josephine waved away the apology. "Mama and Daddy have had that trip to Charleston planned for months, and you've moved Neil around enough. One more move might do him in. How many times have you made him change houses? Nine? Ten?"

Katherine pretended to pout. "I can't help that I fall in love with a new house every year."

"Better houses than men." Both sisters laughed. Josephine lifted the lid on the closest plastic container. A faint moldy scent of items boxed for years wafted out. "I'd forgotten Mama gave me some of Great-Grandma's clothes."

Katherine moved in close beside her sister and touched the navy-blue dress on top. "I bet you're as tiny as she was. You should have a fashion show after we get these to the house."

"Why just me?" Josephine asked with a hint of a smile. "Shouldn't you be subjected to trying to wedge yourself into antique clothing?"

"Not a chance," Katherine said with a laugh. "Not with this bust. No way those zippers or buttons would hold me in. I'd look like a harlot."

A sound between a snort and a laugh rose up Josephine's throat. "A harlot? You know that means 'prostitute,' right?"

Katherine's laugh matched her own. "Poor word choice. But you—these clothes would look great on you. You've got the coveted flapper's body."

"You mean the body you keep reminding me has lost too much weight?" Josephine said, her dark eyebrows lifting.

"We're working on that!" Katherine said lightly. "We can't adjust everything all at once. Some of these changes have to happen slowly. Otherwise it'll throw you into a wild panic, and you'll bolt faster than a wild mustang."

Josephine sighed. "Or sink like a stone."

Katherine nudged her shoulder against Josephine's. "Hey, none of that. You're doing great. Remarkable, actually. Now, let's get these boxes into the truck and ride over to the mansion." Then she laughed. "Don't we sound fancy? Darling, let's return to the mansion, shall we?"

Josephine rolled her eyes as she grabbed the nearest box, but she was smiling.

●●●

ON THE FRONT veranda of the Carter Mansion, Josephine balanced a cardboard box on one hip while retrieving the ring of house keys from her front pants pocket. They snagged on the fabric. She gave the keys a yank and wobbled. Shoes clacked against the front brick stairs. Josephine half turned to ask her sister for help with the keys but didn't get the words out. It wasn't Katherine coming up the steps.

A tall woman dressed in a burgundy cable-knit sweater, pressed khakis, and stylish black boots stepped onto the front porch with a small wave. Her pewter-colored hair was styled into a shoulder-length bob. "Hello, I hope I'm not disturbing you."

Did any polite person *ever* admit they were being disturbed? If Josephine were less courteous, she would wholeheartedly admit to being bothered. Didn't the woman see Josephine was busy moving in? If Josephine's sweaty, disheveled appearance wasn't obvious enough, then the U-Haul and boxes were.

Without waiting for Josephine's reply, the woman held out her hand and said, "I'm Barbara Blanchard. I live up the street, and I wanted to welcome you to the neighborhood."

Josephine repositioned the box on her hip. "It's nice to meet you, Barbara. I'd shake your hand, but as you can see, I have my hands full. It's move-in day for me."

Barbara's burgundy lips stretched into a polite smile. "Of course, of course. What a headache moving is." She glanced toward the U-Haul truck, where Katherine must still be inside deciding what to bring in next. Unless her sister was hiding. "I hope you aren't trying to move all by yourself. I know a great moving company—"

"No, thank you, though. The movers will be here this afternoon with the rest," Josephine said. "I'm Josephine Reynolds."

"So nice to meet you, Josephine. I'm vice president of the neighborhood association. This is a historic neighborhood, you know."

There it was. The real reason Barbara stood on the front porch. She wanted to ensure Josephine knew that there were certain rules to be followed, all of which Josephine had already researched. "Yes, I know. It's a beautiful street, and I'm happy to be a part of it."

Barbara's smile dimmed, and her lips pinched together. "The last owner didn't care much about keeping our street beautiful or about our responsibility to this historic neighborhood."

What could she say to get Barbara off her porch so she could continue moving in peace? "That's unfortunate," Josephine said. "I have all the information about the historical society and its requirements. Thank you so much for stopping by. I look forward to seeing you around the neighborhood." Although she didn't mean it; Barbara didn't seem like the kind of person Josephine could picture herself having a meaningful friendship with. What she was most looking forward to was finishing up today, taking a shower, and falling into bed.

"Donovan Grant was his name," Barbara continued, clearly not picking up on Josephine's social cues or not caring. "Did you know that just before he moved out, he painted some of the trim black on the windows at the back of the house? Only *some* of the trim. Not all of it. And *black.* Why would anyone paint trim black?"

Josephine had noticed the unusual paint job and made a note to strip the paint and match the trim to the rest on the house. "Some historical homes *do* have black trim," she countered.

"Not this one!" Barbara said, a little too aggressively. "And he didn't ask permission. He also added that hideous shed in the backyard, which we repeatedly demanded he remove. Heaven only knows what he used it for."

"A lawn mower or yard tools?" Josephine said, placing the box down on the porch to free her aching arms. This conversation didn't appear to be winding down anytime soon.

"Doesn't matter, because adding an outbuilding is against the codes. And besides, I looked inside the shed after he moved, and you know what was in there? Nothing."

Josephine pressed her lips together before speaking, gathering more courteous words than the options that threatened to tumble out. "Wouldn't the shed have been empty since he moved?"

Barbara huffed. "It didn't look like he'd ever kept anything in there. I'd bet he just added it for spite. And have you *seen* the weather vane?"

Josephine craned her neck as though she could see through the porch roof to the top of the house. "I haven't noticed it."

"It's a turkey," Barbara said. When Josephine laughed, Barbara's eyes narrowed. "It *must* be taken down. He didn't get approval for that unsightly thing, and we didn't notice it until a month or so before he left. When I confronted him about it, he said he'd had it professionally made, as if that makes it okay. And this"—she straight-arm pointed at the front door—"is highly unacceptable. I *know* he replaced the front door with this monstrosity on purpose."

Monstrosity was an exaggeration, but the generic primer-gray front door, probably purchased at a big-box store, was a woeful sight on the stately Carter Mansion. Changing the current front door to a historic one from the late 1890s was a top priority for Josephine once she was all moved in.

Katherine bounded up the steps and lifted her eyebrows in question. Josephine forced a smile. "Thank you for all of this information, Barbara. I'll do my best to bring the house back into line with its historic distinction."

"I certainly hope so," Barbara said, glancing between the sisters. "We take our historic neighborhood seriously."

"That much is clear," Katherine said, "since you've wasted no time in coming over here while we're in the middle of moving in. We appreciate your zeal for neighborhood codes, and if you don't mind, we'd love to keep going. It's already been a long day."

Barbara looked mildly snubbed, but she nodded curtly and walked down the stairs. Once on the sidewalk, she glanced over her shoulder at the sisters, a haughty look on her pinched face, then hustled away.

"I think you offended her," Josephine said, freeing the keys from her pocket, picking up her box, and unlocking the front door.

Katherine shrugged and carried two boxes inside the house. "Her spiel could have waited a day or another week."

Josephine crossed the small foyer and placed her box in the wide hallway that ran the length of the first floor. The switchback staircase took up half the foyer. Directly to her left was an opening to the living room, and the parlor was to the right. Branching off the long hallway were doors to the dining room, a reading and music room, and the kitchen.

Katherine stacked her boxes near Josephine's. "My guess is she's probably busting at the seams to find out who we are and see if we're going to sully her precious neighborhood. I know her type."

Josephine headed back toward the open front door. She knocked her knuckles against it. "She's not wrong, though, about the front door. It is ugly. I can't believe Uncle Donnie got rid of whatever was here before. It had to be better than this eyesore."

"I know a great salvage yard you can check out," Katherine said. "I send all of my clients there. The owner, Leo Freeman, has been in the business for years. He'll know exactly what you need to replace Uncle Donnie's disaster door."

Josephine and Katherine brought in the remaining boxes and smaller items they'd taken from the storage unit. The movers agreed to stop by the unit after leaving the Green Hills house, load up the remaining larger items, and bring everything to the Carter Mansion. Though furnished, there was plenty of room for the antiques and personal items Josephine wanted to add.

At least half of the furniture in the mansion was antique, and why Donnie had left behind such priceless pieces was anybody's guess. It was as puzzling as why he fought viciously to own the house and then allowed it to go into foreclosure.

The dining room table, chairs, buffet, and china cabinet were original to the house, and the end tables, lamps, and a few of the upholstered chairs in the parlor were too. Stepping into those rooms felt like stepping back in time. But the living room furniture was a mishmash of styles and eras. Josephine planned to replace pieces over time and bring more cohesion to the space.

The main bedroom upstairs had updated furniture, but the other two still held their original bedroom suites. With or without permission, Donnie had added an en suite primary bathroom and a Jack and Jill between the smaller bedrooms. He'd also renovated the kitchen and added modern appliances and fixtures. Perhaps those additions had bankrupted him. Josephine knew how expensive high-end taste was. She'd been married to someone with it for fifteen years.

An hour after Josephine and Katherine arrived at the house, the movers parked against the curb. In less than two hours, they unloaded their truck, situated everything inside the house according to the sisters' directions, and drove away with their tip money.

Josephine dropped onto the mauve, floral-patterned couch, a holdout from the eighties. She flopped her arm across her eyes and sighed. "I could probably fall asleep right now."

"The smell of that couch alone would give you nightmares," Katherine joked, lying across the living room rug, arms splayed. "But this rug might be worse. It probably hasn't been cleaned in a decade."

Josephine turned her head to look down at her sister. Love and gratefulness swelled so quickly in her chest that tears stung her eyes. She'd actually done it. She'd sold the house she shared with Nathan, leaving behind his ghost. Leaving behind the dreams they'd had for a future there. Now she was free to start over and, if possible, to attempt a reconnection with something alive and real again. "Thank you. For everything."

Katherine opened her eyes and looked at Josephine. "You'd do the same for me."

Josephine nodded. She would have, but Katherine was the most competent person Josephine knew, possibly had ever known. Katherine always appeared in control and stable, which was the opposite of how Josephine would describe herself recently.

Katherine sat up with a groan. "I'm going to feel this tomorrow. You going to be okay tonight by yourself? Want me to stay over?"

"I'll be fine," she said. After all, she'd been sleeping alone for months, even before Nathan died. He worked so many hours that he often came home after she'd gone to sleep. Rather than wake her, he'd sleep in another bedroom. That thought caused a cramp in her heart. She sat up and rubbed her fingers across her collarbone, looking around the spacious living room. "I've just moved from one big empty house into another."

Katherine's serious expression softened for a moment. "This won't be anything like where you've come from. I have a good feeling about this place."

"Because you won't be the one trying to air out Uncle Donnie's bad vibes? I wish I'd thought to buy sage for burning."

Katherine chuckled. "They call it smudging. The bathroom and kitchen upgrades he did are excellent. Looks like he took care of most of the antique furniture, and as far as I can tell, with the exception of the kitchen, all the original fixtures are still here. Although he wasn't much of a gardener from the state of those rosebushes in the back. They're sadder than a steel guitar in a country song. You can hire a landscaper, unless you're interested in gardening."

Josephine had loved the Green Hills backyard and garden. Though she mentioned to Nathan that she'd like to help with the upkeep and plantings, he insisted on hiring landscapers to come every two weeks. Again he made her an observer rather than an active participant.

Katherine continued, "With a little care, the garden will perk back up."

"Sounds like you're talking about me," Josephine said, trying to make a joke, and yet the truth of her words created a visceral ache inside her.

Katherine stood and reached out for her sister. She pulled Josephine into a sitting position on the couch. "Don't forget to call Leo Freeman next week and get that front door replaced."

Josephine nodded and rolled her eyes. "I won't forget. I gotta get Barbara off my back for a while."

Katherine grinned. "You might be surprised at the wonders changing out a front door can do for a house."

CHAPTER 3

The next morning, Josephine lingered in a slant of sunlight in the kitchen and drank a cup of instant coffee. The light warmed her bare feet on the white tiles. Katherine had helped Josephine find her bed linens and make up the main bedroom's bed before she left last night. By the time Josephine collapsed onto the mattress, she'd been so exhausted she was certain she'd sleep for a week. Instead, she'd tossed and turned all night because of dreams involving being chased by a swarm of bumblebees and standing in a smoky, crowded bar screaming for help, though no one could hear her.

Even now a trace of restless energy coursed beneath her bare feet, a steady hum as though the tiled floor vibrated with impatience and edginess. Lack of sleep was probably to blame. But also the emotions brewing within her.

What had she been thinking, moving into a house too enormous for one person—or even four people? How was uprooting herself from one empty home and planting herself in another a good idea? What would she do with all this space? Open a B&B? Take on renters? Both options were dismal. She didn't want an influx of strangers in her house all the time, didn't want to cook and serve them. Renting rooms sounded even less appealing. The last time she'd shared a place with anyone other than Nathan was in her college dorm, and those memories of no privacy, cramped bathrooms, and unclean living spaces were enough to elicit a firm *no way*.

Josephine didn't need the money. But she wanted to understand why she felt so out of place and alone. Didn't everyone feel a little off when they moved into a new house? *I need to be more patient. There's no way this place could possibly feel like home yet.* But would it ever?

She glanced around the room. Part of Donnie's kitchen renovation included new cabinetry, a walk-in pantry, a butler's pantry, and a laundry room. Unlike many original historic homes, there was plenty of storage space in this kitchen. Boxes labeled *Kitchen Items* were stacked nearby, creating a wall of cardboard squares. She needed to start unpacking them, but the sheer amount of stuff to unpack ignited a spark of frustration inside her.

The terrible coffee added to her darkening mood. Even so, she took a final gulp, grimacing at the lukewarm liquid on her tongue, and then poured the dregs into the oversize ceramic farmhouse sink and washed the basin clean.

Josephine stared at the boxes. She thought about when she and Nathan had moved into the Green Hills house. He'd paid the movers to unpack everything so when he came home from work that day, the entire house was live-in ready. He'd been pleased with the effortless move, but Josephine had spent weeks trying to locate and relocate items.

But here in the Carter Mansion, she could arrange the house exactly like she wanted. She could take her time opening each box and deciding the best placement for everything. This freedom should comfort her, cheer her onward to creating a place perfect for her. Instead, Josephine clenched her jaw at the overwhelming task. If Nathan hadn't died, then she wouldn't be in this house unpacking hundreds of boxes. Annoyed, she kicked the nearest box. She cried out as her toes jarred against the cardboard. Leaning over, she squeezed her aching foot as a column of boxes wobbled, sending the top box falling onto her back.

Josephine groaned and failed to catch the tumbling box. It landed upside down on the tiles. A sound between a laugh and a cry erupted from her lips. Then she righted the box. Handwritten in marker across the top was *Kitchen Linens & Utensils*. She stood and stretched her back, unable to reach the soreness between her shoulder blades where the box corner jabbed her, somewhat thankful it hadn't been a box of china.

Pull yourself together. You made the choice to be here, so unpack these boxes and get on with it. Why did the voice in her head sound like a feisty teenage version of herself? Back when she was so sure of herself, she could have accomplished anything. If her younger self could see her now, lip trembling in the kitchen because of moving boxes, she'd be shamed right out of the house.

"Get on with it," she said, repeating the voice in her head. She could unpack boxes without falling apart or breaking her toes.

Josephine thought about what Nathan would say: *Unpacking yourself? That's ridiculous and a poor use of your time. We could pay someone to do the same job in a quarter of the time.* She imagined her response: *I have all the time in the world now, Nathan.* And she did. No one was depending on her for anything. It baffled her how this new independence felt like a devastating loss when the opposite could also be true. Every single aspect that had controlled and dictated her life was gone. Every choice from this moment on would be hers and hers alone. Some women would fight for and celebrate this kind of release from every obligation, every expectation. But after fifteen years of surrendering her autonomy to someone else, this level of liberation was utterly terrifying. With Nathan she had purpose. Without him, who was she?

Well, for today at least, she was just a woman unpacking boxes.

Josephine grabbed the box cutter and lifted a box from the stack. She placed it on the countertop and slit the tape across the top. After opening the flaps, she pulled out a layer of bubble wrap. Then she paused. *Is that music?* The tinkling of piano keys drifted into the kitchen. Was it coming from outside? From a neighbor's house? She walked out of the kitchen and into the long hallway that stretched from the back of the house all the way to the foyer. But the farther away from the kitchen she walked, the softer the music became.

She returned to the kitchen, and with each step, the music, although still quiet, grew more distinct. Josephine stepped into the butler's pantry and listened. The piano solo was joined by an orchestra. Her eyes darted to the basement door. Before she had moved into the mansion, she and Katherine had inspected the small basement, which was mostly empty except for cobwebs, crumbling wooden shelving, and an assortment of forgotten items such as Mason jars, tools, and a bedframe leaned against one wall.

Josephine wrapped her fingers around the basement door's knob, and a zing rocketed up her arm. She startled at the jolt of energy reminiscent of a static electricity shock. Josephine shook out her arm, then tapped her fingertip a few times against the metal. Nothing happened. She gently wrapped her fingers around the cool knob, but a second sting didn't occur.

When she opened the door, the music swelled into a recognizable tune. "Rhapsody in Blue." She flipped on the switch at the top of the stairs and illuminated the top few wooden steps in a dull brownish glow. The creeping chill of the basement caused her to shiver as she descended the stairs that appeared one by one from the gloom. Her pulse quickened with the rhythm of the song, but when she stepped onto the dirt-covered floor, the music stopped. Josephine held her breath and waited, but the music didn't return.

She glanced around, looking for a source of the music. A radio? But who would have turned it on? Maybe the music hadn't come from the basement at all. She looked toward the ground-level rectangular window at the top of the wall. The glass, barely admitting dingy light, was splattered with mud and grass. Someone could have been walking by listening to music through their phone speakers. *In my backyard? Doubtful.* Who would be blasting jazz this time of day?

Josephine took one more glance around the shadowy space, rubbing her hands up and down her crossed arms, and noticed a sliver of pale light just beneath the bedframe propped against the wall in front of her. She bent over to peer beneath the frame and followed the straight line of light. Was the light coming from outside? *But isn't this wall butted against solid rock? How can sunlight come through? Unless that isn't a solid wall.*

Josephine grabbed the bedframe and heaved it out of the way. Running her finger along the crack at the bottom of the wall, she stopped when she reached the point where the light ended. Then she slid her finger vertically up the grimy wall, creating another line. She stretched as far as she could reach up the wall. A suspicion formed in her mind. *Is there a door here?* She scoffed at the absurdity. Why would there be a door in a solid rock wall?

But at about the position where a doorknob would be, her fingers moved over a papery texture. Josephine pulled out her cell phone and turned on its flashlight. Now she could see a dry substance pasted over the doorknob area. The patch had been painted to match the basement's charcoal gray walls. A subtle vibration radiated up from the packed earth, bringing with it the sensation that a flowing current of energy moved beneath her.

Josephine grabbed a rusted screwdriver from an aluminum pail on the floor and stabbed it into the painted paper. As she suspected, the shaft busted through easily. Josephine tore away the rest of the brittle paper, revealing a hole with light on the other side. She gasped when the music started up again. She leaned her ear toward the wall. The music was coming from the other side of this hidden door.

After a few seconds of being shocked into stillness, Josephine swiped open her phone and texted her sister: Are you free? Right now? Her mind ran wild with possibilities about music playing in a room that had been sealed off. And *why* was the room sealed off? Part of her wanted to flee the basement, but another much more potent desire filled her with the need to know what was happening and how.

Katherine responded: Are you okay? What's up? I can make myself free.

Josephine's heart raced. She texted: I found something in the basement. Can you come over?

Three dots bounced. That sounds ominous. Can you be any more specific? Are we talking dead somethings or Monet paintings? Do I have time to eat breakfast?

Josephine called her sister. Katherine answered immediately. "I hope you're not calling because it's scary option number one."

"I found a door," Josephine said in a rush of words. When Katherine didn't respond, she added, "A secret door in the basement."

Katherine hummed in her throat. "Is your next sentence going to be that you've finally found a way into Narnia?"

"I'm serious."

"So am I," Katherine said.

Josephine explained how she'd found the door, including the mysterious light and music that was still playing. "What do you think? Do you want to come over? Should we open it? It could be nothing."

Katherine chuckled. "How can we *not* open it? But if this door takes us to Narnia, no guarantees that I'm coming back."

"Understood," Josephine said.

"See you in half an hour," Katherine said and ended the call.

●●●

LESS THAN HALF an hour later, Josephine and Katherine stood in the basement staring at the hidden door. The music had stopped almost as soon has Josephine hung up the phone, and it hadn't restarted, which caused Josephine to doubt her sanity. *What if I'm actually losing it and imagined the music? Is that a possibility? Do people hallucinate songs in their heads?* Even so, Josephine hadn't imagined the door that had been purposely hidden.

"Whatcha thinking? Abracadabra? A crowbar?" Katherine asked. She shuffled off through the basement looking for a tool.

Josephine grabbed a screwdriver and shoved it into the mechanism inside the space where the doorknob had once been attached. She wiggled around the tool and then pressed its flat head against the latch, which depressed when she applied force. She heard a confirmation click, and she looped her fingers inside the hole and tugged. The hidden door made a suctioning sound as it unsealed itself and opened just a crack. The unsealed room exhaled a rush of dank, musty air across Josephine's face.

Across the room, Katherine gasped. "How did you do that?" When Josephine held up the screwdriver, Katherine's forehead wrinkled. "You know how to open doors with a screwdriver?"

"When we were renovating part of the Green Hills house, Nathan accidentally shut himself in our bedroom closet that didn't have a doorknob yet." Josephine shrugged. "So I googled it before he lost his mind."

"I'm not going to ask why he closed a door without a knob on it. I bet he lost his mind before you finished watching the how-to video," Katherine joked as she crossed the room to her sister.

"Actually before I could pull up the video, but still I rescued him in less than five minutes. He was too frustrated to be grateful at the time, but later we laughed. The electrical was off in that part of the house, so the closet was extra-dark."

Katherine snorted a laugh. "It must have been awful to be trapped in a cushy walk-in closet for five minutes." She stood beside Josephine. "Smells dank, even more so than this basement."

"Ready?" Josephine asked. Her heart pounded, and she reached for Katherine's hand and squeezed. Then she used the screwdriver to wedge open the door enough to get her fingers around the edge of the cool wood. The tool clanged against the aluminum pail when Josephine dropped it. She opened the door slowly, unsure of what to expect. Her shoulders relaxed as soon as she saw the room had electricity running to it. "The lights are on in there."

Josephine stepped over the threshold with Katherine right behind her. The dimly lit space smelled musky with an aging sent of tobacco and pine. The length and size of the long rectangular space stunned Josephine. Directly in front of them was a substantial wooden bar top at least twenty feet long. Beneath the dust and grime of years passing without use, she could still see evidence of its lacquered finish that would have gleamed in the round pendant lights evenly spaced throughout the room.

Half a dozen round tables, each with four matching chairs, were positioned on the other side of the bar and down the length of the room. There were two additional areas, one with a partially closed door, and the other beyond a large opening in the wall near the back. From where she stood, Josephine wasn't sure what they contained. A tarnished silver mirror the length of the wall hung behind the bar top. Wooden shelves that Josephine assumed once held dozens of bottles were bare except for two lonely, empty liquor bottles, one rum and one brandy.

"Well, I'll be a monkey's uncle," Katherine said. "Is this a bar?"

Surprise laughter bubbled up Josephine's throat. "I think it's a speakeasy."

"No way!" Katherine said, walking to the long bar. Her bright pink nail polish shined as she wrote her name in the dust with her finger. She smiled before wiping her hand against her jeans.

"What else would it be? It's a hidden bar in the basement of a historic home."

Katherine walked the length of the bar top, and Josephine pointed at an antique radio sitting on the end. "Maybe that's where the music was coming from." Relief flooded her. *I wasn't hallucinating!* Maybe the last grief-stricken eight months hadn't permanently broken her. Hope boosted her until Katherine lifted the radio's cord.

"Doubtful," her sister said. "It's not plugged in." The dropped cord slapped against the back of the bar. "Unless this place is haunted."

Shivers ran up Josephine's arms. If the radio wasn't the source of the music, then what or who had beckoned her toward the hidden space?

Lines creased Katherine's forehead. "What's that look on your face? Are you afraid it *is* haunted? Because I don't believe in ghosts."

Ghosts weren't what spiked Josephine's fear. "Do you—do you think I made up the music? Imagined it? Am I . . . losing it?"

"Losing what?" Katherine asked. "Your mental clarity? No, Jo-Jo. Did you imagine the music? I don't know, but whether you did or not doesn't change the fact that you found a hidden door because of it. That's *something*."

Josephine nodded. "I don't think this place is haunted," she said. "But I've *felt* different ever since I moved in."

Katherine's serious expression transitioned into one of understanding. "That's called freedom. This house, your life, your next choices—all yours."

"Freedom," Josephine echoed, the shape of the words feeling strange, almost foreign, on her lips. "Feels like terror."

Katherine walked to her and slipped her hand into Josephine's, the way she used to do when they were little girls. "Sometimes they feel the same. Our perspective is what makes the difference."

Josephine's throat tightened, and she tried to clear it. "You don't know what it's like," she said, her voice almost a whisper. "Losing your anchor. Losing what makes you feel real and connected to the world. My whole life was wrapped up in Nathan. I don't even know what to *do* with myself now."

Katherine shook her head. "You're right, I don't know what it's like to lose my husband. But I know loss, Jo-Jo. I know what it's like to feel panicked when life shifts in a way you never expected, when you feel like the wind has been knocked out of you—"

Josephine rubbed her fingers across her collarbone. "When you feel like you have a hole shot right through you."

"Exactly," she said and squeezed Josephine's hand.

"You say I'm free," Josephine said, "and I am, but I'm also lost. What do I *do* with all this freedom?"

"Maybe it's time to untangle *your life* from what Nathan created for your life. You are still your own person. You used to have dreams—"

Josephine's laugh came out tight and sarcastic. "Dreams? You mean when I was a kid? I don't even remember my dreams, Katybug." She wiped at her wet cheeks, frustrated by her inability to talk about Nathan without crying. Sadness over losing her husband now faded beneath resentment. *If Nathan hadn't expected me to do everything his way, then I'd be different now. I'd be stronger. I wouldn't be this pathetic shadow of who I could have been.* But to blame everything on Nathan also fell short of the truth. Josephine had *agreed* to do everything his way. For years. And whose fault was that?

"You used to talk about working in public relations," Katherine argued.

"I never finished college," Josephine countered. "I've only been an office manager."

Katherine released her sister's hand and huffed. "So what? You worked in Nathan's practice doing more than that. You're the most overqualified office manager I know. You have plenty of work experience, and you're smart and a quick learner. Plus, you're beautiful. Don't look at me like that. You're not as solid as you have been, in my opinion, but you'll get your healthy glow back."

"You act like I might find a healthy glow in one of those cardboard boxes upstairs," Josephine said, trying to joke but sounding dejected.

Katherine ignored her self-deprecation. "You could work in PR or event planning. Lord knows you planned hundreds of parties for Nathan through the years. Or what about fundraising? You could find a nonprofit you support and help them with organizing events or write funding proposals and press releases. Or, worst-case scenario, you could come to work with me and sell houses."

Josephine groaned. "Definitely worst case. I'd be a lousy salesperson."

"You would be," Katherine agreed, but she was smiling. "But I love you, and I'd take one for the team for you."

Josephine couldn't speak around the tightness closing her throat.

Katherine added, "You don't have to decide anything right now."

Josephine tried to remember who she was in college before she met Nathan and even before Seth, whom she'd only dated for a few months. Had she been excited about her future? Had she dreamed of having a career of her own? She could barely recall the young girl she'd been. Life before Nathan felt like it belonged to a woman she couldn't resuscitate.

Katherine walked around the bar and toward the partially open door. She pushed it completely open, poked her head in, and looked around. "Bathrooms. His and hers." Looking at Josephine, she asked, "Why would Grandma have a speakeasy?"

Josephine shook her head. "This probably wasn't Grandma's. Speakeasies came about in the 1920s during Prohibition, so this more likely belonged to our great-grandparents." Katherine opened her phone and started typing. "Who are you texting?"

"Mama," she answered.

Josephine walked the length of the speakeasy and peered into the second room. A sitting area held a few plush leather chairs, four booths, small end tables, and a grimy L-shaped dark-fabric sofa. Wall sconces lit the room in muted milky light. A small rectangle of paper wedged beneath a table leg caught her eye. Josephine tugged it free. She held what looked like a business card. The front of the faded card read *Club Belle Âme*. The back of the card announced Eleanor Baker's membership. The rest of the information was indecipherable, too smudged with dirt.

Katherine followed Josephine into the room. "Whatcha got there?"

She handed the card to her sister. "Someone's membership card to a club."

Katherine pulled out her phone and typed in a search for Club Belle Âme in Nashville, but it yielded no results. "Weird. Maybe it was an informal ladies club, something local, like gardening or volunteer work. Do you think Mama knows about this place?" Katherine asked.

"If she did, then Uncle Donnie would have, but since the door was still sealed up, I doubt it."

Katherine's phone started ringing. "It's Mama. I'll put her on speaker." Katherine held out the phone between them. "Hey, I'm here with Josephine *in the speakeasy*. You're on speaker."

"Hey, sweetheart," their mama said, and by the sound of her softening voice they knew she meant Josephine. "How are you doing?"

"Hey," Josephine said. She skipped right over her mom's question because she couldn't presently describe how she was in a way that wouldn't induce anxiety in her mother. Instead, Josephine asked, "Did you know there was a hidden speakeasy in the Carter Mansion?"

"Are you two pulling my leg? I've been in that basement hundreds of times during my life, and there's nothing down there but junk."

Katherine shared how they stumbled upon the secret door, leaving out the part about Josephine hearing mysterious music, and when Katherine finished the story, their mother exhaled loudly.

"Well, for goodness' sake, I'm just as surprised as you are. But now that you mention it, I do remember a story about my grandma from when I was a kid. It wasn't told directly to me, but I overheard it. I didn't understand much of it at the time. I was so young. It was something about how my grandma once ran an illicit club that the police raided, and she was almost arrested."

"Say what?" Katherine blurted. "We had a rebel in the family, and you're just now mentioning it?"

"Honey, that was a lifetime ago, and I wouldn't have known a speakeasy from a merry-go-round. You could always look it up and see if there are any records, but for all we know, it could have been a nonsense story."

Josephine pulled her cell phone out of her pocket. She typed her great-grandmother's name—Alma Grant—into the search engine and scrolled through the first page of hits. "Nothing for Alma Grant. Nothing scandalous at least."

"No, no, you won't find anything under Alma Grant," her mama said. "Search for Alma Carter. Grant came from her second marriage. I think this would have happened, if it even did, before she married my grandfather."

"Second marriage? This family keeps getting more and more interesting," Katherine teased. "Although it makes sense that she was given the *Carter* Mansion as a wedding gift if she married a Carter. Find anything?" she asked, looking at Josephine.

Josephine scrolled through the new search, and her breath caught, hastening her pulse. "There's an article about a raid on a speakeasy"—she looked at her sister—"at the Carter Mansion on October 9, 1927."

"Well, I'll be," her mama said.

Josephine quickly read the short article. "Members of the Bureau of Prohibition, along with local police, raided the speakeasy, although they didn't find Alma inside. Some people were taken in, but it doesn't appear that anyone was officially jailed. Alma paid a hefty fine, though, since it was inside her house." Josephine returned to the original search and scrolled through the remaining few articles that mentioned her great-grandmother. "The rest of the reports are the same." She clicked off her phone and slid it back into her pocket.

Katherine frowned. "What happened to her first husband? It doesn't mention him."

"He died in World War I. Alma was a widow at twenty," her mama said. "She didn't marry my grandfather until she was in her late twenties, I think."

Josephine pressed her hands against her chest. "Twenty?" As a thirty-five-year-old widow, Josephine hadn't handled losing Nathan with any sort of grace, but did anyone handle losing a spouse well? At least Nathan had left her with enough money to ensure she'd never have to work again unless she wanted to. Josephine couldn't imagine what it must have been like to be widowed in the 1920s, when women's lives were much more oppressed and their choices were far more limited. "That poor woman. How heartbroken she must have been."

"She obviously found a way to survive and not just survive but also prosper," Katherine said. "She found a way to keep this mansion."

Josephine nodded. "I'm having a hard time grasping that our great-grandma ran an illegal bar *in her house*. That's outrageously bold."

Katherine knocked her shoulder into her sister's. "Family trait, boldness. We also exhibit signs of bravery and perseverance." Josephine leaned her head against Katherine's shoulder.

"Hey, girls, I gotta run," her mama said. "I'm meeting Fran for brunch. Jo-Jo, call me, honey, when you have some time. And take pictures for me, but for heaven's sake, don't post anything online. I don't want Donnie finding out what he missed. He probably would have tried to reopen the place."

Katherine laughed, and they shared I-love-yous before she ended the call. Josephine noticed another door near the far back of the room. This door had a doorknob, but it was bolted three times from the inside. A small wooden peg stuck out from the door around eye level. Josephine grabbed the wooden peg, and it easily rocked to one side, revealing a peephole the size of a baseball. She pressed her eye against the hole and looked out into a small room with sunlight filtering into it.

Josephine unlocked the bolts, turned the handle, and tugged open the door. The opposite side of the door was smooth and didn't have a doorknob or a handle. There was no way to open it from the outside. The door opened into a narrow, galley-style space full of old potting tables, gardening tools, and terra-cotta pots. It smelled of wet earth and mulch combined with an herbaceous aroma. Josephine took the few strides straight across the room and opened an unassuming wooden door with a rectangular window—the source of the sunlight—revealing stone stairs leading up to the ground-level backyard garden.

"I think you just found the secret way in," Katherine said. "The patrons couldn't have come in through the front door. That would have been too conspicuous. But if they came through the garden, they could hide what they were doing easier."

Josephine nodded. "And for anyone who didn't know about the speakeasy, this room looked like a potting area for the garden." She walked up the stone stairs and lingered in a patch of dappled sunlight pouring down through the mature oak and maple trees. "Who knows what else we'll find hidden in this house?"

Katherine stood beside her, turning her face up toward the light like a sunflower. "I bet this is only the beginning of the secrets we'll discover."

CHAPTER 4

Katherine left to meet clients who wanted to tour houses for sale in the East Nashville area, and Josephine spent a couple of hours unpacking boxes. She finished the kitchen, and rather than move to the next downstairs room, she wandered upstairs and sat among the boxes from the storage unit containing her great-grandmother's belongings.

When Grandma Dorothy died six years ago, Josephine's mama gathered as many items from this house as she could before Uncle Donnie took ownership of it. Her mama divided up the antique furniture pieces between Josephine and Katherine. Because of the sisters' different tastes, her mama gave Josephine Alma's clothes, photo albums, and a few household antiques, including a daisy-patterned tea set and porcelain planters. Katherine received jewelry and heirloom serving platters and Grandma Dorothy's wedding china.

Alma's armoire had been in storage for years but was now in Josephine's bedroom. Josephine unpacked Alma's delicate clothing, inspecting each piece with gentle hands. She wondered what her great-grandmother's life had been like and where she might have worn each item. There was a variety of styles as well as outfits from different decades. Josephine hung a 1930s deep crimson evening gown with a blouson bodice and flutter sleeves. The cut of the dress accentuated a slim waist, and the silky fabric flowed to the floor. Next she hung a dress from the '40s. Its simple design and army-green color hinted at the atmosphere of the country at the time. The scooping collar and belted waist added slight embellishments, but overall the dress was utilitarian.

There was a rich indigo swing dress with a halter top from the '50s and a sky-blue mini dress with a bow at the collar from the '60s. Alma must have felt a special bond to the '20s, because most of the clothing was from that era, ranging from simple dresses with dropped waists and economical fabrics to more intricate evening wear with beadwork, sequins, and embroidery. Josephine slid the fabric of a forest-green evening dress through her fingers as it shimmered in the light. How glamorous Alma must have looked in that one.

After hanging the clothes inside the armoire, Josephine removed family photo albums from a box. She picked up the one on top and lay across her bed. She smoothed her hand over the aged, cracked leather binding and flipped open the front cover. Alma's signature was scrawled near the bottom of the inside front cover, along with the date 1916. The pages were made of thick black paper, and sepia-tone photographs were glued in place. Some photos were inscribed with black ink, offering names, dates, and locations in cursive handwriting. This album exclusively featured Alma's wedding to Franklin Carter. Josephine had flipped through it after first receiving it years ago, but she hadn't thought of it since. Now she drifted through Alma's memories, mesmerized by the life of a woman she wanted to learn more about.

Pages were filled with smiling faces, which was unusual for photographs of this era. Most vintage pictures revealed people who seemed miserable, uncomfortable, angry, or a combination of all three—and maybe they were. *I can relate.* Alma's more candid images added to the evidence that she wasn't typical. She didn't seem to care about the rules, or perhaps she made up her own.

Waves of joy radiated from the images and surrounded Josephine in a comforting haze. She was drawn into their lives, feeling as if she actually knew these people, as if she had attended their wedding. A shadow of disappointment moved through her when she reached the last page. She sat up and hugged the heavy album against her chest.

Josephine closed her eyes and thought about her own wedding. She'd been dazzled by the entire affair, planned mostly by Nathan's mother, who spared no expense. At twenty, Josephine hadn't known a thing about how to be a wife. She was in her second year of college when Nathan, doing his residency at Vanderbilt, swept her off her feet. She'd never finished her college degree in communications, a decision she sometimes regretted. Instead, when Nathan opened his Nashville practice, she worked as his office manager. He said it would be a temporary job to help him get established. Then she would hire staff and her replacement, and she'd find a career of her own. But Nathan hadn't wanted her to leave, saying she was a vital part of what made his practice one of the most efficient in town. As if "being efficient" was her life goal, she'd continued working as his office manager—and personal assistant, insurance broker, payroll clerk, party planner, and occasionally a wife he noticed—for fifteen years as he became the most-sought-out cardiologist in the state.

Lowering the album to her lap, she placed her palm on its leather cover. Alma and Franklin had been a bright young couple, probably with so much hope for the future. They would have barely a year together before Franklin would be shipped off to France and never return. In less than two years, Alma would be a widow. Josephine squeezed her eyes shut. Her own sorrow blended with the sorrow she imagined Alma must have experienced. A terrible commonality to share. For months she'd been asking herself what the point was of allowing yourself to fall in love. Of giving your heart over to someone only to feel the crushing weight of its inevitable brokenness.

The next album was dated 1917 and followed their first year together. They traveled, attended garden parties, and cuddled before a Christmas tree. They played tennis with friends, and Alma huddled with the same group of women in many photos. Those must have been her closest friends. Alma and Franklin attended outdoor dinner parties and danced beneath oak trees. For all Josephine could see, Alma and Franklin had been blissful honeymooners.

But the next album was dated 1919, skipping an entire year in Alma's life—her first year without Franklin. Josephine wondered if Alma's life had become invisible for a while, too, like hers had, folding in on itself in a swirl of grief and emptiness. Had Alma crafted a plan to open a speakeasy sometime after Prohibition, or had it been an act of desperation for income? Speakeasies were profitable enterprises and probably pulled in more money than an unmarried woman could have made doing anything else at the time. If Josephine had been in Alma's situation, would she have done the same? Would she have had the courage to open a speakeasy? Josephine laughed at the idea of opening and running a bar herself. *I can't even imagine it. And an illegal activity? No way.*

Looking at the beautiful, youthful woman Alma was in her wedding photos, Josephine wouldn't have believed that same woman, with her alabaster skin and big doe eyes, would be daring enough to take such risks. Alma's house had been raided! What

Josephine wouldn't give to have met her great-grandmother, such an unforgettable force.

•••

A WEEK AFTER she moved into the Carter Mansion, Josephine had unpacked every box and put away every item. She hired a cleaning crew that was coming this afternoon. She requested a deep clean of the entire house, a task that would take them about four hours. So Josephine decided to run errands this morning so she could be back in time to let in the cleaners. The broken-down cardboard was in the back of a truck she'd rented for today's tasks. After dropping off the recycling, she planned to visit the architectural salvage yard Katherine suggested.

The first of October brought a crispness with it. Nearly everyone in the city wholeheartedly welcomed the shift in the weather. The pumpkin-spice latte returned with a celebration worthy of its own holiday. Almost overnight, Nashville's trees switched from an array of greens to a colorful display of rich autumnal shades. While loading the back of the truck with boxes, Josephine spotted pumpkins on front porches, and one neighbor had propped a ladder against the side of his house and was hanging oversize spiders in webby gauze large enough to ensnare humans.

Josephine zipped up her jacket and grabbed her purse off the sideboard in the hallway just as her cell phone rang. Katherine was calling. "I was just thinking about you," she said as a greeting. "I'm going to the architectural salvage place this morning."

"I wish I could go with you!" Katherine said. "I love poking around that place. I don't need a thing, but I still like looking and dreaming about a house full of refurbished antique pieces.

I'm calling for two reasons. First, I didn't want you to forget that Neil and I are flying to Tampa today for a week and a half."

Josephine plucked the truck's rental keys out of her purse. "The Realtors convention?"

"Right, which lasts five days, and then he and I are using the rest of the time as vacation. We've rented a condo on the bay, and he might even take me out on a sailboat this year."

"He's not sailing it, right?"

"Lord, no," Katherine said and laughed. "You'd be watching some made-for-TV-movie reenactment years from now about our catastrophe. We'd probably end up on some uninhabited island in the Caribbean, but now that I think about it, that doesn't sound like a bad deal."

Josephine stepped out onto the front porch, then closed and locked the door. "Say goodbye to this front door," she said. "It won't be here much longer. I hope to find something this morning."

"Goodbye, hideous front door," Katherine joked.

Josephine noticed her neighbor had added life-size skeletons to the trunk and some of the branches of the oak tree in his front yard. "What was the second thing?"

"Oh, I'm sending over decorators today. They should be there after lunch," Katherine said.

Josephine paused halfway down the front steps. "Decorators for what?"

"For your housewarming gift," she said. "You asked for outdoor holiday decorations because that wasn't something Nathan ever wanted."

"I'd forgotten about that," Josephine said with a laugh. "I was thinking more along the lines of Christmastime."

"You live on a street where they take their decorating seriously, even Halloween," Katherine said, "and knowing you, you weren't planning on going all out on Halloween décor this year."

Josephine clicked the Unlock button on the truck's key fob. She climbed into the cab. "Not much I feel like 'going all out on' this year."

"Exactly! Which is why I hired people to do the work for you for this Halloween. They're fabulous stagers. I use them all the time for my properties. You don't have to do a thing. They show up with all the décor, put it up for you, and after the holiday they'll come take it down."

"Is this really necessary? I mean, for Halloween? What if we waited until Christmas?" Josephine asked, turning on the truck's engine and switching the air conditioning to low heat.

"Do you really want Barbara, the neighborhood association enforcer, up in your face later?"

Josephine rolled her eyes even though Katherine couldn't see her. "You really think she'll care about my front porch?"

"Are you seriously asking me that?" Katherine asked. "The same woman who showed up on move-in day to complain about your front door and the turkey sitting atop your house?"

"You win," Josephine relented with a chuckle. "And, hey, thank you. Y'all have a great vacation. Drink a mai tai for me."

Katherine snorted. "You don't even drink mai tais."

Josephine smiled. "'Drink a water for me' doesn't have the same pizzazz."

"I'll only be gone a week and a half, okay?" Katherine said. "Call me if you need *anything*, and text me pictures of the decorations."

"I will, and don't worry about me," Josephine said, buckling her seat belt. "What can possibly happen in a week and a half? I'll be fine." She turned on the radio. "Rhapsody in Blue" eased out of the speakers, sending tingles racing across her skin.

●●●

AFTER DROPPING OFF the cardboard at the nearest recycling center, Josephine drove across town to the architectural salvage yard. Calling it a "yard" wasn't quite accurate. Her GPS brought her to the parking lot of an unassuming white building that looked like it had once been a factory or a storage warehouse. Josephine had imagined something more akin to an outdoor junkyard or one of those antique malls advertised on interstate billboards. The kind of places jam-packed with outdated knick-knacks rather than priceless treasures.

A bell jingled when she opened the front door. Warmth from the interior welcomed her inside, and she paused in surprise at the sight of the front area. This place was nothing like a junk-yard or a mall full of tchotchkes. The wall directly in front of her was crowded from floor to ceiling with antique doorknobs and backplates that had been attached to the Sheetrock, giving the appearance of an enchanted wall that could transport you to a thousand different locations. Chandeliers ranging in sizes suitable for hallways to grand foyers hung suspended from the ceiling. Waterfall crystals sparkled in the light, and opaque globes shielded bulbs. There were shiny brass chandeliers and tarnished ones, and others that had been painted multiple times, the evidence a knobby, uneven finish.

Wall sconces, some steel and some dainty enough to hang in a child's nursery, lined a hallway to her right. To her left, intricate scrollwork carvings decorated a twelve-foot long wooden partition. An oversize metal mantelpiece leaned against the partition, half a dozen andirons arranged in front of it. Josephine walked into the next room, which housed more mantels, columns, and a massive assortment of baskets that contained doorknobs, brass plates, skeleton keys, door knockers, and door hinges. The inventory was staggering, and Josephine knew she'd only seen a few of the spaces in this enormous building. People could lose themselves for hours in this place.

The next room held nearly a hundred different stained-glass windows. She marveled at an arched Gothic window that must have been removed from a historic church. It depicted a likeness of Jesus standing among animals. As she leaned over to inspect the design, an older man walked through another doorway and greeted her.

"Good morning," he said. The bear-size man's broad shoulders were slightly stooped, and his tanned skin was deeply lined, revealing a long life, as did his paper-white hair. The gray bandanna tied around his forehead matched his long-sleeve shirt. He moved slowly and intentionally with no signs of the usual rush and hurry people prioritized these days.

Josephine smiled a greeting. "Good morning. I'm looking for Leo Freeman. My sister, Katherine Miller, sent me."

"I'm Leo," he said with a nod. "Owner and preservationist. I remember Katherine. Real estate, right? You two look like sisters. What can I help you with?"

Josephine slid her hands into her jacket pockets. "I'm looking for a door."

He leaned his head toward the opening he'd stepped through and motioned for her to follow him. Josephine walked into a wide hallway lined with hundreds of doors. "Oh, wow," she said. "There are so many. I have no idea where to start."

"That's why I'm here," he said, stopping halfway down the hallway. "Tell me what you're looking for, and we'll narrow it down." He grinned at the amazement on her face. "I don't want to send you into a spin, but this is only a small sample of what I have."

She felt tempted to ask, *"Is there a door that will take me back to the past? Back to when life felt okayish? Before Nathan died . . ."* But how far back would she need to go? When was the last time she'd felt genuinely happy or satisfied? Was that her own fault? How breath-stealing it was to finally understand that *no one* should be or could be responsible for her happiness. No one but her.

Shaking herself out of her thoughts, she answered, "A historic door, preferably from around the 1890s. That's when the home was built, and I'd like something from that era and style."

"The home is here in town?" Leo asked and started walking again. He led them to the end of the hallway and turned a corner.

Josephine gasped at the sheer size of the adjoining room, large enough to drop the first floor of the Carter Mansion into it with ease. There were doors, windows, mantels, finials, cornices, partitions, archways, and more. Her gaze danced everywhere, each item lighting her up with wonder. "This is like Ali Baba's treasure cave."

"Only less shiny," he said with a slight grin. "The home is in Nashville?" he asked again.

"Oh, sorry, I'm so distracted," she said with a shake of her head. "Yes, it's in Belle Meade. I just bought the Carter Mansion. It belonged to my great-grandmother Alma."

Leo's small brown eyes widened, and the lines on his forehead compressed. Josephine couldn't interpret his surprise, and Leo didn't speak for a few seconds. The faint ticking of a clock disturbed the silence. Shivers tickled her skin.

"I know that place," he finally said, breaking the eerie silence hanging between them. "And the need for a new door."

Josephine wondered briefly if Leo knew Barbara. Or maybe Donnie's door was the kind of travesty that spread through historic circles in a bulletin that read: "Historic Home Tarnished by Hideous Modern Door." "My uncle Donnie owned the house, but he went into foreclosure, so that's how I came to buy it. He got rid of the original front door—Heaven only knows why—and he replaced it with a mass-produced one. Not only is this against the historical society's preservation rules, but it's also out of character with the rest of the house. Do you think you have something that will work?"

Leo's slow smile and the glint in his eyes caused prickling on her skin. "I have the perfect door." He motioned for her to follow him again, and he led them to a workshop area in the rear of the massive space. Inside the workshop, Leo removed a heavy blue tarp from an item leaned against a wall. As the tarp fell away, a stunning polished door appeared.

Two rectangular windows stretched from near the top of the door to just below the halfway point. Ironwork scrolled behind the wavy glass panes, adding a simple but beautiful detail. Two inlaid square panels on the lower half of the door were modestly designed. Bronze-colored hinges hung from one edge. The hand-carved door showcased its remarkable craftsmanship, and it appeared to have a functional knob and lock.

"Solid walnut," Leo said, stepping back from the door and admiring it.

Josephine touched the door, caressing the smooth finish. "It's gorgeous, and you're right. It's perfect."

Leo beamed. "Of course it is. This door was handcrafted for that house and until a few years ago was part of it."

Josephine blinked in response, trying to understand his meaning. "You mean this is the one Uncle Donnie got rid of? How did you come to have it?"

"One of your neighbors called me when they saw him removing the door," Leo explained. "They thought I could salvage it."

Josephine's skin tingled. "What are the chances?"

Leo chuckled. "That I'd save the door from the dumpster, never sell it, and you'd end up here years later looking for it?"

She touched one of the decorative hinges. "When you put it that way, it sounds even more unbelievable."

"And yet here we are," Leo said. "My father carved this door."

Josephine's mouth dropped open. "Your father? That must have been . . ." She tried to compute the math in her head but knew it must be wrong. *Could Leo be more than a hundred years old?*

The corner of Leo's mouth quirked. "You're trying to guess my age, aren't you? I can see it on your face." His deep laugh was full of delight. "My father finished the door for Alma in 1922, so more than a hundred years ago. He and my mother started this business as a woodworking shop, but through the years, it evolved into salvaging, preservation, and saving the past. I took over the business when they retired. As for my age, I was the last child of twelve, born when my parents were in their forties, so I'm not as old as I look. Barely eighty-seven."

"Eighty-seven? Leo, you don't look a day over seventy," she said, and they both laughed. "Why aren't you retired?"

"And do what? Besides, I had to be here for when you returned for the door. I knew you would," he said with a wink. He touched the door. "My mother was—what do they call it these days? A spiritual woman, a shaman, a seer? She had special gifts and a deep respect for the sacred. She put a blessing on the door once my father completed it. A protection blessing so everyone within the house would be safe and secure."

Josephine wasn't sure she believed in the power of blessings, but she smiled. *It's a lovely thought, and even if the door is just a door, it's still perfect for the house.* She pointed at the doorknob. "How about the locking mechanism? Should we replace that so I can have one with a key that works?"

"Why would we do that?" Leo asked. "I have the key."

"You have the key to this front door? Of course you do," she said with a disbelieving chuckle. "Leo, I can't thank you enough for saving this."

Leo walked to a shelf that held a wooden case the size of a cigar box, and he flipped open its lid. "Rhapsody in Blue" started playing. He retrieved a small brass key and showed it to Josephine.

"That song," she whispered.

"Alma gave that music box to my mother," Leo said, placing the key in her outstretched hand. "It's wobblier and slower now, but aren't we all? You know the song? One of Gershwin's most popular ones."

Josephine nodded and closed her fingers around the key. The metal felt smooth and cool in her palm. "I heard it recently." Saying the words sent a shiver through her. *It led me to the hidden speakeasy and was on in the truck this morning.* She slid the key into her pocket. "Do you have someone here who can help us load the door into my truck? I don't see the two of us handling this well." Not only was she sure Leo was far too old to carry something so oversize, but Josephine knew she'd probably buckle under the weight of solid wood.

Leo nodded. "Kenny is around here somewhere. He also knows how to install antique doors and build a new doorframe if you want him to help with that too."

"That would be great," Josephine agreed. "And the sooner we get it hung, the better."

Fifteen minutes later, Leo stood outside with Josephine as Kenny carefully loaded the blanket-wrapped door into the back of the rental truck. They scheduled a time for Kenny to come to the house the next day to remove the eyesore and rehang the original door.

"Thanks again, Leo."

"It's been my pleasure," he said. He rested his hand on the tailgate, and he gazed once more at the door lying in the truck bed. "My parents sure thought a lot of Alma. They were so sad when she died. I wasn't born yet, but they talked about her their whole lives, about all she did for the community in her short time here. I grew up feeling like I knew her."

Josephine frowned. "Alma was ninety-eight when she died, long after you were born," she said, offering him a gentle smile. *At eighty-seven, maybe his memory is slipping.*

Leo looked at her strangely before saying, "Alma died in 1927 during the raid on her juice joint."

Josephine laughed but stopped herself quickly, not wanting to offend Leo. "You mean the speakeasy? That's not possible. She didn't die in 1927, because if she had, I wouldn't be standing here."

A hawk screeched overhead. Leo glanced up toward the pale blue sky. He returned his gaze to Josephine's before wishing her a good day and walking away toward the building, leaving Josephine standing beside the truck.

Why hadn't he responded to her correction? A peculiar emotion churned in Josephine's stomach as she drove away. *How lucky is it that I found the original front door? And how odd that Leo believes Alma died in the 1927 raid.*

CHAPTER 5

The next afternoon Josephine stood on the newly decorated front porch while Kenny hung the reclaimed front door. Thanks to Katherine's decorators, the front porch had gone from sparse to an explosion of fall- and Halloween-inspired décor. Chrysanthemums potted in oversize black urns framed the front door. A waterfall of pumpkins in various colors and sizes cascaded down both sides of the front stairs. Wicker chairs with burnt-orange cushions paired with black and white striped throw pillows created a sitting space on one side of the veranda. Dried corn husks wrapped around the porch columns, and a few hay bales were precisely stacked and topped with more pumpkins. "Impressive and over-the-top" was how Josephine described it when she'd texted Katherine photos.

"Let's see if it shuts tight," Kenny said, pulling the door closed and running his hands along the doorframe. He turned the knob and opened the door easily. "Looks good. Sometimes these old houses shift so much that doors never close right or they scrape up the floors. Some people have to saw off the bottoms to make them work, but you're lucky with this one."

Josephine snapped a photo of the door and texted it to Katherine.

Kenny chuckled. "Did I just photobomb your picture?"

She laughed. "Nah, it's for my sister. She'll like the added detail."

Kenny grinned as though he was pleased to be a detail worth noting. "You got the key so we can check the lock?"

Josephine slipped the key out of her jeans pocket and handed it over to Kenny. He locked and unlocked the door to his satisfaction. Then he closed the door, locked it, unlocked it again, and then swung open the door. He handed Josephine the key.

"All done here, ma'am." He reached out and pressed his fingers to the door. "They don't make 'em like this anymore. It's a beaut."

A gust of wind whipped around the side of the house and raced up the porch stairs. Stray pieces of hay tumbled across the boards. Josephine rubbed her hands up her arms and agreed. "Thanks for your help, Kenny. You'll send me an invoice?"

"Yes, ma'am." He gathered his tools and then handed her a business card for the salvage yard. "Leo and I are there pretty much every day. Call us if you need anything."

They said goodbye, and Josephine slipped the card into her pocket. She closed the front door and stepped back to admire it. "Welcome home," she said. Her cell phone dinged.

Katherine texted: Barbara will be tickled pink or at least less pinched around the mouth.

Josephine replied: It's THE door Uncle Donnie tried to get rid of. Found it at Leo's.

Three little dots bounced up and down, and Josephine could practically feel her sister's disbelief. Katherine texted: No way! The speakeasy and now the door. What's next? Maybe you WILL find the portal to Narnia.

Josephine texted back a series of Halloween emojis, and Katherine replied with a sailboat and champagne flutes, along with the words Dinner cruise. Josephine slid the key into the lock to test out the mechanism for herself. One clockwise turn and the lock clicked. One counterclockwise turn, and the lock released. She twisted the doorknob and pushed on the door, but it didn't budge. She pushed harder, leaning her body weight into the door, and it finally released and swung open. Josephine nearly lost her balance as she tumbled forward into the foyer while holding on to the doorknob.

She frowned. The door had opened so easily when Kenny tried it. Maybe it just needed to be opened and closed a few times to loosen up the seal. She swung the door back and forth a few times on its hinges before closing it again. Josephine locked the door, then unlocked it. The mechanism worked well. As she turned the knob, she noticed scratches on the trim framing the left panel window. Josephine leaned closer to the door and tilted her head to inspect the damage.

Except it wasn't damage. Minuscule words had been carved vertically into the thin trim work. Josephine squinted and read the words aloud. "Among the whispering and the stars." Tingles raced across her skin.

Why would someone carve those words into the door? Had it been part of the blessing Leo's mom had said over the door? What did it mean? Josephine turned the doorknob and swung open the door. As soon as she crossed the threshold, she was struck with shortness of breath and dizziness, shivering like someone caught stumbling through a snowstorm. Something was alarmingly wrong.

The interior of the house looked different. *Very* different. For starters, there was a narrow runner in the style of a Persian rug spanning the length of the hallway. Vintage furniture and curiosities filled the living room. She saw a carved wooden sailboat perched atop the picture rail, and a delicate china teapot nestled between leather books near a window, along with a vase of asters. A carved secretary desk was opened, and stationery waited on the desktop to be used. The flamboyant brocade sofa was paired with a red velvet armchair piled with floral cushions and lace doilies, adding a homey touch to the room.

The house seemed shinier, newer, with a high gloss sheen on the exposed woodwork and floors. Sunlight streaming through the windows appeared brighter and clearer, as though the glass panes hadn't yet endured a few thousand sunrises and sunsets. The paint and wallpaper were vibrant and bold. The passing of time had yet to diminish their grandeur.

Jazz music played from one of the rooms, and voices carried from somewhere in the house. *The kitchen, maybe?* Footsteps approached.

Josephine panicked and stumbled backward out the door, closing it quickly. Her heart pounded so fiercely she feared she might pass out, so she inhaled a few deep breaths to calm herself. Reaching out slowly, she turned the knob and eased open the door. This time the interior looked like it had since she moved in. No carpet runner, no music, no voices. A shudder ran through her. *How could I have imagined such detail? Am I sleep-deprived? Hallucinating? Is this another stage of grief, a stage when reality trips over itself and shatters when it falls?*

Josephine pressed her hand against the door. The polished wood felt warm and real against her palm. Catching sight of the tiny carved words, an impulse overtook her. She closed the door and locked it. She examined the key in the palm of her hand, turning it over a few times. Then she slipped the key back into the lock, said, "Among the whispering and the stars," and unlocked the door. When she opened it, breath whooshed from her lungs, and she staggered into the house like a drunkard, quivering and trying to regain her balance on the carpet runner. Jazz music reverberated through the house.

A young woman appeared in the hallway. Dressed in a simple V-neck cotton dress with a green gingham pattern, she smiled and walked toward Josephine. Her thick, wavy dark hair was cut into a bob and parted in the middle. Dark brown eyes, lined in black, reminded Josephine of baby-doll eyes.

"Well, hello there. I admire a bold woman. Someone who marches in without waiting for an invitation," the woman said. She laughed, a cheerful sound. "Did you ring the bell?" She motioned toward the parlor. "The music's loud, but it helps me think. Can't hear much else, though."

"I . . ." Josephine's voice failed her. She blinked a few times, gaping at the woman standing before her. She and Josephine were nearly the same height with similar body types, although the woman had a much healthier glow about her, one that Katherine would suggest Josephine needed to find.

The woman's smile dimmed slightly. "Are you quite all right, darling?"

Josephine recognized her from the faded photographs tucked into her family albums. Could it be possible she was staring at her great-grandmother Alma? The music in the other room swelled with a saxophone solo, and Josephine swayed with disorientation. The woman was at her side in a moment.

"Hattie!" she called up the hallway. "Bring a glass of brandy!" The woman hooked her arm beneath Josephine's elbow and led her into the parlor.

Large sash windows overlooked the front porch and lawn. Dazzling sunlight drenched the room in lemony light. Centered between the windows, a carved wooden side table sat between two upholstered accent chairs with ornate legs. A daisy-patterned tea set and a plate of thin reddish-brown cookies looked as though they had been brought in recently. A swirl of steam rose from one of the filled teacups.

The woman eased Josephine down onto a teal chaise with overstuffed cushions and a curved tufted back. She walked to the radio and turned it down. A caramel-skinned young woman wearing a pale blue wrap dress appeared in the doorway, her glossy dark hair piled on top of her head in large curls. She held a snifter full of amber liquid.

"Ms. Alma," she said, holding out the glass.

"Alma," Josephine whispered the name, and her heart thudded in her chest.

"Oh, thank you, Hattie," Alma said, taking the glass.

"Everything okay in here?" Hattie asked, wearing an expression of concern.

"I'm not sure. Stick close, will you, please?" Alma sat beside Josephine on the chaise and lifted Josephine's hand. She encouraged Josephine to hold the glass. "You're looking pale. Take a sip of this."

Josephine lifted the glass to her lips and sipped. The brandy etched a line of fire down her throat. She rasped a cough as tears filled her eyes, causing Alma and Hattie to chuckle. Hattie composed herself quicker. "Excuse me. I haven't had brandy in years. Now I remember why."

"It's a strong one, but it put some life back into your eyes," Alma said, taking the glass from Josephine and placing it on a nearby table. "You looked about ready to fall over, and dressed like that, did you walk from across town?"

Josephine glanced down at her faded blue jeans and ballet flats. She wore a long-sleeve flannel shirt under her lightweight jacket. *Could it be possible I collapsed on the front porch and this is an elaborate dream?*

"Those aren't any traveling clothes I've ever seen on a woman," Hattie said, and Alma shot her a look.

"We all have different styles," Alma said and patted Josephine's leg once. "And your style must be . . ."

"Workmen's clothing?" Hattie offered through thinned lips. "Mechanic? Someone from the lumberyard?"

Josephine laughed at the absurdity of the moment. Compared to Alma's dress and even Hattie's simple attire, Josephine's clothing looked quite far from what must be considered feminine. This was the oddest, most realistic dream she'd had in years. "It's cold out?" Josephine said as a possible reason.

Hattie's thin brows rose on her forehead, and she cast her eyes toward the windows. "It's not *that* cold, and where are your stockings? Your hair is another matter—"

"Hattie!" Alma scolded.

Hattie huffed and straightened. "I'll be in the kitchen if you need me." As she hurried out of the room, she mumbled, "All kinds of odd birds in this house."

"Please accept my apologies," Alma said gently. Her large eyes radiated kindness. "Hattie speaks her opinion whether I ask for it or not. She means no offense."

"That's okay," Josephine said, and she meant it. She reached up to touch her messy bun, feeling stray hairs sticking out all over her head like a halo of frizz. "I'm a mess. I don't . . . I don't normally look this disheveled." *Except for the past eight months.* She wanted to tell Alma that if she'd seen her a year ago, she might have witnessed someone more alive, more vibrant. Or had Josephine been hollowing out even before then?

"How are you feeling? Better?" Alma asked.

I feel like I'm having an out-of-body experience. Would she wake up soon? Was it odd that she didn't *want* to wake up? That she wanted to spend more time with this dream version of her great-grandmother? "Better, thank you."

"Where are my manners?" Alma said, standing and reaching for Josephine. "I'm Alma Carter, as you must already know, and you are?" She pulled Josephine to her feet.

"Josephine," she answered, purposefully leaving off her last name. *What if Alma knows there are no Reynolds in town? What if she asks about my family?* Her body stiffened.

"Josephine?" Alma said. "That's a lovely name."

"Thank you," Josephine said, focusing on pulling air into her lungs. "I was named after my grandfather."

"Family names are special, aren't they? Josephine, I'm delighted to meet you. Forgive me if we planned to meet today, but I don't have anything on my schedule."

Josephine's mind blanked for a moment, then raced to come up with an acceptable reason. "I'm here to . . . to help." *Not exactly a genius response.*

Alma looked unsure for a moment, and then her expression shifted to one of understanding. "With the upcoming birthday party? Eleanor sent you? She said she had a few ladies in mind who could assist me. I haven't seen you around, but Eleanor has so many friends, I can hardly keep up. Did you meet at the tennis club?"

Alma turned and walked out of the parlor, and she motioned for Josephine to follow. Josephine had no idea who Eleanor was, but she was afraid not to play along. "I'm terrible at tennis," Josephine said to keep the conversation going.

Alma's laugh rang out down the hallway. "I'm dreadful! Absolutely dreadful. Eleanor played once with me and never again. She said I was worse than her nine-year-old cousin. Fine by me, though. I have more interesting ways to spend my time."

Josephine's head swiveled, trying to take in all of the décor and furniture. Framed paintings of landscapes and one of a young girl sitting on a cliff near the ocean hung on the walls. As she passed a grandfather clock, Josephine noticed the time was almost four in the afternoon—the same time it had been *at home*. How could any of this be happening? Could a dreaming mind create such precise detail, down to the shine on the golden face of the grandfather clock?

"I didn't know Eleanor was sending anyone today, but she must have wanted you to have a quick look around so you're better acquainted. The party is in the"—Alma paused at the entrance to the kitchen and glanced over her shoulder at Josephine—"Private room. You haven't been here before, have you?"

Josephine shook her head. The "private room" could be a dozen different places, but Alma was leading her toward the kitchen. *Is she about to take me down into the speakeasy?*

"You look alarmed," Alma said, stepping toward Josephine and touching her arm gently. "Eleanor did explain this to you, didn't she? Please tell me she did."

Josephine quickly nodded. "Yes, I'm sorry. I'm just a little nervous. It's my first time . . ." *Not exactly true.*

"Oh, thank heavens," Alma said, her smile widening. "Tell me, darling, what are you nervous about? Is it the alcohol, the secrets, or the men?"

Josephine laughed unexpectedly. "All three?"

Alma's laugh joined hers. "Oh, I do like you, Josephine. Nothing to worry about for the birthday party. It will be tame compared to anything you've seen or heard about. I don't tolerate screwy behavior. You'll see Club Belle Âme is swanky compared to those dumps your mama warns you about." Alma winked at her and toyed with the string of pearls around her neck.

Josephine's eyes widened. She remembered the tiny rectangle of paper she found in the speakeasy. "You have cards? To the club?"

"Sure we do. Keeps it exclusive," Alma said. "I'll make sure you have one before the bash. Now come with me."

In contrast to the dark walnut grandeur of the front rooms in the house, the kitchen had an airy, fresh feel. The scent of baked bread filled the room, and Josephine breathed it in. Light flooded in through the sash windows, shining off the green-and-white checked floor. Wallpaper decorated with blooming magnolias covered the walls. The antique cast-iron gas stove was almost as beautiful as the furniture. Its white and green details looked like a piece taken from a dollhouse. Although lovely, it was obvious why Uncle Donnie had increased the size of the compact kitchen and added more cabinetry.

Hattie stood sipping tea from a china mug, eyebrows raised at Josephine as though inspecting her. Josephine attempted a smile, and Hattie's lip quirked. *Not a friendly one, is she?*

"Hattie," Alma said, "we'll be right back. Would you mind warming up the tea? I'll take it in the parlor once we return. Thank you."

Alma opened the basement door, flipped on the lights, and breezed down the stairs. This basement version was cleaner, more organized, and packed with canned fruits and vegetables, as well as potatoes and crates of items Josephine couldn't see well enough to identify.

Alma walked straight to where Josephine had found the hidden door. Instead of a dull gray intended to blend in with the surrounding rock, the speakeasy door was polished solid walnut with a proper doorknob and shiny hinges. "This is our door in, but not where the partygoers will enter." She opened the door and stepped inside.

Josephine walked into the speakeasy, and the sight of it took her breath away. Gone were the cobwebs and layers of dust. Gone were the torn upholstery and forgotten furniture. "It's wonderful," she said on an exhale.

"Isn't it just swell?" Alma agreed. She smoothed her hand across the glistening lacquered bar top while she walked into the open area.

The concrete floor was stained a deep crimson. Barstools with black leather seats lined the bar. The tables were polished to a high gleam, and votive candleholders were centered on the tops. Glossy black-and-white photographs of the city and musical instruments hung in frames along the walls. Red velvet curtains held back by tasseled golden ropes framed the private recess. A slightly raised dais against the back wall was large enough to hold a small band. An upright piano sat on the right side of the stage.

Alma pointed toward the door at the back of the room. "That's where everyone will enter. They know the password. Did Eleanor tell you?" Josephine shook her head, and Alma smirked. "Eleanor likes to create mystery. The password is 'among the whispering and the stars.'"

Josephine's heart paused one second, then *whoosh*, her stomach dropped in a freefall. Alma didn't seem to notice Josephine's astonishment. "It's inspired by a fabulous book. Have you read *The Great Gatsby*?" Josephine nodded. "It's scandalous, isn't it? Astonishing, heartbreaking, the cat's meow. Can you imagine going to a party at Gatsby's? Well, this birthday won't be anything like that," she said with a laugh.

Josephine pinched herself and winced. The room before her looked authentic and solid. Alma looked very real and sentient. Curiosity had Josephine asking, "This birthday party you're having, how will I help? Not mixing drinks, I hope." Josephine hadn't made a mixed drink since college, and she had used premade sweet-and-sour mix and tequila.

"A barmaid? Heavens no," Alma said. "Unless you have special talents with bar-keeping."

Josephine shook her head. "Zero talents."

"You don't need them," Alma said with a wave of her hand. "I have the best barkeep in town. Banker by day, barkeep by night, but only here, Thursdays through Saturdays."

"You're only open three nights?" Josephine asked. *Is that normal for speakeasies?* She assumed the ones in New York were open twenty-four hours a day. *Maybe that's just what the movies make you think.*

Alma chuckled. "Three nights is plenty. I don't need people traipsing around my house every single day. Believe me, they would. But having limited operating hours gives me more exclusivity. During the party you'll help bring out food, keep the trays filled, that sort of attention. You can take drink orders if needed, but mostly you'll help me make sure everyone is okay and that Sara is happy." Josephine nodded her understanding. "You'll earn one dollar for helping too."

"One dollar?" Josephine asked, unable to contain her surprise. *Is that all waitresses earn? How much does a dollar equal in present-day money?*

"Eleanor says it's too much, but I don't care," Alma said sincerely.

"Oh"—she walked behind the bar and bent down to retrieve something from one of the cubbies—"Here's the invitation."

Josephine picked up the black invitation embellished with gold metallic ink. The invite was simple enough. It was a birthday party for Sara Stewart to be held at Club Belle Âme from seven p.m. until midnight. But when Josephine's eyes read the date of the party, her hand trembled. "October 9, 1927?"

Alma nodded. "I know what you're thinking. That's a Sunday, and we shouldn't be getting jazzed on a holy day, but Sara is a dear friend, and I promised her brother I'd host it here. We're making an exception this one time."

She had no way of knowing the ninth was on a Sunday. That wasn't why Josephine felt a chill in her bones. Why was that date so familiar? While Josephine searched her memory, Alma continued talking about canapés and festive drinks and what songs the band could play. Just as Alma finished discussing the type of flowers they'd most likely put on the tables for Sara's party, Josephine's breath caught. She recalled standing in the present-day speakeasy with Katherine while Josephine searched the internet for history on her great-grandmother. October 9, 1927, was the day that history recorded the raid on the Carter Mansion speakeasy.

"Any questions?" Alma asked.

So many. But Josephine shook her head, and Alma led them back through the basement, through the kitchen, and down the hallway toward the front door. "It was lovely to meet you, Josephine," she said as she opened the door. "We'll see you next Sunday? Let's say five p.m."

Josephine clutched the invitation, wanting to tell Alma about the raid and yet not knowing *how* to reveal such a knowing.

Hattie stood near the end of the hallway watching them. "Clothes!"

Alma sighed and threw a look over her shoulder at Hattie. When she returned her gaze to Josephine, she was smiling. "The attire for the party is formal. I trust you have something to wear?"

Josephine glanced down at her modern, overly casual clothes and then thought of the antique dresses hanging in the armoire. "Yes."

"Wonderful," Alma said. "See you then!"

Josephine crossed the threshold, heard the door close behind her, and felt the familiar rush of ice in her veins and shortness of breath. A gust of wind pushed across the porch and snatched the invitation from her fingers. Josephine lunged to catch it, but within seconds, the paper had disappeared. Once she stopped shivering, she turned and reached for the doorknob. It turned easily in her hand. When she shoved open the door, she stared at the interior of her present-day house. Alma and the past were gone.

CHAPTER 6

Josephine closed the front door and stood in the foyer, afraid to move, afraid that her fragile reality would completely fracture. She imagined herself as a cartoon character who had one foot on one side of a chasm and one foot on the other, with the gap ever widening.

The October sun set quickly, transforming the interior of the mansion into a house of shadows. Josephine could almost see the past ghosting over the present. Finally she shuffled into the living room and sat on the lumpy mauve sofa she planned to donate soon. In Alma's living room, in a similar location, sat a brocade sofa covered in an exquisite, patterned fabric with a raised floral design probably woven on a loom. Josephine glanced up at the picture rail, now empty, but she remembered seeing a carved wooden sailboat in Alma's room. *But how? How is any of this possible?*

Josephine closed her eyes and rubbed her temples. *Did I black out? Am I still dreaming? Lost in a fog of unreality?* She pulled her phone out of her pocket and swiped it open to text her sister. But she hesitated. She could text: Hey, sis, I just had the most incredible dream, and I might still be dreaming. Do people dream text? Or it could have actually happened. I traveled back in time and met our great-grandmother Alma, and we toured the speakeasy, and she invited me to a party that happens on the night of the raid. And all of this might be because of the enchanted front door . . .

Josephine turned off the phone. What could she possibly write that wouldn't send Katherine into full-blown worry mode? Josephine skipped dinner and opted for a long soak in the tub. Afterward she crawled into bed and drifted off to sleep.

●●●

THE NEXT MORNING, Josephine woke to muted sunlight streaming through her slender bedroom windows. She'd forgotten to close the curtains the night before, and a powder-blue sky stretched across the new day. Somewhere in the front yard a cardinal chirped, then was echoed by another one. A truck rumbled up the street. She sat up in bed and glanced around. The room looked just as it had when she'd fallen asleep after doubting her sanity. No time jumps or great-grandmothers lurking around. No speakeasies or private birthday parties in full swing. Maybe it *had* all been a remarkably realistic dream.

Josephine swung her legs over the side of the bed, stood on the cold hardwood, and stretched her arms high over her head. A feeling of ease filled her, until she noticed a door on the armoire was partially open. It wasn't unusual for antique furniture doors to warp over time and refuse to stay closed, but the armoire had a tiny key that locked the doors and held them closed. Josephine kept the doors locked with the key in the lock, but the key lay on the floor, partially hidden in the shadow below the armoire.

She opened the door fully and sucked in a breath. The armoire had been full of Alma's clothes, and now half of them were gone. Josephine checked the bottom panel of the armoire to make sure they hadn't tumbled from their hangers. Panic seared her, shooting an explosion of heat into her stomach and racing up her spine. Had someone broken into the house and stolen the clothes? But why? Josephine's pulse raced like a frightened rabbit's, and her mouth went dry.

She crept down the upstairs hallway as if the intruder might still be inside the house. Poking her head into the next bedroom, her eyes went wide at the sight of a missing side table. The antique table had been in storage, and it matched the other pieces in this bedroom. The table had a narrow scratch down one of its legs, and Josephine had been careful placing it in the room and positioning the imperfection away from view.

She ran down the stairs like a woman being chased, anxious to check the rest of the house. *Did I forget to lock the doors? Had someone forced entry?* Her panic lessened when she checked the front door—still locked. The back door was also locked, but on her way up the hallway toward the foyer, she noticed the antique sideboard was missing. *No one* could have moved that substantial piece out of the house without her knowing. Made of solid wood and two-inch thick doors, it weighed nearly four hundred pounds. The daisy-patterned tea set placed on the table near the front windows in the parlor was missing, along with a Tiffany lamp and an armchair from the living room. The odd assortment of missing items didn't seem to be connected in any kind of logical way.

Did someone know about the secret outside door in the garden? They might have come up through the basement, but that still didn't explain *how* they'd removed incredibly heavy furniture or *why* they'd chosen to take such random items. Josephine flipped on the light to the basement stairs and slowly took one step at a time. No one waited in the darkness for her. With held breath, she opened the speakeasy door.

She'd already seen the room covered in dust and left to mold, but the sight before her now shocked her immobile. The hairs on the back of her neck stood on end. Shattered bottles—shards larger than a football—littered the space behind the bar. Tables and chairs were overturned, and many had broken spindles and legs. One tabletop was completely cracked in half as though dropped from a great height. Picture frames, with smashed glass, hung crooked on the walls. The room smelled like mildew but also like rot, a stench that turned her stomach. What catastrophe had destroyed the speakeasy in such a way? Josephine backed out of the room, trying to restrain the terror that wanted to spring out of her.

She ran wildly up the basement stairs, stumbling halfway up and knocking her shin against a step, but she winced and kept going. An irrational idea took hold of her, and she sprinted toward the parlor. Josephine had shelved Alma's family albums on the built-ins. She grabbed the first one she saw and sat in the nearest chair. Flinging open the cover, she saw she'd chosen the 1917 album, with photos of Alma and Franklin's travels, parties, friends, and holidays during their first year together. But these photos were not the images Josephine had looked at earlier in the week.

The photo of Alma and Franklin at Niagara Falls was the same, but in the garden party photo, Alma was noticeably absent. This pattern continued throughout the album. Alma with her group of girl friends, then Franklin dancing with another woman under the oaks. Alma opening a Christmas gift, then Franklin and a group of strangers standing near a Christmas tree.

Alma holding a bundle of balloons and laughing, then Franklin standing alone in an empty field, staring out into nothing. Alma was missing from at least half of the photographs. Josephine's hands trembled so hard that the album shook in her lap as if the whole world quaked.

She closed the album, its spine creaking like a lone cry, and stood. She dropped the album onto the chair cushion. Another outrageous idea formed in her mind like an approaching storm. In her mind she saw an image of Leo standing beside her truck outside the salvage yard. She remembered his words about Alma. Josephine returned to the living room and grabbed her laptop from the secretary desk. She opened the search engine and keyed in "Alma Carter, speakeasy raid, 1927." Results populated immediately. The first few hits were articles she'd already read, stating that Alma's speakeasy had been raided on October 9, 1927, but she hadn't been present. However, the next few entries . . . *Oh, my word.* A squeezing sensation constricted her lungs.

The first article she clicked was titled "Local Socialite Dead After Speakeasy Raid." The newspaper clipping detailed the raid on the Carter Mansion and the unintended shooting of Alma Carter as she fled the scene. She died shortly afterward before reaching the hospital. Josephine clicked the next few articles, all variations of the same event. All confirming that Alma Carter was shot and killed on October 9, 1927.

Josephine blinked at her laptop, her mouth hanging agape, her stomach churning. *That's not possible.* Two realities couldn't exist at once. Talking out loud in an attempt to comfort herself, she said, "Half of these articles prove Alma *didn't* die. Also, I'm still standing here!"

But when Josephine and Katherine had searched these articles a week ago, *none* of them had mentioned Alma's death. Because

Alma *couldn't* be dead or else Josephine would never have been born. Josephine felt like someone had poured a bucket of ice water over her head. Words she'd spoken back in the Green Hills house echoed through her mind and then rattled through her entire body. Hadn't she wished never to have been born? And then moments after speaking those words, she'd heard the incoming email about this house.

Josephine closed her laptop and walked into the foyer. She stared at the front door. All of this had started after it was installed. There was only one person she could talk to. Only one person directly connected to this door. Only one person who had mentioned Alma dying in 1927.

●●●

JOSEPHINE SHOWERED AND dressed, skipping coffee and eating a protein bar and an apple while standing in the kitchen. After eating, she wished she hadn't because nausea twisted her gut, and she twitched with nerves. In the foyer, she zipped up her jacket to ward off a chill that had taken hold and intensified throughout the morning, but still she shivered.

On the drive to the salvage yard, Josephine went over a dozen different ways to start this conversation with Leo. Would he think she'd fallen off her rocker? Would he suggest she contact one of those therapists her neighbor had recommended months ago?

Josephine pushed open the front door of the warehouse, and the jingling bell tinkled above her. The wall of antique doorknobs greeted her in the stillness, and she stepped into the warmth of the space. Josephine wandered through the rooms, looking for Leo, wondering if every item in this place might be enchanted.

She was tempted to call out his name. Before she could, Leo appeared from around a corner.

Today a red bandanna wrapped around his tan forehead, and he wore a matching buffalo plaid shirt with the sleeves rolled up to his elbows. "Good morning," he said. "How's the door?"

Josephine's throat squeezed and caused her to stutter. It took a few seconds to regain her composure. "That's why I'm here. I'd like to talk to you about it."

Leo's forehead creased, and the corners of his mouth dipped. "Something wrong with it? Kenny installed it properly, didn't he?"

Josephine tried to inhale, but her lungs felt trapped beneath a pile of bricks. *Pull it together. You can't freak out right now.* She nodded. "Nothing like that. Kenny did a great job." *Maybe too great a job.* "Listen, Leo, I know I'm going to sound like I'm spinning a fantastical story, but I need to ask you something, if you'll humor me."

Leo hooked his large thumbs onto the front pockets of his jeans. Josephine couldn't make her mouth form the words. *I should probably turn around and go straight home, maybe call a therapist or an energy healer or anyone who could help me break through what might possibly be a psychotic episode.*

"What's happened with the door?" Leo asked, encouraging her to continue.

Leo's mother had placed a blessing on the door, which Josephine assumed meant she had believed in the supernatural. If his mother believed in powers greater than humanity's limited understanding, it was possible she'd passed the belief on to Leo. *If not, Leo's about to think I'm at best, bizarre and, at worst, insane.* "Do you believe in magic?" she blurted, and then heat rushed into her cheeks. "No, that's not what I meant. Time travel? No . . . that's not right either."

"What's happened with the door?" he asked again.

Josephine pinched the bridge of her nose and squeezed her eyes shut. What she was about to say might be the most absurd string of sentences she'd ever strung together. "Did you know there are words carved into the door?" Leo nodded. "You did? Do you know what they mean?" Again, he nodded. "So you know about the speakeasy?"

"Yes, and I know about the raid," Leo said. "My parents told me. We spoke about this the day you bought the door."

Josephine shook her head. "You know *one* story, but there's another one. You said that Alma died the night of the raid, but she *didn't* die. She lived and remarried, and they had my grandmother, who had my mother, who had *me*. If Alma had died, I wouldn't be standing here. But yesterday . . . something happened.

"After Kenny left, I noticed the words carved on the door. I read them out loud and unlocked the door, but when I entered the house, it was different . . . 1920s different. Alma was there, *alive*, and I almost passed out. Literally. Alma thought I was there about helping with an upcoming party, so she gave me a tour of the speakeasy, and then she handed me the invitation. The party happens on October 9, 1927. Days ago all I could find about the raid was that it happened, but this morning the same search revealed what *you* said. Alma was shot and died. I know it sounds unbelievable, like maybe I fell and hit my head, and I'd probably agree with you if I hadn't woken up this morning to find things missing from the house."

"Missing?" Leo asked.

"Only Alma's things," Josephine said. "Her clothes, pieces of furniture, photos of her in the family albums." Embarrassment heated her face again. "And there's one more thing. I have an idea why this might be happening. A few months ago, just before I bought the Carter Mansion, I was incredibly depressed because my husband died a few months ago, and I . . . I was a complete mess, and I remember saying that I wished I was never born. And now I'm wondering . . . do you think it's connected to what's happening? But *how* could that be? It all sounds so impossible." Josephine gripped the back of her neck. *How could any of these events be connected? And yet how could they not be?*

"I'm sorry for your loss," he said.

The sincerity in his words stirred the desire in her to cry. She looked away from Leo's compassionate gaze. "I sound nuts."

"No, you don't," Leo said.

Josephine quickly returned her gaze to him. A flutter of hope skittered across her skin.

"Let me tell you what my mother told me about wishes," he continued, "something I've never forgotten. Those made from the deepest part of someone's heart, even the broken pieces, well, they can dramatically change a life. The stronger the wish, the stronger the possibility of change. She said that time listens to our wishes. Time breaks and reforms. Like branches of a river, time can split from a single point where a vital event occurs—when a specific wish is made—and create alternate outcomes simultaneously."

Goose bumps rose on Josephine's skin. "You mean like parallel lives?" Did she believe in those? Could she really answer no after yesterday? After the happenings this morning and reading two different outcomes of the same incident—one when Alma lived and the other when she died?

Leo nodded. "In one timeline, you are Josephine, a grieving widow, living with heartache. But at the moment you wished never to have born, you created a timeline in which you never existed. I'd guess, and this is just a guess, that those two timelines are currently overlapping, because neither one of them is more powerful than the other. Not yet. But it could be that those newspaper articles you read mean that the timeline in which Alma dies is growing stronger. Your wish never to have been born is coming true."

Josephine gaped at him. *This sounds like madness. Utter and complete madness.* So why was her heart hammering in her chest like she was about to leap off a cliff?

"You still have a choice," Leo said, his dark eyes finding hers.

She wrung her hands. "What do you mean?"

"You're still standing here," Leo said simply. "That means you still have the power to change your future, if you want to. Maybe you don't. Maybe you want all of this to be gone. If so, then do nothing. The strongest timeline will always win."

"You think I should go back and save Alma?" Josephine said, wide-eyed and scared, acting as though this entire scenario was actually plausible.

"I think you should do what you want," Leo answered. "Do you want to have a life here? Or do you want time to take back what it gave you?"

What if this was possible? What if dual timelines *could* exist? She thought about all the wishes she'd made throughout her life—birthday wishes after blowing out candles, fingers crossed when hoping a boy would ask her to the dance, Hail Mary requests that her parents wouldn't find her sneaking in past curfew. Had hundreds of her wishes created alternate realities? If the current state at her house with Alma's missing items offered a hint, then the answer was a shouted yes.

Although Josephine had already made steps toward a new life, a life of her own, she'd be foolish to believe she didn't yet have a long way to go to find herself again and sincerely heal her heart and spirit. The idea of years passing before she would feel whole and healthy again exhausted her. Would it be easier to give in to the timeline where she didn't exist?

I can't let Alma die. With a jolt of clarity, Josephine understood she couldn't quit. If Alma died, then not only would Josephine lose her great-grandmother; she'd also lose her mom and sister. All of their lives were in jeopardy because of a foolish wish she'd made while trapped in her shattered heart. "How?" she asked. "How do I change our fates?"

"The door, of course," Leo said. "My mother was a very special woman. That blessing she placed on the door is lending you its power to make a choice. So, what'll it be, Josephine?"

In a move that caused Leo to laugh, Josephine rushed toward him and threw her arms around his tall frame. He wrapped his arms around her and held her like a grandfather. She pulled away, wiped at her face, and gave him a wobbly smile.

"Give Alma my love," Leo said and winked at her.

Josephine nodded and hurried out of the building. *If I'm going to travel back in time and save Alma's life, I have some quick planning to do, starting with a new haircut and clothes.*

CHAPTER 7

The whole idea of what she was plotting made Josephine wonder if she was delusional. If she was, then so was Leo, because his explanation made *sense* even as it shoved against rationality and logic. Josephine wanted to text or call Katherine *so badly*, but there was no way any sane person—other than Leo—would believe her. Even with as much as Katherine loved her, Josephine knew her sister would think her sanity had finally fled. Who would blame her? If the roles were reversed, Josephine wouldn't believe her sister could time jump to save lives. That singular thought pushed a boisterous laugh up Josephine's throat. She caught sight of her wild eyes in the car's rearview mirror and felt like an actress in a movie playing the role of a lifetime.

Soberness halted her mirth. Regardless of *how* absurd this entire situation sounded, there was no denying the unspooling events. Alma's clothing, furniture, and photos were missing—vanished as though they'd never existed. The ruined state of the speakeasy, looking as though a terrible event had occurred, spoke to the truth of a dual timeline, each one potentially trying to triumph over the other. If Josephine's foolish wish came true, how much longer did she have until she disappeared overnight too? *Is that a possibility? Could I vanish? Would Mama and Katherine vanish too?*

If she was going to return to 1927, she needed to look the part. She couldn't stumble into the Carter Mansion wearing worn flannel and jeans again. Josephine pulled out her phone and searched for local vintage shops in or around Nashville. She found two shops that looked promising, so she buckled her seatbelt and drove toward downtown. The first shop sold vintage clothing mostly from the late twentieth century, with a high volume of honky-tonk styles. Those definitely wouldn't work. Josephine didn't know a lot about Nashville in the 1920s, but cowboy boots and rhinestones would turn even more heads than her jeans. When Josephine asked the sales associate where she might find clothing from the '20s, the young woman scrunched up her face and suggested Josephine shop online with larger clothing outlets, try costume sites, or browse boutique websites.

Josephine didn't have time to shop online and wait a week or more for clothes to arrive. Based on the grandfather clock in Alma's house, Alma's time moved in sync with present-day time, so Josephine assumed the days passed together as well. She had five days to stop Alma from dying on October 9.

Josephine got back in her car and drove a few blocks to the second vintage shop. Their selection was more promising. When she admired the fabrics and styles of the 1920s clothes, her fingers tingled.

"That would look gorgeous on you," a woman said. Her shiny black hair was styled into a classic beehive, and with her wide-set eyes outlined in dark eyeliner, she resembled Diana Ross. Probably in her early thirties, she wore aqua culottes and a white blouse tucked in at the waist. Her long legs were on display, accentuated by low-heeled shoes that elongated her entire look. Her exaggerated 1960s-style makeup boasted cherry-red lipstick. "My name is

Lita. Thanks for stopping by my shop today. Can I help you find anything? Are you going to a party?"

Josephine nodded and removed an emerald-green dress from the rack. She held it against her body and admired the way the fabric flowed. "It's an extended party of sorts, so I'm looking for a few items." She glanced up at Lita. "Do you have shoes? Accessories?"

Lita's light brown eyes lit up. "Yes to all of that," she said. "I *love* themed events. People should do more of those, don't you think?" She pulled a blouse and skirt from a rack and held them together for Josephine to see. "The '20s, right? This would be a great everyday outfit." She grabbed another hanger that held a deep crimson dress with a belt. "You have to try this one. With your figure, it's sure to fit you like a glove. Do you need eveningwear too? We have flapper dresses."

Josephine didn't know exactly *what* she needed. One of everything? Alma's collection in the armoire hadn't included flapper dresses. Of course, that didn't mean Alma never owned any. Josephine followed Lita to another rack of sequined and embroidered dresses. "Why don't we dress this way anymore?" she asked wistfully. She understood even more why the clothing passed down to her included so many items from the '20s. The styles were classy, graceful, and had the ability to make any woman look stunning.

"I'll start a room for you and bring you a few more you can try. Tell me your shoe size. Are you looking for jewelry too? Handbags?"

Josephine paused a moment to think through what she needed. "If I'm going to do this, I might as well do it right."

"Amen."

Lita led Josephine to a dressing room and promised to return with more outfits, as well as shoes, hats, jewelry, and handbags. Josephine was surprised by how jittery she felt. As soon as she slipped on the emerald-green dress, the realization of her upcoming challenges started to feel real, almost frightening. *What if I fail? What if I try to go back and the door doesn't work? What if I get stuck in the 1920s? Is that even possible?*

Lita knocked on the dressing room door. "How is the first one fitting?"

Josephine glanced at herself in the mirror and inhaled sharply. The dress was a perfect fit, and for the first time in months, she saw herself as someone who could be beautiful. As a woman who was still attractive, not as someone wasting away unseen. She opened the dressing room door, and Lita's pleased smile was quick and wide.

"Oh, wow, aren't you a doll!" Lita giggled. "That's what they'd call you in the '20s." She lifted two handfuls of hangers with more clothing options. "Let me put these in your room. Don't change yet! I want to grab shoes and a hat for that dress." She hurried away and returned a minute later with the extras.

Josephine slipped on the saddle shoes, and she placed the cloche hat on her head. Lita guided her toward a full-length mirror. She stood just behind Josephine, and Josephine caught Lita's smile in the mirror.

"What do you plan to do with your hair?" she asked Josephine. "Curl it and pin it up?"

"I hadn't thought that far," Josephine admitted. Her mind recalled images of Alma's photo albums. All the women had shorter hair, none longer than their shoulders. Josephine's long hair fell halfway down her back. "I should cut it."

Lita's eyes widened. "You're really going for it."

"It's worth it," Josephine said, even though the meaning was lost to anyone but herself.

"My best friend is a stylist," Lita said. "I send her clients all the time for event hair. Mostly weddings and proms, but also people like you who are going to a theme party and want appropriate hairstyles. I can give you her info if you like."

"Think she has any openings today?" Josephine asked.

"I bet she can work you in! I'll call now while you try on those other outfits."

When Lita returned to confirm that Josephine had an appointment, Josephine wore a long knit shirt, vertically striped in fall jewel tones, with a wide collar and paired with a navy-blue pleated skirt that stopped at her calves.

"Aren't you a sight?" Lita said. "You were made for this era. Do you like themed parties? There's a group of us who like to get dressed up and get together. Sometimes we go out, and sometimes we host parties at our houses. That might not be your thing, but we're always welcoming new people."

The invitation struck Josephine silent for a few beats.

"No worries if you're not interested," Lita said, sensing Josephine's hesitation.

"It's not that," Josephine said honestly. "It's just that no one has invited me out in a long time." *Which might have more to do with me turning everyone down after Nathan died.* Josephine's friends—a term she used loosely—had been Nathan's friends. She hadn't had a friend of her own, other than Katherine, in years. She smiled at Lita. "I'd love to."

Lita clapped. "Let's swap numbers." She ran off to grab her phone so she could add Josephine's number into her contacts.

"We have a '50s get-together planned on Friday at the Pharmacy. I'll text you all the information."

Within moments, Josephine's cell phone dinged with the upcoming event. For months she hadn't wanted to go out and see anyone, but this new group would be different. None of them knew about Nathan or about Josephine's recent slog through life. *I can be anyone now. I can be me.* "Thank you, Lita."

By the time Josephine left the shop, she had a week's worth of clothing, everything from daywear to eveningwear to sleep clothes. Shoes, jewelry, hats, and accessories filled the bags that she loaded into the trunk of her car. She had an appointment in half an hour with a stylist who would cut off at least nine inches of her hair and create a '20s bob, and she also had a budding friendship.

As she turned on the car, her cell phone dinged. Katherine texted: Hey! How's life? Seen Barbara lately?

Josephine smiled. She hadn't seen Barbara, but she'd seen their great-grandmother. She texted: Just went shopping for new clothes. I'm on my way to get a haircut.

Three dots bounced on the screen. Who is this new woman? I love her!

Josephine's heart swelled with her sister's support. How's Tampa?

Hot! But exactly what I needed. I'm here if you need anything.

Josephine wanted to ask for a pep talk. She'd love one of Katherine's encouraging Wonder Woman speeches about having the strength and power to do anything. Instead, she texted,

I love you, Katy-bug. Josephine dropped her phone into her purse and drove toward the salon.

She loved her long hair, so cutting it would be a high-level commitment. All she had to do afterward was go home and get a good night's sleep. Tomorrow she planned to dress in her new clothes, see if she could time jump into 1927, and find a way to save Alma's life without anything going awry. Even to her it sounded like an impossible plan.

CHAPTER 8

Josephine spent the rest of the day at home scouring websites for history on the 1920s. She read everything from Nashville's history to fashion to transportation to etiquette to the day-to-day lives of women to popular foods. How much would it help? She didn't know, but she learned how to properly greet people, according to Emily Post. She also read up on speakeasies, but most of the information focused on the lives of gangsters, money laundering, and murder. Alma didn't fit the stereotype of a speakeasy owner, unless the sweet-spirited, smiling woman Josephine met led a secret life of debauchery and darkness. Josephine shook her head as though answering the question in her mind. *That definitely doesn't resonate as the truth about Alma. Maybe I'll have the opportunity to ask her how all of it started.*

While she researched, Josephine also streamed the movie adaptations of *The Great Gatsby*, *Some Like It Hot*, and *Chicago* for extra inspiration. The movies, although different in tone and storyline, offered Josephine various perspectives on what life *could* have been like during the '20s. Much of that era was so extravagant, especially the parties depicted at Gatsby's. The parties she used to host with Nathan at the Green Hills house could never have lived up to one night in Gatsby's mansion. Josephine recalled the messes she cleaned up after their parties, and yet it still paled in comparison to someone fishing wine bottles out of a swimming pool. She crawled into bed that night with an exhausted mind, hoping for a full night of sleep, but peaceful rest escaped her. She tossed and turned most of the night, fretting about failure or waking up to find the stronger timeline winning—the timeline where her family no longer existed.

After an uneasy night, Josephine was eager to get out of bed and equally anxious about what she planned to do today. Catching sight of herself in the bedroom mirror, she startled, thinking a stranger was in her bedroom. Her reflection lifted a hand and touched her short hair. She'd forgotten. Josephine combed her fingers through her new hairstyle. Sunlight shined against her silky dark hair that now stopped an inch below her ears. This look was drastically different from the long hair she'd worn for years, but the style accentuated her cheekbones and the slant of her eyes. The stylist had shown Josephine techniques for how to add finger waves with hair gel and clips.

Josephine had swallowed down coffee that morning, made a note to buy a new coffeepot and grounds, and eaten a breakfast of oatmeal and fruit. After drinking a few cups of tea while trying not to fret about returning to 1927, she decided to get ready. She now stood in front of a full-length mirror, wearing the long knit, striped shirt and navy-blue pleated skirt. Josephine had never in her life worn stockings with saddle shoes, but evidently women didn't start wearing socks regularly until the '30s. A navy-blue felt cloche hat covered most of her head. She looked the part of a 1920s woman seen in any magazine advertisement for makeup or dresses. The transformation was remarkable. *We'll see what happens when I return to 1927, if I can blend into their timeline.*

Josephine grabbed a handbag and went downstairs, where she paced the foyer. It was half past noon. *Will Alma welcome me in? What's my reason for stopping by? Certainly not the truth.* Josephine wasn't even sure she could get back to 1927.

"Might as well give it a try," she said to the empty foyer. Josephine grabbed the house key and stepped out onto the decorated front porch, hoping no one would see her and question why she was dressed like someone attending a morning costume party.

Josephine locked the door and waited for a few seconds. Then she whispered, "Among the whispering and the stars." She knocked on the door this time, thinking that would be less intrusive than entering uninvited. When no one answered, she unlocked the door and crossed the threshold. Her lungs squeezed, and her veins felt injected with freezing water. She stumbled into the foyer but regained her balance faster this time. The paralyzing chill in her blood gently shifted back to warmth. Relief at seeing she *had* stepped through time was quickly followed by a clutching in her stomach. The plan to save Alma and herself had been set into motion, and the countdown had started.

Josephine closed the door behind her. "Hello? Alma?"

Hattie stepped out of the kitchen at the far end of the hallway. She dried her hand on a towel as she strode with determination up the carpet runner. She tucked the towel into her apron pocket. Her thick dark hair was styled in fat curls on top of her head, held back by a wide band of white fabric.

"Hattie!" Josephine said with too much enthusiasm. She waved at Hattie but lowered her hand when she caught sight of Hattie's deep-set frown. "Hi, hello, I was just out for a stroll."

Hattie stepped into the foyer with one eyebrow raised. Her soft plum lips thinned. "Strolled right on in, I see. Ms. Carter isn't here."

"Oh," Josephine said. She hadn't planned on Alma not being home. "Doing important things, I guess? Party planning or discussing new projects," she said, knowing her esteem in Hattie's eyes was plummeting. *I sound like an idiot.*

Hattie's lips quirked. Was she amused with Josephine's babbling? "If you must know, there was a problem with the band, and she was meeting to discuss it over lunch."

"A problem with the band?" Josephine said. Hope leaped within her, thinking this issue might stop the party from happening. *Act disappointed.* Josephine sobered her expression. "That's unfortunate. Do you think they'll reschedule—"

The front door opened, and laughter burst into the foyer as people entered. Josephine stepped out of the way to avoid being hit with the door. Alma came into view first, followed by two men. Alma's face was radiant. She wore a royal purple low-waisted dress that hung loosely on her small frame. Her hat was identical to Josephine's except in gray wool. A magnetic energy and warmth surrounded Alma, drew everyone right toward her. She was the kind of person at a party whom people constantly ended up standing near, the kind of woman who smiled as though she knew something about the world that you needed to learn.

Dressed in suits, ties, and hats, the two men accompanying Alma looked like they'd walked right off *The Great Gatsby*'s film set.

"Hello, Hattie," Alma said, noticing her standing in the foyer. "Lunch at the Grants was superb, as always." Alma removed her hat and smoothed down stray hairs. "It's the most perfect fall day outside too. I love this time of year when you can *feel* the seasons changing."

Hattie cut her eyes over toward Josephine, who fidgeted beneath the intense gaze. The man closest to Josephine noticed her now and removed his straw boater hat.

"Good afternoon, ma'am," he said in a deep baritone that resonated in the foyer. He wore a three-piece windowpane suit the color of the chewy caramel squares Josephine loved eating at Halloween. His deep brown eyes locked on hers as one corner of his lips lifted in a slow smile.

Wow. Josephine stared at him, unable to return the greeting. Her thoughts went into panic mode and tried to form, then broke apart, then tried to reform, then broke apart again. Alma turned to see whom the man spoke to, and her face lifted in delight.

"Josephine!" she said, coming over and reaching for Josephine's hands as though they were dear friends. "How are you? It's a wonderful surprise to see you, and you look so lovely. I love what you've done with your hair."

"Quite a change, I agree," Hattie mumbled to herself.

Josephine cut her eyes toward Hattie. *She doesn't let up, does she?*

Alma continued as though she wasn't listening to Hattie. "What brings you by today?"

"That's an answer I'd like to hear," Hattie said, still unsmiling.

Repeating her earlier reason, Josephine said, "I was out for a stroll, and I thought I'd stop by and say hello."

"I'm delighted that you did," Alma said, sounding genuinely happy. "Louis, Danny, this is Josephine." She leaned toward the two men and whispered as though sharing a secret. "She's helping out with Sara's party."

Danny, the man who greeted Josephine earlier, stepped closer and gave a nod. Josephine gave him a quick look up and down, stopping on his face. *He is really handsome. Absurdly so.* She guessed his age to be a little older than hers, late thirties. His black hair was thick, slightly wavy, and neatly parted to the side. "Pleased to meet you, Mrs . . . ?"

"Ms. Reynolds," she said before she could stop and think about how much information she should share. Josephine removed her hat and tried not to crush it in her tight grip. She patted her hair nervously.

"Ms. Reynolds," Danny said. "I'm Daniel Stewart, but everyone calls me Danny, and I'd be happy if you did too."

"Pleased to meet you, Danny." *Would you look at that smile?* Josephine forced herself to look away.

The younger of the two men removed his hat and nodded toward Josephine. With fair hair and blue eyes, he had the look of an eager college graduate full of optimism. "Good to meet you, Ms. Reynolds. I'm Louis Grant. How do you do?"

Josephine struggled to keep a composed expression. Louis *Grant*. Grant was her family name and had been her mama's maiden name. *Is this Alma's next husband? Am I looking at my great-grandfather?* "I'm well, thank you. I didn't intend to interrupt—"

Alma shook her head. "Not at all. I'm happy to see you." She looked at Hattie. "Did you hear back from Mrs. Brooks?"

"No, ma'am, I did not," Hattie replied.

Alma's face scrunched in thought; then she focused her doe eyes on Josephine. "You look like someone who knows what to serve at a bash. Would you like to help me create a menu for Sara's party? Any chance I could talk you into staying here a little longer?"

Josephine could be talked into staying as long as it took to change their fates, even though she had no idea where to start. Maybe if she could learn everything about the party plans, she could figure out a way to thwart them. *If there's not a party, then there won't be a raid, and Alma won't be shot.* "I'd be happy to help."

"Swell," Danny said. "You've saved Louis and me from having to choose between shrimp cocktail and cheese balls. We should get back to the bank."

Alma chuckled. "That's positively baloney. Why would I make you choose between shrimp cocktail and cheese balls when we shall enjoy both?" Louis leaned toward Alma and kissed her cheek. He whispered something only she could hear, but whatever it was caused Alma's eyes to dance with delight.

Danny shifted on his feet near Josephine, and she glanced toward him to see he was watching her with his serious brown eyes. "I hope to see you again, Ms. Reynolds."

His sincerity charmed her. She felt seen. *Is this how all men in the '20s make a woman feel?* "Josephine," she said. "You can call me Josephine. Ms. Reynolds sounds like—" She stopped herself before saying, *Nathan's mom.* "Sounds too proper."

"If anything, my mother taught me to be respectful, but I'll honor your request. It was an absolute pleasure to meet you, *Josephine.*"

He spoke her name with such intention that the sound of it created a fluttering inside her. *Oh.* She pressed her hand to her stomach. The grandfather clock chimed the hour with a single gong that echoed through the downstairs and caused Josephine to flinch.

"Tomorrow!" Alma said with excitement. Everyone looked at her. "Don't tell me you forgot. I'm hosting dinner for Eleanor, and she's asked me to invite our dearest friends. That includes you two," she said, pointing at the men. She moved toward Josephine. "You should come."

"Me?" Josephine squeaked in surprise. *I can't meet Eleanor, not when Alma thinks Eleanor was the one who sent me to her in the first place. What will happen when Eleanor doesn't recognize me and reveals we've never spoken a day in our lives?* "I hardly think I'm counted as a dear friend of Eleanor's."

"Oh, applesauce," Alma said with a small laugh. "You'll get on well with everyone, I know it. What do you say? Say yes."

Louis laughed and moved toward the front door. He looked at Josephine and said, "Save yourself some time and say yes. She won't stop until she convinces you."

Alma pretended to pout for a second, emphasizing her full red lips. "Why would anyone say no to delicious food and even better company? We'll have music and dancing. You do dance, don't you?"

Josephine's calm started slipping away. "Dancing, well, I, it's been . . . a while." *When was the last time I danced with anyone?* Her mind wandered through the past. A Christmas party at the Green Hills house six or seven years ago. Nathan had swooped her out of her chair in an uncharacteristic move, saying he wanted to dance to "White Christmas." The cold December night had chilled Nathan's nose and tinged it red. She'd called him Rudolph, and he'd laughed and pulled her closer.

"Danny is a swell dancer," Alma said, grinning at him.

Josephine looked from Danny's handsome face—*was he embarrassed by Alma's compliment?*—to Alma's expectant gaze. It wasn't as though Josephine could turn down any invitation to spend more time with Alma. She must find a way to stop what was coming.

"Thank you, Alma," Josephine said. "I'd be honored to attend your dinner."

Alma squeezed Josephine's arm. "You're a funny one, Josephine. So formal." She turned to see Hattie still standing in the foyer.

"Did you hear that, Hattie? Please add Josephine to our guest list for tomorrow night."

"We should be going," Danny said, opening the front door.

Alma ushered Danny and Louis onto the front porch, thanking Louis for the lunch at his parents' house and for driving her home. Both men put on their hats and nodded goodbyes. Josephine noticed a black Model T parked at the curb outside the house. Alma stood in the open doorway. "We'll see you tomorrow!"

Danny looked at Josephine. "Wouldn't miss it." Then he and Louis were down the stairs, leaving Josephine, Alma, and Hattie standing in the foyer.

Hattie cleared her throat. "Might I speak with you for a moment, Ms. Alma?"

Alma motioned to the parlor. "I'll be right with you, Josephine, and we'll discuss the party."

Josephine walked slowly into the parlor. Hattie might want to talk about something as innocuous as a leaky faucet, but something in Hattie's expression made Josephine want to eavesdrop. She perched just inside the parlor, standing out of sight but near the doorway.

Shoes clicked across the hardwood into the living room then quieted on the oversize rug. Josephine strained to hear Hattie's lowered voice. "What do you know about this woman?"

"What woman? Josephine?" Alma asked.

"There's something about her, Ms. Alma. Something not quite right."

Josephine wrung her hands together and leaned toward the doorway. *What was Hattie's problem? Did she need to play the role of Sherlock Holmes?*

"Oh, Hattie, you worry too much," Alma said. "I have a good feeling about her. She's pleasant and mannerly. What's not right about that?"

Hattie huffed. "You look for the best in people and don't see nothing else. She's not being square with us. That one is hiding something."

Hattie's not wrong.

"We're all hiding something," Alma said plainly. "I've never met a single soul who felt truly free enough to reveal all the things in her heart, especially not a woman. We hide all sorts of things for all sorts of reasons, and each reason is as worthy as the next. If she's hiding anything," Alma continued, "it's nothing meant to hurt you or me. Why don't we welcome her and make her feel safe instead? Lord knows we women need a safe place to be in this world."

Hattie sighed. "Ms. Alma, ain't nobody else like you."

Alma's laugh flittered through the house like butterflies. "I sure hope not! Can you imagine two of me?"

"Lord, help us!" Hattie said, but her voice was full of fondness.

Josephine heard their footsteps returning, so she tossed her hat and purse onto the sofa and hurried to the nearest bookshelf, pretending to be interested in reading the spines while her heart madly thumped in her chest. Alma entered the parlor and caught sight of Josephine.

"Are you a reader?" Alma asked.

I used to be. But she hadn't picked up a book in months, hadn't been able to concentrate on anything for long. "Not recently."

Alma removed a book from the shelf and handed it to Josephine. "Take this one. *The Mysterious Affair at Styles*. Hercule Poirot is the cat's pajamas."

Josephine smiled at Alma's description and thanked her for the book. *Will I be able to take it out of the house? Will it disappear when I return to my timeline? Or might it find itself back on Alma's shelf like it never left?* Time leaping, apparently, was a learn-as-you-go experience.

Alma motioned toward the two upholstered accent chairs near the sash windows. "Hattie will bring us tea." She opened a drawer in an end table and removed sheets of paper and a pencil.

Josephine sat, placed the book beside her on the table, and gazed out the windows at the manicured front yard. There was no house across the street. Instead, wide-open land hosted a variety of trees, pines and deciduous, a scattering of large stones, and the remnants of a low stone wall. At least a half acre of empty land bordered each side of the house. Josephine wondered if this land belonged to the Carters. In her mind's eye, she could see the present-day overlay. Across the street and catty-corner from the Carter Mansion in Josephine's time were houses and a side street that ended in a cul-de-sac. Houses had been built on both lots beside the mansion, and somewhere up the street was where Barbara, the homeowner's association vice president, lived and lorded over her precious historical society rules.

Alma sat with an exhale and positioned the paper in front of her. Her pencil hovered over the top sheet before writing the word *Menu* and underlining it. "Louis razzes me about shrimp cocktail and cheese balls, but those are perfect choices for Sara. She has a fondness for cheese. What do you think about deviled eggs?"

Josephine hadn't attended a single Southern wedding, funeral, party, or holiday gathering without someone bringing or serving deviled eggs. Nathan hated them, hated the sulfurous smell of the yolks. He never let Josephine add them to any catering menu, but without fail, one of their friends would insist on bringing a dish, and that friend always brought deviled eggs.

"I can't imagine a party without them," Josephine said with a small smile.

Alma added *deviled eggs* to the list along with shrimp cocktail and cheese balls. While she wrote, she said, "Tell me something about yourself, Josephine."

Josephine panicked and blurted, "I like the color purple."

Alma burst out laughing and reached over to squeeze Josephine's hand. Hattie entered the room at the same time and positioned a tray with a daisy-patterned teapot, two teacups, and a plate of shortbread cookies on the table between them. She lifted the teapot and began filling a cup with steaming golden liquid.

"Josephine," Alma said, still chuckling, "you make me laugh. I meant, tell me something, like, are you married?" Her eyes drifted to Josephine's left hand.

Josephine had worn her wedding rings like a habit until just before she moved into the Carter Mansion, when she tucked them into the far back of a drawer in her jewelry box. She'd walked around for days feeling as though she'd forgotten something, only to later realize it was her rings—jewelry she'd been wearing for fifteen years. Josephine knew some widows wore their rings for the rest of their lives, but she'd wanted to see if taking off the rings would help her let go of what was to make room for what could be.

Alma's question lingered, and Josephine didn't realize she was rubbing the finger on her left hand until Alma touched her. "Forgive me, dear. I didn't mean to pry."

Josephine's shoulders relaxed and she sighed. "No forgiveness needed. My husband, Nathan, died eight months ago."

"Oh, darling," Alma said, squeezing Josephine's hand and looking at her with compassionate eyes. "I am so very sorry."

Josephine nodded, unable to speak as the familiar sting of loss swelled within her. This time the grief wasn't for the absence of Nathan. *It's for the loss of me.* Hattie paused in pouring tea in the second cup. Josephine glanced up at Hattie's face. *Is that sympathy?* At the very least it was gentleness, the first Hattie had directed Josephine's way.

"How long were you married?" Alma asked.

"Fifteen years."

"Franklin and I were married less than two years, and now he's been gone almost ten," Alma said quietly. The shift in her mood was immediate, like someone had come into her eyes and turned off the light. "Hattie remembers. It was dreadful. I mourned for weeks."

"She did," Hattie said softly and resumed pouring tea. "Heartbreaking for all of us."

"You and Hattie have been together that long?" Josephine asked, looking between Alma and Hattie.

Alma's smile lifted her cheeks and pushed away the sadness in her expression. When she pulled in a deep breath, her mood shifted again and her buoyancy returned. "Since I met Franklin. Hattie's mama was Franklin's nanny."

"She loved that boy," Hattie said, placing a teacup in its saucer and handing it to Josephine, who thanked her.

"Everybody loved Franklin," Alma said. "He was so kind and thoughtful and funny, like you. He made me laugh all the time. Hattie's mama brought her over to help out when Hattie was a teenager. She was here the day I met Franklin's parents in this house. Hattie and I are the same age, and we were friends right away."

"Not right away," Hattie said, but she was smirking.

Alma chuckled. "Nobody becomes friends with Hattie right away, but she saw my finer qualities."

"Hard not to," Hattie agreed. "You need anything, just holler for me."

"Thank you, Hattie," Alma said. Hattie left them in the parlor. Alma sipped her tea, and she and Josephine were quiet for a moment. Then she asked, "What happened to Nathan?"

"Heart attack," Josephine said. "Unexpected and . . . shocking. He was a cardiologist, too, which made the whole thing so ironic."

"Josephine, I'm so very sorry you had to go through that. I wish we didn't share this tragedy, but I do understand. The war took Franklin and so many of our good men. Do you have children?"

Josephine shook her head. Not being able to birth children was no longer shameful in modern culture, but many women—including Josephine for a few years—still suffered a sting of disappointment. Nathan hadn't been upset for long when they realized getting pregnant wasn't an option. He had envisioned having children, but once he saw how much easier his days were without additional responsibilities, he never talked about children or their lack of them. Men were questioned far less than women. She'd been asked hundreds of times why she had no children, and at least half of the people looked at her with sadness, sometimes pity.

"I'm sorry, Josephine. What a bundle of disappointment you've been given. Franklin and I planned to have a big family," Alma said, "and then he was off to war. Who knows if we would have been able to have little ones. I was very angry for a while, but it does fade."

A question left Josephine's lips before she could stop it. "How did you do it? How did you keep going?"

Alma lowered her teacup. "I didn't want to. Believe me, there were days when I lay in bed not wanting to go on one more second. I thought the most dreadful things. How could I be a widow when I was barely a wife? I was a matron without heirs—how could I possibly contribute to society? I would be forgotten."

"I know the feeling," Josephine admitted. In fact, she *did* feel forgotten. Her friends had all been *Nathan's* friends—his peers and the wives of his peers. When she lost Nathan, she lost the person who had connected them all. She was like an anchor cut away from a boat. They kept sailing on, and she'd sunk.

"But Hattie wouldn't let me give up," Alma continued. "And there were others who encouraged me too. They helped me remember my privilege. I wasn't the only person who lost someone in the war, but the Carter family money made certain things easier for me. I wasn't a destitute widow. They convinced me I still had much to offer. Having a reputable family name, social standing, intelligence, and bravery means I can help those around me in a meaningful way."

Josephine nodded and sipped her black tea. It tasted malty, a bit spicy, and had a smoky, rich flavor. Her thoughts drifted to her sister. Katherine continually poked and prodded and sometimes strong-armed Josephine into forward motion. She recalled one of their recent conversations about what Josephine could do with her life now—assist nonprofits or fundraise for charities. Like Alma, Josephine had wealth to keep her comfortable. *But I've been so trapped in my own head. I haven't been thinking about possibilities for how I can use my status and abundance to give back to society.*

Alma filled the silence. "Franklin hadn't made a will, so legally his entire estate went to me. It was more money than I could spend for at least fifty years."

Josephine's eyebrows raised. *Why does Alma need a speakeasy if it isn't about the money?*

Alma continued, "The Carters were terribly disappointed we didn't have children, but Franklin has two brothers and a sister, all married, all blessed with children. I shouldn't have felt so sorry for myself, because compared to many, my life is comfortable. But, Josephine, I was *bored.* Being a widowed housewife without a house full of people to care for is dreadful. I needed interests to keep me alive. You know it's not encouraged for women like us to work outside of the home, but I've found ways to keep myself busy."

Josephine's lips lifted around the rim of the teacup. "Ways such as the Club Belle Âme?"

Alma smirked, and her eyes were alight with mischief. "That's one way."

The whole point of this outrageous time-leaping plan was for Josephine to save the lives of her family by saving Alma's, to erase the despairing wish Josephine had spoken. She had only four days to do this. But as she sat with her great-grandmother, who looked every bit like a well-dressed rebel, Josephine wished she had more time to learn all she could about this fascinating woman.

CHAPTER 9

A phone rang, a shrill noise reverberating in the hallway and foyer, and startled both women. Alma excused herself and went into the hallway.

"Hello," Alma said into the phone. There was a pause. Then she said, "Oh dear, I understand . . . Yes, of course . . . I hope she rests and recovers quickly, and please let us know if you need anything." The receiver clicked against the base, and Alma returned with an expression of disappointment.

Josephine swallowed a sip of tea. "Is everything okay?"

Alma sat again, her forehead creased in thought. She lifted her teacup and sipped. "It will be," she said absently. Then her expression returned to what Josephine was learning to be Alma's natural state—hopeful. "Say, how are you in the kitchen?"

Josephine returned her teacup to its saucer. "What do you mean?"

"Do you know how to cook? And please don't take offense. Many women like us wouldn't trouble themselves to know a saucepot from a cast iron, but I genuinely enjoy cooking. That was Mrs. Brooks's daughter on the phone. Mrs. Brooks has taken ill, nothing too serious, but I was counting on her to prepare all the food for the party. It's too late to find someone now, seeing as how the bash is only days away."

Josephine's pulse increased its tempo. *Without food, would they cancel the party? If they rescheduled to a day when Mrs. Brooks could help, would the raid never happen?* "Could you change the date of the party? Move it to another time when you have everyone you need?"

Alma shook her head. "We've mailed invitations, and there's no reason to cancel. Hattie and I can prepare the food, but it would be so much easier with help."

Josephine tried a different tactic. "What if this is a sign?"

Alma's smooth features wrinkled in confusion. "A sign?"

"A sign that you shouldn't have the party on Sunday," Josephine said.

Alma's face relaxed into a knowing grin. "If I was stopped by every detour, I would have never gotten anywhere. Is this your way of telling me that you're frightful in the kitchen?"

Of course it's not easy to deter Alma. She isn't the kind of woman who hits a speed bump and stops driving. "I can cook," Josephine admitted.

Alma clapped her hands together. "I knew you could. You're not a meek woman, I can tell. Reserved but intelligent and observant." Alma leaned forward and lowered her voice, saying, "I could be wrong, but I bet you're like me. You study people and your surroundings, you learn all kinds of things that others think aren't useful or don't suit their station, and you wind up being able to run the whole show while allowing others to believe they're the ones in charge."

Josephine made a scoffing noise in her throat. *I haven't "run the show" of my life in years.* "I wouldn't dare compare myself to you, Alma. Your bravery alone outshines anything I've ever done."

Alma studied Josephine for a moment before speaking. "You're here, are you not? You lost your husband, your sense of duty, your future, but you are still here, sitting with me, discussing how you can move forward."

Josephine felt the sting of tears, so she glanced out the window. Sunlight streamed down through the tree branches across the street and created patches of light among the browning grass and growing weeds. Alma's vigor for life and her belief in the good of others filled Josephine with guilt about her throwaway wish, her willingness to give up. It threatened Alma's life and every one of her descendants.

She shifted her focus back to the party and the speakeasy. "Don't you ever worry you'll be caught?" She looked at Alma. "By the government or the local police?"

Alma took a cookie from the plate and broke it in half. Soft buttery crumbs fell onto her plate. "Oh, darling, the chief of police visits Club Belle Âme at least once a week." Alma bit into her cookie and covered her mouth when she laughed. "Don't look so shocked."

If the chief of police is a regular patron, then who approves the raid? Who rushes in to stop, arrest, and possibly shoot people the night of the party? The future article stated that the Bureau of Prohibition *and* local law enforcement raided the mansion.

"If you don't mind me asking," Josephine said, reaching for a rectangular shortbread cookie from the ceramic plate, "why do you do it? Drinking alcohol isn't illegal, so what makes you want to sell it and risk getting caught? Is it for the money? I mean, do you *need* the money?"

Alma finished her cookie. "Yes and no. I don't need the money, not right now, but in the future I might. But right now, the money is for others, for the causes I support."

"You're doing all of this just so you can give away the money?" Josephine asked, leaning back in her chair on an exhale.

Alma grinned. "Eleanor says I'm goofy, too, but what's the point of having all of this if I can't do something *good* with it? And people are angry that they're being told what they can and can't do, so they're looking for ways to rebel, have a good time, and live their lives. I'm giving them a way to do that, and they give me a way to help others."

Josephine previously believed speakeasies were dingy, smoke-filled places where people performed acts they were ashamed of, where they hid their secrets and drank themselves into oblivion. Maybe some speakeasies were like that, but Josephine suspected Club Belle Âme wasn't going to be like the dodgy examples she'd seen in the movies.

"Where do you get your supplies?"

Alma sipped her tea. "You mean the juice?" she asked, her voice full of playfulness. "Cecil handles everything. He coordinates the buying and shipping of the alcohol because he knows all the fastest, safest ways to get it here. Most of the time, he's the one who delivers it. He trusts his connections but only so far. He also touts that he's the one who owns the place. Keeps it simple."

Josephine covered her mouth and finished chewing before she spoke. "He pretends Club Belle Âme is his? But it's in *your* house—unless the club isn't really yours. Does he rent the space from you?"

Alma shook her head. "Oh, no, definitely not. Club Belle Âme is mine, but even with our right to vote, you know we women aren't truly seen as capable enough to run a business, certainly not a speakeasy."

"That's ridiculous," Josephine said before she could stop herself.

Alma grinned. "Outrageously ridiculous, I agree. But sometimes we have to play by men's rules. Apply our wit and wisdom to use the system in our favor. You know we are taught we should be well-groomed, demure, accommodating, and present ourselves in a ladylike fashion in public. We should fall in line behind the men."

"And you do all of that?" Josephine already knew the answer.

"I make it appear as though I do, which is why Cecil is ever so helpful. He's also the barkeep. Make sure you try his French 75. It's worth the indulgence. That reminds me. I need to make sure he's placed an order for delivery Saturday. We'll not have enough for Sara's party if we don't replenish." Alma made a note on the paper. "I need to book a new band too."

"Hattie mentioned that the band canceled. Another sign?" Josephine asked.

Alma laughed. "A sign to persevere. Louis suggested another option. They're one of the best bands in town, a local jazz trio." Alma made another note on the paper, then grinned at Josephine. "Can I count on you to help Hattie and me in the kitchen Sunday morning? We won't be making everything, of course. I'll call on a few other friends. I'll find someone to make the birthday cake." She lifted the teapot and refilled Josephine's cup and her own, waiting for Josephine's reply.

Josephine sat mesmerized watching the dark liquid pour from the delicate pot. *As if I have a choice but to say yes.* If she hadn't been trying to save Alma's life, she still would have wanted to spend as much time with her as possible. "Of course you can count on me."

"Wonderful!" Alma exclaimed. She picked up the pencil and talked as she wrote, as though picking up a thread of conversation already running through her mind. "Creamy artichoke and salmon sandwiches are easy and delicious. I'm not sure we can get oysters this time of year, but I'll ask around. What appetizers have you served before?"

Josephine thought of the charcuterie board fascination that showcased all kinds of creative party board ideas. She doubted that a s'mores or a movie-inspired board would make sense to anyone in 1927, but maybe a more traditional one would. "What about a cheese and meat board? Would that fit? It's about the easiest appetizer I can think of, and almost everyone will like it."

"Great idea," Alma said. "I'll add crackers and bread too." After discussing a few other options, Alma's list contained ten appetizers and the birthday cake that a friend of hers would make. Sara's favorite kind of dessert was an upside-down pineapple cake, an interesting birthday cake request in Josephine's opinion. She hadn't researched popular foods in the 1920s, but as Alma explained it, this choice was one of the most requested desserts.

With their tea finished and the menu complete, Josephine felt it would be awkward for her to stay any longer. "Thank you for the tea and cookies," she said, placing her napkin on the table beside the tray and standing. She picked up the Agatha Christie book and held it against her chest. "And thank you for the book."

"I hope you enjoy it, and you're welcome here anytime," Alma said. "I'm grateful for your help with the party and for assisting on Sunday morning with the preparations. You're coming tonight, aren't you? To Eleanor's dinner?"

Josephine tried to keep her expression neutral as her body tensed. Her stomach performed a nauseous roll. If Alma mentioned Josephine's acquaintance or friendship with Eleanor during the dinner, there was no chance Eleanor would play along. *Do I have a choice? Of course I do. I could stay home and lose more time with Alma. So if I want to fix this, no, I don't have a choice.* She *had* to take the chance that Eleanor might expose her lie. If she did, then Josephine would face the consequences.

Josephine forced the sweetest smile she could and nodded. "Yes, I'm looking forward to it." Although she wasn't looking forward to being possibly called out by Eleanor. On the flip side, maybe Eleanor was dense and wouldn't notice or care about a make-believe friendship with Josephine. If it was mentioned, maybe it would go right over Eleanor's head.

"Dinner starts at seven," Alma said, breaking through Josephine's what-ifs. "Dinner attire. I'm sure you have the perfect dress to wear."

Josephine grabbed her hat and bag off the sofa, and Alma walked her to the front door. When the door opened, the outside light moved into the foyer and created a faint rectangular patch of sunshine stretching across the polished wood. A hint of warmth followed it, and birdsong floated in.

"I absolutely adore this weather," Alma said. "It's so full of possibility, and I feel lighter once the heat of summer passes. Don't you?"

Josephine nodded. *I don't miss the stifling humidity of a Nashville summer.* "Southern summers can drain you." *As do months of living beneath a cloud of gloom.* But spending time with Alma had unexpectedly lifted Josephine's spirits, even as she fretted about being good enough to save her family.

Alma's lips turned down slightly as she scanned the front yard. "Are you walking home? It's not too far, is it?"

Josephine hadn't thought of a response to how she came and went to Alma's. She couldn't very well say the truth. "Friends live nearby. I'll walk there and get a ride home."

"Lovely," Alma said, not seeming to doubt Josephine's explanation. "See you soon!"

"Yes, tonight. Goodbye," Josephine said and stepped over the threshold into the October sunlight.

CHAPTER 10

Passing back through time made Josephine's body feel squeezed through a tiny porthole while being encased in ice. This time after leaving Alma in 1927, Josephine stood on the front porch for a few seconds and inhaled slowly, trying to relax her constricting heart and ease her roiling stomach. The freezing sensation zinging through her body made it challenging to stand upright. Her body clenched and curled inward to ward off the chill. Gradually warmth tingled back into her limbs, and her shoulders lowered from her ears. Blinking in the surroundings, she saw the front porch was hers, decorated for the fall. Josephine opened the front door and stepped into her own version of the Carter Mansion. She removed her cloche hat and dropped it, along with the handbag, on the narrow entry table in the foyer.

Josephine still held the book gifted to her by Alma. But when she made the motion to place it on the table with her belongings, she gasped. *The Mysterious Affair at Styles* transformed from almost new in appearance, with a rich golden-brown cloth cover and a black art deco design, to resembling an artifact from a rare bookstore. The cloth cover was worn and had faded to a sickly yellow-brown. The top edge was stained blue. Blemishes marred the back cover, and minor fraying appeared at the bottom of the spine. The interior pages were the color of antique parchment paper. This book was now more than one hundred years old. Josephine carried it into the parlor and gently placed it on a bookshelf. *What is this treasure worth now? What would happen if I took it with me when I return to 1927 tomorrow? Would it age backward, returning to its youth?*

●●●

THE NEXT MORNING, Josephine's alarm went off, and she stirred in bed. After another restless night, she blinked away disorientation, her limbs feeling heavy and sluggish. She'd set an alarm so she wouldn't oversleep, and she was grateful she had because there was no chance she'd have awoken early on her own. Painters would arrive early to begin stripping the paint on the house's exterior trim work, including Uncle Donnie's eyesore of a black paint job on two of the rear windows.

Josephine showered and dressed, finally making herself a mug of tea just before the painters arrived. She walked around the house with the head of the crew. The once springy grass was turning brittle in the cooler October weather, and the blades crunched beneath their shoes.

Josephine and the foreman discussed the scope of the work and looked over paint chips. She verified the option that matched as closely as possible to the original paint—a faint creamy white that complemented the deep red brick. She'd already received approval from the homeowner's association.

While standing in the backyard, Josephine noticed the sadly neglected rosebushes. Withered blooms littered the soil with brown, shriveled remnants of their beauty. Most of the leaves had browned and fallen from the thorny branches as well. *Grandma Dorothy loved those roses and the entire backyard garden.* Josephine smiled. *She called the rosebushes "family heirlooms" like they were furniture or household pieces passed down through the generations.* Josephine assumed that the roses had started declining when Grandma Dorothy died and Uncle Donnie took the house. *Were the roses already in the backyard in 1927, or did they come later?* She made a mental note to check.

As Josephine made her way around the house to the front porch, she groaned. The vice president of the homeowner's association was speed-walking up the sidewalk and waved as though she was vying for someone's attention. It was too late for Josephine to turn and run, so she attempted a pleasant smile and waited for Barbara to reach her.

"Good morning!" Barbara said with a smile that was almost genuine. Her silvery hair was styled to perfection. Wearing a burnt-orange sweater and ankle-length black skirt, she looked like she might be on her way to a fall photo op. "I am thrilled, absolutely thrilled, with your front door. It's such a smart change."

"Did I have a choice?" Josephine deadpanned.

Barbara laughed, misunderstanding Josephine's sarcasm. "Of course you didn't. You wouldn't have wanted that ugly door on your beautiful home. Who would?"

Uncle Donnie did, even if his reasoning was vindictive. "It was the least appealing thing about the house," Josephine said, agreeing that she wouldn't have wanted to keep the door, with or without the preservation rules. "The renovations he did inside are good, though."

"Thank goodness," Barbara said. "I noticed you're painting the house. Good for you! No more black trim."

No secrets with Barbara on the watch.

"And the weathervane too," Barbara continued. "You've been so busy, and we're pleased as punch about everything you're doing to correct mistakes."

Barbara's words jostled something inside Josephine. The woman had *no* idea how accurate her words were. *Correcting mistakes, trying to erase errant wishes.* Josephine frowned. "The weathervane?"

"The turkey," Barbara said and pointed skyward. "You could see that hideous thing miles away. Garish! So glad you swapped it for a more period-appropriate piece. You know how to fit in around here."

Unease slithered into Josephine's stomach. She hadn't changed the weathervane. Josephine craned her head back and walked far enough down the sidewalk to see the weathervane. Barbara was right. The turkey was gone, replaced by a copper weathervane with cardinal points that spun around in high wind.

Barbara's saccharine voice broke through Josephine's thoughts. "Admiring your choice! We love it too. I'd better be going. Just wanted to congratulate you on the wonderful changes. Your porch fits in with the rest of the street and is fabulous, if still a little bare of decor, but I'm looking forward to more!" Then Barbara turned on her boot heels and returned the way she'd come, walking like she was late for an engagement.

"A little bare?" Josephine asked, glancing at her overly decorated front porch. She'd never had so much holiday spirit on the exterior of her house. What more could she possibly add without veering straight toward tacky or unsightly or both? Didn't Barbara appreciate tastefulness? Most people used a light touch when decorating for Halloween. Christmas was the holiday when Josephine saw the zeal for the holidays truly on display. She couldn't imagine how excessive Barbara's expectations would be later this year.

But fall décor was near the bottom of Josephine's concerns. She looked back up at the new weathervane and shivered. *How is the turkey gone? Is this part of the dueling timelines? Are there other alterations I haven't noticed?* Josephine rushed up the stairs and into the house.

She took a quick assessment of the foyer. Everything appeared the same as the day before, but one step into the living room had her faltering. On a table near the sofa, Josephine had arranged a group of framed photographs. There had been five frames, but now there were only two. A Christmas photograph with Nathan was gone, as were two family vacation pictures from Hawaii and California. She quickly scanned the floor around and beneath the table. She yanked and tossed aside the couch cushions. The frames and photos had disappeared.

Josephine picked up the two remaining frames. Her mama smiled up at her from one photo, where she stood among the burst of fall colors painting the trees. It was a picture from their girls' trip to Maine last October. Her mama's smile revealed how refreshed and excited she was, and Josephine remembered how happy her mama had been to share the trip with her daughters. A fellow hiker had taken the picture for them, and Josephine and Katherine had been right there, tucked in on either side of their mama. But now Josephine and her sister were noticeably absent.

The other photograph had been of Josephine and Katherine as young girls in Halloween costumes with their mama, who'd dressed as a bumblebee. Their dad had taken the picture, and Josephine could still hear the echo of his laughter in her mind. Josephine insisted on being a princess that year and forbade Katherine from being one too, which had started a fight that lasted for a week. Now little-girl Katherine sparkled in a princess costume complete with tiara, pink tulle skirt, and scepter, rather than Josephine. Josephine and her mama were missing from the photo, not even a shadow of their presence to be seen.

A tremor moved through her body, shaking the frame in her hand. She placed it back on the table. The sickly squirm in her stomach intensified. *This is all my fault. Mama and Katherine are disappearing because of me.*

A Tiffany lamp replica from Nathan's office had been placed on the secretary desk in the living room. The lamp skewed toward gaudy with its peacock-shaped, bejeweled base and blue and green lampshade dotted with ruby-red jewels. Nathan loved it for its ostentation, for its representation of beauty and confidence. The lamp was no longer on the secretary. It was nowhere, sucked into the void that was erasing Josephine's life.

Josephine sagged onto the sofa as though her bones had gone soft. She sat for a few minutes, her mind reeling, wanting to call Katherine and terrified to call her. *What if Katherine doesn't answer? Or worse, what if she answers and has no idea who I am?* Like a ship unmoored from the harbor, Josephine drifted through the remainder of the rooms, each step twisting her stomach more.

The book Alma had given her, *The Mysterious Affair at Styles*, was nothing but a heap of dust on the bookshelf. Josephine reached out to touch the pile but hesitated, afraid she might turn to ashes alongside the book. The china Josephine received as wedding gifts had been placed in the dining room's display cabinet. She could count on one hand the number of times they'd used the china during the last fifteen years, but she kept it for sentimental reasons. Now the china was gone.

She thought of Alma's missing clothes from the armoire, so Josephine climbed the stairs, wondering if she'd find half of her life vanished too. Upstairs in her bedroom closet, she stood among the clothes. More than half of the hangers were empty, slightly swaying on the metal rod in the rush of wind she had brought in with her. Josephine placed her hand over her heart, willing it to slow down. But when she realized the college sweatshirt she'd been unable to toss out—the one with the fraying cuffs and overstretched hem—was missing, her entire body seized in panic.

Josephine's wild gaze landed on her jewelry box situated on the vanity. She frantically dug through the bottom jewelry drawer. Her wedding rings had vanished, and so had a ruby pendant necklace her mama had given Josephine on her eighteenth birthday. Lightheaded and emotional, Josephine sat on the floor in the closet. Not only was she disappearing, but so was her family and her connection to Nathan. *Is our life together being erased? Who would Nathan have been without me? Would he have married someone else? Would he . . . still be alive?*

Josephine's mind created question after question with no answers. Eventually she got up out of the closet and searched the rest of the house. Along with the significant items that had vanished, other seemingly less important items had, too, like her shampoo and conditioner from the shower, her fuzzy socks with the penguins, and her laptop bag.

Josephine slumped onto her bed. *So it begins. The complete undoing of me.* After losing Nathan, she had more in common with an unraveling sweater than she did with other women. But this . . . this was a complete severing. All those moments when she felt as though she was nothing, forgotten, left to wither, she *had* been something. Something alive and breathing and unique. Was it human nature to *feel* like giving up and yet, when faced with the end, to fight it with a passion so fierce it was breathtaking? *I can't let my family disappear. I can't rob Mama and Katherine of the good lives they deserve.*

A force powerful enough to push her to her feet surged through her body. She stood barefoot on the cool hardwood. *I have to save them.* A bright red cardinal landed on the windowsill outside her bedroom window. She turned her gaze toward its watching eyes. Soft sunlight illuminated the edges of its wings. *And I want this life with my family.*

Josephine would give every bit of strength and cleverness she had to saving Alma so her family could live and love and affect the world. But how? Not having a caterer hadn't deterred Alma. *Can I somehow stop the alcohol from arriving on time?* Alma mentioned that someone named Cecil handled that, and he would be bringing in another shipment on Saturday. *Can I find out when he's arriving? And then what?*

Josephine had a vison of her sneaking down to the speakeasy Saturday night after it closed and collecting all the alcohol. Could she drag out dozens and dozens of bottles without being noticed? She could pour out all the alcohol and leave behind the empty bottles, but what if she was caught in the middle of draining hundreds of dollars' worth? *It might be a risk worth taking.*

What about the band? Josephine might be able to call them from Alma's and tell them not to come. But she'd have to ask Alma for their number, and that would likely lead to a string of questions. *Will a lack of music stop the party?* She thought of all the parties she'd been to when a radio or a record player was all the music anyone needed to provide ambiance. If the band was a no-show, Alma would no doubt use a radio.

Josephine groaned. None of her ideas felt significant enough to change Alma's mind. The most radical idea she had was to tell Alma the truth, but even Alma, with her free spirit and forward thinking, might think Josephine was better suited to a sanatorium. Telling Alma would be a last resort. Perhaps she could learn more about Alma and the party during the dinner for Eleanor tonight, which brought up another problem. *How will I be in the same room with Eleanor without the woman telling everyone she's never met me?* As if Josephine didn't have enough disasters to deal with.

The most important thing Josephine could do now was to settle herself. Her body trembled with a combination of fear and worry. Yet she detected a tiny slip of courage as well.

●●●

HOURS LATER, JOSEPHINE dressed in a hunter-green dress featuring a sheer overlay detailed with delicate floral embellishments. It had a square neckline, ruffled sleeves, and matching layers of soft ruffles in the skirt that started around her hips and swooped back and forth like bunting. She paired the dress with pearl earrings, a cloche hat, lace gloves, stockings, and low heels. She kept her hair simple, opting for soft curls that created a romantic, feminine feel, something she hadn't experienced in months.

Josephine lined her eyes in light brown and added blush and pale pink lipstick. Not knowing what the other women would wear to a dinner party, Josephine didn't want to show up overdressed, even though she'd read that many women in the '20s wore flashy, highly decorated evening wear. Understatement would be a safe option.

Josephine checked the time. Five minutes to seven. She grabbed her handbag and the front-door key, then looked at herself one last time in the foyer mirror, startled by the reflection of a beautiful stranger staring back at her. A small smile played across her lips. *Not bad. I could be someone included in Alma's photo albums.*

One of Alma's girlfriends caught laughing in a photo or dining in the garden among the blooms and butterflies.

When she stepped out onto the porch, the crisp October night air prickled her skin. Across the street, small lights hidden in bushes spotlighted the neighbor's house. The beams pointed toward the skeletons in the oak tree and toward the oversize spider hanging from its web. A cat pranced down the sidewalk and paused to look at Josephine, its tail flicking back and forth, before it continued its prowling.

She turned toward the front door, sliding her fingers across the carved words. Jitters passed through her, making her hands shaky and her breath hitch. *What if Eleanor ruins the whole thing as soon as I arrive? What then?* Josephine had zero backup plans. No plan B or C. She didn't even have a real plan A.

She thought of Katherine, who was the bolder sister, the one less likely to stay on the beaten path, less likely to follow the rules. For years, Josephine stayed the course, even if she didn't like it, if only because it was what someone else said was right. *So what would Katherine do if she felt terrified? She'd do it anyway. She'd close her eyes, inhale a few deep breaths, and run headfirst into the dark unknown.*

Josephine breathed deeply, desperately trying to channel her sister's bravery. She slid the key into the lock and exhaled. Then she whispered the password, knocked on the door, and turned the knob. As soon as she crossed the threshold, the familiar icy chill spread through her veins. Josephine heard saxophone music, laughter, and boisterous voices. She pitched forward slightly but straightened as quickly as she could, even as her body protested. She couldn't be seen hunched over gasping for breath. As she inhaled, she breathed in the scents of roasted meat and baked bread, the wispy hint of cologne and floral perfume.

People came into focus. A small group of men gathered in the living room. Dressed in suits varying in shades between dark brown and navy blue, their backs were toward her. Their voices boomed into the foyer, and Josephine caught snippets of their conversation about money and automobiles. Someone laughed about a newspaper article.

The music flowed out of the parlor, where two women stood with their heads close together and their voices much quieter. Movement on the staircase caught Josephine's eyes. She glanced up to see Alma gliding down the stairs in a silky gray dress that brushed the tops of her ankles. Sequins and beadwork covered the bodice and twinkled in the foyer chandelier like starlight against a night sky. "Josephine!" she called in greeting. "Perfect timing." She reached the bottom and crossed the carpet to grab Josephine's hands in hers. "I didn't even ask how you'd get here. I could have sent someone to pick you up. You aren't driving, are you? Although I wouldn't be surprised if you were."

Josephine scrambled for an answer. "My sister," she said. "Her husband, I mean, they're visiting with friends, and they often give me a lift." None of which was a complete lie. Katherine and Neil had probably made friends in Tampa and could be having a bayside dinner, and they did swing by and pick her up on occasion if they were going to lunch or dinner.

"Swell," Alma said. "If you want to stay out later than they do tonight, one of the men can drive you home. Come, let me introduce you to Sara. You already know Eleanor."

Josephine's body stiffened in panic, but Alma didn't seem to notice. She looped her arm through Josephine's and walked her into the parlor where the two women stood in conversation. The song switched from a slow jazz tune to an up-tempo swing song that matched the quick-step beat of Josephine's heart.

"Ladies," Alma said, presenting Josephine, "I'm so pleased we're all together tonight. Sara, I want to introduce Ms. Josephine Reynolds. Josephine this is Sara Stewart, and as you know, we're throwing her a bash this Sunday. Can you believe it's in three days?"

"So pleased to meet you, Josephine," Sara said. Her cherub face was fair with slightly downturned light brown eyes and Cupid's bow lips. Thin dark brows arched high above her thickly lined eyes, and she'd accentuated her lips in deep red. She wore a maroon dress with so much fringe she looked to be in constant motion, and the short length, stopping at her knees, spoke of a woman who was evolving with the times.

Alma made her way to the sofa and sat. Noticing that Alma hadn't introduced Eleanor, Sara asked, "You two already know each other?"

"Yes, darling," Alma said. "Eleanor is the one who suggested Josephine help out with your party. A wonderful suggestion, too, I might add. Josephine has already been helping me make sure your bash is perfect."

Heat flamed up Josephine's neck, and she could almost feel the color draining from her face. Eleanor was tall and blond, a wisp of a woman, who stood in a way that implied grace and wealth. Her sapphire dress, covered in beadwork and lace, confirmed her obvious affluence. Her matching blue eyes narrowed as she studied Josephine. "I do offer the best suggestions, don't I?" she asked, smiling over her shoulder at Alma, but her voice lacked warmth. She sent a skeptical gaze toward Josephine. "Josephine, dear, do you mind stepping into the foyer with me? I have something I want to discuss, and I don't want Sara to hear."

Sara giggled, probably thinking Eleanor had a birthday surprise. Eleanor looped her thin arm through Josephine's and walked her out of the parlor so quickly that Josephine stumbled over the edge of the rug. Eleanor marched Josephine up the hallway, far from the ladies and the men in the living room.

Eleanor released her arm, and being at least four inches taller than Josephine, she stared down at her with steely blue eyes. "Spill it."

"Uh, what?" Josephine stuttered. The grandfather clock ticked steadily behind her.

"Don't act like a dumb Dora with me," Eleanor whispered, her voice almost a hiss. The scent of her floral perfume and cigarettes permeated the air. "I've never met you, *Josephine*, and I couldn't find anyone to help out with Sara's party, so *I* didn't send you. So level with me or you'll find yourself out of here faster than you can breathe. I won't let you hurt Alma."

Josephine's throat closed, and her heart thumped so hard she thought she might faint. *I can't fail now, not with only three days left to change our fates. Not when half my life has already vanished. What does a woman like Eleanor need to hear?* Eleanor was obviously protective of her friend, so Josephine opted for sympathy. "I would *never* hurt Alma, I promise." *Which is the absolute truth.* "I heard that Alma helped people, women like me. I lost my husband a few months ago—" She paused, trying to summon the tears that had been so easy to locate these days. "I stopped by the other day to speak with Alma, and she was so kind, but she thought *you'd* sent me, and I didn't say otherwise. She told me about the party and the money, and I could use the money. I'm sorry, Eleanor," she said. "I know it's wrong to lie, but I felt so welcome here that I didn't want to tell Alma she was wrong about you and me." *Is that sufficient to convince her? Sincere enough?*

Eleanor listened without interrupting, studying her. Then her pursed lips softened. Her expression shifted from distrustful to understanding. "I believe you, Josephine, I do."

Thank God.

"You don't have the look of a cheat, but no more lies."

Josephine nodded in relief.

Eleanor touched Josephine's arm. "I'm sorry about your husband. That's a tragedy too many of us endure."

"Thank you," Josephine said. "Did you lose yours too?"

"I wish," Eleanor said on an exhale, then kept talking as though she hadn't uttered a shocking fact. "Compose yourself, and let's rejoin the party. You can't return looking like I've stolen your pearls. If Alma likes you, I trust I will too. She's an excellent judge of character, but remember, we have a deal."

Josephine's pulse began to slow, and she offered Eleanor an appreciative smile. "No more lies. I promise."

Eleanor straightened to her full, imposing height. "Excellent choice in handbags. I have one just like that." Then she walked away toward the parlor.

Hattie emerged from the kitchen carrying a pewter tray of hors d'oeuvres. She paused beside Josephine. "You look lovely, Ms. Josephine." Her eyes moved toward Eleanor's retreating back. "Eleanor does not tolerate dishonesty, and neither do I."

Josephine's stomach somersaulted beneath Hattie's intense gaze. *Of all the people to overhear.* "Hattie—"

"I don't trust you, but Ms. Alma does, and I respect her wishes," Hattie said. "But if you mean her harm—"

"I don't," Josephine said, touching Hattie's arm, hoping to convey this deep truth. The tray wavered in Hattie's hand, so Josephine released her. "I promise, I don't."

Hattie hummed as though assessing her belief in Josephine. She walked away without saying anything more, leaving Josephine to stand in the hallway like an outcast. Hattie stopped in the opening to the parlor with the tray of appetizers, and within a moment, Alma emerged from the parlor.

"Let's have a cocktail," she said, walking across the hall to the living room. She caught sight of Josephine and her smile was exactly the sign of warmth Josephine needed. "Josephine, join us! Cecil will make drinks."

Sara, Eleanor, and Hattie followed Alma into the living room. Josephine squared her shoulders and followed. *I can do this.* Whether Eleanor and Hattie believed her, Josephine would *never* harm Alma. The opposite was true. She couldn't let their distrust stop her from doing everything she could to save Alma, but winning their trust might make things easier. She could only do that by consistently proving to them that Alma wasn't wrong to believe in Josephine's goodness.

A broad-shouldered man dressed in a navy-blue suit mixed cocktails at a bar cart. His high forehead, widow's peak hairline, and arched brows accentuated his angular features, with a thin nose, sharp cheekbones, and full lips. He passed a drink to Eleanor and said, "Bee's Knees." She thanked him, and he noticed Josephine lingering off to the side. A quick head tilt and a smile in her direction revealed his friendliness. "You must be Josephine," he said, returning his focus to the bottles in front of him. "What can I get for you?" He held up a bottle of rum. "Favorite drink?"

"Oh, I'm fine, thank you. I don't want to trouble you," Josephine said, but Alma was at her side in a moment, looping her arm through Josephine's and moving her closer to Cecil.

"You are no trouble, Josephine! Cecil loves making cocktails for people. It allows him to display his genius," Alma said and pointed to a sheet of paper on the bar cart. Josephine followed her gaze and noticed a name and phone number scrawled on the paper. "Is that the bandleader?"

Cecil nodded. "I've already talked to him, but I said you'd call and make it official."

"I will. Thank you, Cecil, and please make Josephine your French 75," Alma said. "I was boasting about it yesterday. Go light on the gin, though. Josephine, this is Cecil Miller. Banker by day, barkeep by night. He's my right-hand man."

Cecil's large hands moved in a coordinated rhythm. *So this is the man who provides alcohol for the speakeasy.* "Pleasure to meet you, Cecil. Alma speaks highly of you and says you'll be joining us Sunday night."

"*And* tonight," Alma said, a mischievous glint in her eyes.

Cecil handed Josephine a champagne flute. "Good to meet you, Josephine. First time in Club Belle Âme?"

Josephine took the offered glass and frowned, not following the conversation.

"That reminds me," Alma said, "I need to get you an official card! Cecil, can you make one for her? Josephine Reynolds should be the name on it. Not that you need it for tonight or Sunday, but later, if you want to come back, and I do hope you will."

Josephine's brain finally caught up with the implication. *It's Thursday night, a night when the speakeasy is normally open.* She hadn't been to a bar in more than fifteen years. Sure, she'd gone to restaurants that had a bar, but nothing that compared to a speakeasy in the 1920s, or what Josephine imagined they'd be like. Loud music, flowing alcohol, flappers dancing, people slipping away into shadows to avoid prying eyes. "I hadn't planned on going tonight."

"You should join us," a man's voice said.

Danny stepped into sight from her periphery, and Josephine took him in—the chocolate-brown suit, starched white shirt, and matching brown tie. His shiny shoes were as black as his hair. If Josephine were a character in a movie, she might have swooned at his attention, but in real life his interest unnerved her. She hadn't taken notice of male attention other than Nathan's for almost half her life. She'd almost forgotten what it felt like, the zing of curiosity, the rush of blood, the magnetic pull to another.

"Please say yes," Alma said.

"Remember what I said," Louis said, moving to stand beside Alma. "Save yourself some time and agree."

Josephine inched slightly away from Danny, but his gaze didn't stray from her face. "I haven't been to anything like that in years. I wouldn't fit there. I'd be the 'odd bird,' as they say."

"Horsefeathers!" Alma argued. "You hosted dinner parties when you were married, didn't you?" Josephine nodded, although she didn't see the connection. "It's the same. Socializing with cocktails. Cecil won't allow it to get screwy."

"You'll love it!" Sara chirped, lifting a highball glass full of dark liquid. "It's hotsy-totsy. The best music anywhere."

Eleanor sashayed over to the group, her blue dress swirling around her ankles. She made eye contact with Josephine and said, "We can spend more time with you. Get to know you better." One penciled eyebrow arched, and Josephine understood Eleanor's meaning. "Stay for a few dances."

"Dances?" Josephine blurted.

Alma laughed. "Josephine, your face! You look as though you've been asked to sing for the president. Like Eleanor said, stay for a few dances. If you despise it, you can go."

Josephine looked at all the expectant faces, stopping last on Danny's. The desire she saw flickering in his brown eyes sparked a slow burn deep in her belly. *I'm not afraid I'll despise the dancing.*

I'm afraid I'll look like a complete fool. She had no idea how to appropriately dance in this era. Josephine recalled watching Gatsby's parties in the film and how flamboyant the dancers were, how energetic. *I'm more likely to twist an ankle or fall over if I attempt similar moves.*

"Dinner will be served in ten minutes," Hattie said, placing the tray of hors d'oeuvres on a nearby table.

The others circled around the tray, snacking on shrimp cocktail and canapés. Josephine swirled the liquid in her glass, watching bubbles rise to the surface and pop. Her eyes darted to the bandleader's name and phone number. While everyone was momentarily distracted, she snatched the paper from the bar cart and crumpled it up in her hands.

Cecil returned to the bar cart to make another. He paused for a moment to look up at Hattie. She met his gaze, and the corners of her lips lifted. "I'm expecting dinner to be delicious," he said, keeping his voice low. "It always is."

Is Hattie flustered?

A glance passed between them, and Hattie's posture relaxed. "Thank you, Mr. Miller."

"Cecil," he said. Then he added in a whisper, "Please."

"Cecil," Hattie repeated in a voice meant for intimacy. Then Hattie caught Josephine watching them, and she hurried from the room.

Cecil, oblivious to Josephine's attention, watched Hattie until her form was out of sight. Then he sighed to himself, and Josephine realized there was *something* going on between those two. Or Cecil wanted there to be. *So I'm not the only one keeping secrets.*

CHAPTER 11

The dining room setup was quite formal. The table was beautifully dressed in an art deco style with glassware and polished tableware. A floral arrangement in a pewter vase full of cascading white flowers, pale pink roses, and greenery acted as the centerpiece. Josephine hadn't seen so many utensil options since watching *Titanic*. She would have to pay attention to what the others used for each course so as not to seem unaware of dining etiquette. This proved to be much easier than she first assumed, which was a relief, because the courses came out slowly, and the women were unhurried to lift utensils because of the steady flow of conversation.

They dined on Waldorf salad, roast chicken, and steamed asparagus. Dinner rolls with pats of butter accompanied the meal. The conversation was light and avoided talk of politics, ridicule of any group of people, and pessimistic declarations about the future. No one complained or spoke of hardships. It was the most pleasant dinner party Josephine had ever attended.

Dessert and coffee completed the meal, and although Josephine passed on the ice cream sundae, she sat sipping the best coffee she'd had in weeks. Cecil excused himself before coffee was served because he needed to open the speakeasy and prepare for the evening's patrons. Initially Josephine was averse to joining everyone for a night in the speakeasy, but now she couldn't imagine passing up the experience. This was the first party she'd attended in months, and the first one in a very long time where she felt included and welcomed as part of a cherished group of friends.

Not long after Cecil left, Josephine felt the subtle vibrations in the floorboards as music traveled up from the basement. Alma saw her staring at the floor.

"You get used to it," Alma said. "A pleasant hum, but otherwise you can't hear a thing upstairs. Tonight it's the second-best jazz trio in town. The best will play for Sara's party."

"They're my favorite," Sara gushed. Her flushed cheeks and glassy eyes suggested she'd imbibed a good amount of alcohol tonight.

Eleanor licked ice cream from her spoon. "Will Mark attend on Sunday?"

"Ha!" Sara answered before her face scrunched in annoyance. "He's not invited. Even if he were, he wouldn't set foot inside. He's too good for a life of sin."

"Sara," Danny said in admonishment.

Sara pouted and slumped for a moment in her chair. "What? It's all true."

Eleanor lifted her cup of coffee and sipped. "You and your brother are so different now. I remember him being enjoyable." She returned the cup to its saucer and languidly reclined in her dining room chair. "How did that happen?"

"As soon as he joined the fuzz, he lost all sense of fun. He's made it his duty to enforce Prohibition like it was his idea," Sara said.

Following the conversation, Josephine looked at Danny. "You and Sara are brother and sister?"

Sara's sour expression changed into a delighted one. "Can't you tell by looking at us?" Her laughter bubbled up like a child's. "Of course you can't! Danny looks like our dad, a real stoic, and I got Mother's grace and beauty."

I'd never describe Danny's looks as stoic. Composed and handsome but not stuffy or impassive. "Mark, your brother, is a policeman?" Josephine asked. Danny nodded, and Sara grumbled, "A travesty."

"There are worse things to be," Josephine said, sensing Danny's unease with Sara's mockery of their brother.

"Yeah?" Sara teased. She finished off her martini. "Like what?"

Josephine hesitated and racked her mind for an occupation that might be of poor esteem. "A gangster?"

Eleanor snorted a laugh, and Alma pushed her chair back from the table with a boisterous laugh of her own. "Josephine," Alma said, "I adore you, odd bird or not. Why don't we join the party downstairs? You've promised a few dances before you leave us."

●●●

JOSEPHINE EXPERIENCED A moment of panic when she thought they might go out the front door. *If I step out onto the front porch, what will happen? What if they want to exit through the back door to access the outside speakeasy entrance used by patrons? Will I zip forward through time as soon as I cross the threshold?* Both options filled her body with a sense of being chased by a bear. She grabbed her handbag, which held the front-door key, and hooked it onto her arm. No matter what happened, she could return through time if she had the key.

All throughout dinner she'd been sitting on the crumpled paper that had the band's phone number on it. *What do I do with it now?* Everyone stood and moved toward the hallway. Josephine trailed behind, acting as though she were adjusting her dress and then the straps on her shoes, but Danny slowed and waited for her. In the hallway, after Danny turned his gaze from hers, she tossed the ball of paper into the nearest potted plant. What she'd do now, she didn't have a clue.

Fortunately, Alma made her way through the kitchen and down the basement steps. The dinner party guests traveled like a row of ducklings following their mother down the stairs into the dim basement. The sound of a piano increased as they descended, and once at the bottom, Alma performed a lighthearted dance step over to the door.

Louis stepped around her and flipped the bolt on the door before he opened it. Jazz music and voices flew into the basement so suddenly that Josephine took a step backward. The overpowering stench of cigarettes and alcohol spilled out as well. Her mind created instant images of flappers and men wearing suits and people dancing the Charleston.

Louis motioned with his hand for Alma to enter the speakeasy. "After you, milady."

Alma beamed at him. "Why, thank you, kind sir."

"You two," Sara said with a giggle, following close behind Alma. The fringe on her dress fluttered around her body as though she were caught in a breeze. Louis and Eleanor followed her.

Josephine stood a few feet back from the open door, not making a move to enter. *Is it too late to change my mind?* She'd forgotten Danny was there until he stepped up beside her, his suit jacket briefly brushing her bare arm.

"Having second thoughts?" he asked.

"Nerves," she admitted. She hadn't felt so unsure of herself since walking into her first class in college. "It's been a while since I've done anything like this."

"Think of it like a party where you can get lost in the crowd," Danny said, his baritone resonating in her chest. "No one is expecting anything from you, so you're free to be yourself and relax. No different from what we did upstairs."

"Except for the dozens of strangers, live music, more alcohol, and dancing?" Josephine said, somewhat teasing. Her cheeks warmed when Danny chuckled.

He hooked his arm and offered it to her. "I'll keep you safe."

Josephine looked from his arm up to his deep brown eyes. An excited fluttering exploded to life in her chest like a confetti popper. *There's no way Danny's safe for my heart. But I won't be staying here, so there's nothing to worry about.* Was it possible for her to enjoy herself without worrying? She only planned to spend a few more days in 1927, so a friendly flirtation was harmless. *As if I know how to flirt.* The idea nearly made her laugh out loud. Had she even flirted with Nathan? *No, he'd pursued me fast, never doubting I'd be unable to resist, and I hadn't. His intensity was intoxicating.* She glanced at Danny. Maybe he was only being polite and he was, in fact, perfectly harmless. Even as she thought the word *harmless*, her insides tingled and sparked as if she'd swallowed a live wire.

Here we go. She slid her arm through his and rested it in the crook of his elbow. The solidness of him anchored her. Danny closed the basement door behind them.

Stepping into the speakeasy, alive with people and music and exuberance, far surpassed her expectations. The room throbbed with the pulse of freedom, of secrets, of rebellion. This was a gathering of people who were bucking a system that said they couldn't have something they enjoyed. They were willing not only to pay for it financially but also legally if they were caught, and they didn't seem to care in the least.

A layer of cigarette and cigar smoke hovered near the ceiling like a swirling fog. Josephine fanned her hand in front of her face, but it was useless. A jazz trio—pianist, drummer, and upright bass player—were positioned at the rear of the speakeasy on the raised dais. The room was a blur of sparkling dresses and fashionable suits, a heady mix of perfume and sweat. People huddled at tables in the center of the room, sat at smaller tables along the wall, and lined the bar. Some stood in small groups, talking, laughing, and smoking. Others were coupled and kept their faces close together as though they didn't dare miss a single word. A couple was necking against the wall near the bathrooms. Social habits hadn't changed much in the past hundred years. Josephine smiled.

The basement entrance opened to an area behind the bar, where Cecil was a rush of activity, pouring drinks, taking orders, and talking animatedly with a group sitting at the bar.

"There are so many people," Josephine said, surprised at the number of bodies crammed into the speakeasy.

Danny stepped closer to her so she could hear him over the music and noise. "The capacity tops out at around seventy-five. More than a hundred would like to get in, but once we hit capacity, we turn the rest away." He pointed toward a barrel-chested man standing at the back entrance. The man looked exactly as she had imagined a 1920s bouncer. Intimidating, strong, taller than everyone present, and unsmiling.

"How do they get here without being noticed?" Josephine asked. "Where do they park?"

"Different ways," Danny explained. "Most park a few streets over and take an evening stroll. They cut into the hedges in the gardens behind the house without being seen. Others are dropped off near the open land and traipse through the overgrowth. Though the women prefer the sidewalk to the weeds."

Josephine nodded. "Walking through muck in these shoes would be unpleasant."

Cecil caught sight of them and nodded toward the rear of the speakeasy. He gripped a shaker and shook it a few times before pouring liquid into two martini glasses. "They've gone to the back room. You can stash your stuff under here." He indicated a cubby behind the bar where Josephine saw other handbags and personal items. "No one gets past me. Oh, and this is for you." Cecil pulled a small rectangle of paper out of his pocket and handed it to Josephine.

She accepted the paper and stared down at her own official card to Club Belle Âme. The front of the card had only the club name printed. The back of the card included the membership number and the name of the club again. It also listed the address as "Garden Gate" along with a heart contained in a scrollwork design. Other official numbers were stacked in the bottom left corner, and her name had been written in the bottom right corner. A memory flashed through her mind of the day she and Katherine first entered the speakeasy. She'd found a card just like this one, except the information on the back of the card had mostly faded. All except the name *Eleanor Baker*. Josephine's mouth opened in surprise.

"You're official now," Danny said, misinterpreting her surprised expression as happiness.

She thanked Cecil for the card and slipped it into her handbag before sliding the bag into the cubby.

"What can I get you two?" Cecil asked.

Danny looked at her, and she offered him a half shrug. "Do you like pineapple?" he asked. Josephine nodded. "A Mary Pickford and an Old Fashioned." Danny laid a few dollars on the counter. Cecil nodded. His hands never stopped moving.

"The actress?" Josephine asked.

Danny guided her around the bar, and a group of couples burst into raucous laughter. He leaned closer to her so she could hear him. "She's known for playing characters who are sweet, like the drink. It's a good match for you."

Josephine allowed her gaze to scan the crowded speakeasy. "No one has called me sweet since I was a little girl."

Danny led her through the throng of people. "Because they're preoccupied with calling you beautiful."

Josephine's mouth fell open, and she nearly stumbled. When she glanced up at Danny, he was focused on moving them through the room, avoiding the dancing couples. *He thinks I'm beautiful?* The musicians started in on an energetic swing tune, and women jumped up from their seats at the tables, tugging partners with them to the open area meant for dancing. People flooded the dance floor, and in the crush of bodies, Josephine fell against Danny's side, unable to put space between them.

He slipped his arm around her and continued walking them through the revelers. After they pushed through the high-spirited dancing, she finally exhaled, and Danny released his grip on her. "I almost lost you there," he said, grinning.

"That's the most intense response to a song I've seen since . . ." She couldn't say since the rock concert she'd attended at the outdoor amphitheater in college when people started body surfing the crowd. "Since ever."

Danny's laugh was lost in the noise, but she watched the way it transformed his face. They stepped through the large opening adorned with draping red velvet curtains that led to the more intimate sitting room. Inside the space, the noise level lowered, but only slightly. "The dancing is about as wild as it gets. This place is the swankiest you'll see around here." He looked around the room. "There they are."

Alma raised her hand and waved, and Josephine walked toward where they sat on a plush, L-shaped charcoal-gray velvet sofa. Eleanor sat smoking and chatting with an older man who looked enraptured by her. Her husband? The one she offhandedly said she wished was dead?

Sara sat so close to a young man with dark red hair that she was practically in his lap. Her short dress slid high on her thighs. An imprint of lipstick matching her burgundy shade stained the man's cheek. The young man caught sight of Sara's older brother and promptly put about two inches of space between them. *Wonder what Danny thinks about his baby sister being all over that guy.* He nodded and greeted Danny, and Sara rolled her eyes.

Alma patted the space beside her on the right, indicating where Josephine should sit. Danny took the seat beside Josephine. A moment later, a youthful pale blond-haired woman wearing a gold flapper dress arrived with a tray of drinks, including Josephine's Mary Pickford, and passed one to everyone. Josephine accepted the bright red drink garnished with a maraschino cherry.

Alma gently clinked her highball against Josephine's glass and said, "To friends, love, and prosperity."

Josephine sipped her drink. It was sugary with a hint of the tropics, and the potent alcohol tasted slightly stronger than what she was used to. She'd read about bootleggers who fermented alcohol in their bathtubs. *If the alcohol in my drink is a bathtub concoction, I hope they scrubbed down the tub before starting.* It was probably better if she didn't think too much about the process.

"Good?" Danny asked, breaking through her visions of soap-stained bathtubs full of alcohol.

Josephine nodded. "For homemade alcohol, yes."

Danny shook his head. "That's not bootleg alcohol." He leaned closer to her, and she caught a scent of his aftershave. "The rum's smuggled in from the Caribbean by rum runners. I thought you deserved the real stuff."

Josephine's eyebrows lifted. "Thank you. That was thoughtful, and you're right. It's sweet but good."

"It's my pleasure," he said.

She felt the heat of him beside her, his arm nearly pressing against hers. With the swing music and the overly sweet alcohol and a handsome man staring at her like he'd found something precious, Josephine could lose herself in this moment. For the first time in months, she felt a part of herself unfurling, stretching, as though coming out of hibernation. She hadn't thought about men as dating prospects in more than fifteen years. But Danny piqued her curiosity. *Could another partner for me be possible? Will other men find me attractive?* She pressed her arm against his to see how her body responded. Warmth pooled in her belly. When he smiled at her, Josephine's stomach flip-flopped, and she thought, *Oh, let's do that again.*

A stout man with bushy eyebrows and matching mustache stepped into the room. His suit was a half size too small and barely buttoned over his rotund belly. He motioned to Louis. Louis stood and asked Danny to go with him. Josephine watched them walk out of the room. Alma patted Josephine's leg and said, "Nothing to worry about. That's Mr. Taylor. He runs the bank where they work, and by runs, I mean, he never stops." Alma shrugged. "Most men work all the time, but they're more appealing than the lollygaggers." She lifted her highball and turned to face Josephine. "I believe Danny might be carrying a torch for you."

The conversation switch jarred Josephine. "What?"

Alma's sideways grin caused Josephine to glance away. She focused on a couple sitting across the room from them, but once they started necking, Josephine averted her gaze.

Alma continued, "He's handsome and intelligent and socially agreeable."

A terrible thought knifed through Josephine. She clutched Alma's arm. "He's not married, is he?"

"Oh, heavens no, darling," Alma said. "I'd never encourage your interest in one of those rogues. Danny's wife died during the Spanish influenza outbreak."

Josephine's expression sagged, and Alma's words poked at her own loss. "That's awful."

"Dreadful," Alma agreed, sipping her drink. "She was a handsome woman but always so frail, had been since childhood, I believe. He's quite the match, and his social standing is spotless. He's had many rapt ladies showering him with attention. But Danny hasn't shown much interest in anyone. Until you, that is."

"What do you mean?" Josephine asked, but her tightening stomach already knew the answer.

Alma seemed to sense her unease and reached for Josephine's hand. "It's okay, dear, to find companionship again. It's okay to even *love* again. You are too lovely and much too young to settle for being an old maid."

Josephine couldn't help but laugh. *Old maid?* She supposed in 1927, a woman in her midthirties was no longer marriage material. "What if I'm too old for a new partner?"

"Ha!" Alma said, her smile widening. "You're what, thirty? So am I, or nearly just, and I found Louis. Once you say phonus balonus to what society demands you can or cannot do, you'll see it doesn't matter what others think. They'll soon forget what you've done, and life will go on. Your dearest friends won't care."

The idea that Josephine could have a boyfriend or possibly remarry seemed the equivalent of her traveling to the moon. A far-off dream and not reasonable. Maybe that thought was due to the grieving cloud she'd been suffocating under and not really the truth of what was possible. A month ago, traveling back in time to save her great-grandmother would have sounded like the most outrageously impossible thing. So maybe finding love again wasn't so out of reach.

"I'm thirty-five," Josephine said.

Alma didn't hide her surprise. "Tell no one," she whispered playfully. "You don't look a day past thirty, and you could pass for younger. Danny is thirty-seven, I think, so he's the perfect age."

Why am I even entertaining this idea? "You hardly know me," Josephine said. "What if I'm a terrible partner for him? What if I'm the worst possible option?"

Alma stretched forward to place her empty glass on the low table in front of them. She leaned against the couch and propped her elbow on the low back to face her body toward Josephine. "True, I hardly know you, but I *feel* like I do, and you are nowhere near the worst option. Believe me, there are a few dames who I would beg him not to marry if he ever asked for my opinion. But you, Josephine, have something about you that I trust. I don't think you'd hurt Danny."

"I wouldn't," Josephine answered quickly. *Not intentionally.* "Why would I?"

"Exactly," Alma said, reaching for Josephine's hand. "I've always been able to tell the bad apples from the good."

Alma's confidence in Josephine's goodness filled her with comfort and an expanding feeling of love. "And I'm not a bad apple?"

Alma's laugh forced Josephine's smile to reappear. "Certainly not. You might even be a peach!"

The man who'd been talking with Eleanor stood and straightened his light gray windowpane suit. He was tall and pantherlike with long limbs and slow movements. His heavy-lidded eyes rested on Eleanor, and he held out his hand to her. She allowed him to pull her up, and they stood incredibly close while he whispered in her ear.

Eleanor leaned away from him and turned toward Alma. "Thanks for dinner, darling. We're leaving." Then she let the man put his arm around her waist while he walked them out of the room.

Josephine knew the answer, but she asked anyway. "Is that her husband?"

Alma's sigh pushed her back against the cushions. "Unfortunately not."

"But she's married, right?" Josephine asked.

"Oh, she is, but *that man* isn't her husband," Alma said. "I'm only telling the truth, but I trust you'll keep it between us." Josephine nodded. "Eleanor's husband made his fortune on a silver mine. He went to New York a few years ago to work the books for a steel tycoon, but Charles—that's her husband—has a penchant for horse racing and fast living. He decided he didn't want to return to Nashville, and he never asked Eleanor to join him. Instead, he's gone on living his life there as if she never existed."

Josephine must have looked as shocked as she felt.

Alma touched her arm. "It's not as bad as it sounds for Eleanor. She's set for life financially. She was never in love with Charles. Their marriage was an arrangement made between wealthy families. Now she's free to live however she wants."

Josephine nodded. Not having grown up believing in the idea of arranged, loveless marriages, Josephine couldn't see how anyone had agreed to such traditions. But even in her day, people who chose their marriages didn't always end up happy. At least Eleanor was choosing her own path. "And she's free to be with whoever she wants."

"Exactly," Alma said. "She's happy, though, dear, so don't worry about her. Eleanor knows what she wants, and she's well taken care of."

Before Josephine could say more, Danny and Louis returned with more drinks. Danny sat beside Josephine, and this time when she looked at his face, she saw more than merely a handsome man. She saw someone who had lost a spouse, like she had, someone who had experienced incredible hardship and continued living. *After losing his wife, had Danny ever wished he hadn't been born? Had he ever felt like giving up?* Or maybe Danny and Alma had more in common because of their perseverance and determination not to be defined by tragedy.

Josephine's gaze carelessly dropped to Danny's lips, and he caught her watching him. His mouth twitched before he finished off his drink. Josephine plucked the maraschino cherry from the edge of her first drink, still unfinished, and popped it into her mouth. Danny placed his glass on the table and focused on her.

"I admit I'm less accomplished in social graces than the gentlemen you're used to," Danny said, "but it would please me a great deal if you'd dance with me."

Josephine nearly choked on the syrupy fruit. She coughed a few times in embarrassment, and after she settled, she leaned forward to put her drink on the table.

"Is that a no?" Danny asked, but there was a playfulness in his voice.

"You think too much of the gentlemen I must be accustomed to," Josephine said. "You far surpass most of them in manners, believe me."

"Is that so?" Danny asked, clearly pleased with himself. He stood and held out his hand for her.

Josephine hesitated, but only for a moment. Then she placed her hand in his and let Danny pull her to standing. "Can we make a deal?" Josephine asked, trying to focus on words rather than on the warmth of Danny's hand against hers.

A line of concern appeared between Danny's eyebrows. "A deal?"

"If I'm as dreadful a dancer as I suspect, you won't be too frustrated. Because I did warn you."

Danny's smile sent a shower of heat down her body. He placed her hand on his arm, and with his hand resting atop hers, he led her toward the dance floor. The music intensified in volume as they passed through the slight shelter of the sitting room and entered the larger space. "It's highly unlikely that you're dreadful at anything, and I can assure you I won't be focused on your dancing skills."

Oh my, Josephine thought. She didn't recognize the jazz tune, but it was slow and sensuous with soft brushes sliding across the drumheads, a wavelike rhythm on the piano, and a steady bass line that thumped in tempo with her heartbeat. She quickly glanced at the couples around them to see how they were moving. But when Danny pulled her body against his, she forgot about anything. He enclosed his hand with hers and swayed them to the music. She turned her head to the side to stare at their joined hands and was tempted to lean her cheek against his shoulder. This kind of dancing she could do, but this kind of dancing also turned up the heat of her inner core, which frightened her. She hadn't been with anyone other than Nathan in years, and Katherine was right. Josephine had lost herself in becoming Nathan's wife to the point that she didn't know who she truly was anymore. *Is Danny the kind of man I'd be attracted to if I were confident? Or is he just another man that I would mold myself to please until I fit whatever serves him best?*

Aside from all that, Josephine wasn't meant for this timeline. After she saved Alma, she would return to present day, where

Danny didn't exist and hadn't for at least seventy-five years. *Is it wrong to connect with him in this way now?* If he was feeling the same flicker of passion she was, she couldn't let it continue. But she didn't want to stop.

"Until the other day, I'd never seen you before," he said, leaning down to speak into her ear. His breath whispered down her neck. "Are you new in town?"

Shivers moved through her, and she nodded, then said, "Yes. I've only been here a short time." *The truth.* "I met Alma recently too."

"As I thought," he said. "You couldn't have been here long without others noticing you."

Josephine pulled away so she could look up at him. "What do you mean?"

"You aren't easily overlooked," Danny said sincerely.

Josephine blinked quickly and looked away, trying to focus on something other than the desire increasing inside her. *Stop acting like a wound-up teenager.* And yet she didn't want the surging emotions to stop. A part of her chanted, *More, more, more*.

"I'm a widow, Danny. Too old for people to take much notice of." The words sounded firm yet swollen with grief. Nathan hadn't intentionally overlooked Josephine, but between his work and his social life, Josephine often felt more like an accessory than a partner. After he died, his friends reached out initially, and then Josephine felt released into the void because what did they all have in common now? Without Nathan they were no longer connected.

Danny placed his fingers beneath her chin and lifted her face toward his. "You are a widow, yes, and for that I'm terribly sorry," he said, keeping his eyes locked on hers. "But you are much more than that. You are stunning. I would very much like to kiss you, if you accept."

A tiny noise squeaked up her throat, and because she didn't vocally object, Danny leaned down and kissed her. Josephine naturally pressed toward him, and Danny tightened the arm around her waist. His body felt warm and safe against hers, and the tension and disquiet she felt evaporated. Until an image of Nathan materialized in her mind. Josephine jerked away. Danny startled with a look of concern.

"I have offended you," he said bluntly.

"No!" she said. "No." She glanced down at his chest and tried to inhale a full breath. She touched her fingertips to her lips, still feeling the pressure of Danny there.

Danny looped his arm around her waist and led her to the side of the room. "My apologies, Josephine."

"Don't," she said, pressing one hand against his chest. "I haven't . . . kissed anyone since my husband. I'm sorry. I don't know what I'm doing."

Danny's gentle smile soothed her. "I understand," he said. "It's too soon. But if I may be so bold, you *do* know what you're doing."

Flushed with embarrassment, Josephine covered her face for a moment. Danny touched her hands and slowly lowered them. "Thank you for understanding," she said. *This has gone too far.* "I should probably go home."

"I'll walk you upstairs," he said.

Josephine stopped behind the bar, made eye contact with Cecil, and pointed toward the cubby where she'd stored her handbag. He nodded, and she reached in quickly and grabbed the off-white handbag. Danny opened the basement door and ushered Josephine through. She crossed the dark room in swift strides, her mind leaping from kissing Danny to how to get out of the front door without him following her onto the porch.

What would happen if he stepped out with me? Would he see me vanish? Would he vanish?

Josephine took the stairs as fast as if she was being pursued, but Danny kept up with her. Hattie stood at the kitchen sink washing a platter and looked up at them when they entered. Josephine barely spoke as she passed through the kitchen and into the long hallway.

"Thank you for walking me up," she said with her chest strangely tight. "You can get back to your evening. I'll be okay from here."

Danny reached for her arm and stopped her in the foyer. Although his grip wasn't tight, Josephine understood he wanted her to stop. "Josephine." She chanced a look into his eyes and nearly lost her composure. "Are you quite all right? I didn't mean to upset you."

Her shoulders drooped slightly. "You didn't upset me, Danny," she said honestly. "I'm confused but not upset. It's . . . late, and you've been kind enough to see me this far, but I can handle myself from here."

Danny frowned. "How will you get home?"

"My sister," she answered, continuing the lie from earlier. "She and her husband have a car."

"And they are nearby?" he asked.

Josephine nodded. "Yes, I can walk there."

Danny released her arm and opened the front door. A swirl of cold night air entered the foyer, and Josephine inhaled the coolness into her lungs. "I'll walk with you."

What else can I possibly say to convince Danny to leave me? Her grip tightened on the handbag straps. *This might be the moment when everything goes terribly sideways.* Josephine stepped out onto the front porch and closed her eyes. She heard Danny walk out behind her and close the front door.

CHAPTER 12

Josephine opened her eyes when Danny spoke. "Shall we?"

Too stunned to move, her pulse fluttered like a trapped bird in her throat. Josephine stared out at the dark swath of trees and empty land across the street. A star-filled inky-black sky spanned over the treetops. *I'm still in 1927.* She and Danny were *both* still there. The familiar feeling of time travel—the dizziness and chill in her bones—hadn't occurred. *Why didn't it work? What am I supposed to do now?*

Danny waited for her to respond, his expression sliding toward worry. Maybe she and Danny were both still there because she couldn't time leap with someone else. Maybe if she reopened the front door, she would find herself back in her own time, and Danny would be left on the porch in 1927.

With trembling hands, Josephine clicked open her handbag to grab the front-door key as her mind scrambled to find an excuse to return into the house. The inside of the handbag was full of items she didn't recognize. Face powder, lipstick, a decorative compact, a half-empty pack of cigarettes, and a few dollars. "This isn't my handbag," Josephine said in alarm. *I don't have the front-door key.* "I must have grabbed the wrong one. I have to go back."

"No need to worry," Danny assured her. "Women's bags all look the same to me. Cecil has been watching over them. I'm sure yours is still there."

Josephine whipped around to face the front door. *What happens if I cross the threshold again? Will it rip me back to present day? Without the key, I'll never be able to return to 1927.* Panic caused a revolt in her stomach.

"Danny Stewart?" A man's voice carried up the street, speech slightly slurred but enthusiastic. "That you, Danny boy?"

Danny squinted into the dark. A figure came into focus as the man neared the small circle of dim porchlight shining into the front yard. Danny made a grumbling noise before touching Josephine's arm. "Go on in and look for your bag. I'll be in shortly."

"Yes, thank you," Josephine said, relieved to be free of Danny's focus for a moment.

"Evening, John," Danny called as he descended the porch stairs.

Josephine inched toward the front door. She held her breath as she wrapped her hand around the doorknob. The chilly metal sent a shiver through her. If she time-leaped back to present day, she'd have no way to get back to Alma. Maybe *not* speaking the password would also keep her rooted in 1927. She turned the knob and gently pushed open the door. If she disappeared instantly, not only would she lose the opportunity to save Alma, but she'd lose her only chance to change the future.

Josephine stepped over the threshold and felt the hum of vibrations coming up through the floorboards. She caught a whiff of the evening's meal, a lingering scent of roast chicken and after-dinner coffee. Hattie appeared in the hallway.

"Hattie!" Josephine said, comforted to see Hattie's scowling face. Relief nearly turned her legs to limp noodles. *Time traveling without the key must not be possible.* She couldn't transport out of the past without the key, and she couldn't transport to the future without the key, speaking the password, and entering through the front door.

Josephine lifted the handbag in the air in front of her. "I've picked up the wrong bag. I'll hurry downstairs and grab mine." If she could find her bag, she'd have the key, and she could sneak back out alone while Danny was preoccupied.

Not waiting for Hattie to respond, Josephine practically ran down the hallway, through the kitchen, and down the basement stairs. She opened the door to the speakeasy and was once again hit in the face with the stench of cigarette smoke, alcohol, perfume, and sweat. Music reverberated against her chest. She hurried to Cecil behind the bar.

"I grabbed the wrong bag," Josephine said, and he stopped working long enough to acknowledge her. Josephine knelt and inspected the cubby. There were only two handbags remaining and neither was hers.

Josephine felt the shuddering stop of her heart as her stomach plummeted. She jerked into a rigid stance. "Cecil!" she shouted on a wave of panic.

He slid a drink garnished with a lemon wedge toward a woman at the bar and then walked to Josephine. "What's wrong, honey?" he asked.

"My bag, it's gone," she said, showing him the bag she'd taken by mistake. "It looks like this one, but mine isn't in there."

Cecil shook his head and frowned. "No one's taken anything except you and Eleanor."

"Eleanor!" Josephine said, remembering their earlier conversation. "She said she had a bag just like mine."

"There you go, honey," Cecil said, patting her arm a few times. "Bet she grabbed yours when she left with Anderson. Call her tomorrow."

"Tomorrow?" Josephine said to herself because Cecil walked off to help another patron. *I can't wait until tomorrow. I'll be stuck in 1927 tonight. Can I spend the night in another timeline?* Josephine's head swam with uncertainty.

Someone stepped into her periphery. "Everything all right, darling?" Alma asked. "One minute you were dancing with Danny and the next you were gone."

"My bag," Josephine said on an exhale, her voice skirting the edge of frantic. "I think Eleanor took mine by mistake. She has my house key, which means I can't get home." *Literally.*

Alma's eyebrows raised. "Don't you have a spare?" Josephine shook her head. "Here's an idea. We'll call her in the morning, and you can stay here tonight. I've got plenty of room."

Fear and nerves caused Josephine's body to tremble. The little bit of alcohol she'd drunk soured in her stomach. *What if Eleanor loses the key? What if Eleanor wasn't the one to take my bag?* There was nothing Josephine could do tonight. She looked down at her dress. She had no choice but to take Alma's offer and risk the consequences. "Could I borrow some clothes?"

Alma's easy smile stretched across her lovely face. "I have the perfect outfits for you! Come upstairs with me. Louis is staying awhile longer, but I'm done for the night. If I sit down again, I'll fall asleep in no time." She waved at Cecil. "Talk soon!" He waved back and sent her a wink of understanding. Alma opened the basement door, and Josephine followed. "What did you do with Danny?"

"Do?" Josephine asked, her stomach tightening in an entirely new way. Her mind replayed Danny kissing her. If her body kept responding so intensely, she was going to pass out or be sick. "I didn't do anything with him." *Not the truth. I kissed him like I'd been waiting years for someone to come close enough to get my hands on him.*

Josephine caught sight of Alma's slight smile in the shadows of the basement. "Darling, your face. You can't hide what you're feeling. *Something* happened, but we can discuss that later. I meant what did you do with him after you danced? Did you send him home lovestruck?"

Josephine rubbed her right temple as she slowed her walk across the basement. "Hardly. Someone outside wanted to talk to him. Then I realized I had the wrong bag."

Alma didn't say more as they climbed the basement stairs. She opened the door at the top and spoke to Hattie in the kitchen. "You've been here long enough, Hattie. Why don't you gather your things and go home? Cecil will be up in a few, and he can take you."

Hattie's back noticeably stiffened. "He need not trouble himself. I can walk just fine."

"Of course you can," Alma responded, passing through the kitchen, her heels clicking on the hardwood. "But there's no need to walk this time of night when there's a perfectly suitable ride. Josephine will be staying the night. Eleanor has gone home with Josephine's handbag and house key."

Hattie cut her eyes quickly toward Josephine, probably judging whether she wanted to leave Josephine alone with Alma, knowing she didn't have a choice. Josephine evaded Hattie, breaking eye contact.

"Want me to check that the guest room is suitable before you turn in?" Hattie asked, drying her hands on a dish towel before tossing it into a basket of dirty linens.

"No, but thank you," Alma said. "You go home. It's late. Josephine and I can handle this. I'm sure the room is in excellent order, and Josephine won't mind fluffing her own sheets."

Exhaustion began creeping in at the edges. The late night combined with the stress of the evening slipped weariness through Josephine like a sleeping potion. "As tired as I am, I could sleep on a sofa."

"I'll be a phone call away if you need me," Hattie said quickly.

Alma paused in the kitchen doorway and turned to look questioningly at Hattie. "You'll be back tomorrow morning. What could I possibly need before then?"

Hattie's gaze slid toward Josephine before moving back to Alma. "If you do, call me."

"I will, dear," Alma said.

What does Hattie think I'm capable of? Murdering Alma in her sleep? Stealing her valuables? For a moment Josephine *wished* she could tell them both the truth so Hattie wouldn't be so suspicious and Alma might actually cancel the upcoming party. But the chance either of them would believe her was zero, and she couldn't jeopardize the last few days she had to try and stop what was coming. The sound of the front door opening reached them, and Danny called a greeting from the foyer. Almost in sync, the basement door opened, and Cecil stepped into the kitchen.

Alma reached up to remove one pearl earring and then the other. "Perfect timing."

Cecil's eyes shifted toward Hattie, who appeared unhappy with the way the evening was ending. He looked at Alma. "Garrett will serve the last round, and then everyone will be sent home within the hour. He and Robbie will lock up like usual. We still on for a Saturday delivery?"

"Still as planned, thank you," Alma said to Cecil. "We were saying our good nights. Will you be a kind sir and motor Hattie home tonight?"

"It would be my pleasure," Cecil said with a nod at Alma and then at Hattie.

Hattie turned away and busied herself collecting her bags. She grabbed the linen basket and carried it to a side room that must be where they did laundry. In Josephine's present day, the layout of the kitchen and laundry room had been one of the most dramatic changes to the house, giving these spaces necessary square footage and light. Hattie returned and stood in the kitchen as though she wasn't sure what should happen next.

"Thank you, Cecil," Alma said before walking into the hallway, where she started talking to Danny about Josephine's plans to stay the night. Josephine followed her, abandoning Cecil and Hattie to their awkward silence in the kitchen.

"Good idea," Danny said.

He locked eyes with Josephine, and she felt surprised by the desire to go to him, to replay their kiss. Josephine tried to remember the last time she'd been more than kissed on the cheek or pecked on the lips. In her mind, an imaginary calendar flipped through hundreds of pages. *Months and months. But this isn't my home, not yet, and my focus should be on Alma.* Josephine slowed her pace, keeping as much distance between herself and Danny as she could. Kissing him had been impulsive, and she should probably regret it, but she didn't. Instead, heat flared in her chest. If Danny tried to kiss her right then, she'd let him. In front of everyone. *Pull yourself together!*

Danny's expression matched hers, a fusion of longing and doubt. "The idea of you walking this time of night didn't suit me."

Alma furrowed her brow. "You walking? Tonight? Absolutely not. It's a stroke of luck that Eleanor took your bag. Now you're forced to spend more time with me. You should call your sister, let her know your plans have changed." She pointed to the phone in the hallway.

Josephine's eyes darted toward the hallway phone and then to the crumpled paper she'd tossed into the potted plant.

Danny grabbed his hat from a table just inside the living room and circled it between his fingers. "This is where I take my leave then. Thank you for dinner, Alma and Josephine, I hope to see you again."

Josephine's hand slid up to her neck, her fingers worrying the pearls in her necklace. "Good night, Danny. Thank you for the dance." Inwardly she groaned. *Did I just thank a man for dancing with me?* But Danny's lips lifted in a slight smile. *Is he thinking of the kiss too?*

Hattie and Cecil entered the foyer, and Danny held open the door for them. After saying good night and closing the door, only Josephine and Alma remained in the house. Alma locked the front door and bolted it from the inside.

"If you'll excuse me," Alma said, "I'm going to powder my nose." She pointed to the phone again. "Go ahead and call your sister. I'll be right back."

Alma walked up the staircase, leaving Josephine standing in the hallway alone. Once she heard a door click closed upstairs, she rushed to the potted plant and retrieved the crumpled paper. *I can call and cancel the band.* She glanced at the grandfather clock. *Is it too late to call? Does that matter? I have to try to stop the party.* She smoothed out the wrinkles and lifted the receiver. The dial tone resonated in her ear. Her heartbeat pounded in her chest. She had to do this before Alma returned.

Fortunately, during her research, Josephine had seen how different phone numbers looked in the 1920s. Instead of numbers only, they were a combination of numbers and letters. The bandleader's contact number written on the page read *24-F2.*

Josephine used the rotary dial to input the digits and waited. *It's ringing.*

"Good evening," a male voice said.

Josephine's mind blanked. "Uh . . . hi," she babbled. "Hi, I'm calling about . . . about the party this Sunday."

The man didn't respond right away. Josephine heard her pulse in her ears. *Thump, thump, thump, thump.*

"Yes," he finally said, "is this Mrs. Carter?"

"Yes!" The sharp sting of the lie in her chest startled Josephine. *Keep going!* "We've run into an issue with the party, and we need to—"

"Darling," Alma called from the staircase. Her footfalls grew louder. "Did you get your sister?" Her face appeared as she leaned over the banister to peer down at Josephine.

Josephine locked her eyes with Alma's.

"Hello?" the man asked from the receiver.

"Yes, thank you so much for understanding, Katherine," Josephine blurted. "I'll see you tomorrow, and don't worry about me tonight. I'll be just fine. Good night!" She hung up so quickly that the receiver wobbled on its hook and fell off. She lifted it and returned it to its hook, noticing the visible shake of her hands. She crumpled the paper in her palm.

"Wonderful!" Alma said, coming down the staircase. "I'm happy you'll be here, and we can share coffee and tea in the morning together. It's been so long since I've had overnight company." Alma walked through the house and turned off the lights in the living room, foyer, and parlor, closing the downstairs for the evening.

Then she walked into the darkened parlor and gazed out the windows, invisible to anyone on the outside. Hattie, Cecil, and Danny were gone, already in their cars on the way home.

Josephine stood beside Alma, looking out into the night, urging her heart to calm. *I was so close. Unless I get another chance to use the phone alone, canceling the band won't work.* Josephine focused on another topic to help settle her nerves. "Hattie seems angry you suggested Cecil take her home."

Alma sighed. "They're in love with each other."

So Alma has also seen the attraction between them. How long has their interest been going on? Hattie appeared to be fighting it, but Cecil seemed willing.

"Hattie's not angry," Alma continued. "Not really. You understand the social difficulties with a Black woman and a white man being together."

Josephine nodded her understanding. "And Hattie doesn't want to pursue it?"

Alma smiled. "Oh, she does. She's been fond of Cecil for years now, but she's afraid, understandably so. Cecil cares much less about what people think, but he wants to ensure Hattie feels safe and not threatened by what others might say, so they've kept it quiet mostly." Alma met Josephine's gaze. "We all know, of course, but it's a small circle, so you'll keep it between us, I trust."

Josephine nodded again. "Of course." Even though she and Hattie weren't on the best of terms, she'd never want harm to come to any of them. "Why don't they go somewhere else? Leave the South for a place that might be more accepting?"

Alma chuckled. "I have no doubt they'll eventually do just that. I've encouraged them for years, but believe it or not, Hattie is more stubborn than Cecil. I suspect she'll come around, knowing how much she cares for him. Love is a bit like madness."

"Madness?" Josephine asked, turning to look at Alma's dark silhouette.

"Yes," Alma said, turning from the window. She pretended to waltz with a partner around the parlor. The *click, click, click* of her heels in rhythm with imaginary music. "Fluttering hearts, shortness of breath, sleepless nights, a longing you feel deep down in your bones."

Josephine folded her arms over her chest and rubbed her hands up and down her arms to chase away the slight chill in the air. "Shouldn't love be more sensible?" Even as she spoke the sentence, she felt the lie of it. The wrongness of it.

"Heavens no," Alma said with a short laugh. "You sound like my mother. Shoes are sensible. Never love. Didn't you feel that mad sort of love for your husband?"

Josephine tried to recall *how* she had felt with Nathan. She'd been mired in sorrow for so long that the rest of her emotions felt buried beneath the rubble of grief. "I suppose at first I was caught up in the excitement. But it doesn't last, does it? It fades into routine, and sleepless nights spent thinking about how you ended up sleeping alone *again* in a bed too big for one person."

Alma stopped dancing. She crossed the room to Josephine and touched her arm. "It doesn't have to be that way. You *can* burn with passion your whole life. It's not always a roaring wildfire. Some days it's quiet and gentle, but always there can be passion."

Josephine returned to the windows and marveled at the dark sky with pinpricks of starlight, silver sparkles scattered across a vast blackness. So many stars. Her present-day view was disrupted by streetlights and spotlights pointed toward Halloween décor and manicured hedges. "Maybe not everyone finds that."

"Only the ones who don't believe they will. Or the ones who fight it." Alma joined her and pressed her arm against Josephine's.

They were nearly the same height. From outside the house, they might have appeared to be twin shadows haunting the Carter Mansion, but for how much longer? If Josephine didn't figure out a plan soon, neither of them would be here in a few days' time.

●●●

JOSEPHINE PULLED THE pale pink cotton nightgown over her head, and it dropped to her ankles. Delicate lace framed the square neck, and the flowy sleeves stopped at her elbows. The lack of a waistband reminded Josephine of bathing suit coverups, only this gown was much longer. A full-length mirror leaned against one wall in the guest bedroom. A chunky, six-inch mahogany frame surrounded the silver glass. Josephine gazed at her cleanly washed face as she brushed her fingers against the polished wood, watching her reflection make the same movements. She touched her shortened hair, a change she hadn't gotten used to yet.

Nathan loved long hair and sometimes discussed his lack of understanding about why older women insisted on cutting off their youthful hair. He disliked short haircuts on women. Explaining how hormones and bodies and women's hair changed through the years didn't change his opinion. Nor did giving him examples of how some women looked gorgeous with short hair. At thirty-five, she hadn't yet experienced any dramatic changes with the health of her hair, so keeping it long had been easy. *What would he think about my haircut? Would it have annoyed him?* She chuckled and pressed her hand against her collarbone as a wave of missing him crashed over her. Then she thought about Danny and his kiss tonight. *Why does kissing another man, even with Nathan gone, feel so odd?* As if sensing her question, Josephine saw

Alma in the mirror's reflection. She turned and faced the bedroom doorway.

"We look like twins," Alma said, sweeping her hand down the front of her similar nightgown. "They're not meant for seduction, but they're comfortable. Not that you aren't already aware, but men don't care what you're wearing."

Josephine smiled. "If it's dark, no one can see a thing anyway."

Alma laughed and walked into the bedroom. "Everything to your liking?" She pressed her hand against a pillow on the bed and patted it a few times, fluffing the inside feathers. "Anything else you need?"

Josephine shook her head even as dozens of questions and *needs* raced through her sleepy mind. She needed to know it was okay that she'd kissed Danny, that kissing him wouldn't cause her to lose herself any more than she already had. She needed to know this was going to work out. She needed to know she could succeed without a plan. She needed to know she hadn't ruined everything the night of her wish.

"It's okay about Danny," Alma said, disrupting Josephine's thoughts.

Is Alma reading my mind? "I . . . How . . . I don't know," Josephine stuttered.

Alma sat on the edge of the bed, and Josephine sat beside her. "It's none of my business, but because I've seen that look on your face on my *own* face before, I feel I can offer advice. Would that be all right with you?"

Josephine nodded. The soft mattress indented with the weight of their bodies. Josephine smoothed her hand across the comforter, tracing a fingertip along a line of stitching. "Of course."

"Danny is a good guy. A *very* good guy," Alma said, "but you don't have to like him or ever see him again. It's been, what, almost a year since you lost your husband? That's a long time and yet not long, so it's understandable that you aren't sure how to feel about *feeling* something for another man."

"We kissed," Josephine admitted, causing Alma to smile. Josephine touched her hands to her cheeks, feeling the warmth of embarrassment. "Why am I so uncomfortable about that?"

"Maybe it's not uncomfortable. Perhaps you're embarrassed or excited?" Alma asked. "It's fair to be both. If you're like me, your life stopped for quite some time after your husband died, but the fact is, Josephine, you're still here, and you must start moving again. I don't mean this harshly, but if you were gone and your husband were alive, he *would* find another wife."

Josephine's stomach clenched. She hadn't thought of that. "You're right."

"It sounds dreadful, I know," Alma admitted, "but would you want him alone forever?"

Josephine shook her head. "No, I would want him to be happy and find companionship if he wanted to and not . . . not feel guilty about it."

"It's hard to do the same when it comes to yourself, but the same is true for you." Alma grabbed Josephine's hand.

Guilt was an underlying discomfort, but there was another, much stronger emotion swelling inside her heart. "How do you love someone without losing yourself? How do you become a wife without losing all the other parts of you?"

Alma gazed off for a moment, thinking. "We are taught to release all parts of ourselves when we become wives, aren't we? Or mothers. It's as though those roles are all we're meant to be. So how do we not lose ourselves? It's as easy and as challenging as this: we just *don't*. You can be a wife and a mother and still be Josephine."

Josephine sighed and stared at their joined hands. "I haven't done that well."

Alma smiled sweetly at her. "You can start now. Can I ask how the kiss was?"

Josephine recognized that sparkly glint in Alma's eyes, and it transported her back to high school, when she and Katherine had similar conversations. "It was nice. Surprisingly nice. Until I thought of Nathan."

"That will pass too," Alma confided. "I used to think of Franklin a lot when Louis and I first spent time together, but soon I could tuck away the memories of Franklin in a special place in my heart and make new ones with Louis. One is not better than the other, but different. Louis isn't a replacement for Franklin. They're two separate loves, and I cherish both."

"That's a beautiful way of looking at it," Josephine said, closing her eyes and exhaling.

Alma stood from the bed. "It takes practice. Now get some rest. I'll see you in the morning, and we'll call Eleanor. Good night, Josephine."

"Good night, Alma," she said.

Alma closed the bedroom door behind her. Josephine turned off the overhead light and pulled down the hunter-green coverlet and white cotton sheets. Then she slid beneath the sheets, reached over to the lamp, and turned out the light. The room was instantly dark, the kind of dark she'd only experienced when camping in the wilderness or closed inside a windowless room. Even when the lights were out in the house, there was always some kind of light pollution from electronics, outdoor streetlights, or the city. But here in 1927, the room was pitch black until slowly varying degrees of darkness created the outlines of solid shapes in the room. The dresser near the window. A thin line of lighter black created by the stars and crescent moon outlined the closed curtains.

Josephine thought about what Alma said about finding love again. Josephine had all but forgotten what the exhilaration of a first kiss felt like, but her body hadn't. She'd responded as though kissing Danny was perfectly natural. *Is it wrong that I'm tempted to try again? To see if another kiss will ignite tingles all over my body?*

Kissing Danny again would require more time in 1927. The thought of starting over in this timeline appealed to her. *Could I do that? What would happen if I never returned to my own timeline? Would that be such an awful choice?* But she thought of her mama and Katherine. They'd be devastated to lose her—unless they were already losing her. If Josephine was disappearing, how much longer before they all vanished? What if her staying in 1927 removed all of them completely from the present day? Her family wouldn't grieve the loss of her because they wouldn't have known her.

Josephine's heart ached. *She* would remember, though. She would suffer the loss of them. *Is permanently staying in 1927 worth it?*

"No," Josephine whispered into the darkness. She needed to focus. She had less than three days to save herself. One kiss with a handsome man wouldn't derail her.

CHAPTER 13

Josephine woke up to sunlight pushing its way around the edges of the curtains. For a few moments, she'd forgotten where she was and blinked a stranger's room into view. Remembering she was with Alma in 1927, she slid her legs out from the covers and climbed out of bed. Tugging the curtains aside, she squinted in the bright October morning until her eyes adjusted. At home she likely would have seen joggers or cars rolling past and the neighbors' Halloween decorations across the street. But this morning she saw the empty land across from the house. Tall grass, bleached of green and turning golden in the autumn air, waving in the breeze. Evergreens grew among deciduous trees with scarlet and burnt-orange leaves. Birds darted among the trees and disappeared in the foliage.

A knock sounded on the bedroom door, and Josephine said, "Come in."

The door eased open with a soft squeak, and Alma's fresh face poked through the opening. She wore a simple mauve dress with a drop waist and fluttery scalloped sleeves. Her hair was styled and her makeup applied with a light touch. "Are you decent?"

"That depends," Josephine answered. "Are my night clothes considered decent?"

Alma chuckled. "That depends on who's looking, doesn't it? How did you sleep?" She opened the door wide but lingered in the doorway.

Josephine patted down her unruly hair in response to how composed Alma looked in comparison to her bedhead and puffy face. "I don't remember a thing, so that must mean I slept well. You?"

"Dreamy," Alma said. "Hattie will be here soon. Would you care for tea or coffee with breakfast? Afterward we can give Eleanor a call. I can't call before nine. She likes to lounge about before she starts her day."

"Coffee would be perfect," Josephine said.

Alma walked out of the doorway and crossed the hall to her bedroom. She returned quickly with a blouse, skirt, and a small traveling bag. "These should fit well enough," she said. "Last night's dress is lovely but too fancy for breakfast."

Josephine glanced toward the hunter-green dress she'd draped over a sitting chair in the corner. "You don't wear sequins while you drink coffee?"

"Wouldn't that be a laugh?" Alma said. "I'm half tempted to do it just to see what Hattie would say."

Josephine took the offered clothing. "Thank you for these." She laid them gently on the unmade bed. "I have a few ideas about what Hattie would say."

"You and me both," Alma said playfully. "You're welcome for the clothes. Use the bag to pack up your things. You can bring it back the next time we're together. I'm finished up in the bathroom. It's all yours. Meet me downstairs in thirty minutes?"

Josephine agreed, and Alma closed the bedroom door behind her. Josephine gathered the clothes and went to the bathroom to wash up. Her mind kept tossing up the idea that Eleanor might have lost the key, but Josephine continuously batted it away like a wasp. If she let that thought take root, it would grow rapidly and strangle every bit of hope she had for changing her family's fate. Another thought swelled. If Eleanor didn't have the key, then Josephine would be permanently stuck in 1927, an idea that was becoming more and more appealing. What if she saved Alma, thereby saving her mama and sister, but she stayed in 1927? Was that a possibility?

All of the time travel movies she'd ever seen fast-forwarded through her mind. Although doubtful any of them were scientifically plausible, she remembered enough theoretical science to know that if she altered the past, she would alter the future by default. So if she stayed in 1927, how much of the future, and her present day, would diverge from what she'd known?

Half an hour later, Josephine found Alma sitting in the parlor at the small table near the front windows. Morning light poured through the glass and painted the room in soft light, creating a peaceful, idyllic tableau. In one hand Alma held a smooth, delicate cup encircled with a floral pattern. A matching saucer sat on the table near a plate of fluffy biscuits. Two small ramekins held pats of butter and jam. Alma was bent over a sheet of parchment, busy writing with a pencil.

"Good morning again," Josephine said, not wanting to startle Alma as she entered the room.

Alma glanced up and placed the pencil beside the paper. "I knew those would be perfect for you. I think they fit you even better than they fit me." She motioned to the serving tray. "Coffee and biscuits?"

"Yes, please," Josephine said. She sat in the chair opposite Alma, bouncing slightly on the firm cushion, and unintentionally her eyes went to the parchment. With the writing upside down, she could only read a few words: *children*, *labor*, and *women*.

Alma caught her looking, and Josephine glanced away quickly and reached for the coffee cup meant for her. "Making a few notes before a meeting next week."

Josephine sipped the hot coffee and hummed in her throat. "This is so good. If you don't mind me asking, what kind of meeting?"

"I don't mind at all. In fact," Alma said, reaching for a biscuit and placing it on a small plate adorned with a rim of silver and ivy leaves, "you might be interested in joining us. Although white women have won the right to vote, you know our fight for the equality of all women doesn't end there. It was a wonderful step forward, I'll agree, but there is still much to do to ensure a brighter future." She tapped her index finger against the parchment.

"And the meeting?" Josephine asked.

"We've created a local organization in Nashville that works with other national women's groups," Alma explained. "We don't work exclusively with any one group. Instead, we've taken different practices from each organization and combined the beliefs and missions we feel comfortable supporting. For example, the NWP does so much lobbying for women's rights, but they don't include the Negro community, and that's a topic close to my heart."

"Understandably," Josephine said, looking over her shoulder toward the hallway. Sounds echoed from the kitchen.

"Because of Hattie, yes," Alma said, as though reading Josephine's thoughts, "but also because of many others. If we can vote, why can't they? The Thirteenth Amendment abolished slavery, but you know as well as I do that it didn't end the stunted beliefs or the ignorance. But," she said, pausing to inhale, "I'll stop before I start a speech that I can't stop." Alma split the biscuit down the middle and spread softened butter on one half. "We also focus on child labor and equal rights for women in the workforce. It breaks my heart what some of our children endure, and a third of our women are working now, and they make half as much as men. Half! For the very same work!"

Josephine pressed her lips together to keep from speaking right away. She didn't want to tell Alma that although child labor would end in another ten years, the fight for equal rights and pay might never end. So she focused on the heart behind the conflict. "This work means a lot to you. I can tell you're passionate about it."

"I am!" Alma said loudly and then chuckled as she quieted her voice to add, "It's important to me that I do what I can to move us toward equality, even if the steps are too small to see. Over time I believe those minuscule steps will add up to great leaps."

"They will," Josephine said assuredly. She reached for a biscuit. It was still warm beneath her fingertips. "These are all noble causes, Alma. I admire you for taking a stand."

"I use my social standing as I can," Alma said. "Many women have marched, lobbied, and practiced social disobedience to get their messages heard, which is so admirable, but we're not all created to do the same type of social work. I prefer other methods. I lecture and write letters, both for myself and for those who can't write themselves. I talk to people with money and influence where I can. I prefer a gentler way around the obstacles."

"You don't always have to be a rhinoceros," Josephine said with a knowing smile.

"What a funny way of explaining, but exactly!" Alma said as she beamed across the table at Josephine. "I understand the more vocal and assertive tactics, and each one has its place. But I prefer to distract people with my wit and beauty and win them toward my side of the table. It takes all kinds of people to make changes."

"I have no doubt that you end up with many people on your side," Josephine said. She cut apart the warm biscuit and spread on one side thick red jam dotted with tiny seeds.

"You should join us!" Alma said excitedly.

"Oh," Josephine said, "I'm not sure I have the right skills."

"Baloney," Alma argued. She ticked off on her fingers as she spoke. "You're intelligent, attractive, well-mannered, obviously educated, and I know you have a soft heart."

Josephine blushed beneath the compliments. "That's kind of you to say." She bit into the biscuit to stop her bottom lip from quivering. Why did she suddenly feel assaulted by sadness? Grief often acted like a creature waiting in the shadows, ready to spring out at her just when she thought she was on solid ground again. She didn't feel like *any* of those descriptions, hadn't for months, but the mere idea that she might be someone who could be praised squeezed her from the inside. After she swallowed both the biscuit and the tightness in her throat, she said, "After Nathan died, I stopped. Everything stopped. No going out, no socializing. I barely spoke to anyone, including my family. I could have been *doing* something with myself, but I wasn't."

Alma put down her half-eaten biscuit. "That's quite unfair, Josephine. You *were* doing something. Grieving. When Franklin died, my mother expected me to put on a good face and act as though life were normal. But I didn't. I love my mother, but she's not . . . gentle. She wasn't raised to be. She was taught to be sturdy and strong, capable and obedient. None of these traits are inherently bad, but she doesn't believe in any emotion other than annoyance. She would have buried her sorrow and pushed through. But I'm not her."

Josephine nodded her understanding. "If your experience was anything like mine, it felt like I was living someone else's life. It still feels that way sometimes. How do you push through something you don't even understand?"

"Maybe it's not about pushing through," Alma said with a half-hearted smile. "But allowing yourself to move through at your own pace. I needed to grieve. I didn't want to shove my heartache under the bed or bury it in the yard. I needed to experience it, and I guess you do too."

"As you found yourself again," Josephine said, "is that when you started using your energy to do good things? To help people? To fight for causes?"

"Yes, of course," Alma said. "And you can too. You can start here with me."

"Starting over feels so strange," Josephine admitted. "Like I'm wearing someone else's clothes." She looked down at her borrowed blouse and skirt and laughed quietly. "And I am actually wearing someone else's clothes."

Alma chuckled with her. "What if you thought of it as starting *again*? You're not starting from the beginning but from where you are now."

Alma was younger than Josephine by a few years, but Alma was the wiser of the two. Josephine figuratively walked behind Alma on a path her great-grandmother trailblazed. "My sister has encouraged me to volunteer or offer my assistance to charities."

"Smart woman," Alma agreed, picking up her biscuit again. "Your sister sounds like someone I'd love to meet."

Josephine lifted her cup and sipped the coffee. The dark liquid slid down her throat, smooth and soothing. "She'd love you," she said, knowing Katherine and feisty, passionate Alma had so much in common.

After coffee and biscuits, Alma called Eleanor, who had also discovered she had the wrong handbag. Eleanor arrived at the house around ten, dressed far more elegantly than Josephine had ever seen a woman looking so early in the day. Back home, women in Josephine's neighborhood were far more likely to be sporting yoga pants and tunic tops than pearls and full makeup.

Josephine respected how refined women in the 1920s looked no matter the occasion, how much consideration and intention they put into their appearances. But Josephine also appreciated her comfy loungewear and knowing she didn't have to put on makeup just to drink coffee.

Alma and Eleanor exchanged a few casual greetings in the foyer before Alma showed her into the living room. Josephine stood, clutching Eleanor's bag in her hands. She eyed the lookalike bag in Eleanor's hand. *Please, please, please still have the key.*

"I apologize, Josephine," Eleanor said, holding out the handbag for her. Her fingernails were painted a glossy eggshell color. She and Josephine swapped bags. "I hope it didn't inconvenience you too much."

"Alma was kind enough to let me stay the night," Josephine said. "Thank you for coming over." She unclasped the purse, feeling her pulse quicken. *Thank goodness.* She breathed a sigh of relief to see the front-door key resting inside.

"You really should get a spare," Eleanor said with a hint of reprimand.

Josephine nodded, not wanting to explain the rarity of this key. *Would a copy work as well as the original?* She had half a mind to hang the key on a chain around her neck for the next few days so that it was always with her.

"I've so enjoyed your company, Josephine," Alma said.

"Me too," Josephine said. She knew she should return to present day, but the urge to stay with Alma throbbed her heart. *I won't see Alma again until the party in two days.* She couldn't think of a single reason to come back earlier. "I'll see you Sunday then? Early enough to help prepare the food?"

Eleanor sank into the red-velvet armchair, her pale peach dress clashing with the crimson fabric and floral pillows. She leaned casually to one side, stretching out her long legs before tucking them to the side of the chair. "What's happened to Mrs. Brooks?"

"She's unwell," Alma explained. "So Hattie and I, and now Josephine, will be preparing the food."

Eleanor's smooth creamy features tugged downward. An expression of disdain moved across her face. "Isn't there anyone else who can take on the job? You shouldn't be spending your time cooking."

Alma's cheeks lifted with a hint of amusement, as though this was not a new topic for them. "I enjoy cooking. You know that."

"I can't imagine why," Eleanor said, opening her handbag and pulling out her package of cigarettes. "All that heat and sweat and sticky, dirty hands." She shuddered, causing Alma to chuckle. She removed a cigarette from the pack and held it between her fingers.

Alma tossed a teasing glance at Josephine. "Eleanor is fragile."

Eleanor barked a laugh. "Ha! I know when to get my hands dirty and when to pay someone else to."

"That," Alma said with a nod, "is the absolute truth. No smoking in the house." Eleanor pretended to be annoyed but then smiled at her friend. Alma looked at Josephine. "Sunday around lunch? You can bring a change of clothes and get dressed here if you want."

"What about tonight?" Eleanor asked, looking between Alma and Josephine. She put away her cigarette and placed her handbag on the end table. "Anderson is still in town and wants to come back to the club tonight."

Alma walked to a potted fern sitting on a pedestal near a sunny window. She lifted the ceramic pot gently and rotated the plant before returning it to the stand. "I thought he was going back to Chicago."

Eleanor shook her head. Her drop pearl earrings caught the light before disappearing again behind her hair. "He's leaving Sunday."

Josephine's curiosity heightened. "Is he going there for work?"

"He lives there," Eleanor said.

Is it common for people in this time to have long-distance relationships? It was contrary to what she'd assumed people did. "He comes here for work then?"

Alma walked to the couch and fluffed a throw pillow. A slant of sunlight stretched across the cushions and draped over Alma's torso. "He comes here for Eleanor."

"Oh," Josephine said in response. "He's . . ." She tried to remember how Alma had phrased a man being interested in a woman. "He's carrying a torch for you?"

Eleanor laughed and straightened in the armchair. She clasped her hands together in her lap, looking like an overeager schoolgirl. "Are we discussing our personal lives now? If I answer, do you share your relationship with Danny?"

Josephine's lips parted in surprise. "We don't have a relationship."

Eleanor hummed and quirked an eyebrow. "You kiss men you aren't in a relationship with? Aren't you the progressive woman. I'm a bit surprised, though, because you don't seem like the flapper type."

"Well . . . I . . ." Josephine stuttered. *If I say I don't kiss men I'm not dating, I'll sound like a liar because obviously Eleanor saw me kissing Danny. And if I try to defend that I've never done that before, Eleanor won't likely believe me.*

"Stop teasing her, Eleanor," Alma said.

"Don't look so startled, Josephine," Eleanor said lightly. "I don't care if you kiss a dozen men by Sunday if it makes you happy."

"That would be awful," Josephine said, and both Eleanor and Alma laughed.

"You bet it would," Eleanor agreed. "At least half would be a slobbering assortment. Best to only kiss the good ones. To answer your question, Anderson is carrying an enormous torch for me, and I'm quite fond of him." She batted her eyelashes at Josephine in a playful manner. "Your turn."

Josephine hesitated, but only for a moment. "Danny kissed me. He actually asked if he could, and I didn't know what to say, which he took as a yes."

"And how was it?" Eleanor asked.

"Eleanor!" Alma scolded. "You're relentless."

Eleanor pouted. "Aren't we friends sharing stories?"

Josephine sighed. "It was odd."

"Well, that's not good," Eleanor said with a wrinkled brow. "I would have thought Danny was a good one."

"Oh, he is," Josephine said quickly. "He most certainly is, but I haven't kissed anyone since I lost my husband." Her hands clenched around the handbag.

Eleanor's mischievous smile slipped, and her expression filled with compassion. "I'm sorry, dear. That does take some getting used to."

Josephine nodded. "But you're right about Danny. He's a good one."

"I knew it!" Eleanor exclaimed. "Here's an idea. Let's invite him and Louis to the club tonight. Then the three of us girls can have a swell time. Necking optional."

"Eleanor!" Alma said again and then burst out laughing.

Eleanor smirked at Josephine. "I said *optional*. But my suggestion is to say yes. What do you think, Josephine? Want to join us tonight?"

Josephine's heart answered for her with its quick pace. "Yes."

CHAPTER 14

After leaving Alma and Eleanor, Josephine shivered on the front porch, and her upper torso swayed in a small circle. Her body adjusted to what she was now thinking of as "leaping through time," and based on the way her body responded, she knew the crossing of the threshold into present day was successful. Skeletons climbing the oak tree across the street watched her. Her eyes swept across the front porch covered in fall décor. Brittle brown-orange leaves had blown in from somewhere and huddled against the railing. A small yellow pumpkin had rolled away from its display and stopped against a potted scarlet mum. She was home, back in her own timeline. *Or what's left of it.*

Josephine reached for the front doorknob as someone called her name. Recognizing the voice, she closed her eyes and inwardly groaned. The temptation to fling open the door and pretend she hadn't heard was almost overpowering, but Josephine turned from the door as Barbara stopped at the bottom of the porch stairs.

Wearing a cream-colored wool sweater too thick for the mild weather, and skinny jeans tucked into knee-high brown boots, Barbara looked like someone on her way to pose for family photos among the fall foliage. "Josephine, hello!" Barbara called. "Do you have a minute?" Without waiting for Josephine's response,

Barbara walked up the stairs. "I stopped by earlier, but I didn't get an answer. I'm glad I caught you now."

Does Barbara make neighborhood rounds every day, checking to see if everyone's abiding by the rules? Does she patrol every house or just mine?

"Oh"—Barbara looked Josephine up and down—"Are you coming back from a . . . play rehearsal?"

Josephine laughed. *A play rehearsal? Why in the world would Barbara ask such an absurd question?* Josephine glanced down at her clothing. Shock rushed through her. Her clothing—*Alma's clothing*—had aged drastically. The once white blouse was now dingy, and a few threads were unraveling on one shoulder seam. A missing button caused the blouse to pucker open near her navel. The skirt appeared stiff and starchy against her legs with a fraying hemline. The traveling bag looked like it had been kicked along the highway from Atlanta to Nashville.

Josephine closed her gaping mouth and pressed her lips together for a moment. "Yes," she said, grasping for the fastest half-truth. "I've been invited to a costume event. What can I help you with?"

Barbara's expression was grave. "There's an issue with the door."

Josephine swapped the traveling bag to her other hand and waited for more of an explanation. Barbara stared at her without continuing, as if Josephine had any clue what the woman was talking about. Josephine asked, "What door?"

"Yours," Barbara said as though it was obvious. She pointed at the front door. "You didn't fill out an official form and present it to the preservation board. Any changes to the exterior of the house must be approved. We found your requests for the repainting of the trim but nothing for the door."

Too stunned to speak right away, Josephine blinked at Barbara before looking at the front door. "You mean this door? The door you said you were thrilled about a couple of days ago?"

Barbara's burgundy lips pursed. "Yes, but I didn't realize you hadn't submitted an official form to the board."

Frustration built inside Josephine like a kettle coming to boil. She had more important problems on her mind than submitting paperwork to an uptight preservation board. "Aren't you on the board?"

"Yes, but I don't see *everything* that's submitted," Barbara said. "Some forms can be approved without everyone's signature. But a few of us were discussing the changes you're making, because we're pleased to see the progress, but no one recalled seeing a request to change your front door, which caused us to search for it."

Josephine barely stopped herself from rolling her eyes like a teenager. "You hated the front door that was here, and now you're not happy that I changed it?"

Barbara huffed. "It doesn't matter if I'm happy or not; this is about *the forms*. There is a proper way to follow the preservation process, and you didn't follow it. And after seeing this door, we're not sure it's the right era. We're having a meeting tomorrow afternoon at five, and we have a slot you can take to discuss and defend your changes."

"I don't have time for a meeting, Barbara," Josephine said, losing her patience with the nitpicking woman and her preservation board. "I'll find the paperwork online and send it in."

Barbara hesitated and actually looked uncomfortable. "Well . . . you've already made the changes, so you can't go backward with the process. If you don't attend the meeting, you'll be fined. There will be another meeting later this year when you can defend your reasoning."

The wind picked up, sounding scratchy and crispy as it rustled through the drying leaves still clinging to the trees. Josephine's eyebrows rose on her forehead. "Fined? How much?"

"A thousand dollars."

"A thousand dollars!" Josephine's voice came out as a shout. She kicked aside politeness and jumped straight into outrage. "Did you bother to fine Uncle Donnie for that monstrosity he had hanging here? Or the trim work or the shed?"

"Uncle Donnie . . ." Barbara repeated in confusion. Then her face shifted with surprise. "Donovan is your uncle?"

"Yes, but we're not close," Josephine said angrily.

Barbara's haughty expression flared heat up Josephine's neck. "Yes, we did fine him. Did he pay? Of course not. I guess rule-breaking is an inherited trait."

Josephine groaned, unable to contain her exploding annoyance. "I just can't do this with you right now. This is ridiculous and abusive. This is a perfectly fine door." Josephine pointed straight-armed at the door. "It was hand-carved for the house and hung here for years before Uncle Donnie decided to spite you, so I don't care if you and the board think it's from the correct era. This door is staying."

Barbara took a few steps backward with wide eyes and an open mouth like a guppy. When she spoke again, her voice was timid and hesitant. "Our strict rules and adherence to preservation codes are what keep this neighborhood beautiful, and what we're doing here is probably one of the reasons you chose this house."

Actually it wasn't, but Josephine didn't argue.

Barbara continued, "People like the previous owner of this house, *your* uncle Donnie, would ruin neighborhoods like ours if we didn't enforce the rules."

She's probably right about that. Uncle Donnie has a knack for ruining things. Front doors, family relationships, harmony.

Josephine attempted to calm the raging infuriation inside herself before speaking. "I bought the door from a local salvage yard. The owner of the salvage yard would defend that this is the perfect door for this house, and if I had filled out paperwork, *you would have approved it*, but I don't have time to attend your precious meeting where you sit around and nitpick the lives and decisions of others. Send me a bill."

Barbara's skin pulled taut against her bony facial features as she set her mouth into an expression of displeasure. "You're going to *pay* the fine rather than defend yourself?"

Josephine nodded. "Enjoy your patrol." Then she turned her back on Barbara, opened the front door, and stepped inside without another word.

The interior of the house was cooler than the outdoors. Josephine hadn't switched the thermostat settings for the incoming fall and winter weather, so the air conditioner was still running. The house also seemed emptier than the day before. Alma's house was so full of life and movement and the comings and goings of people, and in contrast, the present-day Carter Mansion was as vacant as a church on Monday. There was more echo, more silence, leaving Josephine more aware of the lack of any presence besides her own. "I'm home," she called to no one. Even her own voice sounded unfamiliar and too loud. She could almost hear an echo returning with, "You're alone."

Josephine had *wanted* to be alone after Nathan died. Being around people had been the equivalent of constantly touching an open wound. How could she ever heal if she was always talking to someone about him or accepting sympathies for such an awful experience? Josephine had pulled way back from everyone, and it hadn't taken people long to get the message and stop reaching out. Eventually being alone disfigured itself into a hollow so vast it had consumed her. Now, after spending time with Alma and her friends, combined with the brief moment wrapped up in Danny's arms, being alone had almost instantly lost its appeal. Standing in a house devoid of vivacity, Josephine didn't like that her life was fading more every day, not only because of her throw-away wish but also because she'd allowed herself to diminish weeks before the wish.

Guilt regarding her attitude toward Barbara pinched the edges of her stomach, but didn't the board allow for judgment when it came to some exterior changes? *Didn't they see I put forth effort to replace the hideous front door left behind by Uncle Donnie's carelessness?* Barbara hadn't mentioned the weathervane, which Josephine definitely hadn't submitted paperwork for because she hadn't even changed it herself. *How much will that cost me? If Barbara knew I am trying to save lives, would the board overlook missed paperwork?*

Josephine almost laughed at the absurdity of the situation as she removed her shoes and left them by the door. If she showed up at the preservation board meeting and told them about trying to save her great-grandmother's life, would they extend her grace? They'd more likely whisper about her sanity and possibly try to find a way to oust her from the neighborhood. Did they have that kind of power? Doubtful, but having Barbara breathing down her neck every other day would make her rethink her neighborhood choice if she weren't so attached to the house.

First things first. Josephine needed to change out of the faded clothing. She moved toward the foyer staircase but caught sight of the living room on the periphery, and something about it stopped her. She turned her full attention to the area. Where the tacky mauve couch had been, now there was open space. Her breath caught. A twisting moved through her gut as if someone were wringing her out. She walked toward the living room and stopped in the opening, leaning her shoulder against the large archway and staring at the emptiness.

Losing the ugly couch didn't bother her. The mounting evidence that Josephine Reynolds was being erased in bits and pieces did. A sweatshirt here, a tea set there. A wedding ring, then a vacation. Josephine didn't want to check the house to catalog what else was missing. What did it matter? She couldn't bring any of those things back unless she was able to change the events happening at the upcoming party.

With a heaviness weighing on her shoulders, she walked up the stairs to her bedroom in search of her phone. She thought of Katherine, and the temptation to call her sister flared again, but . . . Too many what-ifs sprang up in her mind like monsters in a haunted house. If she'd been erased from Katherine's life or Katherine no longer existed, she might completely lose her resolve to keep moving.

Josephine stepped through her bedroom doorway. She'd left her phone charging on the bedside table, and she walked to it. She opened her texts and saw the one from Lita with the details of their upcoming lunch outing. Lita's group of friends would be meeting soon at the Pharmacy, a local burger joint in East Nashville. *Do I really want to go?* Josephine shook her head. Lita's optimism and the idea of making friends had appealed to her at the time, but now, knowing her life was disappearing, the familiar darkening gloom invaded her.

Josephine put down the phone and walked out of her bedroom. She stopped in the hallway. *If I don't go and meet Lita and her friends, then I'm admitting defeat. Admitting that I won't be around to make friends because I can't save Alma.* She marched back into her bedroom, picked up the phone, and texted Lita: See you soon!

Josephine inhaled a calming breath. *I'm not giving up. There's still time to fix this.* She could start by putting herself out there again, by making new friends. Friends that had nothing to do with Nathan. *I can do this.*

•••

JUST BEFORE ELEVEN thirty a.m., Josephine found a parking spot on McFerrin Avenue. Lita mentioned today's lunch was '50s themed, but it was okay if Josephine didn't want to dress up. One piece of Alma's clothing that hadn't disappeared from the armoire was the rich indigo swing dress with a halter top. Josephine was surprised at how well it fit. She paired the dress with sensible flats and a small handbag she'd received for Christmas one year but had never used. The bag was big enough to hold her cellphone and car keys.

Josephine walked up the sidewalk toward the restaurant. For an early lunchtime, there was already a crowd of people dining on the outside porch area. When she opened the front door, more people were huddled around and the bar seating was full. Josephine saw Lita among the people at the hostess stand.

"Lita!" Josephine waved when Lita turned to look at her. "Hey!" She walked toward Lita and her friends. "It's already so crowded in here. Good thing we're here early."

Lita's expression shifted from delight to confusion, and she didn't respond.

A niggling started in Josephine's stomach, an indication that something might be amiss. "Thanks again for inviting me," Josephine continued, pushing through the uneasiness. "I haven't been out in a while, and I'm looking forward to meeting your friends." She smoothed her hand down the front of her dress. "I even found an outfit. It was my great-grandmother's."

The awkward smile on Lita's face sent Josephine's mind spinning. "Uh, hi," Lita said, "I'm sorry, but I don't think we've met. Did someone tell you to meet us here? We're, of course, always open to new people joining us!"

What? Josephine's stomach twisted and then dropped to the hardwood floor. She could feel the sickening thud of her heart. "We met at your store," Josephine said. *Please, please, please remember me.*

"We did?" Lita asked. "Wow, I'm totally blanking. I'm so sorry." Lita touched Josephine's arm as a show of comfort, but *comfort* was the opposite of what Josephine felt.

Josephine backed out of Lita's reach. *She doesn't remember me.* A horrible realization ripped through her. *For Lita, I've never existed. I'm . . . disappearing.* Josephine turned quickly and ran out of the door, nearly bowling someone over on the sidewalk. She ran all the way to her car and then sat in the driver's seat panting and trying not to hyperventilate. When her body stopped trembling enough to drive, she headed back to the Carter Mansion.

Josephine had read in novels about the feeling of "impending doom" but had never experienced something so dramatic in real life. Until now. Now she wondered if she was teetering on the edge of complete disaster.

Back at the house, she plugged her cell phone into the charger in her bedroom and left it on the bedside table. Then she changed out of Alma's dress into a pair of yoga pants and an oversize sweatshirt. An overwhelming urge to call her mama swept through her. When Josephine turned back toward the bed, not only was the phone gone, but so was the charger.

"This can't be happening," she said, pinching the bridge of her nose and hanging her head. "Of all the things you could take, you just *had* to take my cell phone?" Who *you* was in her question, Josephine wasn't sure. God, the Universe, the timeline keepers . . . Regardless, she added her cell phone to the list of items vanishing into the void.

Years ago Nathan had laughed at Josephine when she suggested they have a landline connected in their new house. Landlines were archaic and unnecessary, he'd said. But in this moment, she was thankful that Uncle Donnie had kept the active phone line to the house. After moving in, Josephine bought a simple cordless phone and plugged it in, just in case. She had no idea this *just in case* would present so shortly after moving in.

Josephine returned downstairs to the living room. She grabbed the cordless phone from the cradle and dialed her parents' number by heart, only pausing for a moment when a breath-stealing question struck her. *What if Mama doesn't remember me?*

After a few rings, someone answered. "Hello?" Josephine recognized her father's voice.

"Daddy," she said with both relief and mounting tension. "This is Josephine."

"Yes," he said.

Josephine paced the living room. "Do you remember me?" She stopped and held her breath.

"Of course," her dad answered.

She exhaled, laughing nervously, then started pacing again. "So you remember me and that I'm your daughter and I live in Nashville?"

He paused before answering, and Josephine was afraid to breathe during those lingering seconds. But he finally said, "Do you need to talk to your mom?" Without waiting, her dad's muffled voice called out, "Emily, Josephine needs to talk to you."

Josephine heard the sound of the phone being passed from hand to hand and then her mama's voice. "Josephine, honey, how are you? What a surprise! How's the house? All settled in? You let me know when you're ready for me and your dad to come over for dinner. You need a proper housewarming party. Maybe when Katherine's back from Florida."

Tears prickled in Josephine's eyes. *They remember me.* "I'd like that, Mama. Tell Daddy I'm sorry for being weird."

"What? Why would you say that? He knows his girls are odd," she said with a cheery laugh. "Tell me how you are."

Josephine hesitated. Talking to her mama grounded her again, but it didn't remove the truth that her life was vanishing, that Lita hadn't remembered her—maybe never met her—and that she had no idea how to right this terrible wrong. "I'm okay," she said. "The house is coming along. I've unpacked and I'm rearranging furniture." *Actually it's disappearing.*

"That's great, honey! I'm so happy you're settling in. Is there anything you need? Anything your dad and I can get for the house?"

Josephine allowed a moment of release to soften her body. "Can I get back to you on that? See what happens in the next few days?"

"Of course!"

"Thank you, Mama," Josephine said. "I'm happy you answered. I'll call you in a few days." *If I'm still here.* "Tell Daddy I love him."

"We love you, honey, and we'll talk soon."

Josephine ended the call and stood in a ray of dappled sunlight passing through the maple tree in the backyard and coming through the windowpanes.

Placing the phone on the kitchen counter, she heard the sound of faraway music drifting out from beneath the slight gap between the bottom of the basement door and the kitchen floor.

The hairs raised on her arms and continued up her neck into her scalp. Josephine opened the basement door, and the music crescendoed.

Damp, chilly air billowed up the staircase and encircled Josephine's stockings and feet. The up-tempo jazz song quieted as soon as she placed her foot on the top stair. Josephine flipped on the light switch, illuminating her path down into the dim basement. It appeared nothing had changed until she glanced toward the speakeasy door. In Alma's day, the door was easily spotted and still had a doorknob and bolts to lock it from the inside. The present-day door had been painted and hardware removed to hide it.

But as Josephine looked at the door, the physical aspects shifted in a way that made her doubt what she saw. Wood morphed into stone in a slow, deliberate manner, reminding Josephine of an object sinking beneath sand. The music warbled, sounding like a tune being played from underwater. The rocky earth swallowed the door inch by inch until all that remained was a solid wall of dark gray limestone. The music stopped.

Josephine stood in complete silence, staring at a wall that hadn't been there moments before. With apprehension tensing her shoulders, she walked toward the spot as if she, too, might sink into nothingness. Placing her hands on the wall, the cool rock vibrated beneath her fingers, and Josephine felt like a piece of the limestone lodged in her throat, prohibiting air from traveling up her windpipe.

The speakeasy was gone.

CHAPTER 15

Josephine spent the rest of the day trying not to replay the disappearing speakeasy door over and over again in her mind. Each replay left behind an echo of terror inside her. Even though she knew it wouldn't help, or ease her mind, to take note of what else of hers was missing from the house, Josephine couldn't stop herself from making a mental inventory.

Along with her cellphone and charger, other vanished items included clothing, the few photo albums she'd taken from the Green Hills house, her tennis shoes, Nathan's favorite shirt, and a painting she'd bought on a trip she'd taken with Katherine. A completely random assortment of items, and yet each disappearance made her feel less and less real.

Josephine sat on the front porch and watched the sun set. The falling light tossed ribbons of orange and gold across the coppery sky in broad streaks. Birdsong quieted, and neighborhood lights switched on in the growing darkness. Josephine had experienced so much quiet after Nathan died, but it wasn't the kind of silence that comforted her. Those months were marked by emptiness and the feeling of being nowhere while still somehow existing. Now, sitting here on the porch, admiring the subtle changes in the sky as it changed from pale blue with cotton-ball clouds to vibrant fall colors and clouds like puffs of cotton candy, she knew she would miss this kind of quiet if her life was erased. Her heart craved more of this kind of beauty. How many more sunsets would she witness?

Until recently, Josephine spent most nights alone, drifting from one activity to another, watching a movie she was only half interested in or sitting on the sunporch at the Green Hills house, staring at nothing and losing time just the same. She'd been so secluded so intentionally. Even though her outing with Lita had failed, tonight Josephine had been invited to spend time with people she was beginning to think of as friends, and she wanted to be with them. She wanted to listen to music and eat finger foods and talk about opportunities. It invigorated her yearning to reengage in life. In *her* life. Although her past was fading, she still had two days to change the course of her future. She might yet succeed and overpower the wish she made.

She said goodbye to the sunset, then went inside to shower and prepare for a night in the club with Alma and Eleanor. *And Danny.* Just thinking his name sent up sparks of excitement, a feeling reminiscent of when she was in high school hoping the cute boy would ask her to the dance. This growing emotion pushed aside today's upsetting experiences.

She shouldn't get so attached to Danny or let him get attached to her, because she was leaving—or more accurately, she wasn't *staying* in 1927. Still, a quiet voice in her head whispered she should enjoy the emotion while it presented itself. The feeling of being alive had evaded her for months, and now that it was here, must she push it away?

Josephine chose a deep purple dress for tonight. Extensive beading covered the bodice with sequined accents that glittered in the light. The fringed hem stretched from mid-thigh to her knees. It was a modest flapper-style dress, not as revealing as others she'd seen in the club the night before. She paired the dress with diamond stud earrings, a black cloche hat, lace gloves, stockings, and low black heels. She styled her hair just as she had the night before, with soft curls, because it was quick and easy.

Josephine lined her eyes in a darker shade of brown and added blush and plum lipstick. The makeup was a more dramatic look for her, but it matched the intensity of her present emotions. *If I'm going to be gone in less than two days, why not turn up every part of my life? Why not live louder and bolder?*

Looking at herself in the mirror, admiration filled her for the stylish woman staring back at her. Josephine pointed at her reflection. "I don't know about you, but I'm one click below terrified. What if I can't pull this off?" Another thought echoed through her mind and relaxed some of her muscles. *But what if I can?*

Josephine looped the front-door key through a long chain. Then she grabbed her handbag and stepped out onto the porch. The evening air brushed across her flushed skin, cooling her slightly. Her hands trembled, probably because her emotions were all over the place, a tight tangle of anxiety, excitement, fear, expectation, and hope. Josephine inhaled to calm her nerves, but it did little to settle her vibrating insides. She heard Katherine's voice in her head, *"Take the leap."* Josephine unlocked the front door, spoke the password, and knocked on the door.

After twisting the doorknob, she eased it open and stepped her heeled shoe across the threshold. Her body whirred with the leap across time as a rush of cold flooded her veins and disoriented her for a few seconds. Her response time quickened, and she found herself stabilizing faster than ever before. The chill gripping her body released its hold.

The warmth of the house surrounded her, and the sound of a piano solo danced through the room. Josephine stepped onto the foyer rug, her heels silent against the woven threads. She slipped the long chain around her neck, tucking the house key beneath the neckline of her dress. The cool metal dropped against her breastbone and rested there, hidden away. Voices drifted from the living room, a mix of baritones and higher-pitched altos. Heavy footsteps sounded behind her on the porch, and before she could close the door, a man rushed up the front steps.

"Where's Danny?" the man demanded. His tan skin was pulled tight across angular, irritated features. Thick coal-black eyebrows creased low over his even darker eyes, and his scowl marred what Josephine was sure could have been a handsome face. The navy suit was an inch too short at his ankles, the fabric faded at the knees and frayed along the cuffs. Either he didn't have the money for a new one or he was the kind of man who didn't purchase anything new until the old completely unraveled. Standing on the porch now, his scowl more pronounced, he repeated, "Where's Danny?"

"I don't know," Josephine said, taking another step backward into the house. "I just arrived." She gripped the edge of the door and moved to close it.

The man stepped toward her in an aggressive manner. "Don't cover for—"

"Mark," Danny said, appearing beside Josephine. His presence hastened her heartbeat. "This is a surprise. I hope you're well. Can I ask what you're doing here?"

Now Josephine remembered Mark was Danny's brother, the policeman. She quickly scanned Mark's features again and saw similarities in the shape of the brothers' eyes and facial structure.

But Mark's strained face looked more worn, more lined with stress and unhappiness than Danny's.

"I know what you're planning," Mark said, his jaw clenching and releasing. No pleasantries for Mark. He obviously didn't have time for manners.

Danny stepped slightly in front of Josephine as if protecting her. "Could you be more specific?"

Mark made a growling noise. "Everyone knows," he said derisively. "The whole department. It's a disgrace. It's *illegal*, Danny. Don't you care about the law? And dragging Sara into it. You should be guiding her, not encouraging her to blatantly break the law. You need to be careful. I'm here to warn you. Call off the party on Sunday."

Danny's fists clenched and unclenched at his sides. "Sara is an adult. She makes her own decisions."

Mark stomped his foot on the porch boards like a child throwing a tantrum. "People aren't ignoring lawbreakers anymore. They're tired of allowing debauchery and evildoing to persist. Don't you think it's time you stop wasting your life? Alcohol is a sin, and it will rot your entire life. What would Margaret say if she were alive?"

Danny moved toward Mark lightning fast, so fast that Josephine barely registered he'd moved away from her. Danny shoved his finger into his brother's chest, and palpable fear flashed across Mark's face. "Don't you ever speak her name in such a way again. She's not some pawn you can use to validate your arrogant disregard for others' choices. I would knock you off this porch if there wasn't a lady present. It's best you leave."

Mark backed away slowly, fear still present in his shadowed eyes. Halfway down the porch stairs, he turned to look up at his brother. "You've been warned." Then he rushed down the stairs, jumped into the car parked at the curb, and drove away.

Danny turned to look at Josephine still standing in the open doorway. "My apologies, Josephine. I could have handled that better, but Mark has always known how to rankle me."

According to Alma, the chief of police was a regular patron at the club, so he wasn't likely the one who would participate in a raid. *Could Mark be behind it? Would he be such a zealot that he'd raid his sister's party and be the reason Alma is shot?* The possibility unsettled Josephine. The fierceness and fury behind Mark's warning heightened Josephine's resolve to ensure Alma's safety. *If I can't stop the raid, I will stop Alma from dying.*

Danny touched her arm, bringing her back to the present. "Are you upset with me?" he asked.

"No, of course not," Josephine said, trying to relax her expression. "Mark was aggressive, and I don't blame you for responding like you did." She paused for a second before asking the question she knew the answer to. No man would have responded so furiously unless it was about someone he loved. "Was Margaret your wife?"

Danny nodded and stepped into the house. He closed the door behind him and flipped the lock. "She loved Mark, showed him kindness and compassion, even though he's hotheaded and reckless. He acts without thinking, always has."

"Sounds like a bad combination for a police officer," Josephine said.

Danny shrugged his shoulders. "From what I've heard, he's an excellent officer. Just not an excellent brother, not lately."

Josephine tried to offer Danny an understanding smile. "His coming here tonight could be his way of showing you he cares. That he doesn't want you or Sara to get in trouble."

Danny rubbed the back of his neck before dropping his hand again. "You have a kind heart, Josephine, but Mark's reasons for coming here have more to do with shame."

"What do you mean?" she asked.

"He's ashamed he has a brother and sister who have chosen to live sinful lives. He fears his reputation is ruined because his family isn't righteous enough."

Josephine almost rolled her eyes in response, but Danny looked sincerely bothered by his brother's close-mindedness. "You know that's baloney, don't you?"

An expression of appreciation moved across his attractive face. "I do. You look beautiful tonight."

"Thank you," she said, glancing down at her shoes in a moment of shyness. She removed her hat and smoothed her hair. "You look nice too. Handsome, I mean." In his dark gray suit and starched white shirt, Danny's good looks would cause any woman to pause and admire. *Could he be any more striking?* Then he smiled at her. *Yes, he certainly can.*

Danny reached for Josephine's hand, and she allowed him to take it. "Can you forgive my lack of manners with my wayward brother?"

Josephine squeezed his fingers. "There's nothing to forgive."

Danny gently tugged her toward him, and a flame of desire flared in her. He leaned toward her, and she knew what he wanted. *Yes, kiss me.* Her eyes fluttered closed.

"Josephine!" Alma's exuberant voice filled the foyer. "Aren't you two a dashing pair?"

Josephine dropped Danny's hand, and he moved away slightly.

"Come into the living room," Alma continued. "Eleanor was just asking about you."

Eleanor lounged on the couch with Anderson, sitting close enough to him that not even a sheet of paper could be passed between them. She laughed at whatever he was saying, and Josephine had never seen Eleanor so happy, so unconcerned with her environment. Her black mini dress, covered in sequins and fringe, showcased her long legs. She'd styled her hair in swooping waves that were pinned to one side with a feathery clip. Anderson looked like a posh businessman in a black suit that coordinated with Eleanor's outfit.

Louis, wearing a pinstriped midnight-blue suit, sat in the velvet armchair with floral throw pillows shoved to one side, as though sharing space with frivolities. His drinking from a highball glass made the scene almost comical. Alma announced Josephine's arrival, and everyone turned their faces to her and said hello.

The floor started vibrating, and Josephine glanced down, understanding the speakeasy band was starting their first set of the night. She couldn't hear the music because of the radio playing upstairs.

"How about we leave your bag and hat upstairs this time?" Alma said. "Then you'll know exactly where it is. Want to leave your gloves as well?" Alma leaned toward her, and Josephine caught a whiff of her sweet perfume with hints of rose. "You look so lovely tonight, and Danny can't take his eyes off you." Alma gripped her arm as if sensing Josephine's nerves. "Don't panic. He's a real gentleman, and he'll only go as far as you let him."

Josephine's eyes widened, and Alma burst out laughing as she took Josephine's bag, hat, and gloves. She crossed the room to a sideboard, and Josephine followed. Alma opened one of its doors and placed Josephine's things inside. She stood and leaned her hip against the furniture.

"I didn't mean anything unseemly, Josephine," Alma said playfully. "You're a sweet woman, I can tell. I only meant that he's not the pushy, aggressive sort."

"Like Mark?" Josephine said before she could stop herself.

Alma's smile slipped. "You know him?"

Josephine shook her head. "He showed up here when I did, and he and Danny had a heated conversation."

Alma's lips turned down. "Mark isn't like Danny and Sara. He's much more challenging to like, and, yes, he's considerably more aggressive, which only enhances his unlikability. But I do try to be courteous when I see him." She lowered her voice to a whisper. "He's intent on closing down every speakeasy in the city, but there are powerful people in play here who don't agree."

The tightening of Josephine's stomach caused her to shift on her feet. Eleanor burst into laughter across the room, and Danny poured himself a drink at the bar cart. "Do you worry about what he'll do?"

"What good would that do?" Alma asked. "I can't control what he does or doesn't do, and if I worried about everyone and everything, I'd be a shaking mess in my room. Now, enough about Mark and his unattainable ideals. Let's enjoy the evening." Alma hooked her arm through Josephine's and walked her back to the group. "Who's ready for an evening in the club?"

A chorus of yeses rang out, and everyone stood to make their way downstairs. Josephine wanted to stop worrying about Mark and enjoy the evening, but she couldn't shake the upsetting awareness that in a matter of days, all of their lives could drastically change.

●●●

MORE BODIES CROWDED Club Belle Âme tonight than the previous evening. People bellied up to the high-gloss bar, where Cecil tossed around a shaker that moved like a blur of silver while he mixed drinks. The quartet playing at the back of the room had a pianist, a drummer, an upright bass player, and a trumpeter. The tables nearest the bar had been pushed closer to the walls to accommodate the dance floor, covered in dancers swinging, swaying, and pressing themselves together in a riotous affair.

The enthusiastic music beat against Josephine's body, wave after wave of an up-tempo rhythm that made her toe tap in sync. She flinched when someone grabbed her hand, but realizing it was Danny, she relaxed somewhat. Holding hands with Danny didn't exactly calm her. Instead, a fiery energy thrummed through her body. Eleanor, Anderson, Louis, and Alma were calling out their drink orders to Cecil. Danny leaned down so she could hear him, and his voice tickled her ear.

"Mary Pickford for you? Or something different?" he asked.

With how jittery her insides were, Josephine wasn't sure she wanted to add alcohol to the mix. So she shook her head and declined. Danny ordered an Old Fashioned, and Alma motioned for them to follow her to the separate sitting room. Dozens of people stopped them to speak while the group made their way across the floor. How anyone could hear and understand conversation with the level of music and the rising and falling of voices, Josephine didn't know.

Once they stepped into the separate seating area, the crowd noise diminished slightly, but people still leaned in close to be heard, making the entire room appear full of people locked in intimate conversation. The places where the group sat the night before were empty, and Josephine questioned how that was possible with the number of people in the speakeasy. How had no one else taken these spots?

Eleanor dropped down on the couch and patted for Josephine to sit beside her. "This area is always saved for Alma—Cecil's orders." Josephine lifted her brows in question. "You know people think this place is Cecil's, right? But it's still Alma's house. Even the drunken ones respect that rule. We don't have to push and shove for a spot."

Josephine's lips lifted on one side. "I doubt you've ever had to push and shove for anything."

"You're a clever one, Josephine," Eleanor said with a sly smile. "Alma mentioned Danny was carrying a torch for you, but dear, I think it might be a brazier."

"An inferno," Alma said, joining the conversation.

"Stop, you two," Josephine said. "I can barely keep my hands from shaking. You're making it worse."

Eleanor chuckled and placed her hand on Josephine's. "You'll be fine. Don't think so hard."

"Let it happen naturally," Alma agreed.

The trumpeter rang out a series of notes that kept tempo with Josephine's heart. She looked between the two of them. "Let *what* happen naturally?"

"Necking, of course!" Eleanor said, and Alma laughed.

"You're frightening her," Alma said. "Start with dancing. See if you enjoy his company."

"She wouldn't be shaking if she didn't enjoy his company," Eleanor said. "Oh, look, he's coming now. Smile, Josephine. You look like you're about to be arrested."

Josephine attempted to shift her expression into one of calmness, but for all she knew, she might resemble a department store mannequin with frozen features. The upright bass coaxed dancers onto the floor with a sensual song meant to call forth slow movements and bodies pressed together.

Danny held out his hand toward Josephine, and she lifted hers to meet him. He pulled her to her feet, asking, "Would you like to dance?"

She nodded, and Danny led them to the crowded floor. Tossing her gaze over her shoulder, both Eleanor and Alma grinned at her like they couldn't be more excited to see what happened next.

Danny was a few inches taller than Josephine, and when he pulled her close to him, he pressed his chin gently against the side of her head while they swayed to the music. She closed her eyes and relished the feeling of closeness, surprised by the intensity of attraction electrifying her. They were tucked among dozens of others all moving intentionally to the music. Every so often an elbow or a shoulder would bump into them, but people didn't seem to care, aware of how little room there was for everyone.

When the couple in Josephine's direct line of sight started kissing, she turned her head quickly and knocked her forehead into Danny's cheek. "Sorry," she said, embarrassed but also laughing.

"I spot an empty table," he said. "Let's give ourselves some room."

Josephine didn't want to stop dancing with Danny, but he grabbed her hand and pulled them through the mass of dancers. The table for two was situated in a corner of the room, and both chairs were on the same side of the small round table. Whoever had been sitting here wanted to be as close to their partner as possible. The leather seat still felt warm beneath her as though recently vacated. Danny didn't move his chair away from Josephine's, so their knees pressed together beneath the table.

A waitress came over and placed Danny's Old Fashioned on the table, which was a little unnerving. *Cecil must keep track of where everyone is. Maybe that's part of his job, to keep a watchful eye at all times.* Danny took a small sip and then focused his attention on Josephine.

"Where did you live before coming to Nashville?" he asked her.

Josephine couldn't say "across town," so she recalled when she was younger, still living with her parents. Her dad had taken a job in Georgia when she and Katherine were children. Everyone in her family had eventually moved back to Nashville, and

Josephine had been in Tennessee for almost twenty years now. But she answered, "Atlanta."

"I've heard the population has continued to grow rapidly, far surpassing what people predicted," Danny said. "Momentous growth in agriculture and industry."

Josephine nodded. "Atlanta is a sprawling city," she agreed, having no idea what 1920s Atlanta would have been like, but knowing modern Atlanta supported a massive infrastructure.

Danny lifted his glass to his lips. "What part of town do you live in, if you don't mind me asking?"

Josephine had anticipated this question. She was thankful she'd taken the initiative to research all she could about Nashville leading up to 1927. "East of Hillsboro Road. It's a newer set of lots and houses."

Danny's expression revealed his interest. He slowly spun the glass between his fingers, turning it in a steady circle. "Do you mean the Green Hills Subdivision? Developed by Calhoun?"

His knowledge of the area instantly made her uncomfortable. *What if he knows more about that area than I do?* "Yes," she said, hoping he wouldn't press for details.

"That's a fine area," Danny said. "I can picture you among the shade trees, lounging in a pleasant backyard. May I ask if you have children?"

Josephine almost smiled. *So people in the 1920s ask all the same questions. First they ask if you're married; then they ask if you have children.* Easy enough conversation, but also some of the most loaded, most emotionally charged questions to ask anyone. A lifetime of baggage and heartache could be attached to them.

Josephine shook her head. "We didn't." She didn't elaborate. *I doubt people are as aware and knowledgeable about fertility and reproductive systems as they are in my time.* It saddened her to think that in the 1920s the women probably carried blame and shame if they were part of a childless couple.

"Margaret and I didn't have children," Danny said, which surprised her. "She was unable to carry any babies to full term."

Josephine's expression fell. "I'm so sorry Danny, for both of you. That must have been so difficult and heartbreaking."

A boisterous quick-stepping song started, an odd pairing with the tragic topic, but welcome for it kept the conversation from feeling too grave. Danny nodded and cast his gaze across the room as though pulling up a memory in his mind and watching it play out. "If we had a boy, we were going to name him Elliott," he said. "Elliott Daniel Stewart."

"That's an excellent name," Josephine said. His vulnerability strengthened the longing in her to be close to him, to learn all she could. She had assumed men in the '20s were more closed off and certainly not open to sharing intimate and emotional details of their lives. Maybe Danny was an exception to stereotypes, or maybe Josephine's assumptions were based on movies and men she'd known in her own life.

"My grandfather's name was Elliott. He was a good man," he explained. "I wanted to give my boy a strong family name."

Josephine had a few questions too. Questions she couldn't ask Eleanor or Hattie without raising suspicions, but maybe she could ask Danny. She wished she'd ordered a drink so she'd have something to do with her hands. "Alma mentioned she doesn't worry about getting in trouble because the chief of police is a patron." Danny nodded. "Is there anyone else who might not keep her secret? Another patron or someone else who doesn't agree with the chief of police? Someone who might support the Bureau of Prohibition?"

Danny's brow furrowed. "Not a patron. I see where you're going with that because we've both heard it happen before, but those instances are when a patron and the owner had a falling out, and everyone loves Cecil and Alma." He glanced around at the crowd. "This isn't a troublemaking group."

"What about other local law enforcement?" she asked, treading as lightly as possible, not wanting to speak ill of his brother.

Danny shook his head. "I've seen almost the entire police force in here at one time or another. But not tonight. They won't be at Sara's party either. She's not close friends with any of them or their wives."

So Mark was still a possibility and could be working with the bureau. If he knew no officers were present tonight, then he wouldn't be risking his career if he planned tonight for the raid. Betraying his brother and sister would be a great loss, though, but Josephine didn't want to press the subject.

Danny asked, "Will you continue to live where you are without your husband?"

Dancers moved round and round, shuffling in a lopsided circular motion across the stained concrete floor. In her real life, she'd already left the house. Even in a fabricated house in a neighborhood that she only fake inhabited in this timeline, she knew she wouldn't stay there without Nathan. "Probably not."

Danny appeared distressed for a brief second. "Where will you go?"

Josephine didn't know how her life would play out in 1927 or in present day. Everything depended on what happened at the party in two days. "I don't know."

Danny's hand covered hers, his fingers wrapping around her palm and holding on. "I would very much like for you to stay awhile."

Josephine's heart pumped so quickly that she worried she might swoon. "Stay where?"

"In town," Danny said. "In Nashville so that I might see you more often. Would that please you too?"

How can he talk in a way that sounds like an actor in a classic black-and-white movie? How can the heroine not fall for his sincere expression while he delivers perfect lines? Her gaze locked with his, and when he moved his face closer to hers, Josephine knew what was coming, and she welcomed it. With his lips brushing hers, he asked again, "Would that please you too?"

"Yes," Josephine whispered back, and Danny kissed her.

His hand moved to her cheek before sliding toward the back of her head, where his fingers moved beneath her hair. She rested her hand on his other arm still propped on the table and leaned closer to him. Suddenly an image of Nathan appeared in her mind, and Josephine paused, but for only a second. Then she gently pushed aside the image, remembering Alma's wisdom. Josephine could care for both men. She wasn't choosing one man over the other. She was continuing to live and honoring her life too.

When Danny pulled away, the look of pleasure in his eyes turned up the flame burning inside Josephine, and she enjoyed it. She hadn't felt this much passion in more than a year. It reminded her of when she and Nathan first met, when he couldn't keep his hands off her, and they kissed every chance they got.

He reached for both of her hands. "I'm not the kind of man who dallies with many women."

Josephine couldn't help but laugh. "That sounds like you know a scoundrel or two."

Danny looked momentarily embarrassed but chuckled. "What I mean is—"

"I know what you mean," she said, wanting to relieve him of having to explain he wasn't a rogue. "Alma mentioned you aren't the type."

He nodded. "I haven't had much interest since Margaret." Josephine understood. "But I'd like to see you, as often as you'll allow me."

Josephine's heart swelled and then squeezed. She wanted to see more of Danny, too, but in two days she would be gone, whether because of failing to save Alma or returning to her own time. It wouldn't be fair to lead Danny on, but she couldn't tell him the truth. Turning him down was a hurtful option, especially with all the hope she saw on his face. *If I'm successful, will all memories of me vanish from their days? What if Danny never remembers a woman named Josephine Reynolds?*

"Take your time," Danny said, sensing her hesitation and thinking she might not be ready to date anyone.

Josephine smiled at his kindness and reached up to touch her hand to his cheek. "I like you, Danny."

He placed his hand over hers, and a dimple appeared in his cheek. "I like you, Josephine."

She opted for truth. "And I'd like to see you as much as I can for as long as I can," she admitted.

Danny's delighted expression made her reconsider *not* returning to her timeline even if she saved Alma. "And I'd like to kiss you as much as I can for as long as I can."

Josephine laughed and felt an ache in her cheeks from smiling. "Starting now?"

Danny leaned toward her and kissed her again.

CHAPTER 16

Josephine awoke Saturday morning feeling like a love-struck teenager. She marveled at how the giddiness of new love transformed her and instantly transported her back to youth. No longer could she relate to the grief-laden woman she'd been, the one who seemed to age in fast-forward. Her first impulse was to call Katherine, to talk to her most trusted confidante about this resurgence of feeling. But she couldn't. *What if Katherine doesn't answer? What if the number is no longer hers? Or worse, what if Katherine doesn't recognize me?* Instead of falling down that black hole of what-ifs tangled with sadness, Josephine closed her eyes and refocused her thoughts on Danny.

She and Danny had spent most of the night sitting at that corner table laughing, talking, and kissing. The votive candle on their table had burned out before they ended the evening. He'd spun her around on the dance floor to at least a dozen songs, but they always ended up back at the table. She'd asked him so many questions about himself, everything from the ordinary (What's your favorite color?) to the intimate (What are your dreams?), and she could almost forget she was out of place in 1927. For long stretches of time, she felt like she truly belonged there with him. Just a man and a woman getting to know each other with the enthusiasm new couples have for a possible future together.

Hazy sunlight filtered through the sheers covering her bedroom windows. Josephine stumbled in so late the night before, she hadn't bothered pulling closed the heavier drapes. She'd had just enough energy to wash her face, change out of her evening dress, and pull on a T-shirt before crawling into bed. Just before closing her eyes, she'd glanced at the bedside clock to see it was nearly two in the morning. When was the last time she'd seen the world after midnight? Josephine grinned and hugged the feather pillow against her chest. *Not in the last ten years, and possibly not since college.*

Part of her knew it was absolutely ridiculous to allow herself to feel so much excitement and happiness about Danny. Sunday night, their worlds would shift. She'd never see him again, so why permit him to occupy so many of her current thoughts? Why daydream about him, about the way he held her on the dance floor, about the way it felt to kiss him?

But there was another part of her, a part that had fallen into hibernation until now. *That* part sounded like a cheerleading squad rooting for her inside her heart. So Josephine gave herself permission to enjoy this lightness coursing through her, even if only for a little while. She deserved a little joy after so much sorrow.

Josephine was shocked to see it was almost nine a.m. She hadn't slept that late in years. She had nothing planned today. Instead of feeling uncomfortable with her lack of direction, Josephine decided to enjoy the freedom, and she did something she hadn't done since living at home with Katherine. She grabbed the Bluetooth radio-and-speaker combo from her closet and spun the tuner until she found the local station that played oldies. Turning up the volume, she danced around her bedroom, tossing her arms around in wild abandon, unable to stop smiling.

Josephine skipped her way to the bathroom, humming a tune she'd danced to with Danny. She brushed her teeth and showered, her heart buoyant until she turned off the shower faucet. The radio had gone off, and the sound of water flowing continued through the pipes—a new sound since she'd moved in. Then Josephine heard an odd noise coming from downstairs. It was reminiscent of a water feature at a spa. She dried off quickly and dressed before rushing down the stairs. The sound of running water grew louder and sounded more like a waterfall the closer she got to the kitchen.

Josephine gasped. Instead of Uncle Donnie's tasteful farmhouse sink was a gaping hole in the cabinetry and a ruptured pipe. Water burst up and arced out like a fountain from the exposed plumbing. An inch of water covered the kitchen tiles and soaked everything in a fifteen-foot radius. Josephine scrambled toward the cabinets and turned off the water supply. The powerful rushing water slowly lessened until it became a drip and then completely stopped. Kneeling in the deluge, she soaked her jeans and shivered from the icy water. When she stood, she realized the refrigerator was gone and the laundry room looked like the contractor had framed it and never returned to finish the job. Even the Sheetrock and washer and dryer were gone.

Josephine sloshed barefoot toward a kitchen chair and dropped into it, her dizzying thoughts making her lightheaded. *Am I losing the fight to survive? Is the timeline when I don't exist going to win out before I have a chance to save Alma tomorrow?* The Carter Mansion was removing Uncle Donnie's additions bit by bit.

"Please give me until tomorrow," she said to no one and yet to *anyone* who might be listening. "*Please.*"

When her feet were almost numb, she got up and moved the kitchen chairs out into the hallway. She couldn't lift the kitchen table alone, so she had no choice but to leave it and clean up the water as best as possible. The mop had vanished, but Josephine found a broom and swept the water out the back door. It spilled down the brick steps like a waterfall, soaking the red bricks and flowing out into the browning backyard grass. Josephine dried the rest of the floor with towels and then hung them outside to dry.

She wondered if she should call a plumber, but what could they do? She didn't have a replacement sink, so she didn't really need running water in the kitchen right now. As long as she could use the bathrooms, Josephine could manage the next couple of days. She had no idea why the upstairs shower would have caused the pipe to burst in the kitchen, but expecting logic in the middle of her current situation was pointless. Josephine was, after all, living out the most illogical moments she'd ever experienced.

She moved through the rest of the day with a tightness threading through her muscles. *Will I round a corner and find another part of the house gone? What if my belongings vanish one by one until I can't make it to the party tomorrow night because there's nothing left? Will the timeline be so cruel as to give me an option and yet not? Will it bring me almost to the end and make the choice for me?* The notion that she might never see Alma or Danny again, or any of the others, not even one last time, filled her with a melancholy ache faintly similar to losing Nathan. She'd grown too attached to them, she knew that, but how could she not? Josephine had been wandering so long in the dark, so far removed from friends and *life,* that now being welcomed and included by Alma and her friends, Josephine resembled a crocus pushing up through the winter soil at the birth of spring.

●●●

LATE AFTERNOON ARRIVED, staining the sky in shades of indigo, violet, and the palest of pink. Josephine sat in the parlor, staring out the window. The house phone rang and she startled at the sound. *Who would be calling me? And on this phone? Who even has this number?*

"Hello?" she answered.

"How's your experiment going?" a man asked.

After a few seconds, Josephine recognized the voice. "Leo?"

"Mm-hmm."

"How did you get this number?" she asked.

"It's been the same for years," he said. "How's the experiment going?"

Josephine exhaled. "Honestly, Leo? I don't know. One minute I feel like everything's going to be okay. I'm loving spending time with Alma and her friends, and I think I can change what happens. The next minute, for example this morning, I'm standing in the kitchen and the sink is missing, a pipe is bursting, and the laundry room has reverted back to when Uncle Donnie started building it. The house appears to be taking back anything that is part of the timeline when I succeed. If Alma dies—" Her throat tightened, and she couldn't continue for a moment. "If I fail, then her future family doesn't exist, which means even Uncle Donnie and his changes vanish."

"Hmm . . . time is short but not finished. The party is tomorrow night, right?"

"Yes."

"And you have a plan for how to stop the party or keep the raid from happening?"

Josephine hesitated. "Not really," she admitted. "I'm kind of winging it." She didn't want to admit she'd spent the entire night thinking about Danny and not once trying to come up with a plan for Sunday. "Alma won't be deterred by any hiccups. After the caterer canceled, I suggested she reschedule, but she's not easily discouraged. I tried to cancel the band, but I was interrupted. And I can't think of any other ways to change her mind."

Leo's concern deepened. "Have you thought about telling Alma the truth?"

Josephine pressed her lips together. *Yes, of course I've thought about telling the truth—as an absolute last resort. Maybe I'm there already.* "She'll think I'm completely bonkers. Why on earth would she believe such a story? I can hear her now saying, 'That's phonus balonus, Josephine,' and then laughing because she thinks I'm joking."

"What if you had a way to prove it to her?" Leo asked.

Josephine frowned. "How would I do that?" *Surely he doesn't expect me to show Alma how I can time leap.* That kind of proof seemed *too shocking*.

Josephine gazed out the window toward a rising crescent moon. The streetlights cast a blue-white glow onto the sidewalk. Faint stars had started to appear in the darkening sky.

"I know a secret or two about that house. Maybe one of them could prove to her you're telling the truth. Do you mind if I ride over? I need to show you."

"Tonight?" she asked.

Leo nodded. "Do you have another plan?"

Josephine laughed dryly. "We've established I have no plan, so please, come over and share these secrets." She hung up the phone. *What secrets could possibly convince Alma that I'm her time-leaping great-granddaughter?*

●●●

LEO PARKED ALONGSIDE the curb in front of the house, and Josephine met him at the front door. Streetlights cast a long shadow that preceded him as it stretched up the brick stairs. She flipped on the porch lights and welcomed him in, but he paused and admired the Halloween and autumn decorations crowding the veranda.

"Festive," he said with a look of approval. Amusement also flickered in his deep brown eyes.

Josephine stepped out onto the porch and swept her hands back and forth as though showcasing the décor. "My sister's doing. She hired people for me because she said this neighborhood would expect it. She's not wrong. Barbara already gave me pointers for how to amp up what's already here."

Leo's booming laugh spread across the porch and echoed into the foyer. Before crossing the threshold, he stopped momentarily to admire the door his father carved. Josephine closed and locked the door behind them. Leo paused in the foyer, looking around with childlike amazement. She could almost see the little boy he'd been.

"This brings back so much I remember about this house," he said. "It hasn't changed too much, mostly aged and more lived in. I was in here only a few times, but I thought this house was grand."

"It's still grand," Josephine agreed. "If you overlook all the missing pieces—" Her voice stopped when she saw the secretary desk in the living room was gone. The room was becoming bare enough to resemble a ballroom instead of a cozy place where people gathered and spent time together. "The secretary vanished in just the last couple of hours. I loved that desk." She crossed the room and squatted down to run her fingers over the indentions in the rug where the feet of the desk had been pressing in for years. "Leo, I'm running out of time." She inhaled a shuddering breath as tears stung her eyes.

Leo walked into the nearly vacant room and stood in the center, turning a slow circle before facing Josephine. "Not as comfortable as I remember."

Josephine wiped at her cheeks. The last two picture frames she'd placed on the table near the sofa had vanished. "There was a couch there," she pointed, "but you're not missing anything. It was ugly and smelled like it hadn't seen sunlight in decades. But *me*, Leo, my things, my life, my photos, they're disappearing. *I'm* disappearing." Fear knotting with sadness crowded her body and forced more tears from her eyes.

"Hold on a minute before you get too far into that," Leo said, aware that Josephine was on the verge of breaking down. "Let me show you something."

He knelt slowly at the edge of the thin Persian rug and started rolling it up. After a couple of feet, a hidden compartment in the floor revealed itself. Josephine rushed over and knelt beside Leo. He smoothed his large hands over the square piece of wood that disrupted the vertical wood plank pattern. Then he hooked his finger around the metal loop pressed into the top of the compartment lid and lifted it. The door opened with a soft whoosh of air as the unused hinges squeaked.

Inside the square space, no larger than two feet square and barely a foot deep, laid an assortment of items. Josephine reached in and pulled out yellowed papers. She recognized the handwriting as Alma's. The papers looked to be ordinary lists, but part of Josephine cherished them as precious items. A chocolate-brown leather-bound ledger contained financial details about liquor purchases, as well as other items bought for the speakeasy like food, furniture, and payments to musicians. Leo unrolled a set of architectural designs for the speakeasy. Blank membership cards to Club Belle Âme were scattered throughout the space.

Josephine picked up one and rubbed her thumb over the faded paper.

Leo handed Josephine an aging, brittle-edged postcard. A black-and-white image of the Eiffel Tower filled one side of the card. The backside of the card was addressed to Alma in Nashville and sent by Franklin Carter. The message he'd written to her was short, but he called her "*belle âme*."

"She named the club after this," Josephine said, showing Leo the writing. A warming sensation coursed through her. Even after tragedy, Alma had taken the beautiful parts of her life with Franklin and added those memories to her present and future. "This must have been his nickname for her."

"Beautiful soul," Leo said, translating the French phrase. He removed the final item from the space, a miniature carved wooden horse resembling a knight piece from chess. The polished wood still gleamed.

Josephine rocked back on her heels and stared at the items they'd removed from the hidden space. "How did you know about this?"

Leo handed her the carving. "This piece was mine," he explained. "I spent an afternoon with Louis—"

"Louis?" Josephine asked. She was just now putting together that Alma died before Leo was born, which meant Leo's visits to the Carter Mansion happened years after Alma was gone.

"He took over ownership of the Carter Mansion as a way to secure Alma's memory," Leo said.

Josephine frowned and rubbed the spot between her eyes. "Leo, I've just realized something. When we first met, you said a neighbor called you about the front door after Uncle Donnie removed it." Leo nodded. "But that would mean my uncle Donnie was born, which is only possible if Alma lived—but you also told me that Alma died in 1927, and you only knew about her through your parents' stories." He nodded again. "*How* is that possible?"

Leo stood and stared at his hands as if there were answers carved into the lines on his palm. "It would appear I am also living two timelines." His chuckle surprised Josephine. "I guess this is how you feel—I have two sets of memories that both feel real but can't possibly have both occurred, and yet they have."

Josephine sighed. "It's bizarre. What do you remember about the day you were here?"

"I don't remember why I was here or much about that day other than this hidden compartment. Louis showed me the secret space and made me promise that I'd never tell anyone, because it was full of Alma's important documents. This horse was my favorite toy at the time. I wanted it to stay with her things. Louis tried to talk me out of it. I'd wondered what became of everything they put in here, including my horse, but everything looks the same as the day he showed me."

Josephine rubbed her fingers over the smooth, rounded edges of the horse. "Did your dad carve this?" Leo nodded. "It's incredible, all the detail on such a small piece. But how is knowing about this secret space going to help me?"

Leo's bushy white eyebrows lifted. "Tell Alma the truth. Show her you know about this."

Josephine knew Leo was right about her needing proof if she hoped to convince Alma. She returned the horse to Leo as an idea came to her. "What if I added something of mine to it? Do you think it might still be there in 1927?" But then Josephine frowned. "No . . . that won't work. My present-day house things don't travel back in time with me, only what I have on my body or am holding in my hands seems to go with me. But," she glanced at Leo, "maybe I could take something with me in my purse."

Josephine hopped up and rushed out of the room and across the hall. In the parlor she pulled one of the only remaining photo albums off the shelf and flipped through it until she found an envelope of family photos her mom had given her. Josephine had never gotten around to placing them in the album. Would the photograph she sought still exist? She flipped through the pictures, hoping she could find it. It was a photograph of Alma the last time Josephine had seen her, when Josephine was about seven. When she saw it, her heart lifted. Standing with Alma were four generations of women: Alma; her daughter, Dorothy; Josephine's mother, Emily; and Josephine and Katherine as young children.

Josephine hurried back into the living room. Leo had returned the items to the hidden space and was closing the lid when she entered. "What about this?" She handed him the photograph.

Leo studied the photo. "How strange to see Alma as an old woman. That's you?" he asked, pointing to the tallest girl in the photo. Josephine nodded. "Use both. Show her the compartment and this photograph."

"I'm going to sound so irrational."

"You say that like this whole experience doesn't defy logic," Leo said with a sly smile that lifted his cheeks, almost hiding his eyes. "How much do you want to save her and yourself? And maybe the rest of us too?"

Josephine reflected his smile even as her body tensed with the unknown. "You get right to the heart of the matter, don't you?"

Leo gave her a knowing look. "Call me Monday and let me know how it goes."

Josephine's eyebrows lifted. "You're certainly hopeful."

Leo winked at her. "Is there any other way to live?"

CHAPTER 17

A wild, unexpected thunderstorm swept through town right after the grandfather clock chimed midnight. Josephine barely slept. Most of the night she lay awake, listening to the wind howling in woeful bursts. Lightning flashes illuminated the house in strobe light patterns, followed by boisterous booms of thunder that rattled windows and dishes in the cabinets. At some point in the wee hours, the storm quieted, and Josephine drifted off to sleep.

But the next morning, the bedsheets were tangled around her body as though she'd been wrestling all night. She awoke groggy with the niggling worry she'd forgotten something vital. Then she fully awakened. Today was October 9, the day of Sara's party. The day of the raid.

After unwrapping herself from the sheets, she sat on the edge of the bed, apprehension seeping into her thoughts and sinking into her bones. *What else might be missing from the house today? Will I be given the chance to live my way through the evening and the opportunity to save Alma? Or will time be stolen from me?* Just thinking about Alma possibly being shot in less than twenty-four hours filled Josephine with a sickening dread.

She brushed her teeth and showered without catastrophe. No bursting pipes or water flooding the house. After a tentative search of the house, she determined nothing else seemed to have gone missing, not anything she could immediately spot. Josephine dressed, wrapped herself in a wedding ring quilt, and sat on the back steps in a patch of sunlight. She drank green tea from an oversize ceramic mug Katherine had gifted her a few Christmases ago. She cupped her hands around the smooth, red-glazed finish, and her fingers warmed. Tea was the only hot beverage option she had in the house other than another instant coffee packet. She couldn't handle another cup of bitter coffee, and she hadn't had time to buy a coffeepot and coffee grounds. The tea tasted grassy, and she'd steeped the bag too long, giving the warm drink a potent and slightly unpleasant bite.

The withering rosebushes still needed tending, and bare patches of hard earth spotted the dying, browning Bermuda grass. Skinny weeds grew along the fence line, and she wondered if she should hire a yard service. *But won't the weeds be dead from the cold in another few weeks? Will I even be here then?*

She shook her head as though trying to jiggle loose the negative thoughts. She couldn't think like that. She *had* to believe she could save Alma tonight. Josephine closed her eyes and imagined the yard in 1927. She'd caught glimpses of it outside the kitchen windows and knew it was considerably more thriving then than today. She thought about the people who sneaked through the tall hedges that used to be in the backyard as they'd made their way to the speakeasy's secret entrance. Which caused Josephine to wonder if the exterior basement door was now gone. *Has the door hidden in the potting area also vanished?*

She walked halfway down the length of the house and took the stairs to the potting room just below ground level. It looked much the same as it had the day she and Katherine found the speakeasy, full of broken terra-cotta, dirt, and potting tools. But there was no trace of a door. Josephine pushed her fingers through a small pile of dirt on a potting table, drew a question mark in the mess, and exhaled loudly. Though it surprised her, she'd grown to love Alma, and the thought of her great-grandmother not getting to live past tonight unleashed a swell of sorrow inside her.

How could such a stupid, heartbroken wish cause so much devastation for so many people? Josephine had only met a few of Alma's closest friends, but she knew dozens and dozens of other people cared about Alma. Alma must be impacting lives all around her, and if the world lost Alma tonight, they would lose more than Josephine could even imagine. The number of lives Alma's death would alter was staggering. Josephine couldn't even process the loss of her mama and sister and all the people who would be affected without them.

"I can't fail," she whispered to no one. "I can't."

Josephine finished her tea and returned into the house. While washing the tea dregs from her mug, she felt the urge to research the raid one more time. Why, she didn't know, because she'd already read the articles a half dozen times to glean as much information as she could, which wasn't much. There was no record of who shot Alma or why they would have used gunfire to shut down a relatively harmless speakeasy. As far as Josephine knew, the club members weren't wanted criminals, and there was no overt illegal activity happening inside. Club Belle Âme wasn't a haven for gangsters or gamblers. *Why would someone need to wield a gun and then fire it at people, whether they were running away or not?*

Josephine grabbed her laptop and sat in the only remaining piece of furniture in the sparse living room, an uncomfortable armchair in need of firmer padding in the seat cushion. She typed her keywords into the search bar and hit Enter. Many of the same previously read articles populated the search. But her eyes landed on a piece of information she'd never seen. A time stamp. Josephine clicked open the article and scanned it, then read out loud.

"At 11:22 p.m. on the night of October 9, officials raided the Carter Mansion after receiving a tip regarding illicit activities." The rest of the article read the same—Alma was shot fleeing the scene and died before arriving at the hospital.

Josephine sat back in the chair and stared at the screen. Now she had a precise time. Now she knew exactly when she would have to alter the future. *Can I put my faith in the hope that the time will remain the same, that the past won't shift again?* All she could do was trust she was meant to find this information today because it was crucial to her success. Whatever plan Josephine came up with, she needed to implement it *before* 11:22 p.m.

It was time to get ready to return to 1927 so she could help Alma prep food for Sara's party. Josephine put away her laptop while this bonus information zinged through her like a jolt of electricity on a loop. She changed into an era-appropriate blouse and skirt set. When she applied makeup, she wished she could share a laugh with her sister about how women in the '20s wore makeup to drink coffee. She was currently putting on makeup to make finger sandwiches. Katherine would find that both ridiculous and hilarious. An ache for her sister constricted her heart, but Josephine assured herself she'd make everything right again.

She packed a small leather travel bag with clothes and accessories for the party, and she grabbed her dress, leaving it on the hanger. She made sure to tuck the photograph of her family into her handbag. The last thing she did was slip the long chain holding the house key around her neck. Looking down, she held the key in the palm of her hand and then pressed it against her chest, closing her eyes and tossing a prayer into the heavens.

While standing in the foyer, she glanced up at the chandelier, around at the front rooms, and then down the hallway. "Wish me luck," she said and then opened the door and stepped out onto the front porch. The previous night's storm had left behind a mess of saturated leaves that clumped together on the porch stairs and sidewalks. Fallen branches littered the street, and a few skeletons had been torn from the oak tree across the street. Their bodies were scattered around the yard, leaving behind an even more macabre scene. Her porch had fared better, but strands of hay ripped from the bales speckled the boards and tangled in the chairs. She'd clean it up later, but for now, she needed to get to Alma.

Josephine faced the front door and locked it. Her heart beat as if she'd been sprinting, so she pulled in a deep breath, but still her hand trembled, excess energy humming through her, as she unlocked the door. She spoke the password in a whisper, knocked on the front door, and then twisted the knob like she'd done half a dozen times before. But this time felt monumental, crucial, like her whole life depended on it. Because it did.

CHAPTER 18

Josephine stepped across the threshold. The force of today's time leap was intensified, and she staggered beneath its icy grip, which stiffened her muscles, making her body as rigid as a frozen sculpture. For a few seconds, Josephine couldn't inhale, and the sensation of choking shot panic through her body. Almost as suddenly, the seizing of her body decreased, and she gulped air. Without meaning to, she released her travel bag, and it thumped loudly to the floor, alerting everyone to her presence. Her fingers couldn't keep hold of the clothes hanger, and she helplessly watched her lovely dress create a scarlet puddle of fabric on the floor.

Alma popped out of the kitchen at the end of the hallway, wiping her hands on a towel. Alma's dark hair was held back by a white elastic band. A polka-dot apron covered most of her wrap dress. Hattie followed right behind Alma. Josephine caught a glance of Hattie's downturned mouth before her vision blurred. Church bells rang in the distance, a slow, steady cadence ringing through the chilly morning.

"I knocked," Josephine croaked. When she straightened after bending down to retrieve her belongings, her body moved in jerky motions, and she nearly tumbled to the floor.

The rush of feet sounded down the hallway, and then Alma was at Josephine's side, gripping her by the elbow and standing her upright. "Darling, are you okay? What's wrong?"

Josephine placed her hand against her forehead and blinked a few times. The coolness of her fingertips instantly lowered the heat flushing her skin. Josephine's vision cleared, and Alma came into clear focus with her large, dark eyes wide with concern. "I'm all right," she said, placing her hand over Alma's for a moment. "I must have stood up too quickly, and the blood rushed to my head."

Alma released her hold on Josephine's arm. "You sure?"

Josephine nodded, noticing smudges and stains on Alma's apron. Someone had stitched Alma's name at the top left of the bib. "I'm sorry to worry you. It happens sometimes."

"Mama has the same thing happen when she's been sitting too long," Hattie said. "She stands up and tips over like a reed in the wind."

Josephine bent over to grab her handbag. She wanted to see if the photograph had crossed the threshold with her, but she couldn't in front of Alma and Hattie.

Alma picked up her dress. "This is gorgeous," Alma gushed. "Won't you be a doll tonight!" Then her voice regained a serious tone. "Are you quite sure you're okay?"

"I'm already feeling better," Josephine said, which was a half truth. A tinge of terror spiraled through her, causing her pulse to leap. *Was the time jumping worse because I'm nearing the end of my ability to move between the timelines?* Tension stiffened her chest, and she wanted to rub it away but feared Alma's worry might increase. "Where can I put my things?"

Hattie reached out her hand for Josephine's bags. "I'll take them." Josephine hesitated. She couldn't check the photograph if

Hattie took the bags, but how could she say no? She passed her bags to Hattie. Alma handed Hattie the dress. "Best you get back to the kitchen and show Josephine what we're doing. We need to keep moving if we plan on finishing before the party."

Alma waved her hand through the air in a dismissive motion and smiled at Hattie, who started up the staircase. "We'll be done in plenty of time."

"Not if we're standing around fainting in the foyer," Hattie said without looking back at them.

"I didn't faint," Josephine mumbled.

Alma hooked her arm through Josephine's and led her up the hallway. "Of course you didn't," she said, her voice regaining its usual lightness. "Now, tell me, how are you with canapés?"

Josephine couldn't help but smile at Alma. "I'm good with eating them."

Alma's laugh sent happiness flowing all around them, and Josephine wished she could be embraced by this joy forever.

•••

AROUND LUNCHTIME, TRAYS of cheese balls, deviled eggs, creamy artichoke and salmon sandwiches, cucumber canapés, and sliced meats and cheeses were put into the icebox. Josephine noticed peeled pink shrimp already inside the icebox when Hattie opened the door to find room for their prepared food. On the dining room table, a mix of pewter and porcelain trays were arranged with crackers, baguette slices, shortbread cookies, and mini buttermilk biscuits. There were bowls of cocktail sauce, creamy dips, and mixed roasted nuts.

"What's next?" Josephine asked, surveying the assortment of offerings they'd assembled in the last couple of hours.

"I'll make sweet tea and lemonade," Hattie said, standing in the dining room doorway. "But how about I make lunch first? You ladies hungry?" Someone knocked on the front door, and Hattie's head turned in that direction. "You expecting company?"

Alma shook her head. "No one other than Josephine this morning," she answered. She pressed her hands together and bounced once on her toes. "But I do love a surprise visit."

Hattie moved around Alma so she could answer the door. "Heaven knows we get all kinds of people walking up in here like this is their place." She looked pointedly at Josephine.

Josephine wouldn't be walking into 1927 for much longer. The sting of truth drooped her shoulders before she could stop it. Spending time with Alma was wonderful but also wrapped loosely with a ribbon of gloom. Josephine wanted to stretch these days out until the timeline snapped apart. *In a few more hours, everything will change.*

Hattie opened the front door, and male voices boomed greetings into the foyer. Alma made a noise of glee and hurried out of the room saying, "That's my Louis." Josephine followed Alma out of the dining room, watching Alma skip up the hallway like a little girl. "This is unexpected but a real pleasure. Whatever are you doing here?" she asked Louis.

"Good day, Hattie," Louis said, and Hattie returned the greeting. "We wanted to drop off a few things for tonight's party. I hope that's okay."

Josephine might never get used to the way men dressed so formally in the 1920s. Louis wore a beige windowpane suit with an off-white button-up shirt beneath his jacket. His high-shine dark brown shoes reflected the midday sunlight streaming in through the open door. Lemony light sharpened the edges of the outdoors, outlining the day in brightness. Louis shifted the box in his arm, removed his boater hat, and propped the hat on top of the box. Then he reached for Alma with his other hand. She wound her arms around his waist as he tugged her against him in a hug. He looked as pleased to see her as she was to see him.

Standing just behind Louis was Danny, his arms full of bags and boxes. Josephine's heart performed a quick *rat-a-tat-tat* in her chest and turned her insides to jelly. She wanted to scold herself to pull it together, but then she thought . . . *why? Why not enjoy every second of his handsome face?* His dark-eyed gaze met hers, and Josephine swayed where she stood, remembering the moment when she'd *known* she was falling hard for Nathan. It felt almost exactly how she did now. Like her body was transforming into air. She'd never have believed anyone could form an actual crush so quickly, especially not her. With Nathan it had taken her weeks to relent to his steady pursuit of her. But when Danny smiled at her, Josephine's body was propelled as if by an invisible current.

"Good morning," Danny said to Josephine and then glanced toward Alma. "A few things Sara asked me to bring and some gifts from the family."

"Of course, of course," Alma said, motioning for Louis and Danny to come inside. "We've just finished preparing the food for the party and were discussing lunch. Would you like to join us?" Alma stood in the doorway gazing out into the front yard; then she closed the door and whirled around. "I have a swell idea! Why don't you stay for lunch—you will, won't you?—and let's dine outside in the backyard. It's a gorgeous day."

Louis chuckled. "What if I told you I had plans?"

Alma pressed a hand to his chest and grinned at him. "I'd ask you to please change them and have lunch with me first." She looked at Danny. "You too."

Danny nodded once. "It would be my pleasure."

"Here, let me help you," Josephine said, reaching for some of the items in his arms. "Where should we put these?"

"Presents we'll leave upstairs," Alma said. "What else have you got there?" She rooted through the box in Josephine's arms. "Party decorations! Yes, let's put those downstairs. We'll decorate later this afternoon. Hattie, would you prepare lunch for us? Let's use the leftovers from our food prep this morning. Sandwiches, fruit, and light hors d'oeuvres. After you drop those off downstairs, Danny, you and Louis can help set up the table and chairs outside."

"Yes, ma'am," Danny said. "Louis, you can leave that box upstairs. Those are gifts, and, Alma, there are hostess gifts for you."

"That wasn't necessary," Alma said, "but Sara is such a dear to be so gracious."

Hattie walked toward the kitchen, and Josephine followed her with Danny close behind. They left Alma and Louis in the foyer, discussing what they'd both been doing this morning. While Josephine and Danny walked up the hallway, he said, "It's good to see you."

She tossed a glance at him over her shoulder and slowed her pace. "It's good to see you too." And she meant it. She wanted to imprint in her mind the way her body vibrated with pleasure at the nearness of him. "A swell surprise, as Alma likes to say."

In the kitchen, Hattie opened the basement door for them and flipped on the light. Josephine made her way down the stairs and placed her box on a nearby shelf so she could unlock and open the speakeasy door. Danny thanked her and walked into the club, where he unloaded the bags and boxes on the bar top. Josephine put her box beside the others. He sorted through what to leave and what to bring back upstairs.

Josephine's gaze landed on a few boxes full of liquor bottles stowed behind the bar. *This must be from Cecil's delivery yesterday.* Her mind quickly wondered what might happen if she poured out the booze. *Would they immediately suspect me?* She glanced toward the bathrooms. *Could I pour enough of it down the toilets to cause the party to end early? If they ran out of liquor, would people go home?*

Danny separated presents from party decorations. "Do you mind filling that bag with the gifts that go upstairs?"

Josephine's mental plan paused. She started filling a bag with the gifts so they could be carried back upstairs. *How can I get Danny to go upstairs without me?*

"That's everything," he said, glancing one last time at the items. "Sara is thrilled about this party. She talks about it every time I see her. It might be the only thing she's been thinking about for days, weeks even."

Josephine could relate. Thoughts of the party, the raid, and saving Alma consumed her, creating a perpetual tension in her body. "It's a special day," she said, aware of the layers of meaning in an innocuous statement.

Danny stepped toward her, and when Josephine understood the expression on his face, her breath hitched. His fingers found hers. "I can't stop thinking about you, Josephine."

"Me too," she said and then shook her head. "I mean, I've been thinking about *you*. Not me thinking about me."

Danny laughed and slipped his arm around her waist, pulling her against him. "You bring me happiness. I hope I do the same for you."

She nodded without speaking, and then Danny's lips were against hers, kissing her, making her forget anything but the two of them. Tension eased from her body as his touch electrified her every nerve. Kissing Danny was like jumping off a cliff and realizing she had wings. Heart-stopping and then exhilarating.

"Hey!" a voice called from the top of the other room. "Are you two coming back upstairs?"

Danny reluctantly pulled away and pressed his forehead against Josephine's while he calmed his breath. Then he moved his face from hers and shouted, "Be right there!" Before releasing Josephine, he kissed her quickly on the lips.

Her breath shuddered, and she knew she could kiss Danny for the rest of her life—even as she knew she couldn't.

"You okay?" he asked, touching her cheek.

Josephine closed her eyes at the ache of unwanted tears. "Breathless," she whispered. When she felt certain she wouldn't cry, she opened her eyes and looked up at him.

Danny smiled and straightened his suit. Then he grabbed the bag of gifts off the bar. "We'd better return or Alma will send Louis to get us."

Josephine nodded but didn't take Danny's offered hand. "I need to . . . powder my nose. I'll be right up."

Danny nodded his understanding and walked out of the speakeasy, leaving the door to the basement open for her. Josephine made a show of walking toward the bathrooms, but she listened to the sound of Danny's feet on the stairs, waiting for the opening and closing of the kitchen door. When she was sure she was alone, she hurried back to the boxes of liquor behind the bar.

How much time will I have before someone comes looking for me? Josephine grabbed two bottles and ran to the bathroom. She closed the doors behind her and unscrewed the bottles as quickly as she could. Then she poured them out into the toilet, her heart pounding frantically in her chest. She flushed the toilet, watching the amber liquid swirl away down the pipes. *What about the bottles?* Maybe she could bury them in the bottom of the trash can behind the bar.

Josephine walked out of the bathroom area, holding the empty bottles, and found Hattie standing behind the bar, looking at her. Josephine stopped immediately, her brain leaping forward with any excuse for what she was doing.

"I just found these in the bathroom!" Josephine said, pitching her voice high with forced shock. "Do you think someone brought extra booze into the club? Is that allowed?" Her heart pounded so hard that Josephine felt an explosion of heat in her chest, pushing its way up her neck and into her cheeks.

Hattie frowned but then shrugged. "People do all sorts of things. I wouldn't be half surprised if they bring in their own juice." She pointed toward a place behind the bar. "Toss them in there."

Hattie grabbed a shaker from behind the bar while Josephine tossed the liquor bottles into the trash bin. She hoped Hattie couldn't see the way her body trembled. Josephine glanced at the nearly full boxes of liquor for Sara's party. There was no way she'd be able to sneak back down to the speakeasy alone to finish her plan. *With all of that booze, no one will leave the party early tonight because of an alcohol shortage.*

They locked up the speakeasy and made their way up the stairs and into the kitchen, where Hattie had pulled together a buffet-style lunch. Hattie left the shaker on the counter, mentioning to Louis where he could find it. With Alma's direction, Louis and Danny set up a wooden outdoor table beneath the sugar maple tree in the backyard. Its gorgeous fall leaves ranged in color from brilliant yellow to burnt orange. The table had enough room for six people to dine. They invited Hattie to join them, but she assured them she would rather stay inside and continue preparing for the party.

Josephine stood near the kitchen windows and watched them setting up as her pulse slowly calmed. She'd nearly been caught pouring out the alcohol. *What would Hattie have done if she'd been the one to catch me? She might have ruined everything.*

Josephine excused herself to wash up before lunch. While away from the group, she slipped the chain and front-door key from around her neck and tucked it into her handbag upstairs. She could walk out the house doors and not be transported back to modern day as long as she didn't have the key. While dropping the key inside her bag, she checked for the photo she'd brought. Josephine exhaled a sigh of relief and eased the photograph out of her bag. There was a smudge at the corner where the photo image was rubbed away. *It must have been damaged in my purse, but most of the photo still looks untouched.* She studied the family smiling back at her. Seeing Alma as a woman in her eighties bolstered Josephine's courage that a future for Alma was possible. She returned the photo to her handbag and hurried downstairs to join the others.

Outside, the table fell into a large pool of shade offered by the maple as the sun traveled high in the sky. A white cloth draped the table, and an etched glass vase of freshly cut pink roses sat in the center. Platters of food filled the middle of the table, and place settings of everyday china, silver utensils, and glasses created a fancier affair than Josephine had anticipated for outdoor dining. At the parties she and Nathan hosted at their house, she used melamine dishes only. After years of people accidentally breaking dishes and glasses, she no longer needed to impress anyone with a place setting. But today's table was a lovely, special occasion for Josephine: her first and last outdoor picnic-type lunch with Alma, Louis, and Danny.

Josephine borrowed a lightweight shawl from Alma to ward off the slight chill in the air. Fallen leaves carpeted the ground and crunched beneath their shoes as they gathered around the outdoor dining area. They sat at the table, Louis and Alma on one side, and Danny and Josephine on the other. Just as they started filling their plates, Louis said, "I've nearly forgotten! I have a surprise for you, dear. Danny, you remember *the thing* I put in one of those boxes?" He moved back his chair and stood. "Excuse me for a moment."

"Sounds mysterious," Alma said playfully as she used a pair of mini tongs to place a tea sandwich on her plate.

Danny nodded. "I'll need to go with you. It'll take you too long to find it among all the other things Sara sent. I think I know what box I put it in." He placed his napkin beside his plate and stood. "Please excuse us, ladies."

Josephine reached for a few slices of apple and lined them up on the edge of her plate. She added a mini buttermilk biscuit to her plate and separated the top and the bottom to create a place for her to add toppings. When the men disappeared inside, Alma lifted her glass of lemonade. "Here's to us," she said, smiling across the table at Josephine.

Josephine lifted her glass, which caught a ray of sunlight that glinted off the rim. "To us." After taking a sip, she said, "Thank you, Alma. For all of this. For including me in your life, for letting me take part and enjoy your company." Her throat tightened, forcing her to stop talking.

"Darling," Alma said, reaching across the table for Josephine's hand. Josephine met her halfway and joined their hands. "You are so very welcome, but you should know, I have adored every moment. I think Danny would say the same." Alma winked at Josephine.

Her body loosened for a moment when she released a quiet laugh. "I really like him."

Alma sighed dreamily. "I remember when Louis and I first met. I tried to push him away in the beginning because I was nervous, but once I let myself *enjoy* him, then we bloomed like a rosebud opening, slow and glorious. I look forward to spending my life with him."

Josephine's smile wavered at thoughts of the future. "You think you'll get married?"

"Oh, yes, I *know* we will," she said. "I'd also like to . . . to have children if we can. I do want a family."

Josephine's heart quivered. She desperately wanted Alma to have the future she dreamed of. Not only because Alma's future secured Josephine's, but because Alma *deserved* the magnificent life waiting for her. The life that existed before Josephine altered it. Guilt slithered into Josephine, whispering that this was all her fault. *If I hadn't been so careless, there would be no chance of Alma's life meeting a tragic end. But I'll fix everything. I'll ensure Alma has a future.*

"Whatever are you thinking about, darling?" Alma asked before taking a bite of smoked salmon on a cracker. "You look fretful."

Josephine laughed away her worry and rubbed the spot between her eyes. "Sometimes my mind takes off without my permission and frets about the future."

Alma's expression revealed her understanding and her compassion. "It will all work out just as it should. You'll see."

"I hope you're right," Josephine said.

"Darling, I *know* I am."

Danny and Louis emerged from the house and rejoined them at the table. "For you, dear," Louis said, placing a curious contraption on the table in front of Alma.

Alma wiped her hands on her napkin and then picked up the vertical, leather-covered wooden box. There were two dials on the front and a lens, along with a thin metal handle coming out of one end.

"A camera?" Alma said with wide eyes.

"An Ansco Memo," Louis confirmed. "First of its kind, and I've already loaded it with film."

Alma moved back from the table and slid out of her chair. "I love it! Let's take a picture!"

Danny reached for the camera so he could take a photo of Louis and Alma. "Stay in the shade. The guy we bought this from said harsh sunlight produces a poor photograph."

Alma latched onto Louis's arm and leaned into him, smiling at Danny. Danny counted to three and snapped the picture with a soft click. Alma motioned for Josephine. "Come get in one with me."

Josephine balked. *I can't be photographed in 1927, can I? What will happen to the photo? Will I disrupt the timeline if I'm captured here?* "I don't photograph well," she said, hoping to change Alma's mind.

"Horsefeathers!" Alma said. "Do this for me, please."

Louis was right. No one could say no to Alma. Not easily. Josephine awkwardly pushed back from the table as one chair leg sank into the ground and wobbled sideways. Danny was at her side in a moment, offering his steady hand. She thanked him and walked over to Alma. Louis moved out of the picture, and Alma grabbed Josephine's hand.

"Thank you," Alma said. "I don't ever want to forget this moment, when the four of us are having the time of our lives and happy, and now we'll always have something to remember it."

Josephine looked over at Alma and felt a surge of admiration and love for this woman. "I know I'll never forget it."

"Look at the camera, you two," Danny called and then counted down to one. After he snapped the photo, Alma rushed over and took the camera, saying Danny needed to stand next to Josephine.

It was too late to stop what was happening. Josephine had already been photographed with Alma. *How can I say no to being in one with Danny?* If only she could take these pictures with her when she left, but they'd be trapped in a roll of film until the entire roll was used and developed. Josephine wondered what the developer might find. *Will he see two people standing together on a beautiful day? Or will he find one person photographed alone?*

Danny's hand in hers abruptly stopped her questioning thoughts. "I don't smile in photographs," he said.

Most men didn't, even in Josephine's modern times. "You should," she said. "You have a great smile."

Danny squeezed her hand. "You make it easy."

Click. "That's going to be a favorite!" Alma said, having snapped a photo of them looking at each other. "Now look at me!"

Josephine and Danny obeyed Alma, and even though she couldn't tell if Danny was smiling, she grinned happily at the camera, shoving down any thoughts that pulled her out of this moment standing close to Danny and looking at her beautiful new friend and one-day great-grandmother. In this moment, life was both complicated and achingly exquisite.

CHAPTER 19

About a half hour before the start of the party, Josephine emerged from a guest room wearing an elegant beaded and sequined scarlet dress that hugged her body, stopping at her knees. This was her favorite dress among the ones she'd bought, with its V-neck design in both the front and back, the stunning silver-sequined peacock pattern stretching across the bodice, and its irregular slant of tassels that started at one hip and swooped downward diagonally. She wore a headband adorned with a small peacock feather on one side and ruby stud earrings.

Hearing voices and music coming from downstairs, Josephine slowly walked down the stairs, her heels quietly clicking against each step. She soaked up the surroundings—the band playing on the radio, the scent of lemon and wood polish, the chandelier bulbs casting dazzling light in the foyer. She wanted to always remember the Carter Mansion as it was when Alma lived in it. Swing music flowed out of the parlor, and laughter carried down the hallway. The atmosphere *felt* like a party, charged with excitement and enthusiasm, the awareness that something grand approached. Josephine paused on the bottom stair with her hand resting on the glossy finial post that hadn't yet been worn down by a thousand touches. She gazed at the front door. Outside, the sun had set, and the darkened windows reflected the lights inside the house. How grateful she was for this second chance. How hopeful she was that she could make a difference tonight.

"Josephine," a male voice said from the foyer. Danny wore a three-piece black pinstriped suit with a white shirt and black tie. He looked at her as though enchanted. "You are breathtaking."

She walked to him. Long ago she'd heard mention that once you stopped looking for love, it would find you. That couldn't be truer with Danny. Her resurrected heart was the last thing she expected to encounter in 1927. Yet here she was, gazing up at a handsome man who looked at her with adoration and wonder and an undercurrent of desire.

"That dress," he said, still staring at her with his mouth slightly agape.

An unexpected burst of playfulness overtook Josephine, and she twisted her hips right and left, causing the scarlet fringe to wiggle and wave. Danny's raised eyebrows brought laughter up her throat. She boldly placed her hand on his chest. "You look incredibly handsome."

Danny leaned over and kissed her cheek. "Thank you, and forgive me ahead of time if I can't take my eyes off you tonight."

"Josephine!" Alma's voice called out from behind them as she walked up the hallway in a beaded silver dress that glittered as if woven of starlight. "Just when I think you can't possibly be more beautiful! That color is divine, darling!" Alma embraced Josephine in a hug and then stood back to admire her.

Alma complemented her dress with a long strand of pearls that she'd coiled around her neck a few times, creating multiple loops. Her dark eyeliner traced her doe eyes, and plum lipstick accentuated her full lips. Three pearl bracelets on one wrist clacked together every time she moved her arm. She grabbed Josephine's hand and spun her in a low circle.

"Thank you, Alma," Josephine said. "You look as bright and lovely as the moon."

Alma's smile stretched across her face. "It takes real beauty to *see* beauty. Isn't she gorgeous, Danny? Aren't you a lucky cat?"

"Luckiest one in town," Danny agreed. "With the exception of Louis, of course."

Alma laughed and gave Danny's arm a playful pat. "Always the gentleman."

The grandfather clock in the hallway chimed the half hour, and Josephine clasped her hands together, the chimes grounding her. She wasn't only attending a party. She was also trying to mend time. "How can I help? Anything you need me to do for the party?"

Alma shook her head. "You've already done enough."

"But I was supposed to help out with serving," Josephine said, reminding Alma of their earlier arrangement.

Alma waved her hand through the air. "I've hired someone else. You, dear Josephine, are an invited guest now. So you must come down and see the decorations. Hattie and Cecil have been down there for the past hour, and I had a peek. Sara is going to think it's the cat's pajamas!" Alma started down the hallway, and Josephine and Danny followed.

Danny grabbed Josephine's hand and entwined his fingers with hers. Josephine glanced down at their joined hands. An ache started in her stomach, whispering that in a few hours Danny's warmth would be gone. *But not now*, she argued with the discomfort trying to spread through her. Now she was still with Danny, and Alma was still joyful and unaware of the coming raid. Josephine refused to let the inescapable future spoil these moments with the people she cared so much for.

The transformation of the speakeasy into a birthday party was remarkable. White, red, and black streamers swagged from nearly everywhere—from corners, across lights, around hanging frames, along the front of the bar, and across the shelves behind the bar. White balloons scattered across the floor like fallen clouds, and as they walked through them, balloons lifted and bounced, creating momentary pathways before falling back onto the concrete floor. A *Happy Birthday* banner draped across one wall, and the band was setting up on the dais. Vases with a mix of white daisies and red roses adorned every table, and the end of the bar was a depository for wrapped presents.

The separate seating area had been rearranged as a buffet station, and the food they'd prepared earlier now filled a few tables. A pineapple upside-down birthday cake had been placed on one end of a table, with candles pressed into the centers of the caramelized pineapple slices.

Cecil and Hattie emerged through the door at the back of the room, both carrying boxes of bottles that clinked when they walked.

"Last shipment," Cecil said. Balloons bounded out of his way as he walked toward the bar.

"It looks amazing," Josephine said. "I couldn't even have imagined this."

"Hattie has a way of making everything lovelier," Alma said.

"Everything," Cecil agreed as he tossed a look at Hattie and then placed his box on the bar. He took the other box out of Hattie's hands, and she smiled at him before looking at Alma.

"Anything else you need from me down here?" Hattie asked.

Alma made a shooing motion with her hands. "Thank you for everything. Now go get ready because I fully expect you to join in this party."

"Yes, ma'am," Hattie said with a quick smile before disappearing through the basement door.

Cecil started unloading the boxes of bottles and finding space for them on the shelves or in the cubbies behind the bar. Even if Josephine had poured out more bottles earlier, this extra shipment of alcohol would have covered the party tonight.

"Robbie will be here shortly," Cecil said. "He has the list of invitees and knows what to say to anyone who tries to squeeze in who isn't on the list. We have about half an hour before they start arriving."

"Thanks, Cecil," Alma said. "What would I do without you?"

"Hopefully not bartend," he joked. "You can do a lot of things, but mixing drinks isn't one of them."

Alma laughed. "Too true." She spun in a full circle, taking in the decorations again and clasping her hands at her chest. "Isn't this swell? It's going to be a memorable night. I can *feel* it."

Josephine's stomach somersaulted. "It sure is," she said softly.

●●●

BY NINE THIRTY p.m. the club was practically bursting with revelry. The voices of about fifty people filled the rooms, and the band had been playing nonstop since seven. Couples danced, swinging each other around the floor, then pressed their bodies close together when the rhythm slowed. Partyers hooted their pleasure and shouted boisterously across the room at one another. Balloons drifted around the bodies and bounced off tables and walls. People volleyed them across the room, seeing how long they could keep them aloft.

Sara, dressed in a tight black dress covered in fringe, wore a bejeweled tiara someone had brought for the birthday girl. Sara knew the gems weren't real, but she modeled the gift as if it were on loan from the British collection of Crown Jewels. Her face alight with a perpetual smile, Sara appeared delighted by the attention and celebration of her birthday.

Josephine had been helping Alma and Hattie replenish the food trays as needed and mingled with the partygoers, making sure everyone was satisfied, grabbing drinks when asked. Danny stayed close to Josephine and tried to get her to dance a few times, but she'd stayed focused on helping Alma and keeping track of the time.

Alma stepped onto the dais and borrowed the bandleader's microphone. "Excuse me, everyone! Thank you so much for coming out and celebrating our beautiful friend and sister, Sara. We couldn't be more grateful for you! Now if you'll please make your way into the other room"—she pointed toward where they'd set up the food—"let's light the birthday candles and cut the cake!" She covered the microphone with one hand, but her muffled voice carried through the speakers. "Take a fifteen-minute break. Get yourselves a drink. Sound good?" The band members nodded and smiled gratefully.

People shuffled toward the room in a mass of bodies and squeezed around the space to make room for as many people as they could. People spilled out the doorway, and Josephine lingered on the fringes. Someone pressed in beside her, and she gazed up at Danny.

"You promised me a dance," he said, leaning over to whisper in her ear.

Inside the room, Josephine heard Alma's voice and then Sara's. She couldn't see the cake, but it sounded like they were lighting candles.

"I did," Josephine agreed. She lifted his arm and looked at his wristwatch. *Nine forty-five p.m. I have time for a dance or two.* "After they cut the cake?"

Danny nodded and the room started singing "Happy Birthday." Josephine and Danny joined in, and his warm baritone surprised her. When they were done singing, a cheer rose from the crowd joined by applause. People started moving out of the room and spreading back out into the club.

"You have a nice singing voice, Danny," Josephine said. "You could have had a career as a singer."

Danny laughed. "The life of a musician wouldn't have suited me, and"—he slipped one arm around her waist—"I might not have been here to meet you."

Josephine's insides melted, and she pressed her cheek against his chest, holding him close for a few moments.

A man's garbled voice pulled Josephine's attention. She turned her head to see a dark-haired woman with heavy makeup and a gold flapper dress standing beside a slender man. His suit jacket was unbuttoned and flapping open to reveal a leather gun holster strapped over both shoulders. One of the holsters held a gun.

"Lower your voice, Tommy," the girl hissed. "We're here to have fun, not have you stirring up trouble."

Tommy puffed out his chest in an almost comical way. "I'm not afraid of trouble."

Josephine's eyes widened, but Danny caught her gaze and shook his head. He stepped them a few feet away just as Tommy buttoned up his suit, hiding his gun from view.

Danny quieted his voice so only Josephine could hear. "Tommy is a showoff. All talk, if you know the type."

Josephine's heartbeat pounded inside her chest. "But he has a gun." Panic surged through her, and in her mind, she could hear the ticking of a clock.

"Hey," Danny said, touching her arm, "it's okay. I wouldn't say Tommy is harmless, but he's not going to use that thing tonight."

"How can you be sure?" Josephine said, watching Tommy and his date push through the crowd toward the food table. The need to be near Alma intensified. "Let me make sure Alma and Hattie don't need help with the cake, but once the band starts up again, I promise we'll dance."

People were already eating slivers of cake served on party plates. Hattie sliced the cake, and Alma helped pass out plates to those who were waiting. Josephine walked over to Sara and touched her arm.

Sara turned her glassy gaze toward Josephine. "Swell party, isn't it?" She forked a bit of cake into her mouth. "My favorite," she said as she covered her mouth to chew.

"Happy birthday, Sara," Josephine said. She wanted to add, *I hope you still think it's a swell party after what happens soon,* but she didn't. Even thinking about the imminent raid tautened every muscle in Josephine's body. She had to stay focused, so she tried not to allow thoughts of Tommy's gun to run rampant.

Josephine walked to where they were serving the last pieces of cake, and Hattie handed Josephine a slice. "Oh, no thank you," Josephine said. Her uneasy stomach didn't want food in it.

"That's not for you," Hattie said with a smirk. "Take that to Cecil . . . please," she added, looking as though saying the words pinched her face.

Josephine shook her head. "Your sincerity is overwhelming." Alma snorted a laugh, which caused Hattie to chuckle.

Josephine moved around the people on the dance floor who waited for the band to resume. She slid the party plate onto the bar and called Cecil's name. He walked to her while tossing a shaker back and forth over his shoulders. "Cake from Hattie."

He lowered the shaker to the bar top and grinned at the plate. "She's a real doll."

"That's one way to describe her," Josephine said before turning her back on Cecil and scanning the room.

The band was gathering back on the dais, and the crowded room swelled with pleasure. The moment felt like an out-of-body experience, her watching and knowing in a short time a raid of men would rush in and throw this celebration into chaos. Josephine had been unable to stop the party, and seeing everyone's happiness, a part of her was thankful for her failure. But she still had a chance to change the ending of this night.

She thought of the photograph in her purse upstairs and the hidden compartment in the living room floor. Telling Alma the truth was now her only option, but at least she had proof to support her outlandish story. She could let the party go on for a little longer, and then she'd do her best to convince Alma to make everyone vacate the house. If the bureau men raided at 11:22, they'd find the speakeasy empty. There was no way to hide evidence of an illegal bar, but at least the partygoers would be safe.

Danny walked through the crowd, parting people and balloons, and moved straight toward Josephine leaning against the bar. She pushed away from the bar's edge and met him on the dance floor just as the band started playing again. The tempo required fast feet and swinging hips. Josephine had been watching the dancers and studying some of their moves and thought she might be able to twirl around the floor in a similar manner without crushing Danny's feet.

"As long as you lead, we should be fine," she said, stepping toward him and holding open her arms.

"As long as you're with me, I'll lead us anywhere," he said, and Josephine closed her eyes and smiled. *Where did he come up with these lines? It's like he's read a manual on how to properly woo a woman. Who wouldn't fall hard for Danny Stewart?*

Danny moved her around the floor, and by the time the song was over, Josephine's cheeks were sore from nonstop smiling, and frantic thoughts had been pushed to the back of her mind. They danced through three more songs back-to-back before Danny insisted he needed a rest. Perspiration dotted Josephine's forehead, and she grabbed a napkin off the bar and blotted her face before using the flimsy paper as a makeshift fan. Danny ordered drinks, and she found an empty table in the corner. Danny removed his suit jacket and hung it on the back of a chair. Cecil waved at them from the bar, and Danny retrieved their drinks.

"Water," he said, placing the heavy glass of water down in front of her. The water sloshed from side to side with the movement, catching wavering dots of light on its surface. "Cecil wanted me to pass along that he's *never* served water from the faucet to anyone in the club as long as it's been open."

Josephine laughed as Danny sipped his Old Fashioned slowly. "Thank you," she said. "Hydration is important." Danny chuckled and leaned back in the chair, stretching his long legs out in front of him. "It's been a great party. I'm so glad I'm here," she said. Even with the impending raid that brought anxiety, these last few days with Alma, Danny, and the others had been life-changing.

He sat up and scooted his chair closer to hers, their knees touching beneath the table. "I haven't had this much fun in ages.

In fact, days of fun seemed gone years ago, and I hadn't expected them to return."

Danny's wife had been gone since 1918, almost ten years ago. "Did you not want to remarry? Not to be presumptuous, but most men would have already found a new wife." Even in modern times, it was rare for a widower to stay single unless he truly wanted to be.

Danny took another sip of his drink, allowing moments of silence to pass between them while the party raged on. "I thought about it, but not as often as people assume. I had a wife, and I loved her. For all the women who came around after Margaret, none of them caused me to wish for marriage again. I stopped believing I'd have that desire again. Until you."

Josephine recognized that look in Danny's eyes, the one that spoke of yearning. When his hand clasped hers and he leaned closer, she welcomed him, closing her eyes and waiting for the feel of his lips against hers. She didn't wait long. Danny's kisses swept her away to a place where her rush of thoughts turned wispy and then disappeared. She'd never kissed anyone in a bar in front of dozens of strangers, until she met Danny. Maybe she felt freer in a time not her own, or maybe Danny and his kiss made her believe nothing else mattered outside of the space they occupied right now.

When he stopped kissing her, she wanted to pull him back again, but he held out his hands and pulled her to stand. "I want to dance with you," he said. "And feel you close."

Josephine reached for his wristwatch to check the time. Ten fifteen. She wanted to talk to Alma by 10:45 because it might take some time to convince Alma and then more time to herd everyone out of the speakeasy before 11:22.

"Got somewhere else to be?" Danny asked teasingly.

"Not yet," she answered and followed him onto the dance floor. Josephine gave herself permission to dance with Danny for another half hour before she disrupted their lives forever.

●●●

BETWEEN DANCES, DANNY ordered another cocktail, and he brought Josephine one last Mary Pickford. She almost said no, but perhaps it would give her the courage to tell Alma the truth. Josephine finished the syrupy sweet drink too quickly. A welcome fuzziness that bent time and swirled the colors around her cushioned her thoughts while Danny spun her and then held her close again. They swayed on the dance floor among a throng of others while the band played a blues song meant for heartbreak and loneliness.

Josephine stared up at Danny, and his deep brown eyes looked as lost in the moment as hers. A body bumped into Josephine and jostled her attention. Eleanor leaned close and laughed. Anderson held Eleanor in a close embrace. "Look at you two," Eleanor said, her voice slower and lighter than usual. "What a swell pair. From strangers to lovers."

"Lovers!" Josephine blurted before she could stop herself. Heat flushed her cheeks, and the back of her neck burned. Danny's arms tensed around her body.

"Shhh!" Eleanor said, leaning close and attempting a whisper. "Your secret is safe with me. Great party, isn't it? I can't believe it's almost over."

Almost over. Josephine jolted from her love haze. She yanked at Danny's arm to check the time on his wristwatch. "It's eleven!" she nearly shouted. "How could I lose track of time?" She stumbled backward out of Danny's arms and slammed into the couple behind her. Amid their complaints and grumbling, jerking her head left and right, she searched the room for Alma, seeing nothing but a sea of unfamiliar faces. "Where's Alma? I have to find Alma."

"Josephine," Danny said, grabbing her wrist, "what's wrong?"

She pulled out of his grip. "I have to find Alma!"

"Is she plastered?" Eleanor asked.

"Josephine?" Danny asked again.

Josephine didn't answer him. She couldn't. The only thing that mattered now was finding Alma before it was too late. *Have I already failed?* Her heart slammed hard in her chest as she took off running.

CHAPTER 20

Josephine rushed off the dance floor, looking at every couple and scanning faces. She ran to the back of the club and checked everyone at the tables. The bandleader looked down at her with a questioning expression and then returned his focus to the music. The trumpet solo swelled in volume, making her head throb. Josephine entered the seating room where the food had been arranged. Now only a scattering of options and crumbs remained. People lounged around the room and had no awareness of the imminent threat. Still no Alma. Josephine checked the restrooms, knocking on the stall doors and calling Alma's name, but she wasn't there either. Josephine ran to the bar and failed to slow enough before slamming into the polished edge of the bar top. Air whooshed from her lungs on impact. She gasped and then called out to Cecil.

"Have you seen Alma?"

He shook his head. Then he held up one finger, saying, "Actually, yes. I saw her go upstairs, and I haven't seen her return."

Without thanking him, Josephine burst through the basement door, slamming it behind her, and flew up the stairs to the kitchen, shouting Alma's name as she ran through the house. She sprinted past the grandfather clock in the hallway, refusing to glance at the time and panic further. She ran through the dining room. The modest chandelier cast a halo of light onto the empty table. She rushed into the parlor, her eyes roving over the bookshelves, the sofa, the chairs near the darkened windows, but no one was there. The living room was also empty. Then she leaped up the stairs two at a time, shouting Alma's name, out of breath and wheezing, her head spinning from the alcohol and fear slamming through her veins.

After searching the upstairs bedrooms, Josephine stood at the top of the staircase sucking in air and feeling like she might either throw up or faint. Her chest squeezed so tightly she could hardly breathe. She couldn't give up now. Josephine scrambled back down the stairs and into the hallway, and that's when she noticed the back door in the kitchen was slightly ajar.

Josephine's heels slammed against the hallway runner. She flung open the back door and almost tumbled down the stairs in the dark. Her heels sank into the soft earth. Outside in the cold, she shivered in the night air. "Alma?" she called, her voice pinched and frantic. She almost shouted in relief when Alma's voice returned her call.

"Josephine? Are you quite all right, darling?" Alma emerged from the darkness and was at her side, a shadow in the chilly night. Louis materialized at Alma's side. The air around them smelled of cigarette smoke and ashes.

"No," Josephine said in a rush of breath. Her body trembled so hard that she felt Alma's hand vibrating on her arm. Her thoughts were coming too fast, rushing over her like she'd been thrown into river rapids. "You have to get out of here! Everyone has to get out of here! They're coming soon, and I wanted to tell you earlier, but I couldn't because I didn't think you'd believe me, and then I lost track of time, and we must leave now."

"Hold on a minute," Louis said, stepping in closer. "Has something happened at the party?"

"Yes, I mean, no. Not yet. But it's going to happen," Josephine said.

"I don't understand, Josephine," Alma said, her voice taking on an edge of worry.

"Government officials, they're coming. A raid. They're going to raid the speakeasy," Josephine said. Full-blown panic ricocheted through her, muddling her words.

Louis's chuckle would have been offensive if Josephine hadn't already anticipated it. "How could you possibly know that?"

"Josephine, did someone tell you this?" Alma's face turned toward Louis. "Would they do that?"

"Of course not," Louis said with surety. "The chief is one of our biggest supporters."

"It's not him," Josephine argued. And although she couldn't be sure, she added, "It might be Mark, working with the Bureau of Prohibition."

"My brother?" Danny asked. "What about him?"

Josephine whirled around to see Danny coming down the back steps followed by Eleanor. The light from the kitchen cast them both in a rectangle of yellow light that disappeared a few feet into the backyard.

"What's going on here?" Eleanor asked, her face covered in night. "Josephine, you ran out of there like your dress was on fire. What's happening?"

"It's—it's just a guess that he's leading the raid because he's angry, and he threatened you," Josephine said.

"He threatened you?" Louis asked, now a trace of concern in his voice.

"Mark's a hothead, you know that," Danny said. "What raid?"

"Tonight," Josephine said. "I know it sounds like baloney, but it's true. I swear it." She grabbed Alma's hand. "You *have* to believe me."

Danny stood rigid beside Josephine, all hints of their earlier closeness gone. "Mark wouldn't raid his own sister's party."

"Mark *does* know about the party, though," Eleanor said.

Josephine's mind began clearing as her thoughts gained traction. She could convince Alma. "I can prove it!" She tugged Alma toward the house. "Please, Alma. We have to hurry."

Thankfully, Alma hesitated for only a second before she followed Josephine into the house. Josephine nearly dragged Alma down the hallway into the living room with the rest of the group following close behind.

"Stay here," Josephine said. "I need to get something out of the bedroom upstairs." While Josephine ran out of the room, she heard Eleanor say, "Should I say what we're all thinking? Josephine's had too much to drink. She's hallucinating."

"I don't know," Alma said. "She doesn't sound drunk, and it's not like her."

Josephine flew up the stairs and carelessly ripped open her handbag. Lipstick, eyeliner, and a compact flew into the air before hitting the hardwood and scattering. The front-door key and chain bounced off the bed, and Josephine grabbed it and shoved it beneath a pillow. The photograph fluttered to the floor. She scooped it up and ran out of the room.

By the time she returned to the living room, out of breath and pulse sprinting, Louis and Danny stood near the bar cart fixing themselves a drink, while Eleanor lounged in the red velvet chair. The three of them looked as if they had all the time in the world to listen to a ridiculous story told by a possibly drunk woman. Alma was the only one pacing, her features drawn in alarm.

"Danny, what time is it?" Josephine asked.

He paused in pouring gin into a lowball, the pale yellow liquid swirling around the bottom of the glass. He lifted his wrist and checked his watch. "Eleven ten."

Josephine's stomach dropped into her feet. She held out the photograph for Alma, who took it, and then Josephine went to the edge of the living room rug just as Leo had shown her. Josephine gripped the edge of the rug, closed her eyes, and inhaled a deep breath. The next few moments were either going to save her life or end it.

"That's a picture of my family," Josephine said to Alma. She started rolling the rug toward the center of the room.

Eleanor sat up in the chair. A floral pillow fell to the floor. "What on earth are you doing, Josephine?"

Without responding, Josephine continued, "That's four generations of my family. My great-grandmother, my grandmother, my mom, and me and my sister. Look closely at the oldest woman, she's standing on the far left."

"Alma," Louis said, finally noticing what Josephine was doing. His heavy glass clinked against the bar cart's top shelf. A few more rolls of the rug, and the secret compartment was revealed. "How did you know about that?" he asked accusatorily.

"I told you this one couldn't be trusted." Hattie's voice startled them as she entered the room, pointing at Josephine. Her distinct frown exhibited her disdain.

"You're not wrong, Hattie," Josephine admitted, much to Hattie's surprise. "But not for the reasons you think. I know about this"—she knocked her knuckles against the secret lid—"Because the same one exists in my house."

Eleanor stood from the armchair. Her fair skin paled further as her forehead creased. "What are you talking about? Alma, what's going on?" Eleanor looked at Josephine. "Be square with us. You remember our deal? You promised not to lie to me or Alma again."

"Again?" Alma asked.

Eleanor motioned to the space between herself and Josephine. "We don't know each other, Alma. I'd never even met her until dinner last Thursday, but she said she needed the money for working the party, and she didn't want to tell you otherwise since you assumed I sent her to you."

"Is that true?" Alma asked.

Josephine nodded. "Yes. I'd never met Eleanor, but I wasn't here to work the party, though that's what you assumed. I needed an excuse to be with you. I *needed* to save you tonight."

Alma's face scrunched in confusion. She moved the photograph closer to her face. Then she lowered the image, and her gaze locked on Josephine's. "Half of this photograph is missing. It has something smudged all over it."

Josephine stood, leaving the secret compartment unopened. "What? No!" She took the offered photograph from Alma, and her body seized with fear. Alma was right. A black smudge smeared across more than half of the photograph, completely removing Alma, Josephine's grandmother, and her mother. The only two people left in the photograph were Josephine and Katherine. "No, something's happened to it. When I got here today, there were other people in that photo, including my great-grandmother. Alma Carter Grant."

Eleanor snorted a laugh, and Hattie laughed with her. The sarcastic sound rankled Josephine's nerves, but Alma wasn't laughing. Her wide eyes studied Josephine.

"Me? How could that be possible?" Alma whispered. "That little girl." She pointed at the photograph in Josephine's hands.

"That's you?" Josephine nodded. "She has your eyes. But it's impossible. And this photograph . . . is this real color?"

"Absolute baloney!" Eleanor said. "Alma, you can't possibly believe this. *You* can't be this woman's great-grandmother."

Eleanor's use of *this woman* stung Josephine, but she'd known there would be raging doubts. If someone told Josephine this story, she might have reacted the same before experiencing this for herself.

"She's probably been casing the house," Hattie agreed. "To steal from you!"

"Why would I show you the secret compartment so I could steal from you?" Josephine argued in frustration. "I would have already stolen whatever I wanted, and I certainly wouldn't bring you in here to reveal it." Josephine reached out to touch Alma briefly. "Please, you must believe me. I can explain later, I promise, but right now, we need to get you and everyone else out of the house by 11:22."

Louis walked to Alma's side. "Dear, perhaps it's time for Josephine to go home. It's been a long day for all of us."

"I know this sounds completely insane," Josephine said. "I get it. I would think you'd lost your mind if you were telling me this story, but look at the picture, Alma." She handed it back to Alma. "*Really look at it*. That's me, and my great-grandmother was in the photograph, too, when I got here. But time is erasing me—erasing *us*. I swear it."

Alma looked at the picture again. The color photo trembled in her hand. "Is this like *The Time Machine* by H. G. Wells?"

Eleanor laughed again. "That's a work of fiction!"

Alma glanced over at her good friend without a bit of humor in her face. "Aren't all fictional stories based on some seed of truth?

Isn't that where every story starts? What happens at 11:22?" Alma asked Josephine.

Danny had inched closer to the group, his drink forgotten on the cart. "That's in ten minutes."

Josephine swallowed and stared into Alma's eyes. "A raid happens, and you get shot. You die before you get to the hospital. If you die, I die. I swear I'm telling the truth."

"Complete foolishness," Eleanor said. She turned her back on Josephine and strode across the room.

"What have you got to lose by believing me?" Josephine pleaded.

Josephine could see Alma had started to tremble, could see Alma felt the truth of Josephine's words reverberating inside her. The two women locked eyes, and Alma mouthed, *Only everything.*

Louis stood so close to Alma that he must have sensed her fear too. "Just to be safe, let's get you out of here."

Alma nodded. "Louis, you and Danny get *everyone* out. Hurry!"

Danny's body tensed as he looked from Louis to Alma. He pulled his car keys out of his pocket and handed them to Alma. "Go to my house. Eleanor, go with them. Hattie, you too. My car is about a block up the street to the east."

Hattie harrumphed. "Are you serious? We're trusting her?"

"Get Alma out of here!" Louis shouted.

His outburst echoed through the house and shocked everyone, but Hattie stood at attention. "What about Cecil?"

"We'll get him," Danny assured her. "Louis and I will meet you at my house once everyone is gone. Go!"

Danny didn't look once at Josephine. *Is he angry or distrustful? What did I expect? That he'd be thrilled to find out his new love is either a horrible liar or a time traveler from the future? That if Alma is Josephine's great-grandmother, then he's decades older than me, too, and probably not even alive in my timeline? That is, if he even believes my story.*

But they would. They'd believe her as soon as the police showed up. Josephine couldn't concern herself with Danny's feelings. The most vital thing was to get Alma safely away from the house.

Louis kissed Alma's cheek and ran off toward the kitchen, where he'd no doubt do his best to stress the emergency to the partygoers. Danny rushed through the house, turning off every light and sending the interior into near darkness.

"Leave the doors open and unlocked," Alma shouted at him. "I don't want them breaking down my doors. Make it easy for them to find whatever they're looking for."

"But Alma," Hattie said, "when they find the club, they'll arrest you."

Alma looked in Hattie's direction even though their faces were deep in shadow. "Better arrested than dead. Now let's go."

The four women hustled out of the house, down the porch stairs, and down the sidewalk. Before they found Danny's Model T, snippets of voices could be heard. The women stopped and all turned their heads back toward the house. Dark shapes shot out from around the house, the shadows of people fleeing the speakeasy. Some ran down the sidewalks; others darted across the street into the empty land and disappeared into the overgrowth and trees. Car engines turned over, and Josephine felt a mild sense of relief knowing people were listening to Louis and Danny.

Sirens wailed in the night. Headlights lit up the shadowy street, and six black cars pulled to a stop in front of Alma's house and partially blocked the road. The car in front was illuminated by the others, revealing a cop who jumped out of the driver's seat without closing the door. He was lit up by his own headlights before disappearing into the dark.

"Run!" Eleanor screeched.

The women took off running, and then a gunshot blasted through the night, followed by another and another. Alma's scream was short but ripped a chill through Josephine. Josephine turned and saw Alma had fallen onto the sidewalk. Josephine rushed to her side, panic nearly blinding her.

"Alma!"

Alma was pushing herself up with her hands and groaning. Josephine scanned the concrete below Alma's body, looking for a dark stain that would reveal Josephine had failed.

"Oh, no, no, no, are you shot?" Josephine cried.

"No," Alma said, reaching for Josephine's hand. Josephine slowly pulled Alma to her feet. "My heel broke, and I tripped." Her torn dress revealed ripped stockings and scraped knees.

Hattie and Eleanor rushed to their side. "Alma, are you okay?" Eleanor's voice sounded thick with fear.

"I'll be fine," she said, leaning on Josephine for support.

Another gunshot echoed through the night, and the women flinched. "We have to get out of here," Josephine said.

They hurried the rest of the block to Danny's car. Eleanor opened the passenger door and Hattie climbed into the backseat. Eleanor heaved herself into the passenger seat, scooped up her dress, and closed the door. Alma opened the driver's side door. In her trembling hands, the car keys jangled and then dropped onto the pavement. Josephine bent down and retrieved them. Josephine closed her hands around Alma's.

"You can do this, Alma," Josephine said. "You can do anything. I'd offer to drive, but I have no idea how to drive this kind of car."

"I suppose you only pilot time machines?" Alma said, trying to joke, but her voice cracked, and Josephine saw a glint of wetness on her cheeks.

"Something like that," Josephine said.

Alma leaned over the front seat and slid the key into its place. She turned it slightly. Then she walked to the front of the car, and Josephine followed her.

Josephine stood with Alma facing the front fender. "What are you doing?"

"I have to pull the choke and crank it," Alma said.

Josephine stared open-mouthed at the grate on the front of the car. "You crank it from out here?"

"Your time machines have cranks on the inside?" Alma pulled at a knob on the front of the grate and then grabbed the crank hanging down in front. She rotated it once, and nothing happened. When she turned it a second time, the buzz of an engine started.

"Let's go!" Alma said.

Josephine crawled into the backseat and sat beside Hattie, who slid as far as she could from Josephine, hugging the edge.

Alma climbed into the driver's seat, adjusted the key in the opposite direction, and then moved the throttle as the engine shifted to a soft hum. With her hands on the steering wheel, Alma pushed the gas, and the car rolled forward. Another gunshot sounded over the rumble of the car's engine.

"Drive!" Eleanor demanded, and Alma obeyed. She turned the car onto the next street and drove away from the scene unfolding behind them.

After a few minutes of silence, Hattie turned her expressionless face toward Josephine and said, "You were telling the truth."

Josephine nodded without speaking.

CHAPTER 21

Josephine recognized nothing as they drove. Nashville in 1927 was an unfamiliar landscape and a dark-sky space. Danny's Model T didn't have a roaring engine like a modern-day car, so riding a short distance was slow and tense. *How far are we from the Carter Mansion? Far enough away not to arouse suspicion that we're fleeing the scene?* But no one pursued them, and after about fifteen minutes, Alma pulled up to the curb in front of a grand Craftsman-style shingle-and-stone house.

Lantern lights burned on either side of the double front door. Alma turned off the engine and pulled out the keys. The women climbed out of the car and made their way up the stone steps. Their ghostly reflection cast back to them from the windowed doors. Alma tried a few keys before finding the correct one. She pushed open the door and stepped inside, then walked to the nearest wall and switched on the foyer light. She'd either been inside Danny's house before or instinctively knew the layout.

A small, burnished metal chandelier illuminated the wide hallway. Its burnt-orange sconces cast a warm glow. The low ceilings lacked the grandeur of the two-story foyer in the Carter Mansion, but the woodwork was remarkable. Layered crown molding and one-foot-high baseboards were stained dark walnut and ran the length of every room Josephine could see. Matching wood columns defined the two front rooms off the left and right of the hallway, and in one room Josephine spotted barrister bookcases, wainscoting, and stained-glass windows.

"Let's wait in here," Alma said, walking into the sitting room. A large overstuffed cream-colored sofa and a matching love seat anchored a beige, faded blue, and cream patterned rug. Two tan, tufted wingback chairs framed a stone fireplace topped with a chunky wood mantel. A faint scent of woodsmoke lingered. Alma switched on two pewter-based lamps that sat on a credenza against the wall, and two circles of pale light barely lit the room.

"Don't you want to clean up those scrapes?" Hattie asked, looking pointedly at Alma's knees.

Alma shook her head. "I'll be fine. It only stings a little now. I'd rather wait for the men to arrive."

Eleanor flopped onto the sofa and leaned heavily against the arm. Her eyes closed when she leaned back her head. "This feels like a dream. Will I wake up tomorrow to our life as it was before this madness?"

Alma sat down beside her and patted Eleanor's leg. "I don't want to think about tomorrow. I only care that everyone will be okay tonight."

Hattie sat on the other side of Alma, and the three women passed glances at one another before looking at Josephine, who lingered in the sitting room doorway, unsure if she should sit with them or keep her distance. *This whole mess is my fault.*

"Josephine," Alma said, "come in. Sit. You look ready to bolt."

Josephine thought she'd feel completely relieved now that Alma was safe, but her insides continued to quiver, and she worried about the men. What if removing Alma from the scene had caused someone else to be shot and killed? She had heard five shots fired. Who was shooting and why? Had the bullets hit anyone? Josephine sank into one of the armchairs across from the women.

"Why don't you tell us how you knew about the raid?" Eleanor said, pursing her lips. "Did someone tip you off?"

Josephine shook her head. "I told you the truth."

Eleanor huffed. "You expect us to believe you're a time traveler?"

Alma looked at Eleanor. "You didn't see the picture. That was *her*."

"From what I heard, it was a ruined photograph," Eleanor said. "How convenient. It might have been of anyone. Why would any of us believe *you* were the missing great-grandmother? Hattie, you're mighty quiet. What's your take on this?"

Hattie folded her hands together in her lap, staring down at her tan fingers. "Something ain't right about this whole thing." Her eyes met Josephine's. "And not only because Josephine has been lying, but it's the way she *shows up* at the house, like she pops in from nowhere. Like . . ."

"Like she's traveling through time," Alma whispered. Eleanor laughed again, but Alma shushed her. "Josephine, why don't you tell us—"

The front door swung open, and male voices followed. "Alma! Eleanor!" Someone shouted. "Hattie!" No one called Josephine's name. Louis, Cecil, and Danny stepped into view and caught sight of the women, who all stood as soon as they heard voices. Alma rushed to Louis and threw her arms around him. He embraced her so tightly that her feet lifted off the floor. For once, Hattie didn't seem to care if anyone saw her affection for Cecil. He crossed the sitting room in a few strides and wrapped his arms around Hattie.

"You're okay. You're okay," Hattie whispered against Cecil's shoulder.

Danny remained in the doorway with his eyes on Josephine. He didn't move toward her, and the tiniest fracture cracked her heart.

She averted her gaze and walked toward the windows that looked out into the front yard. Her sad-eyed reflection gazed back at her.

"What happened?" Alma asked when she pulled away from Louis, brushing her hands over his chest as if to ensure he was unharmed.

"It was Mark," Danny answered. Josephine jerked her head in his direction and found he still watched her.

"No," Alma said in shock. "He wouldn't."

"He did," Danny said.

"Did you see him? Are you certain?" Alma asked.

"After we convinced everyone to leave, which was easy once we said the fuzz was coming—" Louis started.

Cecil interrupted. "I've never seen people run so fast. They nearly trampled one another trying to get out. Robbie kept it from dissolving into complete chaos. We let the band go but made them leave their instruments. I doubt the police will confiscate those. If they do, we promised we'd buy new ones."

"We heard gunshots," Eleanor said.

"Tommy Lyons," Louis said. "Fool brought a gun to the party."

Josephine caught Danny's eye, but he glanced away.

Louis continued, "He shot at the cops, and they shot back."

"It's a miracle no one was killed in the crossfire," Danny agreed.

Alma locked eyes with Josephine. "It's a miracle we all got out of there." She looked at Danny. "And Mark?"

Unhappiness pulled his features into an expression Josephine had never seen on him before. "We were already out of the house, hiding far enough away, but I heard his voice, and then I saw his face." He finally spoke to Josephine. "You were right."

Everyone turned their attention to her standing by the windows, separated from the group.

"I didn't want to be," Josephine said.

"I think I—*we*—deserve an explanation," Danny said.

Eleanor groaned. "She's only going to tell you that she's a time traveler."

"Be that as it may," Danny said, "she saved all of us from possible jail time and maybe saved Alma's life. Hear her out."

"I need a drink before we start story time," Eleanor said. "Danny, where's the hard stuff?"

●●●

JOSEPHINE STOOD IN the large open doorway to the sitting room, facing the group as though she were about to deliver a speech. Louis and Alma sat on the couch, Hattie and Cecil on the loveseat, and Eleanor yawned in an armchair. Danny stood at the fireplace, arms crossed over his chest and shoulder leaning against the mantel. Cecil had fixed drinks and surprised Josephine by offering to make her one, but she declined. With her adrenaline tanking, she didn't want to add one more thing to her crashing system.

While everyone watched her, Josephine started from the beginning, from the moment she made the errant wish. Then she took them on a journey from buying the house to searching for a new front door, leaving out details that might affect the future should she give them too much knowledge while in the past. She explained finding the door carved by Leo's dad and blessed by his mom. Alma gasped when Josephine mentioned this.

"I've never told *anyone* about the blessing," Alma said, visibly shivering. Louis wrapped one arm around her and rubbed his hand up and down her arm for warmth.

Josephine continued, telling them how Alma's belongings and evidence of Josephine's life started vanishing. She explained the front-door key, the minuscule words carved into the wood, and what happened the first time she time-leaped into 1927.

"Wait," Alma said, stopping Josephine midsentence. "There are no words carved in the door."

"There are," Josephine said. "They're carved into the left side of the window pane. They're tiny and look like scratches until you get close. Speaking the words out loud is part of what makes the door work."

"What do the words say?" Danny asked.

Josephine glanced at him and felt an ache in her stomach. She wanted to go to him, to apologize and beg him to understand, to consider forgiving her. "Among the whispering and the stars."

"Ha!" Eleanor said, her eyes fluttering open. While appearing to be dozing, she'd obviously been listening. "The password for the club?"

Alma's face pulled downward in an uncharacteristic frown. "I'd never carve the password into the door."

"Well, someone did," Josephine said. "In my day the words are there."

"In your day . . . ," Danny repeated. "And what year exactly is that?"

Josephine hesitated, feeling the intense stares of five sets of eyes on her. "Almost a century from now."

Danny's eyes widened, and Hattie inhaled sharply. They all gaped in disbelief, a mix of expressions on their faces. Some looked shocked into acceptance while other faces clouded with doubt.

"You mean to say we're a hundred years old *in your day*?" Eleanor asked with a lazy laugh.

Danny pushed off the mantel and gripped the back of his neck. "We'd be older than a hundred, Eleanor," he said, his voice stiff and unhappy. "And if any of what Josephine is saying is true, *we're* not even alive then." He walked past her without making eye contact and stood in the foyer, staring at his own front doors as if they, too, might be enchanted.

He was close enough for her to reach out and touch him, and she desperately wanted to, but Josephine pressed her hands against her body, watching him in an uneasy silence.

Finally Danny turned and addressed the group, looking past Josephine at his friends. "I suggest we all stay here for the night. We can return to Alma's tomorrow and assess what's happened. There are plenty of rooms upstairs for everyone. Take your pick." Instead of moving toward the stairs, he walked down the main hallway, turned a corner, and disappeared from view.

In the sitting room, Eleanor stood first and waved good night to everyone, stopping to kiss Alma's cheek and hug her briefly. Eleanor's whispered words were lost to Josephine, but Alma's gaze drifted toward her, making Josephine think Eleanor was talking about her. They all had plenty to say about her now. Whether they believed Josephine didn't matter anymore. She had accomplished the one thing she'd set out to do.

Hattie and Cecil stood from the loveseat, and Cecil placed his hand on the small of Hattie's back, guiding her toward the staircase. She rested one hand on the finial post and glanced up the staircase uneasily, as if deciding whether staying the night in Danny's house was a good idea, but like the others, what choice did she have? Louis passed by Josephine and politely wished her a good night. Alma was the only one who paused long enough to engage her in conversation.

Alma's hand was warm against Josephine's. The gentle touch reminded Josephine of Katherine, who often showed this kind of affection. "This is a lot to take in. A lot to believe. If I can be honest, I *want* to trust you, because it doesn't make sense for you to make up this wild story for nothing, and you did get everyone out of the house. If someone tipped you off to the raid, it still doesn't jibe for you to create this other story about time traveling. What would be the point? And then there's the strangeness of the photo and you knowing about the secret compartment in the living room." Alma paused and inhaled a slow, deep breath. She reached up to twist the pearl earring on her left earlobe. "Do you really live in my house in the future?"

Josephine nodded. "I do."

Alma's smile reappeared as quickly as it had faded. "Is it still lovely?"

"It is," Josephine said, squeezing Alma's hands. "The rosebushes need some work, but I hope to bring them back to life so they can be as beautiful as yours."

Alma shook her head, a calm sway back and forth. "It's like a dream, all of this. You're right, I might never have believed you, given more time to think about it."

"Are you coming, dear?" Louis called from the staircase.

"Be right there," she answered. "Josephine, no matter what happens next, thank you for tonight, for keeping us safe. Try to get some sleep. We'll figure everything out tomorrow." She joined Louis on the staircase, and they retreated to the second floor.

Josephine walked into the sitting room and wrapped her arms around her stomach, hugging herself for warmth and comfort and failing to feel either. *What did I think would happen? They'd throw a ticker tape parade in my honor? It was a miracle they even listened to me and vacated the mansion.* But the rejection still hurt, knowing most of them thought she was either a liar or out of her mind. Exhaustion moved swiftly through her limbs and an ache throbbed at her temples. Josephine sat on the edge of the sofa, but as soon as she felt her body sinking into the cushions, Danny appeared in the doorway. She lurched to her feet, swaying off-balance for a moment.

"Can we talk?" he asked. He stepped into the room with a tentative gait. He had removed his suit jacket, vest, and tie. Wrinkles creased his white shirt, and a streak of mud striped the toe of his left shoe. "Sit," he said, motioning for her to return to the couch. He sat down across from her in one of the wingback chairs. Leaning forward, he propped his elbows on his thighs and stared down at the rug. *Are there answers there? Is he gathering the courage to express how angry, disappointed, or repelled he is by me?* He exuded displeasure, but Josephine wasn't sure it was directed at her.

The silence dragged on, and Josephine's heart couldn't handle the continued distance between them. "I'm sorry, Danny," she said, her words tumbling out in a stream. "So very sorry."

Danny lifted his head slowly, his brown eyes finding hers. "Let's pretend I'm entertaining this story of yours. That means you knew the whole time that you weren't staying here. You knew this *trip* was temporary."

Josephine nodded. "But I didn't know how attached I'd get to everyone," she admitted. "Certainly not to you."

He sat upright and then leaned back against the chair. His hands gripped the armrests. "Meaning what?"

Josephine squirmed on the couch and clasped her hands together to keep them from trembling. "I didn't plan on you," Josephine said. She sighed and hung her head, unable to hold the intensity of his gaze. "I didn't actually have any sort of plan. I just knew I needed to save Alma. But then I met you, and I knew I shouldn't spend so much time with you, but I couldn't stop myself."

"Couldn't or wouldn't?" he questioned, causing her to lift her head. His expression was hard and filled with confusion and perhaps a hint of pain.

Frustration combined with her own heartache and reared up inside her chest, shoving words out before she could stop them. "What woman in her right mind *wouldn't* want to spend time with you? Looking like you do and talking like you do, you're a human dreamboat." She pressed her lips together to stop the flow.

Danny's laugh surprised her. "A dreamboat? Is that a literal thing?"

A fragment of tension broke off from her shoulders at the sound of his laughter. "No. It means a handsome man. I really am sorry, Danny. I meant everything I said to you."

"Other than where you're from, what you're doing here, and who you really are," he said, seriousness returning to his posture and voice.

"Most of what I said was true," Josephine argued. "I did live in Atlanta for a while, and I also lived in the Green Hills area before moving into the Carter Mansion. I am a widow, and I haven't been with anyone since Nathan died. And how I felt—no, *feel*—about you, all of that is true. I couldn't have told you I was from the future. You wouldn't have believed me."

"I'm uncertain I believe you now," Danny said.

Josephine's shoulders sagged forward. "I understand. Making sure Alma was saved is the only thing that matters. I can live with the fact that none of you believe me. I'll be gone tomorrow anyway, and you can all go back to your normal lives, the way they were before I came."

Danny's jaw clenched and released. Then he stood and walked toward her, surprising her by sitting on the couch. When he grabbed her hands in his, Josephine's body stilled as the moment suspended between them.

"How could I possibly return to a life before you?" Danny asked. "The very idea is impossible."

Josephine looked down at their clasped hands. "I'm learning nothing is impossible."

Danny's thumb moved over the back of her hand, launching tingles along her skin. "Then it's improbable. Say I don't want to return to a life before you? What if I don't have to?"

Their eyes met. "What do you mean?"

"If you've been coming and going between now and the future," he said, speaking the words slowly as though the sentence only came to him a piece at a time, "what if you stayed? With me?"

Josephine's heart nearly burst from her chest in rapid beats, causing her stomach to sink. *Stay? In 1927?* "I . . ." *I what? Couldn't? Wouldn't? Is it possible to stay in 1927?* "I've considered it," she said honestly.

Danny's back straightened, and his grip tightened on her hands. Hope radiated off him. "Consider it more. We would be happy, Josephine. I know we would. I could make you happy."

Josephine slid her hand out from Danny's and touched his cheek, the faint scratch of stubble appearing on his warm skin. Looking into his eyes, she wanted to say yes. She wanted to agree to spend the rest of her life with him, even as she knew that kind of commitment should not be made on impulse. Would she be repeating the pattern of becoming whatever a man wanted, rather than staying true to herself and what was best for her life? She'd always be an outcast here. An anomaly who knew too much about unfolding events. How would that affect her relationships? How would it change her? And there was the question of whether she could actually *stay* in 1927. She wasn't even sure what might happen by morning. Now that she'd altered the timeline, Josephine had no idea what else was already changing.

"Oh, Danny, I know I'd be happy with you, but—"

He didn't let her finish. He leaned forward and kissed her, stopping any more words from leaving her lips. Silencing any reason why she couldn't stay with him. Josephine angled closer to him, relishing his kiss and the way her body responded to his closeness. Kissing Danny usually made her forget everything, but the weight of decision pressed heavy in her mind, and she couldn't entirely block it out. But she tried, focusing on the warmth of his hands and the way her body felt lighter and full of air.

Minutes later when Danny pulled away, Josephine was dizzy with desire and exhaustion. He brushed his hand down her cheek, down her shoulder, and slid it down the length of her arm until he held her hand. "You don't have to decide tonight, but think about it. Please."

Josephine nodded, afraid to speak. Danny leaned over, gave her a quick kiss on the mouth, and stood.

"You look about ready to pass out," he said.

She smoothed her hand over her hair as if that might help the fatigue she knew was evident on her face. "Just what every woman wants to hear."

Danny chuckled. "There's plenty of room upstairs for you to sleep."

"Thank you," she said, folding her hands together in her lap. "I'll be up in a bit."

"Good night, Josephine," he said.

Josephine felt squeezed into her skin, as though one more emotion might cause her to burst. "Good night, Danny. And thank you."

"For what?" he asked.

For kindness. For kisses. For asking me to stay. For wanting *me to stay.* "For everything."

His smile was small but genuine. He turned toward the staircase, and she watched him climb the steps until he was out of sight. Then she fell over sideways on the couch and pulled her legs onto the cushions, lying with one cheek smashed against the fabric, staring at the ashes in the fireplace, wondering how she could possibly stay in 1927 and how she could possibly leave it.

CHAPTER 22

"Josephine?"

The voice traveled from a great distance, pushing through the murky darkness of Josephine's mind. Her exhausted body tried to respond to the call, but a heaviness pushed down again as she slipped back toward sleep.

The voice called again, louder, more distinct. Josephine forced her eyelids open and was blinded by a startling brightness. A blurry figure, a shadow contrasting with the light, was just out of focus. *Katherine? Had it all been a dream?* For a moment she wondered if this was the day she'd moved into the Carter Mansion, and exhaustion had caused her to fall asleep on the living room couch. But memories of 1927 and Alma and Danny and the raid swiftly filled her mind, too real to be a dream. *Have I been transported back into present day?* Her heart leaped with the hope that she'd saved everyone, including her immediate family.

"Josephine?"

Josephine pushed her body into a sitting position, momentarily confused by her surroundings. She wasn't in the Carter Mansion, and the woman before her wasn't her sister. *Alma.* While she wasn't disappointed to see Alma, the hope she'd been feeling at the possible presence of her sister evaporated.

Josephine's right arm cramped from lying on it, and she tried to rub away the soreness. Her legs ached, as did her ankles and feet, because she'd fallen asleep wearing her shoes. Memories of last night surged as the dam of sleepiness released.

Alma sat down beside her on the couch. "Good morning," she said quietly. "When I didn't see you upstairs, I was afraid you were gone."

Alma still wore last night's dress, but her face had been washed and her hair brushed. Her skin glowed fresh and clean. Josephine touched her cheek, feeling the rough imprint of the upholstery on her skin. She probably looked as much of a mess as she felt.

"I meant only to lie down for a minute," Josephine said.

Alma shifted on the couch. "I'm glad you're still here." She slid her fingers along a chain she wore around her neck. "Did you sleep well?

Josephine gazed around the room and then leaned over to unbuckle her shoes. Her ankles cracked as she rotated her freed feet in small circles. "I don't remember anything after closing my eyes. Did you?"

Alma hummed in her throat. "My mind was alive with thoughts and questions most of the night, so it would be too generous to call it restful sleep." She toyed with beading on the skirt of her dress. "What happens next?"

"I go home?" Josephine said, not confident of anything.

"It's as simple as that?" Alma asked.

Josephine massaged the side of her neck. "None of this is simple." She cut her eyes over to Alma and then studied the stonework around the fireplace. When she spoke again, her voice was quiet. "Danny asked me to stay."

Alma sighed, the weight of her thoughts mingling with Josephine's. "I'm not surprised. I wanted to ask you the same thing."

Astonishment rushed through her, jolting and earnest. "You did?"

Alma's gentle smile lifted her cheeks. "Of course." Then the smile waned. "But you have a life there, and you deserve that. Asking you to stay makes it easier for us, I suppose, because we've grown fond of you. You have friends there, don't you? And a family?"

Friends? Not really. Not anymore. There was that almost-moment with Lita, but it had vanished. Josephine did have a family, and they were the main reason she felt compelled to return home. "I have parents and a sister, Katherine."

Alma nodded. "They would miss you greatly."

"A part of me wants to stay here, Alma," Josephine said. "It's so tempting, but in my heart, I know it isn't right. This is *your* timeline. I don't belong in 1927. I've been so lost ever since Nathan died, but being here with you has helped me see that starting again, choosing a new life, is possible. You've shown me that I could be happy again, and Danny . . . Maybe I *can* fall in love. Maybe my heart still works. My home life isn't perfect, but it's *mine*, and I'd like to give myself another try at choosing a life that makes me happy."

Alma reached over and took Josephine's hand. "I want you to have all of that, Josephine, and you will. I've known you were special since the moment I met you."

Josephine smiled. "Even though Hattie thought I was bad news?"

Alma laughed quietly. "Hattie knew, too, didn't she? In her own way, she knew something wasn't on the level. Where she saw an impostor, I saw you. Someone who was a lot like me, and it makes sense knowing we're family."

"So you believe me?" Josephine asked. "You believe all of this is true?"

Alma shrugged one shoulder. "It's not easy to believe, but it adds up. The strangeness of everything is difficult to ignore. It would be simpler to go with a logical explanation, but some things in this world aren't logical."

Alma reached for the clasp at the back of her necklace and unhooked the chain. The necklace had been tucked into her dress, but as she held it out to Josephine, Josephine now saw the chain had a ruby pendant hanging from it. Her eyes widened. "This is the same—" Josephine stopped herself from saying the ruby pendant necklace was the same one her mama gave her on her eighteenth birthday. The same one that had vanished a few days ago from her jewelry box.

"The same what?" Alma asked. "You've seen this before?"

Josephine pressed her lips together and shook her head.

Alma chuckled. "Josephine, your face always shows what you're feeling. Do you have the same necklace at home? You must. What else can you tell me? Do I marry Louis? I do, don't I? You called me Alma Grant." She pressed her hands to her cheeks and grinned widely. "I can't wait for that life, and oh! I have children. *We* have children." Tears gathered on Alma's lower lids, and her hands covered her lips for a moment. "I have a family. Why hadn't I thought of that until this very moment?" Alma leaned over and wrapped her arms around Josephine, pulling her into a tight hug. When she pulled away, Alma took the necklace from Josephine's hands and hooked it around Josephine's neck. "It was always meant for you. And, Josephine, thank you for saving my life."

Josephine lifted the pendant in her fingers and stared at the light sparkling in the crimson stone. "I wouldn't have *had* to save you if I hadn't caused the whole mess in the first place."

"You needed to cause this whole mess," Alma said confidently. "You needed this journey to rediscover life and to see that your life and *you* are so special. Not just anyone could have done this. You are very brave."

Gratefulness tightened Josephine's throat. "You sound like Katherine. She seems to believe there's a brave person somewhere inside of me."

"I couldn't agree more," Alma said.

"I'm going to miss you. All of you," Josephine said, her voice quivering. "What will I tell Danny?"

"The truth. He'll understand eventually," Alma said. "You've done him a kindness too. Danny didn't believe he would ever open his heart again, but you showed him he was wrong. Just like he showed you that you were wrong about finding love again."

Josephine allowed her body to fall back against the couch cushions as she exhaled. Alma patted her leg. "It will all work out. I have a good feeling about it. Let's get you home, Josephine." Alma stood and held out her hands. "But first, let's get you cleaned up. You look like you spent all night at Jay Gatsby's."

Josephine snorted a laugh and grabbed Alma's hands. "But did I enjoy it?"

Alma grinned. "It was a night to remember."

●●●

BY THE TIME Josephine was washed up and dressed again in last night's dress, which mildly stank of cigarettes and sweat, everyone was awake. When she came downstairs looking for Alma, she found Cecil and Hattie drinking coffee in the sitting room. They glanced up at her but didn't say anything. Josephine caught sight of Eleanor through the windowed front door. She stood on the front porch, smoking and talking with Louis in the brilliant light of a crisp morning. Alma's voice traveled up the hallway, so Josephine followed the sound to the kitchen.

Sunlight flooded the kitchen through a bank of square windows with panes of wavy glass welded together with lead. An open doorway led to a sunporch a few steps down from the kitchen level, bringing more light to the area. The kitchen smelled like baking biscuits with an overlay of cooked fruit. Josephine also inhaled the scent of coffee.

Alma chatted with a rotund older woman with paper-white hair pinned up in a braided bun. So many smile lines framed the creamy white skin on her cherub face. She wore a floral apron as she filled a plate with biscuits straight from the oven. Alma looked over as Josephine entered the kitchen. "There she is, the last of our group," Alma said. "Josephine, this is Mrs. Millie. Mrs. Millie, meet Josephine Reynolds."

Mrs. Millie wiped her hands on the hand towel hanging from the apron pocket. "Nice to meet you, Ms. Reynolds. I haven't seen so many people in Mr. Stewart's house in years. It's a nice sight to see all this company."

"Nice to meet you too," Josephine said. "Could I have a cup of coffee, please?"

"Yes, ma'am," Mrs. Millie said, filling a mug with coffee from a kettle on the stovetop. "Here you are."

Josephine thanked her and brought the cup to her lips, inhaling the warming aroma of a rich blend. The liquid heated her throat as she swallowed. Alma motioned with her head toward the sunporch, and Josephine walked to the doorway. Danny stood facing one of the tall, rectangular windows that revealed a gorgeous, sun-drenched fall morning.

An array of houseplants grew in porcelain containers and wooden boxes. A cream sofa was flanked by two wicker chairs with tan cushions. A glass door with an accompanying screen door led to the backyard covered in fallen leaves, a carpet of reds and golds. Josephine stepped down into the room.

"Good morning," she said softly, not wanting to startle him.

He turned his face to look at her, and her breath held for a moment. His expression was one of weariness. Had he slept at all last night? Guilt rippled through her at the knowledge that his hurt was because of her.

"It is morning," Danny said before returning his gaze to the backyard. "Whether it is good or not is still up for debate."

Alma's words from this morning returned to her. Josephine had to tell Danny the truth, had to get it over with and tell him she couldn't stay. Not because she didn't *want* to be with him, but because it wasn't right. "Danny, I thought about what you asked—"

"I know you can't say yes," he said, interrupting her.

He faced her. A bluebird swooped past the windows, a streak like a ribbon of royal blue.

"You do?"

"It was selfish of me to ask," he said.

Josephine put her coffee down on the nearest table and walked to him. She reached for his hands, and he didn't pull away. "You're not selfish," she argued. "If anyone is selfish, it's me. I shouldn't have let things go so far between us. I *knew* the truth, and I let all of it happen anyway."

Danny's hand on her cheek stopped her from saying more. His eyes stared into hers. "I wouldn't change any of it."

"Even though I'm leaving?" Tears pricked her eyes. He nodded. She moved forward, wrapping her arms around him, and Danny held her. Tears leaked down her cheeks. Leaving Danny didn't feel like losing Nathan, a cavernous wound into which everything had collapsed. Leaving Danny was sharp, like running through thorns, quick and painful but not deep enough to scar. If anything, opening her heart to Danny had renewed her love of life and possibility. She unwrapped her arms and swiped at her cheeks as she stepped away from him.

"Josephine," Alma called from the doorway, "Louis is ready to drive us home."

"I'll come too," Danny said.

"What about the authorities?" Josephine asked. "Will they be waiting for us?"

Danny shook his head. "Doubtful, but they'll be back."

"No matter what happens," Alma said, "Cecil *will not* take the blame."

Danny nodded. "Louis and I will stay with you. Until then, I can help clean up or . . ."

Alma's expression exposed her concern. "I don't know what we'll find."

"What do you mean?" Josephine asked, reaching for her mug and sipping coffee.

Alma's forehead creased. "I'm trying to be hopeful it's not a disaster."

"Why would it be?" Josephine asked. "Would the men have wrecked the place?"

"Angry people do hurtful things, Josephine," Alma said. Then she quickly glanced at Danny. "Not to suggest Mark would allow it, but . . ."

Danny nodded. "After last night, I see that Mark is capable of things that shock me. I'll go with you."

"Thank you, Danny," Alma said. She made eye contact with Josephine. "Ready?"

"As ready as I can be." Josephine tossed a glance over her shoulder at Danny, who joined her. They walked up the stairs into the kitchen. She wanted to ask him if he believed the police, or his brother, would have destroyed Alma's house, but she was also afraid of the answer. The raid was inevitable, regardless of the timeline, so why was she gripped by guilt and melancholy as though she had caused it?

CHAPTER 23

Someone had closed the Carter Mansion's front door, but it was unlocked. Wind rustled through the dry leaves still clinging to the trees across the street. A mockingbird called, and a blue jay screeched an answer. Otherwise the morning was calm and quiet, the opposite of last night's affair. Louis and Danny entered the house first.

Louis held out his hand in a sign for Alma and Josephine to stop. "Wait here."

Alma nodded. Until Alma reached for her hand and squeezed, Josephine didn't realize she was holding her breath. "No matter what," Alma said, "we'll be all right."

The men disappeared into the house, walking through the downstairs rooms first. Danny took the stairs two at a time and scouted the second floor. After a few minutes, they met in the foyer and spoke in quiet voices. Louis opened the front door wider and motioned for the women to enter.

"Most everything is undisturbed," Louis said with an expression of relief.

Alma tensed beside Josephine. "Most?"

Danny pointed to the hardwood floors. Josephine noticed dozens of shoe prints all over the foyer floor, as if a dance party or a stampede had taken place. "Mud's been tracked in all over the place," he said. "Upstairs too. Why they needed to search the second floor is beyond me, but after a good cleaning, the house will be okay."

Josephine's heart sank. "They went upstairs?" She'd left her personal belongings in one of the bedrooms. "I left all my things up there." *The key.*

Danny shook his head. "I don't think they took anything, and they'd have no interest in your makeup."

"If they didn't steal the silver," Louis agreed, "they aren't interested in your sundries."

Danny pointed down the hallway. "Let us check the club. You two stay up here."

"Why can't we go with you?" Josephine asked.

"I second that," Alma said. "My biggest worry was the house. I can handle whatever we find in the speakeasy."

Louis touched Alma's arm. "I don't want to upset you."

"This entire situation upsets me, Louis," she said firmly but without anger. "I knew when I started the club that this could be a possibility." She motioned toward the kitchen. "But you two can go first. Josephine and I will follow."

Louis closed the front door and turned the lock. Then Josephine and Alma followed the men down the basement stairs. The door to the speakeasy was open, and the stench of cigarette smoke and spilled booze overpowered the damp, earthy smell of the basement. Louis stopped abruptly as soon as he stood in the doorway, causing Danny to bump into him. Alma gripped Josephine's forearm. The image of the destroyed speakeasy from Josephine's day flashed in her mind. Had the authorities completely wrecked the room? Had they overturned tables and chairs, torn the framed art from the walls? Were bottles shattered, leaving behind deadly shards of glass sitting in puddles of spoiled liquor?

"Is it awful?" Josephine asked.

Danny peered around Louis's shoulder. "A mess."

Louis walked through the doorway with Danny close behind. Alma and Josephine swapped glances and followed. Alma's sharp intake of breath wasn't surprising once they saw what had been left behind.

Birthday streamers ripped from the walls littered the ground in tangles of wet, torn paper. Shriveled white balloons, half the size from the night before, collected against the walls and under tables. The Happy Birthday banner dangled toward the floor, one end still stuck to the wall. The letters D, A, and Y had torn away and lay on the floor covered in shoe prints. Only a few chairs were overturned, but half of the flower vases were smashed. Crushed and trampled daisies and roses added to the disarray.

The worst of the damage appeared to be in the bar area. Most of the liquor was gone, probably boxed and carted away by the police. A few bottles had been either dropped or thrown, as evidenced by the shattered glass and wet floor behind the bar. The bar top was unscathed, as was most of the glassware. Napkins that had been stacked on the bar for patrons now covered the concrete in a sticky carpet of dirty shoe prints.

The separate sitting area where they'd arranged the food and party favors was a mess of scattered food, soiled napkins, and damaged paper plates. Alma stood with fisted hands on her hips, surveying the room. "Must they have made such a mess of everything? Was it necessary to throw plates and napkins all over?"

Josephine stood beside her. "It could have been much worse." The current state of the club was a relief compared to the future version she'd seen—the violent version that included the loss of Alma.

"You're right," Alma said. "But still, it's so much chaos. I know all of this can be cleaned. The most important thing is that we're all okay. Thanks to you."

"What will you do with the club now?" Josephine asked, bending down to pick up a torn piece of wrapping paper. She traced her fingertip across the polka-dot design. "You won't be able to keep it open, will you?"

Alma shook her head. "We knew this was temporary, at least until Prohibition ends. Tell me it ends," she said, allowing herself to smile for a moment at Josephine.

"You know I shouldn't reveal anything else about the future," Josephine said. "I have no idea how I might have already changed things."

"Blink once if it ends. Twice if it endures into your day," Alma persisted.

"I can't say anything," Josephine said, but then she winked once at Alma.

Alma heaved a sigh of relief. "It's good to know some foolishness dies out in the future."

"We have our own kind of foolishness," Josephine said. "So what will you do with the club?"

Alma shrugged. "We could turn it into a dance hall, serve seltzer and lemonade. Or I could close it up for good."

The sound of someone playing the piano reached them, and Josephine's body stiffened at the tune "Rhapsody in Blue." Someone was playing the starting clarinet solo on a piano instead. "That song," Josephine said, walking out of the separate room as though in a trance.

Alma followed her. "It's one of my favorites."

Danny sat at the piano, his long fingers moving over the keys. He played the song that had called to Josephine from the basement, the one that led her to the speakeasy.

"The band's gear looks untouched," Louis said, meeting Alma and Josephine in the center of the room.

"Danny plays the piano?" Josephine muttered in shock, staring at his profile as his hands glided over the keys.

"He's good, isn't he?" Alma said. "I've begged him dozens of times to play, and he always says no. But he must have been 'moved by the Spirit' today, as my mama likes to say."

Shivers rippled over Josephine's skin from her scalp to her toes, filling her insides with fluttering. "It's perfect," she said quietly.

Alma stood next to Josephine. "I hope you'll let go of the idea that you created a mess here. You might have made a wish that disrupted our lives, but"—she nodded toward Danny at the piano—"you've changed us in remarkable ways and set some of us free."

Josephine wiped tears from her cheeks. "I think I set myself free too."

"I know you did." Alma leaned her head against Josephine's shoulder the way Josephine and Katherine often did with each other. The familiarity of the gesture and the force of love behind it wasn't lost on Josephine.

●●●

JOSEPHINE GATHERED HER belongings from the upstairs bedroom. Sliding her grasping fingers beneath a pillow, she exhaled in relief when she found the chain she'd shoved under there the night before. When she pulled out the necklace, the house key dangled and spun on the twisted chain. Josephine hung the necklace around her neck and pinched the key between two fingers before resting it against her palm.

Danny appeared in the doorway. "Find everything?"

She nodded and let the key fall from her palm. It bounced against her chest. "Danny, I . . . I'm going to miss you."

He stepped into the room. "I know you must return, but can you come back? Are you able to visit us?"

"I don't know," she said honestly. "I have no idea what will happen when I return. I don't even know what I'll find there." *Will the Carter Mansion have reverted to what it was before Alma's and my belongings started vanishing? Will the renovations Uncle Donnie made be there?* She tried to smile at Danny, but uncertainty pursued her.

Danny moved closer to her and leaned down slightly to kiss her forehead. "Let's get you home."

As they walked down the stairs, Josephine saw that Eleanor, Hattie, and Cecil had rejoined them. "What are you doing here?" Josephine asked.

Eleanor's expression was a mix of amusement and skepticism. She watched Josephine come down the steps. "And miss the time traveler's exit?"

Josephine couldn't tell if she was being sarcastic or if Eleanor sincerely wanted to see her off. "When you see that I'm telling the truth, I'll never be able to hear your apology."

Eleanor smirked but didn't reply.

Alma crossed the foyer to stand with Josephine. Unexpected tears gathered in Josephine's eyes, and Alma's bottom lip trembled. "I know your leaving is for the best," Alma said, clearing sadness from her throat. "I'll still miss you, but I'll see you again one day."

Josephine wiped her cheeks. "You will."

Alma's eyes widened, and she jerked her head toward the living room. "The hidden compartment," she said, walking away from Josephine and standing on the living room rug. She whirled around with a grin of excitement. "Could I leave something for you? Could you find it in the future?"

"I don't know," Josephine said. "So many things can happen between now and then. I also don't know if any of you will remember me."

"How could we forget?" Danny asked, his face pulled into a deep frown.

Josephine shrugged. "I don't know how any of this works. I won't forget. I know that, but I don't know how you'll be affected." She looked at Alma. "But we can try."

Alma rushed back over and grabbed Josephine's hands. "Yes, we can try. Check it, will you? When you get home, go straight there and see what I've left for you."

Josephine nodded. She released Alma's hands and glanced around at the group, her gaze lingering longer on Danny. His smile was slight and his expression like someone trying to mask emotion. For once Hattie didn't appear angry at or skeptical of Josephine. Instead, she looked curious. "I have no doubt you'll continue to be a wonderful friend to Alma," Josephine said to her, and Hattie nodded.

Is that respect I see on Eleanor's face? What will Eleanor say to them once I'm gone?

"You could leave your note of apology in the compartment too," Josephine said to Eleanor, causing Eleanor to bark a laugh.

Josephine hugged Alma one last time, squeezing tight. She wanted to say something comforting or brilliant to Alma, but the words jumbled together in her mind, and she couldn't bring any of them out. Josephine pulled away and picked up her bag from the floor. Lifting her hand, she offered everyone a weak wave before turning toward the front door. Her hand hesitated on the doorknob, but only for a second. If she waited any longer, she'd never leave.

Josephine opened the front door. Sunlight and a strong breeze pushed through the open door. She stepped over the threshold, closing the door behind her and leaving 1927. Her lungs expelled all her air as a freezing sensation rocketed so forcefully through her body that she pitched forward. Her legs buckled, and her knees slammed against the porch boards. Josephine doubled over with the sudden pain.

When she opened her eyes, her surroundings blurred in and out of focus until finally she could see clearly. Skeletons clung to the oak tree across the street. Burnt-orange leaves collected in a pile at the curb. Turning her face, she saw pumpkins and hay and an urn of chrysanthemums nearby. *I'm home.*

Josephine stood slowly and rubbed her knees. Comfort entwined with loss. Danny's question returned to her. *Could I go back and visit?* Josephine spoke the words carved on the door, unlocked the door, held her breath, and twisted the knob. When she pushed open the door, she saw her own version of the Carter Mansion. Alma, Danny, and the others were not waiting for her on the other side. She closed the door, locked it, and tried again.

The second try yielded the same results. Heartache combined with understanding swelled inside her. No longer could she travel back to 1927. She would never see Alma or Danny again. In Josephine's present day, Alma was already gone, but there was a shred of comfort knowing that the Alma she'd left in 1927 would see Josephine again in another sixty years.

Josephine stepped over the threshold and closed the door behind her. Her mouth fell agape when she saw the living room. Nathan's replica Tiffany lamp in the shape of a peacock sat on the secretary desk, both returned from the void. The gaudy couch was also back in its spot, along with framed photographs sitting on a table nearby. Josephine rushed over and grabbed one. A half laugh, half cry erupted from her lips. In the photo, she and Nathan smiled up at her from beside the last Christmas tree they'd decorated together. The next photo of the girls' trip to Maine included her mom, Josephine, and Katherine again, all three of them smiling in mutual joy. In every photo, every original person had returned.

Josephine walked down the hallway to the kitchen. The grandfather clock ticked steadily. The farmhouse sink was positioned where Uncle Donnie had installed it, the refrigerator hummed in its cubby, and the laundry room was fully functional. She glanced at the basement door and crossed the room to open it. After switching on the lights at the top of the stairs, Josephine hurried down into the basement. The once hidden speakeasy door had returned, no longer swallowed up by the limestone. She dropped onto the bottom step, letting her head fall between her knees so she could calm her breaths.

When she stood to walk to the speakeasy door and inspect what the club now looked like, a faraway ringing phone pulled her attention. Josephine paused, turned her ear toward the staircase, and listened. *Is that my cell phone?*

Josephine flew up the basement stairs, sprinted through the downstairs, and hurled herself up the staircase to her bedroom. Her cell phone was lit up and ringing on the nightstand. Just as she picked it up, the ringing stopped, but not before she saw the caller's name. *Katherine.*

Josephine nearly dropped the phone from her shaking hands. She dialed her sister's number and waited, gulping air.

"Hey! I was leaving you a voice mail," Katherine said. "Where have you been? I've been calling you."

"Katherine!" Josephine said. Her legs wobbled, so she sat on the edge of the bed. "It's so good to hear from you."

"Why do you sound so out of breath?"

Josephine laughed and then sucked in more air. "I was in the basement, and I ran for the phone."

"What were you doing in the basement? Everything okay?" Katherine asked. "And where have you been? I was starting to freak out. Mom said she heard from you a few days ago and you sounded troubled."

Josephine closed her eyes and inhaled slowly before speaking. She wanted to tell Katherine everything, but she couldn't. "My phone . . ." *Disappeared? No, I can't say that.* "Died."

"That's why they have phone chargers," Katherine said. "Or do you mean *died* died?"

"Yeah that," Josephine said, avoiding the truth. "Sorry to worry you, but everything is fine now."

"Now?" Katherine asked, picking up a deeper meaning.

"Yeah," Josephine said. "Everything is okay, or it will be." All of which was true.

Katherine exhaled loudly. "I'll be home tomorrow. Want to grab dinner this week? Or I can bring something over if you don't want to go out."

Josephine thought of Alma and her friends. She thought of sitting with Danny at a corner table in the speakeasy. "No, let's go out for dinner. I've trapped myself inside long enough."

Katherine didn't respond immediately. Then, without asking for an explanation or acting as though Josephine's new attitude was shocking, she said, "I love you, Jo-Jo."

"I love you, Katy-bug. Be safe coming home. Call me this week." Josephine disconnected, holding the phone and staring at the home screen's image. A subtle thrill started in her chest and spread outward. She *could* feel excited about her life again. Alma would tell her the possibilities were endless if only Josephine would open herself up to them, open her heart to them.

Thinking about Alma triggered the memory of Alma asking Josephine to check the hidden compartment in the living room.

Josephine hesitated. She wanted to run downstairs and open it, but more than that, she really wanted a shower and a change of clothes, because last night's dress had done all it could for her.

●●●

JOSEPHINE ROLLED UP the living room rug and exposed the hidden compartment. She hooked her finger around the metal loop and lifted the lid. It opened with a squeak. *Did Alma and the others even remember me after I returned to present day? Did their memories of me vanish?* Inside the hidden compartment, the contents looked much the same as they had when Leo first revealed it to her, but Josephine saw something new. Lying next to a stack of papers was an envelope with her name on it.

Josephine reached in and pulled it out. She broke the envelope's seal and removed stationery she recognized from the same design Alma kept on her secretary. Josephine sat on the floor and unfolded the letter. The date 1931 was handwritten in the top right corner.

Dearest Josephine,

I hope this letter finds you well and happy. I know I said I would write immediately, but I kept putting it off, not knowing quite what to say or how to say it, and knowing I had plenty of time to put something into our secret spot.

I think of you often, more often than I share with anyone. We did not, in fact, forget you. Our memories were not wiped clean of your presence in our lives. This has been both a gift and a heartache. I miss you, but I am always hopeful that your life will be flooded with joy and love and that you will cherish our time together as I do.

Louis and I were married less than six months after you left. Perhaps you already know this, but you didn't hear it from me, so it feels right to share it with you this way. We have a son, Charles Joseph Grant. It felt right and good to name him after you. He's a year old and learning to walk. I always wanted a family, and I am eternally grateful to have been given the opportunity to have one.

I don't know if you're curious about the others, but I feel I must share news of their well-being. They rarely talk about you. The day you disappeared was quite shocking even for those of us who believed you. It's as though if we admit it really happened, we are somehow forcing ourselves to believe in other impossibilities. This is unsettling for most.

Eleanor is as lovely and as complicated as ever. She and Anderson are still together. He bought a house in Nashville, and he spends half the year here and half the year in Chicago. I expect one day Eleanor will leave for Chicago and make a home there or he will sell his home in the city and settle fully in Nashville.

Cecil and Hattie wed in a private ceremony that included only family and very close friends, and although they do not yet have the freedom to openly speak about their marriage, I hope they and their children have a better future ahead.

Danny speaks of you sparingly but more than anyone else. How could he not? Don't feel guilty for this, Josephine. Your love was a gift for all of us, and Danny will move forward. He might even find love again now that he sees it's possible. I hope you will too.

Louis thinks I should not dwell long in the past since you are also in our future, and although I would love to write to you often, perhaps he is right. Our lives are better left to carry on separately for now. Until I see you again, I am sending my love to you, Josephine, and I am forever grateful.

Yours always,
Alma

Josephine reread the letter twice, until tears dropped from her eyes and splashed the paper. She wiped away the splatters so the letter wouldn't be ruined. Then she held the pages to her heart as if she could absorb Alma's love through the ink.

CHAPTER 24

TWO MONTHS LATER

"When do you officially start event planning for Nashville's Spring Art Gala?" Katherine asked, tugging the fleece blanket tighter around her shoulders.

"Yesterday," Josephine said.

Katherine smiled at her over the top of her holiday mug. "And you're holding tickets for Neil and me, right?"

"I don't know, Katy-bug," Josephine said, feigning doubt. "It's an expensive event, and I've committed to raising thousands of dollars for art education. Giving away free tickets sounds contrary to my goal."

Katherine poked Josephine's arm. "I'll buy two pieces of overpriced artwork."

"Deal," Josephine said with a laugh. Her cell phone dinged, and she fished it out of the folds of her blanket. Lita texted: Reminder about our totally rad 80s Christmas party. 7 this Saturday night. Josephine smiled and texted back: I'll be the one wearing the most offensive fluorescent colors imaginable. She looked up at Katherine. "You're still coming to Lita's party, aren't you?"

"And miss wearing a side ponytail and neon leg warmers? Not a chance. I'm definitely going. And speaking of going, it's freezing out here. Any chance we can get going inside?" Katherine's knees were tucked into her chest and hidden beneath layers of bright blue fabric covered in white puffy snowflakes.

The sisters sat on the front porch of the Carter Mansion in cushioned wicker chairs. A Christmas quilt draped Josephine's shoulders, and a red hoodie loosely covered her head. She sipped hot cocoa from a ceramic mug decorated with snowmen wearing various hats and scarves. "It's forty-five degrees. Freezing is thirty-two."

Katherine rolled her eyes. "Excuse me, *I'm* freezing out here. Why are you forcing me to drink my coffee outside?"

Josephine stretched her legs out from the blanket, admiring her fuzzy winter socks and buffalo plaid flannel pajama bottoms. Katherine wore matching pants and a green hoodie. "My holiday bucket list. We've just crossed off 'drink hot cocoa outdoors in the snow.'"

"Technically, we're not in the snow," Katherine grumbled.

Patches of white snow covered the sidewalks and front lawns. The inflatables covering the neighbor's yard across the street were weighed down with last night's snowfall. Nashville rarely got snow, but these three inches had every kid outside today, trying to sled down the nearest hill on a baking sheet or building snowmen barely a foot tall. Their delighted voices carried down the streets.

"Fine," Josephine said, "we can go back inside."

"Thank you!" Katherine said, standing so quickly that coffee sloshed from her mug. She danced out of the way of the splash. "I can barely feel my toes."

Josephine pulled the quilt around her shoulders as she stood. A brilliant red cardinal landed on a nearby holly bush and chirped.

"Excuse me," a male voice called from the sidewalk.

Josephine couldn't see him, but Katherine looked down the front stairs at someone and spoke. "Yes?"

"Is this the Carter Mansion?" the man asked.

"Yes," Katherine said. The fleece blanket dropped from one shoulder, and she held her coffee high while she grabbed the blanket. "And it's not for sale."

The man chuckled. "I don't want to buy it. I just have a few historical questions, if you have a minute."

"Oh," Katherine said, glancing over at Josephine. "You'll want to talk to my sister, then. She knows all the history about this place. She and Leo are a local dynamic duo on all things historic Nashville and the Carter Mansion."

"Don't forget we have a fondness for the '20s," Josephine added.

Katherine smiled. "Have I told you how funny you two are? You buy a door from Leo, and you're best friends for life."

Josephine laughed. "It's something like that."

Katherine motioned with her head. "Come on up."

Josephine stepped into view to see the man coming up the front steps. When he caught sight of her, he stopped halfway up and stared. Josephine's heartbeat paused and then increased momentum in her chest. The dark-haired man looked about her age. He wore a brown leather jacket zipped nearly to the top. A hint of a gray shirt peeked out near the collar. He wore jeans and thick-soled boots with a leather satchel strap crossing his chest.

Katherine looked between the two of them. Two narrow lines creased between her brows. "Are you okay?" she asked the man.

He broke eye contact with Josephine and glanced down at his boots before continuing up the stairs. On the porch he flipped open his satchel and reached inside. He pulled out three rectangular pieces of paper. "I'm sorry for staring," he said to Josephine.

"It's just that you look a lot like a woman in these pictures. It's uncanny. Maybe she's family?"

He held out the papers, which Josephine realized were black-and-white photographs. Josephine took them, and Katherine pressed in close so she could see too. Josephine couldn't breathe. She couldn't even think. She could only stare at the faces. In the top photograph a woman with short dark hair stared up at a man in mutual adoration. Even from the woman's profile, Josephine knew it was her. *This was taken during the outdoor lunch I had with Danny, Alma, and Louis before Sara's birthday party.*

In the second photograph, the man and woman looked directly at the camera, and Josephine couldn't deny the face was hers.

"She looks just like you, Jo-Jo!" Katherine said. She grabbed the photograph from Josephine's hands and walked to the edge of the porch and held the photo in brighter sunlight. "The man kinda looks like you."

He nodded. "Now you see why I was shocked to see your sister."

Josephine stared down at the third photograph, which was of her and Alma, both smiling at the photographer, who Josephine knew had been Danny.

Katherine returned to her side and gasped. "That's Alma!"

The man stepped closer to them. "You know the women?"

"We know that one. She's our great-grandmother," Katherine said, pointing to Alma. She looked at her sister. "Who's the other woman, and why does she look like your 1920s doppelganger?"

Josephine laughed away the nervousness squeezing her throat. "Maybe a distant relative?"

Katherine shook her head. "So bizarre."

"Where did you get these?" Josephine asked. She also wanted to ask why he looked so much like Danny, but didn't.

"They were passed down through the family," he answered. "My mom had them last. Those pictures, I think, were taken in this backyard. My grandfather used to tell me stories about this house. They were told to him by his dad."

Josephine met the man's gaze. "What kind of stories?"

He pointed toward the front door and then rubbed his bare hands together to ward off the cold. "One was supposedly that my great-grandfather carved secret words into the front door."

Katherine laughed, but Josephine's body swayed, and her vision blurred. She tilted sideways, bumping into Katherine, causing her to spill more coffee onto the porch boards. The Christmas quilt hanging around Josephine dropped to the porch. "Whoa, Jo-Jo, are you okay?"

The man reached out to steady Josephine. His hand on her arm sent an electrical pulse racing across her skin. He seemed to feel it, too, because he jerked away his hand and stared at his palm before opening and closing his hand.

"Who . . . who was your great-grandfather?" Josephine asked. Her heart knew the answer before he said the name.

"Daniel Stewart," the man said. "But everyone called him Danny."

Josephine put down her mug and walked to the front door. She slid her fingertips across the minuscule words, closing her eyes and feeling into the steady, strong beat of her heart. Alma had thought it was absurd that anyone would carve words into the door. Josephine assured them *someone* had carved them because that was part of how the enchantment worked. That night when she told her story after the raid, Danny had been the one to ask what the words said.

Danny carved the words into the door.

Josephine sensed the man stood near her. She opened her eyes and met his. "It says, 'Among the whispering and the stars.'"

"Wait," Katherine said, stepping closer to them. "There are actually words carved into this door?"

The man leaned closer to the door and tilted his head to better read them. "Incredible," he said.

"What do those words mean?" Katherine asked.

"It's from *The Great Gatsby*," Josephine answered. "It was one of Alma's favorite books."

Katherine's eyebrows lifted. "How do you know that? And why would your great-grandfather carve words into someone else's door?"

The man said, "The story is that my great-grandfather did it for a woman he loved."

Josephine's breath caught.

Katherine sighed. "It's always about a woman, isn't it?" she joked.

Then the man caught Josephine's eyes. "I'm Elliott, by the way. Elliott Stewart."

"Elliott," Josephine said, her voice breaking slightly. "That's an excellent name."

Elliott's smile spread across his face, reminding her so much of Danny. "I was named after my grandfather. He always said it was a strong family name."

Josephine placed her palm against the door and sent out a silent thank-you. The wood warmed beneath her skin. She twisted the doorknob and pushed open the door. "You said you have stories about this place?"

Elliott nodded. "Many."

"Why don't you come in? I'd love to hear them," Josephine said. "Katherine needs more coffee anyway."

"So we're just letting strangers into your house now?" Katherine teased, but there was a hint of seriousness in her tone.

Josephine picked up the Christmas quilt and draped it over one arm. Then she grabbed her mug and closed the door once Elliott and Katherine were inside. "He has a photograph of my doppelganger. Aren't you the least bit curious?"

"You win," Katherine said, walking up the hallway. "I'll start another pot of coffee. Why don't you get the fire going?"

Elliott stood in the foyer and shoved his hands into his jeans pockets as he glanced up at the chandelier. "Some of these stories are far-fetched; some might say they're impossible."

Josephine smiled at Elliott and motioned for him to follow her into the living room. "I have some experience with the impossible."

AUTHOR'S NOTE

By the time this book releases, it'll have been more than fifteen years since I walked into the architectural salvage yard that eventually inspired this novel. I love historical objects, even knickknacks collecting dust on shelves or in boxes. Flea markets and antique malls fascinate me with their collections. I'm the one flipping through a random basket jammed full of loose photographs, some more than one hundred years old, and wondering about the stories the people in the pictures would tell me if they could.

Years ago, when I was wandering around the gargantuan salvage yard, I came across a massive, solid wood door adorned with hand-carved details and inlaid glass panels. The attached ticket stated the door was from the late 1800s. Looking at the door, a wisp of a thought entered my mind. *If I walk through that door, what's on the other side?*

I tucked that imaginative idea away in my pocket for many years. Then during a lunch meeting with my editor, Laura, we discussed ideas for my next book. She simply asked, "What about time travel?" I love time travel stories, but I'd never written one or even entertained the idea. But her question kept echoing through me until it bounced against the memory of that door in the salvage yard all those years ago.

Instantly, I saw that door on a house, and I knew that it was an *enchanted* door. What was on the other side? The Roaring 20s! Isn't it amazing how long we carry around stories, not even remembering they're still living somewhere inside of us until they resurface again? Until someone else knocks lose a memory or sparks a flame in our own imagination?

I'm so grateful for that simple "time travel" question and for Josephine, who's also been drifting around inside of me since I was very young. It was the perfect time for an enchanted door and Josephine to come together and share their story with all of us.

ACKNOWLEDGMENTS

Lots of writers will say that working on a book is solitary, like writing on an island somewhere with great distances between yourself and the rest of the world. I don't feel that way because if I'm actively writing, I'm encircled by my characters who, believe me, have a lot to say. I also feel surrounded by a team of people, who are all actively working (often behind-the-scenes) to help me create the best possible story I can.

Working on this book, which I lovingly call *Josephine*, has been a fun and challenging way to stretch myself into a new fictional space: time travel. There are always those who keep you sane during the flailing times, those who are willing to brainstorm no matter how wacky the idea, and those who pep talk you into leaping back into a story that might feel like a wild mustang running free.

Buckets and buckets of thank-yous to Jason, who has been listening to me yammer about stories for a gazillion years and who listened to my first summary of this book and agreed it was definitely worth writing. Thank you for being you: essential, unrepeatable, forever kind.

A confetti parade of thank-yous to Rea whose voice notes are life! Thank you for encouraging me to trust my inner knowing, for comforting me when my heart tumbles out of my chest, for keeping me jazzed every day about the infinite possibilities, and for following the pings with me on the greatest adventures. I know there are more to come!

Thank you, Laura Wheeler, foremost for being the most supportive, encouraging, and rockstar editor a girl could have! Thank you for tossing "time travel" into my imagination. Josephine wouldn't be here without you. Thank you for helping pull the strongest, most creative ideas out of my head and get them onto the page in a way that makes me so proud of this book and so grateful to have the opportunity to work with you.

Speaking of rockstars: Cue the fireworks for Harper Muse! This team deserves more thank-yous than I can say in a day. They are such a supportive, professional, encouraging, funny, intelligent, creative, and fabulous team. Pretty sure I won the jackpot with them. I literally would not be here writing this if not for them. Amanda Bostic, thank you for giving me a place to share my dreams. You are the best. Sincerely. Savannah Breedlove, Natalie Underwood, and Laura, thank you for being a top-shelf editing crew. You make me look good! Jere Warren, Patrick Aprea, Kerri Potts, and Colleen Lacy, I am so very grateful for your marketing magic and expertise and for all the ways you get my books out into the world so that the perfect people can find them. Margaret Kercher and Taylor Ward, thank you for working so unbelievably hard and with such persistence that helps create the most wonderful happenings for me. Thank you to Halie Cotton for your creative genius and gifting me with the most stunning covers. No one ever sees my books without commenting on how beautiful they are. Thank you sincerely to HarperCollins for continually breathing more life into my dreams.

Thank you, Jackie, for your brilliance that is only trumped by your kindness, for being my earliest reader, and for helping me shape my first draft into a manuscript I felt sincerely proud of. I adore working with you. Thank you, Erin, for your amazing editorial eyes, for helping me elevate my writing, and for sharing your genius with me. I am so grateful we get to work together.

An overflowing heartfelt thank-you to my family, for believing in me no matter what, for picking me up when I faceplant, for loving me just the way I am, and for celebrating with me. In the family lottery, I've won a million times over! I love y'all to the moon.

Finally, to my readers, thank you for opening your hearts to me and to this story. May you find the same wonder and hope and enchantment in these pages that Josephine does. This story is not just mine, but ours, a shared dream woven with threads of magic and love.

DISCUSSION QUESTIONS

1. At the beginning of the story, Josephine starts out in one state of mind—stuck in a dark place—but throughout the story, she begins to truly see herself and a future. How does Josephine's character evolve throughout the story, and what significant events contribute to her growth?

2. Family dynamics play a significant role in this story. Discuss the relationship between Josephine and her sister. How does their bond influence Josephine's decisions and actions? How does Josephine's bond with Alma change the course of her life?

3. What did you learn about the Jazz Age and its cultural significance? What details made this era come alive for you?

4. There are so many ways the past affects the present and the future. When time travel becomes a piece of this story, the past and present entangle and complications can arise. What

are the implications of Josephine altering the past? How does this theme of cause and effect resonate with you?

5. How does meeting Alma change Josephine's understanding of her family history and herself? Discuss the importance of ancestry and legacy in the book.

6. Josephine faces difficult choices in her quest to save Alma and herself. What ethical considerations does she grapple with, and how do these shape her actions?

7. Themes of grief and healing arise in the book. How does Josephine's journey through time help her cope with her grief and loss? How do her encounters with people in 1927 affect her growth and healing? In what ways is the house a metaphor for her healing process?

8. Courage and resilience are common threads woven throughout Josephine's and Alma's lives. Discuss Alma's character and the risks she takes running a speakeasy. How do her courage and resilience inspire Josephine?

9. How are love and relationships depicted in the book, both in the past and present timelines? How do these relationships influence the characters' motivations? Which relationships were your favorite?

10. What does the original door symbolize in the story? How does it function as a portal between past and present, and what does it represent for Josephine?

11. How does the book explore the theme of choices and their consequences? Do you agree with the decisions Josephine makes throughout her journey? Why or why not? What might have you done differently?

12. If you could invite characters from this novel out for dinner, which characters would join you at the table? Why did you choose them?

ABOUT THE AUTHOR

Photo by Matt Andrews

Jennifer Moorman writes enchanting novels inspired by the everyday magic and whimsy in the world around her. She is the bestselling author of the magical realism Mystic Water Series, *The Baker's Man*, and *The Magic All Around*.

Born and raised in southern Georgia, Jennifer has a deep love for nature, a fondness for honeysuckle, and childhood memories of whippoorwills singing her to sleep. She is a foodie, a self-taught baker, and has a travel bag ready for her next adventure. She can always be won over with chocolate, unicorns, or rainbows.

When she's not writing, you can find her testing a new recipe, chasing rainbows, or stargazing. She lives in a magic house in Nashville, Tennessee.

Connect with Jennifer at jennifermoorman.com
Instagram: @jenniferrmoorman
Facebook: @jennifermoormanbooks
BookBub: @JenniferMoorman

“Sometimes, the impossible can become possible. I was hooked from the very first enchanting page.”

—KRISTY WOODSON HARVEY, *NEW YORK TIMES* BESTSELLING AUTHOR OF *A HAPPIER LIFE*

CAN ONE THOUGHTLESS WISH ERASE A LIFE?

Widowed at thirty-five, Josephine Reynolds wishes she could disappear, but her concerned sister convinces her to buy their ancestral home, a Craftsman bungalow in disrepair and foreclosure. It’s a welcome distraction, and Josephine can’t believe her luck when she finds the home’s original door in a salvage yard.

When she installs the door and steps through it, Josephine is transported into 1927, where she meets her great-grandmother Alma, a vivacious and daring woman running an illegal speakeasy in the bungalow’s basement. Immersed in the vibrant Jazz Age, Josephine forms a profound bond with Alma, only to discover upon her return to the present that history has been altered. Alma’s life was tragically cut short in a speakeasy raid just a week after their fateful meeting.

Josephine has a chilling revelation—her own existence is vanishing—and she must race against time to rewrite history. Josephine is desperate to not only save Alma but save her own future in a time-bending journey where past and present intertwine in a desperate battle for survival.

INCLUDES DISCUSSION QUESTIONS

HARPER MUSE

Visit us online:
@HarperMuseBooks
harpermuse.com

FICTION
USD $18.99 / CAD $23.99
ISBN 978-1-4003-4363-8
51899
9 781400 343638

Cover design by Lindy Kasler